Enjoy reading

Gazda

Trevor Johnson

Trevor Johnson

See more at https://trevorjohnson.net

Gazda

A writer is someone who has taught his mind to misbehave.
Oscar Wilde

Table of Contents

Drifting ...
No ...
Floating ...
No ...
Falling ...
Floating and falling ...
Falling and floating ...
Bright lights ...
Coloured lights ...
Ruby red, emerald-green ...
Not lights ...
Not lights ...
Reflections ...
Dazzling, coloured reflections.
Nude nymphs tossing a bloated ... bearded ... severed head ... between them.
An albino ... half man ... half gorilla snatches the head
A huge, bloodshot eye ... behind a thick lens ... looks down from the sky
Multicoloured liquids wash over the picture ... they can't make it go away.

Christopher's eyes shot open. He didn't recognise the picture. Yes, the bed, the door, but not his bed and his door. He'd gone from deep dream, to fully awake without passing through the usual drowsy stage. The dream, which had seemed so real, was rapidly disappearing.

A flow of cool air across his torso told him he'd forgotten to put his pyjamas on, something he'd never done before. And he could never remember waking up with both arms above his head, like babies often sleep. Turning his head much too quickly he saw his wrists were handcuffed to the bedposts: not his bedposts.

Cold sweat prickled his forehead. He closed his eyes and rested his chin on his chest. The nausea passed and he opened his eyes. The flimsy curtain, not his curtain, was no match for the bright sunlight outside; sunlight that highlighted the starkness of the room: definitely not his room. He saw the not unusual sensation of a semi-erect penis was not the result of erotic dreams, but a pink ribbon tied in a neat bow at the base.

He closed his eyes and tried desperately to think. Multiple images flashed before him, but nothing made sense. He stiffened when something moved and brushed against his leg. With the slowest movement possible he turned his head and squinted.

A deep breath escaped from the figure beside him and made its lips tremble. No, not its, her. Same honey-blonde hair as Lisa. It is Lisa! He let out a yelp as he forgot the handcuffs and obeyed the instinct to hide his nakedness. This brought back the nausea, and he slowly filled his lungs with air three times.

He looked again towards Lisa. She was still not conscious, and he didn't resist another instinct: to let his eyes roam over her body. The black bra, pushed below her breasts and suspender belt complete with stockings made his constricted penis twitch. He looked away, guiltily. The thought 'not a natural blonde' increased his embarrassment.

A key turning in the lock, sent Christopher's feet searching desperately for any covers at the bottom of the bed. He found nothing.

The Theft

4 February to 3 September 2008

"Is somebody meeting you?"

"A secretary."

"Not the dark-skinned beauty you've always talked about having as a secretary?"

"No, a) unfortunately it's no longer PC to even think such things, and b) it's not my secretary. In this company we share secretaries."

"Really!"

"Dream on, Martin."

They presented their passports to the unsmiling Grenzpolizei with the peaked cap pulled low over his eyes, and passed into the baggage collection area.

Martin's case was almost the first to slide down the chute and land with a thud on the carousel. Even though he was on a tight schedule for a meeting, his curiosity made him fiddle with some papers until Christopher's two pieces and a box arrived. "Did you have to pay excess baggage?"

"Yes, but what could I do? I tried to bring the minimum clothes and what I thought I'd need until I can get back to the UK to collect the rest."

"When do think that will be?"

"Two or three months."

They passed through customs and the lazy but analytical gaze of the official, into the usual airport throng of drivers and guides holding up name cards. Christopher did a one-hundred and eighty degree scan and found the letterhead of ZFFM.

"Welcome to Switzerland, Mr McLendi. I'm Lisa Stern, Herr Muri's secretary."

'Five two, natural blonde (I would guess), with bulges in all the right places, and very attractive, except for a nose a little too large' was how Martin would describe Christopher's welcomer to his former colleagues.

"Thank you."

"I guessed you'd have a lot of luggage, so I parked outside the terminal, illegally I'm afraid. So, if you wouldn't mind, we should hurry. I don't want to overstretch the generosity of the nice, young policeman who said he'd watch over the car for a few minutes."

"Of course. Bye, Martin, I'll keep in touch."

"Bye, Chris, good luck with the new job." As they shook hands he whispered, "Nice, very nice."

The young policeman had taken it on himself to do more than 'watch over' the BMW. He was directing traffic around it. He seemed so pleased with himself that Christopher felt sure he would have helped Lisa load the luggage if Christopher hadn't been there. He held up the line of cars so Lisa could pull out and received a demure smile.

"This is your car, Mr McLendi."

"Christopher, please."

"The garage called yesterday and said it was ready, so I thought I'd bring it and you won't have to change over all your luggage."

"Thank you."

"There are just a couple of forms to sign when we get to the office and then you can legally drive it."

"I presume my British licence is OK?"

"For now, but we'll have to get a Swiss licence for you." Lisa was aware that her skirt had ridden up when she sat down. She discreetly tugged at the hem.

"As you know, Mr Mc– Christopher, we have put you in the flat the company has opposite ZFFM until the end of the month. You can move into your apartment on the first of next month. I've–"

"I can't remember, are there shops nearby?"

"I've asked the putzfrau, the cleaning lady, to put some basic supplies in for you. I can't guarantee that you'll like what she's chosen, but it should get you through at least until tomorrow. Herr Muri would like you to have dinner with him tonight."

"OK, that's all the formalities, you're now official. I'll take you in to see Herr Muri now."

"Christopher, welcome to–"

Lisa soundlessly closed the door between her office and that of the CEO. She clicked one of the word icons at the bottom of her screen. The document filled the space.

```
ZFFM Zürich Flasche Fullungs Machinen
Personnel Department
Summary sheet of new employee

Name: Christopher McLendi
Nationality: British
Age: 40
Marital status: Bachelor
```

```
Position: Head of Technological Development
Qualifications: BSc Packaging Technology (1992)
Salary: Access code needed
```

Lisa had the access code but the number didn't interest her.

```
Assessment: see H-P Schuster report
```

She clicked on it.

```
Schuster Search AG
Report on Christopher McLendi
```

She scrolled down to the 'Summary/Opinion'.

```
    Christopher McLendi is an independent-minded
and strong-willed person, but at the same time a
team player. His natural shyness can make him seem
aloof at first, but one quickly recognises he is a
person who is easy to get on with.
    His parents' financial situation forced him to
leave university after one year. He studied part-
time for a degree and has moved rapidly up the
professional ladder through hard work. Anecdotal
evidence suggests he gets on well with his
colleagues and earns their respect.
    Definitely worth taking a look at for the Head
of Technological Development.
```

"Has he arrived yet?"

Lisa put her index finger across her lips and pointed with her other hand to the inter-office door.

Erna lent and whispered. "What's he like?"

"Mr McLendi, the Head of Technological Development, seems like a nice person."

"'A nice person', what does that mean?"

"Exactly what it says."

"Don't be so annoying, Lisa. We're all curious to know about our new colleague."

"'We?' You mean 'I' don't you?"

"I, we, what does it matter."

"As I said, he seems like a nice person."

"So nice that you're keeping him for you?"

"Not my type."

4

"Ah, that tells me something."

"What?"

"I thought everything in trousers was your type."

"Erna, I don't think that's—

"OK, OK stay cool. If you don't want to tell me …"

"What do you want to know? As if I couldn't guess."

"Married?"

"Exactly. Erna, I've only saw him briefly when he came for the interview, and today I just drove him from the airport – hardly enough time to get his life story."

"No, but you have access to his file."

"Good thing you don't. Does it make any difference anyhow?"

"What?"

"Whether he's married or not?"

"Different strategy."

"No, if you must know."

"What did you mean 'not my type'?"

"Seems a bit 'bookish'."

The inter-office door opened. Erna straightened her skirt, flicked her hair back and moistened her lips. Lisa rolled her eyes and rose.

"Lisa, you can take Mr McLendi over to the flat now. Get him settled in, and I'll pick him up later."

"Yes, Herr Muri."

"Ah, Erna."

"Herr Muri."

"You should meet a new colleague. This is Christopher McLendi our new Head of Technological Development. Christopher this is Erna Sameli. Erna is a team leader in the purchasing department, dealing with items for R&D. You'll probably have a lot of contact with her. Whatever you want, Erna can get it for you."

Lisa tried and almost succeeded in suppressing a guffaw. The unsuppressed bit ended as a cough, which brought a look of concern from Herr Muri and a scowl from Erna.

"Well, I don't agree."

"Rudi, you can't just keep saying 'I don't agree'. How about some alternative suggestions?" Christopher managed to turn a clenched-fist, table-banging gesture into an open-palm, gentle tapping.

"I just did."

"Did what?"

"Say I don't agree."

Christopher wondered if it was time to take a break. They'd been going now for almost an hour and a half, most of that time on the same topic. New Product Steering Committees weren't a collection of people who automatically agreed, that was the idea of having many different inputs. But this was the third meeting of this particular task force and they kept getting stuck on the same topic again and again.

"Let's get some input from a different perspective. Bernard, how do you see this from production's point of view?"

Bernard coughed three times, which he always did, before answering. "It's difficult to say." Fence sitting was another Bernard characteristic. "I mean there are advantages and disadvantages on both sides."

"Yes, but the advantages of what Rudi is suggesting give us far more flexibility for the future."

"Thank you, Hans. I don't agree with you, but–. You've got me saying it now." Christopher smiled in Rudi's direction. Rudi ignored it. "but tell us why you think that."

"From what Rudi's told us about what's happening in the market, and he should know as the Marketing Manager, our competitors are already reacting more quickly to customer needs than we are. It seems to me that we must leave as many options open as possible."

Christopher glanced at Rudi; now he was smiling. Although Hans Struber, the Quality Control Manager, did not have any decision making power on this committee, as the person who had been around ZFFM the longest he did command a large degree of respect. "But what I'm suggesting will give us that flexibility in–"

"In ten years."

"Let me finish, please, Rudi. What I'm suggesting will give us far greater flexibility in the future, and–"

"We can't be sure of that."

"Gentlemen, we seem to have the good, healthy, traditional clash between marketing and development." Herr Muri stepped into the discussion. It was unusual for him to take part in the Steering Committee at this early stage, but with the entrenched positions at the previous two meetings Christopher had asked him to be present. "I'm not here to act as referee. I can't make the decision, that's what I pay you gentlemen for. If I may make a suggestion. The only two people sitting around this table who have the marketing and technical knowledge to make the basic decision about the fundamental direction for the future are Rudi and Christopher. I suggest you suspend the committee until they make that fundamental decision. Rudi, Christopher let's meet in my office."

"Come in Rudi, Christopher's delayed." Herr Muri knew that Rudi would arrive a little bit early so he could claim the chair opposite his desk: pole position. That would leave Christopher the chair slightly to one side. Herr Muri had also deliberately given Christopher a time of fifteen minutes later.

They spoke in English, the company language, even though both were Swiss-German mother tongue, albeit Züri and Bern Deutsch.

"That was a big order yesterday from Hungary."

"Something we've been working on for a few months, Herr Muri."

"I know. Well done. You'll be going to the show in Frankfurt next month of course."

"Of course."

"I'm trying to rearrange one or two things so I spend a couple of days there rather than one."

"That would be good."

"Well, you know I miss getting out and meeting the real, live customers."

"I know."

"Feeling you've got your finger on the pulse of what's happening."

"It's the only way to know what the customers want."

Herr Muri nodded. "Of course, the question has always been, do the customers know what they want."

Rudi Affolter had guessed where this conversation was going. "There's no doubt in my mind the best source of information of what's happening in the market is the customers, not some–" He'd planned to stop himself even if Herr Muri hadn't interrupted.

"Oh I'm sure you're right about what's happening in the market now, but does that tell us about the future?"

Rudi nodded.

"Sorry I interrupted you, you were saying something about 'not some'."

"Was I? Can't have been important."

"I'm sure we agree that we have to be open to new technology."

"Providing it brings something."

"Of course. That's why we brought Christopher on board."

Rudi nodded.

"In the six months he's been with us he's already made suggestions that will result in significant savings in production. They should give you more flexibility in certain price negotiations."

"My team doesn't negotiate on price, Herr Muri, we sell quality."

"I know."

"Something I've been doing for twenty years now."

"I know."

"Successfully for twenty years. So I think I know a little bit about this business, more than ..."

"Someone who's only been here a short time?"

"To be honest, yes."

Herr Muri let the heat that was building cool a little. "When my father started this business there wasn't much technology in filling glass bottles; just simple automation of the manual methods. Nowadays, as you well know, our customers' production lines have become more sophisticated, which puts high requirements on our machines. Technical innovation is going to be the key to the future success of this company. I want–"

"I know that better than anyone, Herr Muri, and my market knowledge will keep us–"

"Let me finish. I want to let Christopher run with this project. I've talked to a few people outside and got some good feedback."

There was a knock at the door.

"Come in. Ah, Christopher, come in." Herr Muri rose, Rudi didn't. "Take a seat. Rudi arrived a bit early so we've just been talking about the Steering Committee. We've agreed" Herr Muri paused, looked at Rudi, and waited for him to nod, "the final decision on this particular project will be yours. I'm sure you'll want to use Rudi's extensive knowledge of our customers, but you'll have to guide us to the future, right Rudi?

"Of course, Herr Muri."

"I hope you have a good crystal ball, Christopher."

"And that you don't drop it." Rudi tried to make his comment light, with a smile, but it came out as a teeth-baring grimace.

"OK, gentlemen, I think we'd better get back to work."

"Oh, Christopher." Lisa's call stopped Christopher just as he and Rudi reached the outer door of Herr Muri's office suite.

"Yes, Lisa."

Rudi paused also, looking as if he was holding the door open for Christopher.

"Accounts called about the money you're taking to Uzbekistan. It's a bit more cash than they normally hand out, so they want you to sign for it personally. Sorry, even I can't overrule the self-appointed gods of the accounts department."

"That's OK, I'll collect it now."

"Lisa, I've got a problem."

"Tell me."

"My briefcase has disappeared from my office."

"Disappeared?"

"Gone."

"When did you last see it?"

"About an hour ago, just after lunch."

"Was there anything important in it?"

"Everything for my trip tomorrow, my wallet with all credit cards, my passport, the dollars I picked up from accounts, and some papers from—"

"I'll call the police."

For Christopher what happened was much more than a theft, it felt like an invasion of his person. But for the police it was just one of the hundreds of such incidents that occurred every day.

"I'm sure you understand, Frau Stern—"

"Fraulein."

"I'm sure you understand Fraulein Stern, if we were to send someone to investigate every incident, we would need a police force ten times the size we have."

No, she didn't understand. However the friendly but firm tone of Constable Roth left her no choice, and she wrote down the address of the police station where Christopher could go to report the 'incident'.

After cancelling all the credit cards and starting the process of getting a new passport, Lisa, Erna, Christopher and a few others took up the police suggestion of making a search of the building: 'people who do this are often just looking for cash, and discard the wallet or bag quite quickly'.

Erna found Christopher's briefcase jammed behind a toilet bowl, on the marketing and product management floor, the cash, passport and wallet were all gone.

Christopher's main concern was getting his passport replaced. Whether it was his charm or he found the right person on good day he didn't know, but the British Consulate in Zurich worked miracles. They issued a temporary passport and he could make the important trip to Uzbekistan with only three days delay.

At eight o'clock on the morning of Christopher's return Lisa was in his office before he sat down. "Gute Morge, how was your trip?"

"Good, very good. An intensive couple of days, but we have full access to the technology, and I think they'll be more."

Unusually, Lisa closed the door and sat in the chair in front of his desk. "So, here's where we are."

"Where we are with what?"

She looked puzzled. "The investigation of course."

"What investigation?"

"Christopher, you had your briefcase stolen, remember."

"Ah that, well you heard what the police said, little chance of finding the contents of the wallet, and no chance with the cash."

"That's just their excuse for not doing anything."

"Well if they don't do anything I don't know who can."

"Us."

"Us?"

"Yes, us."

Christopher expression said he didn't understand and there was just a trace of uneasiness.

"Look, someone took your briefcase from your office, right?

"Right."

"And your office is on the fifth floor of the building."

"Yes." The uneasiness in his face was beginning to predominate.

"So, the chances of anyone walking in off the street and stealing it are small."

"I'm not sure I like where you are going with this, Lisa."

"But the conclusion is obvious, it must have been an 'inside job' as they say in the movies."

"Now I know I don't like where you've arrived."

"But it's true isn't it; one of our so-called colleagues is a thief."

"'Thief' sounds a bit strong."

"You can find another word, the result is the same. Someone took your personal property without your permission."

Christopher steepled his fingers and looked at her over the top of them. "I've got a new passport, the credit cards were all cancelled, and the company's insurance will cover the lost cash."

"So, what, no harm done?"

"I don't think we can have a big investigation."

Lisa pushed back the chair, almost jumped to her feet, and headed for the door. "So, we just wait until it happens to someone else. I hope it's not me."

Christopher rose and moved round his desk. "Lisa, wait, come and sit down."

She turned, but didn't move.

"Lisa I don't want this to happen to someone else, it's a horrible feeling, but—"

"but you don't want to do anything about it."

"I don't want everyone to feel under suspicion, we have to work together."

She came and stood behind the chair. "I know, but you agree we should find out who it is."

He gestured to her to sit. He took a deep breath. "I agree, but we must be discreet."

"I agree with that. I said the same to Erna."

Christopher grimaced, "Erna's involved?"

"Of course, she was the one who found your briefcase after all."

"OK, but discreet is the word."

"I thought grease was."

"Sorry?"

"Grease is the word, is the word."

"I'm not with you."

"Never mind."

"So, tell me what you've discovered so far."

Lisa looked at him over the top of her glasses. "You're sure you want to hear?"

"Is it that bad?"

"No. First we tried to make a list of everyone who was here that day. Well not everyone clearly, but certainly those people we saw on this floor."

"All the people who work here I would assume."

"Yes, plus three reps from our suppliers, and that quick visit in the afternoon from those Koreans."

"I hardly think they could be suspects."

"No, but you have to work by a process of elimination."

"You sound like a detective."

"I'm not, but I have connections, and I'll come to that in a minute."

Christopher had heard Lisa described as 'hartnäckig' on his first day in ZFFM. His schoolboy language knowledge did not extend as far as a meaning, but it was one of those German words he found comical for some reason. Despite his promise to himself not to, he looked it up in the dictionary. 'Tenacious' was the best translation.

"A few of the evening cleaning staff were here earlier than usual, but whether they arrived before or after your briefcase disappeared we're not sure, they said after."

"You've asked them?"

"Yes."

"That's not what I mean by being discreet."

Lisa shrugged. "We didn't exactly give them the third degree."

"No, but–"

"Anyway, there was no one else other than the staff, that's why we think it's an inside job."

"And 'we' is you and Erna?"

"And my police connection."

"Who is?"

"A cousin of Erna's."

"Oh!"

"Don't say 'oh' like that. It's a distant cousin, and Erna doesn't know I contacted him."

"But you know him?"

"Just after I joined ZFFM I went out with Erna, and we met him in bar. He chatted me up. Is that expression still used? I was probably a bit vulnerable because I was still going through my divorce. We went out a couple of times.

"I didn't even know you were married."

"Why would you? We divorced three years ago."

"I'm sorry."

Again the shrug. "It happens. I made a classical mistake I suppose, a cross-cultural marriage."

"Not always a mistake. Not that I have any personal experience, of cross-cultural relationships or marriage."

Lisa made a mental note, for Erna. "I once had job at Aston Villa Football Club, Andre was one of the up-and-coming stars of the Swiss national team. We married a few months before his transfer back to Zurich. I'd only met his family briefly before we moved here. 'I'm marrying the man, not his family' I said to people who tried to give me words of caution. His mother, I never met his father, was what you would call traditional Swiss. She believed the man goes out to work and the wife stays at home and keeps house. I wanted something more challenging. Sorry, I'm sure you don't want to know all this."

"No, please finish. If you want to."

"Well, to cut a short story even shorter, despite his international experience, Andre agreed with his mother. We separated and started the divorce. ZFFM took a chance on the little English woman who had not so much work experience and didn't speak German. There you have it, the story of my life, at least part of it."

"Sorry to hear that."

"So, anyhow, back to my police connection. As I said we went out a few times, but he was not tall, dark and handsome enough for me. We parted friends, although he did try a couple of times to resurrect our relationship He's in the Kriminalpolizei, KRIPO, and I felt I could call him to ask his advice about this theft.

"He said most of these types of thefts are by people who you know. And before you say anything, no, I didn't prompt him. He told me to become observant, discreetly, to see if anyone is suddenly spending a lot of money. You can't trace cash, but there might be a trail if he uses the credit cards."

"Assuming it is a 'he'."

"There are only two women on the list."

And I thought we cancelled the credit cards?"

"We did. You are no longer liable, but the thief can still use them. He told me not all places that take credit cards connect to the credit card company's computer. Many still use the hand machine. The information about cancelled cards can take several days to get to these places."

"And who pays for that?"

"The insurance companies, I suppose. The credit card companies have to report any illegal use, so the police will let us know."

"So, what about this list?"

"The list of suspects."

"Lisa!"

"I know, I know, be discreet. I told you, we made a list of everyone who was here. Erna and I are the only two women who could have got into your office during the time in which the offence took place."

"You're sounding like the police now. Who else is on the list?"

"Herr Muri, you—"

"Herr Muri! I hardly think he would steal my briefcase."

"You never know."

"Why?"

"For the thrill, film stars steal socks from shops."

"And me, I'd steal my own briefcase?"

"Unlikely, I admit."

"Thank you."

For the next few days Lisa observed their colleagues and Christopher observed Lisa. He told himself he could control the situation and if it got too intensive he would tell Lisa to stop. Two unexpected things happened. First he became more intrigued with finding out if it was 'an inside job' as she called it. Second, rumours started going around and eventually got back to him that with all the 'meetings' he and Lisa were having, there must be something going on between them.

She gave him an update at least once a day, always closing the office door and speaking in hushed tones. Mainly she reported who had a new tie, a new jacket, a new suit. Each was a minor event, she admitted, but together they might add up to something.

The police received information about the use of one of the credit cards, on the first weekend after the theft, in a hotel restaurant, and two men's clothes shops in Basel.

After two weeks, Lisa and Erna asked to see Christopher.

"We've reached a conclusion," said Lisa.

"A conclusion?"

"About whom the thief is," said Erna.

"'May be', who the thief is 'may be'," added Lisa.

Christopher focused his eyes on the space between Erna and Lisa. They looked at each other, and Erna nodded slightly.

Lisa took a deep breath. "We think it's Rudi, Rudi Affolter."

Christopher jumped, as if being awoken from a sleep. "Rudi Affolter? Why?"

Lisa nodded, and Erna continued. "He's had some new clothes recently, he's been acting suspiciously–"

"What does that mean, 'suspiciously'?"

Erna looked at Lisa. "Not normal?"

"You'll have to come up with a better definition than that."

Lisa had told Erna Christopher would not just accept 'not normal', although it was true. "He's been avoiding people. Normally, as you know, he's very gregarious, but lately we've hardly seen him. He sits in his office all day."

"Well, I must admit I haven't had much contact with him since the last New Product Steering Committee, perhaps he's not feeling well."

"Perhaps, but there's something else. Everyone around here feels bad about what happened to you, having something stolen from your office after only a short time here. It doesn't happen in this country."

"And everyone's expressed their sympathy."

"Except?"

"Except?"

"Rudi Affolter?"

Christopher thought for a moment. "I don't remember Rudi saying anything, but I couldn't make a list of who did and who didn't. But what possible motive could Rudi have?"

Lisa let the question hang for a moment. "The Steering Committee, the decision made by Herr Muri?"

"You're not suggesting that ... to get back at me ... seems a bit petty."

"But it could happen."

"In your long experience of such cases, Inspector Stern."

Erna giggled, Lisa allowed a small smile at the corners of her mouth.

16

Christopher quickly ran the facts through his head. He and Rudi Affolter had rarely agreed, but their differences had always been professional. Herr Muri had given him the authority to decide about the new product. Rudi had been there when Lisa had told him about the cash waiting for him in the accounts department. "But as far as I know Rudi's a respected member of his commune. Isn't he a member of the council or whatever it's called?"

"Gemeinderat."

"Thank you, Erna. Well?"

Lisa shrugged. "That doesn't automatically mean he's not a thief"

"Can we stop using that word, a person's innocent until proven guilty."

"All I mean is that Gemeinderatmitgliede are not always honest."

"Hardly ever in my experience. I knew–"

Yes, thank you Erna, that's exactly what we don't need to know."

"But I was only going to say–"

Lisa touched Erna on the arm and shook her head. Christopher allowed the silence to settle over the situation that was developing.

Erna sighed and turned towards the door. "I'll see you later, Lisa."

"I warned you this could cause problems."

"She'll be OK. She's just trying to help."

"But you, we, can't start adding two and two together and getting five."

Christopher could see from the look on Lisa's face that she didn't agree. "We don't need to get five, four's enough."

"Lisa– "

"Yes, I know."

"I need to see Herr Muri, can you try to fix up something for this afternoon please."

"So, you don't think we should do something?"

"About what?"

"Rudi Affolter."

"Lisa … " Christopher took a deep breath, which brought his voice down to normal from the shout that was developing. "… let's drop the subject."

"If you say so, Mr McLendi." Her body language sent a different message.

"Constable Roth?"

"Yes."

"Lisa Stern."

"Good afternoon Ms Stern what can I do for you?"

"You told me about the use in Basel of one of the credit cards stolen from Mr McLendi."

"Yes."

"So the signature was a forgery. Do you have a description of the person who used the card?"

"I can't tell you that."

"Why?"

"Because the description may not be accurate and might lead to false suspicions or accusations."

"Will you be trying to find this person?"

"We don't have the resources to do that. If something more concrete came up later we would match the description against any suspect."

"Just tell me, was it a man with a small beard?"

"I can't say. ... Do you have someone in mind?"

"We have our suspicions."

"We?"

"My colleagues and I."

"May I ask who?"

"I don't think I can say, 'it might lead to false accusations'."

"It might be withholding information from the police."

"One of our colleagues, Rudi Affolter."

"Why do you suspect him?"

"He has a new suit, bought in Basel."

"Is that all?"

"We've always suspected his involvement in some funny business."

"'We' again? Funny business?"

"Well, I then. He seems to have a lot of money, big house, big car."

"The proceeds from stealing people's briefcases no doubt.

"Goodbye, Constable."

The First Abduction

5 September to 15 September 2008

Late on the next Friday, Lisa strode into Christopher's office, this time alone, and said she needed to talk to him. She didn't wait for him to answer, and closed the door. "There have been some developments."

Christopher had been half expecting this and had decided that he wasn't going to react. His thought was that as long as there was no disruption in the company he would let Lisa play amateur detective until she became tired of it. "Tell me."

"We know that his new suit came from Basel."

"Who's new suit?"

"Rudi Affolter's."

"How? Did you get a look at the label when he took his jacket off? Or has Erna been getting closer to Rudi?"

Lisa ignored Christopher's smile. "I just happened to overhear a conversation he had with Hans Struber."

"'Just happened to overhear'?"

"Yes."

"So, he shops in Basel. I think you'll find a few thousand other people do also."

"But that's where someone used your stolen credit card."

"Hardly a watertight case is it?"

"And that's not all."

"No?"

"No. We think he's involved in something more than just stealing from colleagues."

Now Christopher did react. "What?"

"We think he may–"

"Who is 'we'?"

"Erna and I."

"Erna and you."

"Yes. We saw some funny people going into his house, the night before last."

"You did what?"

"We saw some– "

"Yes, I heard that bit. My question is, how did you see?"

"We happened to be in that area."

"Lisa, sit down, I said to be discreet. What do you mean 'we happened to be in that area'?"

"Looking for a restaurant."

"Did you find one?"

"No."

"Did you expect to?"

"We were not sure."

"So you just drove–"

"Walked."

"Walked around near Rudi's house."

"Yes."

"Did anyone see you?"

"No. Almost the only other people around were the strange people going into Affolter's house, and they were in too much of a hurry."

"What do you mean 'strange'?"

"A little guy and a very tall lady."

"Lisa–" The telephone buzzed. "What if someone had seen you sneaking around?" The telephone continued to buzz. "Christopher McLendi ... yes, Rudi, good afternoon ... fine, fine, and you? ... yes, you're right, there's been no time since I got back from Uzbekistan ... oh that's OK ... nothing particular ... well, yes, thank you ... I'm sure I'll find it ... Lisa? ... I don't know, I can ask her ... yes, OK, thank you." Christopher smiled.

"What?"

"What?"

"You'll ask Lisa what?"

"He said he felt embarrassed that I have been here over six months and he hasn't invited me over to his place. He's having a few friends round for dinner tonight and wondered if I'd like to join them."

"And what's that got to do with me?"

"Almost as an afterthought he said if you would also like to come along there would be at least two faces I knew."

"Wow."

"Yes, wow. Doesn't sound like someone who stole my briefcase, does it? Would you like to go?"

"Yes," said without a moment's hesitation.

"I'll pick you up at seven thirty."

"Might be better to take a taxi. I went to a ZFFM barbeque at his house some years ago, I remember he was generous and insistent with the drinks."

Rudi's house was near the airport in what would have been a small village before the Zurich urban area spread. The taxi driver had said it would take about twenty-five minutes. Christopher had learnt that this meant exactly twenty-five minutes.

Although she'd only had a short time after they'd left the office, Lisa looked different to how he saw her every day. He'd always thought she was attractive. He remembered Martin's comment the first day he'd arrived in Switzerland, 'Nice, very nice.' But she seemed to deliberately dress down in the office, as though she didn't want to stand out. Tonight she looked … 'stunning' was the only word he could think of.

"Have you ever seen Rudi outside the office?"

"No, have you?"

"As I said, he invited the management team for a barbeque a couple of years ago. We'd just got some big order. But other than that, no. I thought he might have suggested going out for a drink or something with you."

"No. From what I've seen in the short time I've been here, work colleagues and social contacts seen to be two separate things in Switzerland. Totally different to England."

"That's true. I've heard many stories about him with beautiful girls in some of the best restaurants in Zurich."

"Really?"

"Yes, difficult to believe perhaps."

"Why?"

"Well he's not what I would call the most attractive man."

"Beauty is in the eye of the beholder."

"Yes, but he's short, overweight, greying, stupid little beard and … well, ugly."

"Not your type then?"

After a bright September day, dusk was descending when they arrived. There were no lights on in the house.

"Sorry, I only have a two-hundred franc note." said Christopher paying the taxi driver. "Are you sure this is the right house?"

"Ja."

"No, I was asking the lady."

"I'm sure."

The taxi driver grunted and gave Christopher his change in twenty franc notes

It was an old, impressive house. Three, possible four, stories high, with large windows on the ground floor. It stood in its own grounds, surrounded by a chest high wall. A pathway snaked across the fifty metres of garden between the road and the house. In many places, houses like this would have implied wealth of the occupier, but in Switzerland most of them had been in families for years. The closed shutters on all the upstairs windows gave the house a slightly sinister feel in the fading light. The creaking of the wrought iron gate added to the feeling.

They heard nothing when Lisa pushed the doorbell. She tried a second time and a third. A light went on over their heads. The frosted glass panels in the door glowed.

"Lisa, Christopher, good evening, welcome, come in, come in." Rudi Affolter shook their hands and clapped Christopher on the back. "Did you ring more than once? We're out on the terrace, trying to pretend it's not the end of summer."

They followed him down the long corridor, through a living room and out onto the terrace. The sound of laughter grew louder as they approached. What Rudi had called the 'terrace' was a large conservatory. The glass walls were open. The long garden, illuminated with coloured lights hidden in bushes and trees, descended in layers. The other guests rose from leather-upholstered, wicker, garden furniture as they entered.

"So, let me introduce you. My friends, these are my colleagues Lisa and Christopher. Lisa and Christopher this beautiful lady is Ekaterina."

The heavily-bejewelled hand held out to them was small and delicate, which was in contrast to the height of the lady behind it. Slavic cheekbones gave her natural beauty.

"Ekaterina's husband, Herman."

" Good … evening." Lisa managed to suppress a giggle. For some reason the name Herman said Herman Munster to her, but this was far from the figure that took her hand and raised it towards his lips, but did not caress it. He was one of the few men Lisa had met who was smaller than her. His blond hair, cut in the style of the Beatles, and heavy glasses made him look like a little schoolboy, which he obviously was not. His voice was deep, but squeaky "Have we met before?"

"No, I don't think so." But Lisa was not so sure: something nagged at the back of her brain.

"I never forget a face."

"It's true. He remembers people he's only passed on the street." Lisa thought Ekaterina was going to pat him on the head, but her hand brushed his shoulder.

"I'm sure I've seen you somewhere recently."

Rudi waited for a response from Lisa. When none came he continued with the introductions "And these two delightful creatures are sisters Nicole and Sandy visiting from the USA."

How does he do it thought Lisa. The blond-haired, blue-eyed nymphets, dressed in identical backless, almost frontless mini dresses, looked young enough to be his daughters or even granddaughters. Giggles issued from their pouted lips instead of greetings.

"And finally, my good friend, Mikos."

Now that's Herman Munster thought Lisa. But there was no bolt through his solid neck, only over six feet of rippling muscle, accentuated by a tight-fitting, beige suit. That he wore dark glasses was no surprise.

"Now, we have about an hour before we eat, so plenty of time for a few drinks."

Ekaterina slipped her arm through Christopher's. "So, you're the English expert on glass. Rudi talks about you all the time. I've been looking forward to meeting you. I know nothing about glass, except that it breaks. I would love you to tell me all about it." The breathiness of the last sentence would have sounded cheap had it come from Nicole or Sandy, but Ekaterina's heavy Eastern European accent made it impossible not to be flattered by it. And, surprising himself, Christopher was. Ekaterina guided Christopher to a couch in the corner of the conservatory.

Lisa had not been anxious about coming to the lair of the man she knew was guilty of the theft, but without Christopher by her side she suddenly felt exposed.

"So, you're also English." said Herman.

Rudi said the plan had been to eat outside, to keep it informal. However, as a cool breeze had developed, he had moved it inside.

When Lisa saw the dining room she suspected the plan had never been 'to keep it informal'. Seven-piece, silver, place settings and white, linen napkins sat evenly around a large, circular dining table. Rudi gave the impression that he was randomly suggesting where people might like to sit. However, on the plate where each of the ladies 'decided' to sit was a white orchid: one of Rudi's hobbies. Christopher was between Ekaterina and Nicole, and Lisa between Mikos and Herman.

The food was magnificent: another of Rudi's hobbies.

Herman kept Lisa fully engaged in conversation. To her surprise, after her first reaction, Lisa soon warmed to him. He had an opinion about everything. Out of the corner of her eye she could see Christopher fully engrossed in Ekaterina.

Rudi reached across Sandy and Herman to clink glasses with Lisa. "How long have you been with us now Lisa?"

"Three and a half years."

Herman also clinked Lisa's glass. "So you like living in Switzerland."

"Yes, certainly."

"I'm not surprised, it's much safer than England. You don't feel as though you're going to have something stolen from you at any minute here."

Lisa's eyes flicked to Rudi, who was concentrating on cutting his duck breast. He spoke before lifting the piece. "It still happens through. Just a few weeks ago, our friend Christopher here had his briefcase stolen from his office

"What, here in Zurich?"

Rudi looked at Lisa, who just nodded. "Yes, right here in Zurich."

"But, Rudi, I thought your offices are on the fifth floor of the building."

"They are, but it still happened."

"Does anyone suspect anybody from inside?"

"I don't know. Lisa probably knows more, she dealt with the police."

Lisa blushed. "I … I … don't know. They didn't say anything." She took too many short sips of wine, which caused her to cough.

Herman patted her gently on the back. "Are you OK, my dear?"

"Yes … yes, thank you." She took a bigger sip.

"You have to be careful. A friend of mine had difficulty with a piece of asparagus once …"

For Christopher it was a new and, if he was honest, exciting experience to be talking to someone who hung on his every word. No matter which way Ekaterina took the conversation with her questions, the technology of glass-making, living in Switzerland, working for ZFFM, his answers seemed to fascinate her. During the dessert he felt a hand on his leg. When he smiled and she didn't react, he stupidly realised the hand was on his right leg, the one closest to Nicole. He didn't look round, and after a while the hand was no longer there.

"You are married, Christopher?"

"No."

"No, not yet?"

"Most people would probably say I'm married to the job."

"I thought perhaps … " Ekaterina inclined her head towards Lisa.

"Lisa? No … no … Lisa's a colleague."

"Excuse me for being personal."

"That's OK. No, Lisa's a colleague … a very helpful colleague, but just a colleague."

"I see."

"She's been particularly helpful recently dealing with my theft."

"You had a theft, in Switzerland?"

"Yes, someone took my briefcase from my office."

"That's bad when that happens. It is easy to start suspecting your colleagues."

Christopher lowered his voice. "That's what I've been telling Lisa. She's becoming a private detective."

The excellent wines flowed freely, but the buzz of conversation, although growing louder, remained with Rudi, Lisa and Herman on one side of the table and Christopher and Ekaterina on the other. Lisa saw how Mikos followed both conversations, but never said a word. Wicked thoughts passed through her head about the purpose of Nicole and Sandy. Decoration only? Or most likely entertainment for Rudi and Mikos later.

"Now my friends what would you prefer, sit here for our coffee or get more comfortable in the lounge?"

The guests looked at one another and gestured 'I don't mind'. Ekaterina spoke. "Rudi, darling, I love your dining room, but I do find these chairs a little uncomfortable darling."

"So, to relieve Ekaterina's posterior we will adjourn to the lounge."

Lisa tried to get close to Christopher as they changed rooms, but Ekaterina commandeered him once again. She steered Christopher to one of the deep, leather couches in the darkest corner.

"Herman, you know where the drinks are, would you like to see what everyone wants while I look after the coffee. And don't be mean with measures, these are my bottles, not yours."

"Christopher?"

"No nothing for me, thank you."

"Oh but you must, Rudi will be upset if you don't choose something from his vast array of liquors from around the world."

"Don't force him, Herman. But if I may suggest, Christopher, you should try the Bulgarian mulberry Rakia. I brought it as a gift for Rudi. It is very special. Try just a little bit, please, for Ekaterina."

The 'little bit' arrived in a large brandy glass, which disguised that it was the equivalent of a quadruple in English terms.

Herman arrived with a glass containing a good measure of a golden liquid for Lisa.

"What is this?"

"Something that I am sure you have never tried and something that I am sure you will like."

Lisa lifted the glass to her nose, and immediately recoiled.

"Yes, I know it has a strong smell, but taste it."

Lisa took the tinniest sip possible. The effect of the thick, golden liquid sliding down her throat was warming, comforting, uplifting. "Magical," she said.

"I've never heard it described like that before, but yes, 'magical' fits."

The grandfather clock in the corner sounded its resonant midnight, but no one noticed. Herman continued to regale Lisa. She was vaguely aware of much laughter from Ekaterina, and tried to ignore it. Mikos sat apart from the rest, and still had not spoken more than half a dozen words all evening. Rudi sat in a king-sized, black, leather armchair with Nicole and Sandy perched on the arms. Count Basie played softly in the background.

"Are you a jazz fan Rudi?" Christopher asked.

"Yes, but more trad jazz than big band. And you?"

"Big band when possible, but if not blues."

"You'll have to excuse me for a moment." Lisa struggled to stand from the deep cushions of the couch, and Herman pushed on her elbow.

"Up the stairs and first on the left," said Rudi.

Turning right at the top of the stairs, which had seemed unexpectedly difficult to climb, Lisa opened a few of the doors on the corridor. She turned at the end and saw Sandy, or was it Nicole, at the top of the stairs.

"Lost your way?"

"Eh … yes."

"This is a rambling house. I often lose myself."

"Really."

"Yes. The toilet's this way."

Lisa stood at the top of the stairs. It looked a long way down. Swaying slightly, she gripped the banister. Hushed voices floated up from below.

"It's difficult to tell."

"I know but we have to find out."

Lisa waited a few seconds before descending slowly.

As she approached the lounge Lisa knew there was something she should remember, but couldn't work out what it was. The trip jogged her memory. She took a couple of staggered steps, but recovered by taking hold of the back of Rudi's chair.

"Careful," said Rudi. "Why these old houses have steps at the entrance to every room I don't know."

Lisa rested for two breaths. Herman was smiling at her, obviously expecting her to go back to sit with him. She looked if there was room for her on the couch where Christopher and Ekaterina sat. It was tight, but she managed to squeeze herself between Christopher and the arm. "We didn't have the opportunity to talk during dinner, Ekaterina." The light in the corner was just strong enough for her to see the 'so what' expression on the sophisticated face.

Lisa realised this was the closest physically she had ever been to Christopher. Whether it was that or the alcohol or Ekaterina's presence or all three she was not sure, but she found herself smiling at him and touching his arm to emphasise what she was saying. Erna would have called it flirting, and would have been jealous.

Somewhere a clock struck … what time? Christopher was not sure. His eyes couldn't focus on his watch. Was the clock inside the house or outside? He felt a bit squashed between Lisa and Ekaterina. He tried to reach his glass on the low table in front of the couch.

"Allow me," said Ekaterina.

Lisa beat her to it. "What are you drinking, Christopher?"

"Something special I recommended to him."

"You should try it Lisa, it's very nice." Christopher offered his glass to her.

"It may be too strong for her Christopher."

Lisa grabbed the glass and took more than a sip. "Delicious."

Herman appeared at Lisa's side. "Can I get you anything else?"

"I think I would like to try some of what Christopher's drinking."
Ekaterina smiled.

"And for you Christopher?"

"Well, just a small one."

"Oh don't go, we're just getting to know one another."

"Now Ekaterina, if Lisa and Christopher want to leave, don't you stop them."

"But Rudi …"

"No Ekaterina." Rudi leant closer to her and said in a stage whisper, "maybe they have other plans."

Lisa clung on to Christopher's arm. Christopher squeezed his eyes closed. "We must be …"

Drifting ...

No ...

Floating ...

No ...

Falling ...

Floating and falling ...

Falling and floating ...

Bright lights ...

Coloured lights ...

Ruby red, emerald-green ...

Not lights ...

Not lights ...

Reflections ...

Dazzling, coloured reflections.

Nude nymphs tossing a bloated ... bearded ... severed head ... between them.

An albino ... half man ... half gorilla snatches the head

A huge, bloodshot eye ... behind a thick lens ... looks down from the sky

Multicoloured liquids wash over the picture ... they can't make it go away.

Christopher's eyes shot open. He didn't recognise the picture. Yes, the bed, the door, but not his bed and his door. He'd gone from deep dream, to fully awake without passing through the usual drowsy stage. The dream, which had seemed so real, was rapidly disappearing.

A flow of cool air across his torso told him he'd forgotten to put his pyjamas on, something he'd never done before. And he could never remember waking up with both arms above his head, like babies often sleep. Turning his head much too quickly he saw his wrists were handcuffed to the bedposts: not his bedposts.

Cold sweat prickled his forehead. He closed his eyes and rested his chin on his chest. The nausea passed and he opened his eyes. The flimsy curtain, not his curtain, was no match for the bright sunlight outside; sunlight that highlighted the starkness of the room: definitely not his room. He saw the not unusual sensation of a semi-erect penis was not the result of erotic dreams, but a pink ribbon tied in a neat bow at the base.

He closed his eyes and tried desperately to think. Multiple images flashed before him, but nothing made sense. He stiffened when something moved and brushed against his leg. With the slowest movement possible he turned his head and squinted.

A deep breath escaped from the figure beside him and made its lips tremble. No, not its, her. Same honey-blonde hair as Lisa. It is Lisa! He let out a yelp as he forgot the handcuffs and obeyed the instinct to hide his nakedness. This brought back the nausea, and he slowly filled his lungs with air three times.

He looked again towards Lisa. She was still not conscious, and he didn't resist another instinct: to let his eyes roam over her body. The black bra, pushed below her breasts and suspender belt complete with stockings made his constricted penis twitch. He looked away, guiltily. The thought 'not a natural blonde' increased his embarrassment.

A key turning in the lock, sent Christopher's feet searching desperately for any covers at the bottom of the bed. He found nothing.

The figure in the doorway gave a small cough and said in heavily accented English, "Excuse me, sir, I thought something might be wrong, checkout is by noon."

Christopher automatically said, "What time is it?"

"One-thirty, and we do need the room." A lecherous smile flickered across the man's face as his eyes roamed over the two bodies on the bed. "Unless you'd like to stay for another night, sir."

"No, we'll be leav– Just a minute ... what are you talking about? ... Where are we? ... " Christopher's wrists struggled against the handcuffs.

"In a hotel, sir."

"What?"

"In a hotel, sir."

"What are we doing here?"

The man's eyes did another scan of the bed. "I'm sure I wouldn't like to say, sir."

Christopher struggled again and the metal dug into his skin. "Call the policed

"If you say so, sir, but I don't think they'll have the keys for those." He nodded towards the handcuffs.

"Call the police, something terrible has happened."

"It doesn't look as if it was that bad, Sir."

Christopher threw his leg over Lisa to hide the most embarrassing parts of his and her nakedness. "Just call the police."

"You sure you don't want me to wait for a few minutes, Sir, until you've completely finished."

"Just call the police."

"If that's what you want, Sir." He licked his lips and gently closed the door.

"Lisa, Lisa. Lisa, wake up."

No movement, only deep breathing.

He strained against the metal around his wrist and moved his head as close as he could get to hers. "Lisa, Lisa wake up."

She began to stir.

"Lisa, wake up."

"Mmm, Christopher."

"Lisa, please wake up."

"Christopher ... Christopher ... Christopher?" She was immediately aware of her exposure and scrambled to grab the under sheet and pull a bit of it around her. Only then did she look at him. "Christopher, what's–" She giggled. "What's going on?"

"See if you can find some keys for these things."

She looked around for something to cover more of her body and saw a blanket on a chair by the window. She was halfway to the chair when the door flung open and two uniformed policemen stepped in. She froze in midstride with one arm across her breasts and a hand over her pubes.

"Going somewhere, Fräulien?"

Lisa ignored the question, reached for the blanket and wrapped it around her, all in one swift movement.

"Guten Tag, mein Herr, wie gehts?" The older of the two policemen smiled down at Christopher, his eyes focused on the pink ribbon.

"This is not the way it looks," said Christopher. "Something crazy has happened here."

"Something has happened, I would agree, but what is crazy?

"Er meint 'verrückt', Politzeimeister."

"I know that, Schmidt. What I mean is, what is crazy to one person, may be normal to another."

"Could we have this philosophical discussion some other time. Can you get me out of these things?"

The hotel employee picked up a small key from the bedside table. "Would this help, Sergeant?"

Once released, Christopher wrapped himself in the sheet he'd been lying on, and rushed to Lisa's side. She was starting to shake, and he put his arm around her, mainly to stop the blanket slipping off her shoulders.

"I think we'll leave you alone for a few minutes, Mr McLendi. Get dressed and telephone to the reception when you are ready. I'm Sergeant Grindel and this is Constable Schmidt by the way."

The two policemen turned and left, but the man from the hotel hovered by the door, staring at Lisa and licking his lips in an exaggerated way.

"Out!" Christopher ordered.

As soon as the door closed, the tears Lisa had been holding back flooded out, and Christopher had to support her to the bed to stop her collapsing onto the floor. "What happened?" she said between sobs.

"I don't know. My mind's in a whirl. Let's get dressed and maybe then we can think more clearly."

"Dressed in what?"

"Our clothes must be somewhere."

He was right they were scattered around the floor. Lisa gingerly picked up her skirt and immediately dropped it: It was damp and smelt repulsive. Christopher looked in the wardrobe, and found it empty. He caught a glimpse of his left arm in the door mirror: there was a large bruise above and below his elbow. Lisa was reluctant to go anywhere near her clothes, but the choice was simple, wear either them or a blanket or a sheet for the police interview. They both opted for the latter.

They sat in silence waiting for the police to return.

"So, Mr McLendi and Miss ?"

"Stern, Lisa Stern."

"Miss Stern. What people get up to in their own homes or hotel rooms is nothing to do with us. So, we could just leave you now, but you asked the hotel to call the police. Now I'm obliged to find out why."

"Perhaps you can tell us where we are for a start, Inspector." Despite the swirling in his head, Christopher tried to put as much dignity into his voice as possible.

"Sergeant, Sir. You don't know where you are?"

"I wouldn't be asking if I knew, would I?"

"Hotel zum Kirsch, Sir, just off the Niederdorfstrasse. Almost as an afterthought he added, "Zurich."

Christopher glanced at Lisa. She had stopped shaking, but from the look on her face it could start again at any time. Her bedraggled hair, smudged make-up, and drooping eyelids must have confirmed what was surely the policemen's opinion: it had been a night to remember or a night to forget . He assumed he looked the same, although without the make-up, he hoped. "I've no idea how we got here, Sergeant."

"By foot according to the man on the desk. And you Miss Stern, have you any recollections?"

Lisa's voice was thick and barely audible. "No."

"So now you see why I asked him to call the police. Something's wrong here, surely you see that, Sergeant."

"Once again I say, it's not for me to judge what is right or wrong, Sir. Do you remember anything about what happened before you got here?"

Christopher screwed up his eyes. "Nothing that makes sense." He turned again to Lisa. She was just staring into the middle distance.

The constable had been moving around the room. He'd picked up two champagne bottles off the dressing table and pointedly turned them upside. He retrieved one of the two, empty, litre, bottles of vodka from the waste bin and let it swing between his thumb and forefinger.

The heavy knock on the door snapped Lisa out of her trance.

"Come in." said Christopher and the sergeant together.

"Sorry to disturb you." The man from the hotel looked disappointed that Lisa now had a sheet around her, although he still licked his lips when he looked at her. "I need to know if these people are leaving, Sergeant. They only paid for one night and I have to let the room." He looked at Christopher. "Sorry, but I have a job to do."

"What do you mean, 'they only paid for one night'?"

"Cash, when you arrived on Friday night."

"Friday night … and what is it now?"

The man looked at the sergeant, the constable and back to Christopher. "Saturday afternoon."

"Look, Mr McLendi I think the best thing is for you and Miss Stern to put some clothes on, and have some coffee, probably black. Think about what happened here, and come to the station if you still want to talk to us about it."

"You still don't believe we know anything about this, do you?"

"I've told you, Sir …"

"I know, I know, you're not here to judge."

"Just ask for Sergeant Grindel."

"Where is the station, I guess it must be close because you arrived here so quickly."

"Oh no, it's on the other side of the river. My inspector sent me to a possible disturbance in the Niederdorfstrasse, but it was over when we got here."

Constable Schmidt looked puzzled.

Lisa had started shaking again and didn't stop until she got into a hot bath. An odd thought struck her: if they'd had a night of sex, as the scene suggested, why didn't she feel sore. Had they really come to this hotel? Why couldn't she remember?

Christopher felt like lying back down on the bed, but decided movement, slow movement, was more likely going to clear his head. He picked up the scattered underwear between thumb and forefinger and dropped it into the waste bin, added all the bottles, and covered them with a blanket. He found his wallet on the floor. A quick check showed all his cards were there. The large number of twenty-franc notes in the cash compartment puzzled him. He forced himself to think, which only brought on the nausea again. An image of a taxi flashed through his muddled brain.

"Lisa, can you hear me?" He thought she might have fallen asleep, so he tapped gently on the door. "Lisa?"

"What?" a soft voice said. "Who?" louder "Christopher is that you?"

"Sorry if I woke you. I'm just going out to find something to wear that we can walk out of here in. I didn't want you to think I've left you."

"OK, lock the door and don't be long."

"I don't think anything more will happen now the police have been here."

"No, but—"

"I'll be as quick as I can." He reluctantly pulled on his trousers, decided against the shirt, and turned the lapels of his jacket inwards to cover his chest. The smell made him boke.

He was back in twenty minutes with two, belted raincoats and two pairs of sneakers. The shop assistant had said the coats weren't really unisex when Christopher told him he also wanted a smaller size for his wife. The sneakers were two sizes too big for Lisa, and the coat drowned her. With the collar turned up she almost disappeared, but she was glad of the extra anonymity.

Christopher would have preferred to take a shower before leaving the room, but clearly Lisa wanted go as quickly as possible. They bundled their alcohol soaked clothes into the plastic bag from the shop, and hurried through the small reception area. Out of the corner of her eye Lisa caught the leer of the man at the desk. She was sure he could see through the coat to her nakedness.

Without discussing it Christopher gave the taxi driver the address of Lisa's apartment. They made a brief stop at Christopher's where he hurriedly threw some clothes and a bottle of cognac into a suitcase.

As soon as they reached her apartment Lisa disappeared into the bathroom for over an hour. Still not having showered Christopher was reluctant to sit down, but this gave him time to pace the room and try to remember what happened.

When he eventually emerged from the shower he could smell the coffee. Lisa, in a large, white, towelling dressing gown sat hugging herself on the couch. "I hope you don't mind that I haven't dressed."

"Of course not." He poured two large cognacs and sat in the chair opposite her. "How do you feel?"

Lisa slowly shook her head. "I'm not sure how to answer that at the moment."

Christopher nodded. "My head feels like a hangover, but my stomach's OK."

The silence hung heavy, both staring into their glasses and giving the amber liquid a swirl more often than necessary. When they did speak it was at the same time and with the same thought.

"What's the last thing you clearly remember?"

Lisa looked at him for the first time since they'd left the hotel room. "If I'm totally honest, being in your office late yesterday afternoon."

"We went to Rudi Affolter's."

"Did we?"

"I think so. You don't remember?"

"Now you mention it, vaguely."

The silence descended again. From the way their eyes closed and eyebrows knitted they were both trying desperately to remember.

"There were other people there," said Lisa, almost to herself.

"Yes, but who?"

"And we had something to eat."

"I'm sure you're right, but I can't remember." He poured more cognac without asking. "We could 'phone Rudi and ask him."

"Hmm."

"That didn't sound like a yes."

"Well …" She took a larger sip than intended and started coughing.

"Are you OK?"

"Yes, it just went down the wrong way."

"Have you got his number?"

"Who?"

"Rudi."

"Christopher, don't you think we should try to remember more before calling him. Won't it be a bit embarrassing to tell him we woke up in a hotel room with …"

"I wasn't planning to tell him all that. Just say we had a good time and enjoyed meeting the other people; hope we didn't stay too long."

"Fishing."

"Something like that. So, do you have his number?"

She concentrated on the cognac. "No."

"We could try directory enquiries." He reached for the cordless telephone on the table beside him.

"He's ex-directory."

"How do you know?"

"I heard him say once in the office."

Christopher tried to see her eyes, but she kept her head down, studying the drink. "You don't think I should 'phone him, do you."

She looked up. "Christopher, doesn't something strike you as a bit strange to say the least? We're suddenly invited to Affolter's house and the next thing we remember is waking up in a seedy hotel." The memory of a pink ribbon made her smile. "wearing almost nothing, and there's enough empty bottles of champagne and vodka for a birthday party."

"Of course it's a 'bit strange' as you put it."

"Even more strange when it happens after being at the house of the person who stole you briefcase and– "

"Lisa, we talked about this before. There's no proof that Rudi stole it."

"Proof? What proof do you want? I told you about all the new clothes he's bought. It was him all right and now he's done this to us."

"Why?"

"Why what?"

"Why did he steal my briefcase and why–"

"I told you, the decision in the Steering–"

"Yes, I know to get back at me, but that still seems petty to me. And now you're suggesting he did something to us and dumped us in that hotel. Why?"

"I don't know, yet, but it was him, I know."

"OK calm down, we're trying to remember exactly what happened."

Silence. Pictures flickered in Christopher's head, but he couldn't hold on to them.

"I told you that Erna and I saw some funny people going in and out of his house."

"Lisa, I didn't think this was something we should be discussing before, and after what's just happened I certainly don't think we should be discussing it now. Would you like another cognac?"

"No, thank you. Maybe you're right … but why would Rudi suddenly invite us? Did he want to find out if we suspected him?"

Christopher could see she wasn't going to let it go. He poured himself a small measure. "OK, supposing you're right, I still don't see what that's got to do with us waking up in that hotel?"

"I don't know … at the moment."

"Anyhow, we have something more urgent to think about: are we going to go back to the police?"

"You have your doubts?"

"You saw the reaction of the sergeant, he–"

"I must admit, I wasn't taking too much notice of anybody's reactions."

"Well he clearly didn't believe that we don't know how or why we were in that hotel."

"But we don't."

"You know that and I know that, but you can see how it must look from the outside."

"We can't just forget the whole thing."

"No, but we need to try to remember more about yesterday evening before we talk to the police again. I suggest we try getting a good night's sleep, see what the subconscious mind can come up with."

"I'm not so sure I'm going to get much sleep."

"Another cognac might help."

She held out her glass. "It might."

Silence.

Lisa shook her head, "All those empty bottles in the room; we can't have drunk that much champagne and vodka. Can we?"

"As I said, my head feels like a hangover, but–"

"Mine too, but we're drinking cognac on Saturday afternoon. I wouldn't be able to do that after all that the night before."

"Me neither, but I think the shock of waking up in that posit– that situation might have sobered us up."

"Even so."

They sipped slowly, but steadily. "Christopher can I ask you something?"

"Of course."

"I know there's no danger, but if I start to remember, depending on what it is … well I must admit I'm more than a little bit frightened. Would you … would you mind staying. I'll make us something to eat and there's a half decent bottle of wine, more alcohol, that I've been saving for a special occasion. I think this more than qualifies as special, although not in the way I originally intended."

"Of course I'll stay. That couch looks comfortable enough, especially after this much cognac and wine. And if our subconscious minds don't provide the answers we can always probe Rudi on Monday."

He was wrong, the couch was not comfortable. The alcohol had not stopped the question swirling around his mind. How had he come to be in that hotel, on that bed, with Lisa? The memory of Lisa on the bed caused part of his body to react in a way that made him embarrassed, even in the dark.

Think, think. It must be possible to remember something of what happened. It's in the memory somewhere; just a question of making the right connections. But how? … … Nothing! No pictures, no sounds, nothing, absolutely nothing.

He screwed his eyes tighter, until they hurt, but still nothing.

The cognac was starting to have its soporific effect.

Rudi … Rudi asked me to dinner … suggested I bring Lisa. OK. Where does he live? … in an apartment … in Switzerland, obviously .. which floor? … I remember looking up … third or fourth … no … not an apartment … a house with four stories … how did we get there? … an aeroplane? … Rudi lives in Switzerland … I saw an aeroplane when I looked up .. his house must be near the airport.

He opened his eyes.

We went by car … where's the car now? … a taxi? …we went by taxi. Phew this is hard work. All this effort and I think I know we went to Rudi's big house near the airport by taxi.

He could not stifle the yawn, but he kept it quiet.

At least it's a start, I suppose.

His eyes started to close.

Leave the rest until morning.

As the cognac finally did its job and he drifted off, the image of Lisa on the bed floated once more into his head.

The hypnic jerk brought him half-awake.

A bodiless head floated past: a bearded, bodiless head. Nymphs hovered around the shoulders of a gorilla: nude nymphs. Above them multicoloured liquids poured out of an eye.

The blanket covering him slipped onto the floor.

His eyes flickered open and his hand immediately went to the cold, damp sensation on his forehead. All the images of the dream fast-forwarded through his head. I mustn't lose this. "Pen, paper." He reached out his arm to the left. No table. "Where's the pen and paper?" He reached further and rolled off the couch.

Many experiences of being aware of having good ideas while asleep, only to have them fade by the time morning came had taught him to keep pen and paper by the side of the bed. Some of the best themes for the short stories he wrote came from those ideas.

He groped around Lisa's flat in the half-light, trying to keep the images in his head. In the kitchen he found a board on a hook on the wall. He could just make out the words 'coffee' and 'nail polish'. With the attached felt-tipped pen he quickly scribbled key words, bodiless head, nymphs, eye, multicoloured liquids.

In the bedroom Lisa tossed and turned. Every time she closed her eyes Rudi Affolter's face greeted her, as if etched on the inside of her eyelids, so she lay with her eyes open. Normally she was very good at remembering exactly what she wore and what she had to eat, but both pieces of information were missing in connection with the visit to Rudi's.

I think I made a special effort when I was getting ready. But why? Not for Rudi that's for sure.

She couldn't help a shy smile when she remembered.

Because I was going with Christopher. Careful Lisa, he's your boss. But it was the first time I'd been with him outside the office, and he is ... what? ... he's ... attractive. Ekaterina thought so. Who? Ekaterina? Who's Ekaterina?

Lisa closed her eyes and the picture of Rudi reappeared.

Ekaterina? Where was Ekaterina? ... Of course, at Rudi Affolter's. Tall, elegant, beautiful Ekaterina, how could I forget her? What about her and Christopher? ... I can't remember. Why can't I remember?

She lay on her back and stared at the ceiling. What did we have to eat? If I could remember that it might trigger some other thoughts. We had a lot to drink, that I do remember. ... 'A piece of asparagus?' What does that mean? We had asparagus to eat? No, not to eat, but choking on asparagus. ... I choked on some wine and he said something about choking on asparagus. Who? "Are you OK, my dear?" Of course, the little guy ... what was his name?"

As she succumbed to the light stage sleep, the image of Rudi Affolter floated away. Voices drifted in and out, 'briefcase', 'spying', 'magical fits'.

"What would you like for breakfast? Are you still on English or have you adapted to the Swiss style of bread, cold meats, cheese, and jam?"

"English still I'm afraid, but not bacon eggs etc."

"Just as well, the closest I could get would be two eggs and even they may be off."

"Just cereal if you have it, Otherwise toast and tea."

"Muesli?"

"Just toast and tea."

They ate in silence, both trying to understand what had come to them during the night.

"Did you remember anything?" They spoke at the same time.

"Yes." Again synchronised.

Lisa put her mug down with more force than she intended. "I'll get a pen and paper."

Christopher closed his eyes. "What I actually remember is not very much. We went to Rudi Affolter's by taxi. He lives in a big house near the airport—"

"I know, I've been there before, remember."

"Spying, with Erna."

Lisa glared at him. "And the ZFFM barbeque."

"I did have a weird dream about—"

"I know there was an Ekaterina at Rudi's"

"Ekaterina?"

"Yes, tall, elegant, beautiful Ekaterina."

Christopher shook his head.

"And a little guy. I remember I almost choked on some wine and he said 'are you OK, my dear'. I don't remember his name."

"So, between us all we remember is Rudi's house, beautiful Ekaterina and a little guy."

"It's a start."

Christopher shrugged. "I suppose."

"I heard voices."

"Voices?"

"As I drifted off to sleep last night, 'briefcase', 'spying', 'magical fits'.

"The 'briefcase' sounds like your overactive imagination again. My dream was weird, with some strange images." He retrieved the kitchen board from beside the couch.

"I wondered where that had gone."

"Sorry. I needed something to write on." He told her about bodiless heads, nude nymphs and coloured liquids pouring out of an eye. "When I'd written it down I realised I'd had a similar dream, immediately before waking up in that hotel."

The thought of 'waking up in that hotel' brought images of a pink ribbon before Lisa's eyes and she suppressed a giggle and blushed. "Obviously your dream needs interpretation."

"Obviously."

"Let's try."

"Do you know anything about dream interpretation?"

"We had a class on Freud at school."

"It might not be enough."

"Let's try. Tell me more about last night's dream and perhaps it will trigger some details of the first dream and mean something to us."

"Let me see, what came first? The floating, bodiless, head ... a bearded head."

"What colour was the beard?"

"Colour? I don't know ... grey."

"Rudi Affolter."

"What?"

"Rudi Affolter."

"Yes, I know, that's what we're trying to find out: what happened at Rudi Affolter's."

"No, I mean the grey-bearded, bodiless head, that's Rudi Affolter."

"There's no reason to think—"

"Did the head have shifty eyes?"

"No, why?"

"Affolter does, a thief's, shifty eyes."

"Lisa."

"OK, OK. Carry on with your dream. I won't interrupt again."

"I told you it was weird."

"And what about the first dream?"

"The same characters, but even more weird. It might make a good story."

"You mean for the newspapers?"

"No, perhaps you didn't know that writing short, fiction stories is my hobby."

"No. How would I?"

"I've just remembered something. In the first dream the nude nymphs were tossing the head between them."

"Sounds like an erotic dream, tut, tut."

"Not really an erotic dream."

"Nude nymphs tossing a head about, doesn't sound like a normal dream."

"It definitely wasn't 'normal' ... Blonde."

"Sorry?"

"Blonde hair, they both had blonde hair.

"So, what–

"Just a minute ... Nicole–"

"and Sandy. Rudi's two playmates."

"Yes, the nymphets."

Lisa smiled. "See, that's another part of the puzzle."

"You're enjoying this aren't you?"

"Enjoying is the wrong word, but I do want to understand how we came to be in that hotel."

"Me too."

"You don't seem to have Ekaterina in your dreams. Do you remember Ekaterina?"

Christopher concentrated. "'Just try a little bit, for Ekaterina'."

"Sorry."

"That's what she said, 'Just try a little bit, for Ekaterina'."

"I think that's a big part of the problem, we tried more than a little bit."

"Yes, Ekaterina, I think I talked to her a lot."

Lisa nodded. She realised that was what she was trying to remember last night before going to sleep. Ekaterina and Christopher.

Now she remembered and wanted to move on. "So, who else have we got in your fantasia?"

"The gorilla?"

"Anything special about it?"

"No ... no, I don't think so."

"And an eye in the sky."

They talked for another half-hour, Lisa trying to get Christopher to remember more details of his dreams.

"I'm exhausted," said Christopher. "Let's summarise, again, what we've got."

"Me too. OK, we went to Rudi Affolter's house, near the airport by taxi. We met some people there: two blond nymphets; tall, elegant, beautiful Ekaterina, who got her claws into you– "

"That might be a bit of an exaggeration."

"No, believe me, I remember that."

Christopher was a bit taken aback by the note of jealousy in Lisa's voice.

Lisa took a not too well hidden deep breath. "An eye in the sky, and a little guy."

"And a gorilla."

"Doesn't sound like much after all this effort."

"No, but more than yesterday."

"The question is, how will it sound to the police?"

"As I said yesterday 'if we go to the police'."

"You still have your doubts?"

"I was doubtful when that policeman left us in the hotel room. 'Come to the station if you still want to talk to us about it' he said. He obviously thought it was just the end of a wild night."

"But why would you ask the hotel to call the police?"

"It was a mistake? A reaction on waking up? To protect ourselves? Who knows?"

"And what we've remembered so far isn't going to help our credibility: nymphets, a gorilla, a beautiful woman, and a little guy"

"Exactly, we'd look foolish."

"So, what are we going to do?"

"We have to talk to Rudi. I don't see any other way to get some idea about what happened."

Lisa sighed.

"You really don't like him, do you?"

"He's never liked me for some reason. After what's happened I don't trust him."

"We've been through this. We don't know that anything's 'happened'."

"So you say, but if he had anything to do with us ending in that hotel, he'll pay."

"Let's talk to him tomorrow."

"OK."

"But in a calm way, we don't want to start accusing him of anything."

"Not yet."

Lisa said she felt OK to be by herself. Christopher could see anger at Rudi Affolter was replacing her nervousness. He knew he would have to try to get some 'control' over her the next day. He still didn't believe that Rudi had had anything to do with the theft of his briefcase. Or, was it that he didn't want to believe? As for what had happened between Friday night and Saturday afternoon, how could Rudi have anything to do with that? However, the fact was that something happened for which he had no explanation.

When he got home and consulted his diary he saw that tomorrow was the second Monday in the month: the day of the production-R&D review. The meeting would last two hours. How was he going to ensure that Lisa did not start giving Rudi the third degree during that time?

He didn't want to have the dreams he'd had the night before, so he took two of the sleeping tablets the doctor gave him to help him sleep on long flights.

Christopher put his head round the door of the marketing department not expecting to see anyone at seven fifteen, but one of the senior assistants was already there. "Good morning, bright and early this morning."

"Good morning, Mr McLendi. I find it easier to concentrate at this time, before the telephones start ringing."

"I was going to leave a message on Rudi Affolter's desk, but perhaps you can ask him to call me as soon as he gets in."

"Christopher, it's Rudi, you wanted me to call you?"

"Rudi, good morning. Yes, I wanted to suggest you come to the production-R&D meeting this morning, we could do with your input on the 9410 product."

"How long will it last?

Lisa hovered in Christopher's open door

"About two hours."

"OK, I have a meeting at eleven thirty."

Christopher replaced the receiver. "Come in, Lisa. You're here early."

"I thought we'd catch Affolter before many other people arrived."

"That was Rudi on the telephone, I've invited him to the meeting."

"But I want to be there when you confront him."

"Lisa, neither I nor you are going to 'confront' him. I promise I won't mention Friday until we have a chance to thank him together."

"When will that be?"

"After the meeting."

"What time?"

"It should take about two hours."

Lisa turned and mumbled something Christopher could not hear.

"Oh and Lisa, I think it might be better not to talk to anyone about what happened, especially Erna." He took her lack of response to mean she would be ignoring the advice.

Christopher could tell from the puzzled looks on the faces that no one from production or R&D could understand why Rudi Affolter was at the monthly meeting. As it was his meeting, he didn't feel obliged to offer any explanation. This also surprised the participants.

Although the meeting was much shorter than usual, as they came out of the conference room they almost bumped into Lisa.

"Christopher, Rudi, I was just on my way … to the post room."

"Via the long route," said Rudi.

"Sorry?"

"I'm sure I don't have to remind you the post room is at the opposite end of the building."

"Ah, no I have to collect something from … from down here first."

Christopher jumped in quickly to save Lisa any further embarrassment. "But this a good opportunity for us to thank you for Friday night."

"Yes, thank you so much, we really enjoyed it."

"I'm glad you both could come."

A silence stretched beyond the five-second awkward point. Christopher could see Lisa dying to saying something, but, with great difficulty, holding herself back.

"Did you get home all right?" Rudi must have seen the glance Lisa and Christopher exchanged.

"Why do you a– "

Christopher jumped in again. "Yes, yes, of course, no problem."

"Good."

The silence started to descend again, but Rudi interrupted it. "Well, I must get on."

"Yes, me too." Christopher started to turn, but stopped when Lisa spoke.

"I hope we didn't outstay our welcome, I've no idea what time we left. I know it was late."

"I've no idea either, and no, you didn't, what did you say, 'outstay' your welcome. I've not heard that before, 'outstay', very descriptive."

"I think we were the first to leave weren't we?"

Christopher was getting more nervous with each question from Lisa and tried to catch her eye to signal they should go, but she never took her eyes off Rudi's face. He stared back at her. "Oh, Nicole, Sandy and Mikos were staying with me, and Ekaterina and Herman left soon after you."

"We enjoyed meeting everyone." Christopher placed his hand as discretely as possible under Lisa's elbow, but she took a half step away.

"Was there any particular reason you asked if we got home all right?" Clearly Lisa realised time was running out for her interrogation.

"Well, after Christopher had fallen– "

"I fell?"

"Yes, don't you remember?"

"Oh ... yes ... of course."

"I felt a bit guilty. Perhaps I'd been too generous with some of the drinks, I know not everyone drinks as much as some of my friends and I. Mikos picked you up and put you in the taxi."

"Oh yes ... yes, that was kind of him."

"I should think you've got a few bruises though."

"I survived."

"I was sure you would, Lisa said she was going to ... 'take care of you'." Christopher caught the wink from Rudi, and it made him even more keen to get away.

Safely back in his office, Christopher paced up and down. He expected the knock on his door. A head appeared between door and jamb.

"Come in Lisa, and close the door."

"We didn't find out much, did we?"

"Even with your probing."

"Just a few innocent questions."

"I hope Rudi thought so."

"I don't care if he did or not."

Christopher drummed his fingers on the desk. "Hmm."

"What does that mean?"

"It means what happened might be a lot less mysterious than we were thinking."

"Why do you say that?"

"Didn't you see him wink?"

"Who?"

"Rudi."

"Wink?"

"When he said, 'Lisa said she was going to take care of you'."

"No."

"What if we did have too much to drink, which we did, and decided, and I use the word in the loosest possible way, to spend the night together in a hotel?"

"Having too much to drink doesn't make you lose your memory."

"Have you ever had that much to drink, Lisa?"

"I'm sure I have, but perhaps not that combination of drinks."

"Exactly."

"But I don't believe any amount of alcohol can make you do something completely out of character."

"Meaning?"

"I'm not in the habit of jumping into bed with …"

"With?"

"Strangers."

"Hardly strangers."

"With my boss then." Lisa felt the blush starting.

"Me neither, I mean not with my boss, but with my …" Now Christopher blushed. "However, after that much drink …"

"No, I'm sure we didn't decide, someone put us there, I feel it."

"Makes going back to the police a little more difficult though."

All morning, Lisa had avoided going anywhere near Erna. On one side she was dying to tell her what happened. On the other she knew Erna would ask lots of questions, which she couldn't and didn't want to answer. Despite what she'd said to Christopher, she realised there was the slim possibility of an outside chance she had jumped into bed with her boss. If anyone could worm a confession out of her it was Erna. And in Erna's eyes it would be more than 'a slim possibility of an outside chance'.

Erna was hovering in the corridor connecting Christopher's office with Herr Muri's. "Hi, Lisa, did you have a good weekend?"

"Not bad, and you?"

"OK. Did you do anything special?"

"No, did you?"

"I heard you went to Rudi Aff–"

"Where did you hear that?" came out much more sharply than Lisa intended.

Erna held up her hands. "Sorry, I didn't realise it was a secret."

Lisa rubbed the top of Erna's arm. "Sorry, didn't mean to snap. Let's go for a coffee."

Lisa guessed Erna must be near to bursting. "So, yes I did go to Rudi's on Friday."

Erna's 'go-on nod' brought no reaction. "And?"

"We had a pleasant evening."

"'A pleasant evening'"

"Yes."

"Lisa, you are so annoying. What happened?"

"Happened?"

"Grrrr."

"OK. We were invited to–"

"We?"

"I meant I."

"No, you said 'we'."

Lisa's deep breath was mental rather than physical. "Mr McLendi and I."

Now a smile accompanied Erna's nods.

"Don't smile like that. Just work colleagues getting together."

"Who else was there?"

"Some friends of Rudi's."

"No one from ZFFM?"

"No, as it happens."

More smiles and nods from Erna. "Nice."

"It was."

"Did Mr McLendi see you home afterwards?

"Look–"

"OK, OK. Of course I'm interested how your first date with–"

"It wasn't a date. That's an old-fashioned word anyway."

"Date, rendezvous, stelldichein call it what you like: going out with your boss for the evening. Did you invite Mr McLendi in for coffee?"

Lisa knew she had to stop this. "Rudi told the other guests about the theft of Christopher's briefcase."

"How did he look?"

"Look?"

"You know, pleased, sorry, embarrassed ... guilty?"

Lisa thought about it "Sympathetic if anything, I suppose."

"Any signs of new clothes or anything."

"Erna, I'm not familiar with Rudi Affolter's wardrobe to know what's new and what isn't."

"What did Christopher wear for your date?"

Lisa stood. "I have work to do."

Erna remained sitting. "So do I. Are you seeing him again?"

"Erna–"

"OK. You can tell me about it some other time."

"And I'm sure you'll ask another time, but there still won't be any answers."

"We'll see. By the way did you tell your Mr McLendi what we saw at Affolter's house."

"Yes, and he wasn't pleased that we'd been there."

"So, are we dropping the investigati–"

The face of Sergeant Grindel loomed into Lisa's mind and she shuddered. "No, no."

"Lisa, are you OK?"

"Yes. No, we should still keep an eye on him."

"So, you still think he's guilty?"

"Oh, he's guilty all right."

Erna couldn't know that Lisa was thinking about pink ribbons and empty bottles not briefcases.

Lisa hurried back to her office. There was something she needed to do while it was fresh in her mind. Down one side of a piece of paper she wrote the names Rudi had just mentioned of people at the dinner party: Nicole, Sandy, Mikos, Ekaterina and Herman. Down the opposite side she listed the characters she and Christopher had come up with. "Nicole and Sandy are the nymphets. Ekaterina is Ekaterina. That leaves Mikos and Herman. Herman, Herman monster, must be the gorilla. So, Mikos is the little guy.

A delegation from an important, German customer was visiting the Zurich factory, and Rudi asked Herr Muri and Christopher to join them for lunch. Several times during the long, drawnout meal Christopher felt Rudi looking at him, but his head turned away whenever Christopher glanced in his direction. On one occasion Christopher thought he saw a small smile.

After lunch Rudi, Christopher and a team from production met with the delegation to discuss a possible joint project. An hour and a half into the discussion, the four Germans said they needed some time alone to answer a question from the production people. Rudi and Christopher retired to Rudi's office.

"How do you think it's going?"

"Oh they'll agree."

The usual marketing optimism thought Christopher. "It's an interesting project, but will it be profitable?"

"I think so."

"Are they going back to Munich tonight?

"No. I've arranged something very special for them tonight at a club in town; it should help them to agree. Do you want to join them, I can't?"

"Thanks, but I'm still feeling the effects of Friday to be honest. Having a drink at lunchtime didn't help. By the way, thanks once again, we enjoyed it."

Rudi didn't look up from the papers he was studying on his desk. "My pleasure. We'll have to do it again. We'll make it a bit less alcoholic next time." Now he looked at Christopher. "As long as you both enjoyed it."

Even through the beard Christopher could see the corners of Rudi's mouth turn up in something between a grin and a smile. Curiosity got the better of the caution he'd told Lisa to excise. "I noticed your wink in the corridor, when you said something about Lisa was going to take care of me', and your little smile now. Is there a reason?"

Rudi busied himself with the papers again. "No."

"No?"

"It's nothing to do with me."

"What isn't?"

"Look … as I say, it's nothing to do with me, but I'm pleased you and Lisa are getting on well."

"Why do you think we are?"

"The way you were on Friday, during the evening and when you left."

Christopher made a quick decision; Lisa would have been proud of him. He closed Rudi's door. "Actually, between you and me, we did spend some time together. We woke up in a hotel, but neither of us can remember how we got there. Did we really have so much to drink?"

"Depends what you mean by 'so much'."

"Well, speaking for myself, I wouldn't say I was a big drinker, but not a novice at the same time."

"Different drinks affect people in different ways, and at different times."

"All the same …"

"I must admit that Ekaterina sometimes spikes people's drinks, for fun she calls it, but she promised me she wouldn't do anything on Friday. I'll ask her, if you like."

"No, don't do that. It would be embarrassing if she knew what I've just told you."

Rudi got up and approached Christopher. His tone was conspiratorial. "So, you woke up in hotel."

"Yes." And that's going to be the limit of your knowledge thought Christopher. He moved away from Rudi.

"What's the last thing you remember?

'Arriving at your house' would have been the honest answer, but Christopher said, "Walking out of your house."

"And falling?"

"No."

"And then a blank."

"Essentially."

"I could give you the name of the taxi company I called. The taxi driver might be able to fill in some gaps. But is it worth it? Put it down to a few lost hours and a good time, which unfortunately you don't remember." Again the wink.

The taxi company was Rudi's 'local'. Christopher and Lisa decided Lisa should call them a) because her German was better and b) the story would sound better coming from a woman.

Surprisingly the person who answered the 'phone remembered the call out on Friday. "I did the job myself. It's my company, but it had been a slow night and I'd sent all the drivers home."

"Could I come and talk to you?" If Lisa had been doing this in English she would have used a 'little girl lost voice', which was not easy in German.

"I'm rather busy, could you tell me what it is about?

"It's a bit embarrassing, I'd rather come and see you."

The tone of her voice was obviously working better than she thought it was because he agreed to meet her at his office.

The 'office' was the garage of an ordinary house. There was one taxi parked outside.

"Was kann ich für Sie tun, Fraulein?"

"Wie gesagt, es ist ein bisschen pienlich und mein Deutsch ist nicht so gut."

"You can speak in English if you prefer."

"Thank you. You picked me up on Friday night?"

"Ja, at 42 Jacobstrasse, with a man."

"Do you know the owner of the house?"

"I would not say 'know', we pick up people there before."

"Roughly what time was it?"

"I can say you exactly." He made a few mouse clicks. "We have the call at one thirty-eight, so I pick you up at quarter to two."

"And where did we go?"

"You do not know?"

"That's the embarrassing bit. I don't remember anything after leaving my friends'."

"Something bad happened to you?"

"No, why do you ask?"

"You ask many questions, a ... how do you say 'Gedächtnisverlust'."

"'Memory loss'."

"Your German is better than my English. Memory lost is normal after good night, Nein?"

"As I said, nothing happened. I, we, because the gentleman I was with can't remember either, just want to fill in the gaps." They'd not discussed this part of the story, but Lisa wanted to stop the taxi driver feeling that he might become involved in something strange.

"You said to go to Zurich. I asked where, and you said to tell me later. The man, the gentleman, was quiet, or shocked after falling perhaps. You talk to him, but I do not know what you say. At Zurich I still not know where to go. On the Limmatquai you suddenly say stop. The man say something about walking and listening to jazz. You both had a 'taumeln'."

"'Taumeln'?"

"Crazy walk."

"Which direction did we go in?"

"The Niederdorfstrasse."

"Did you see anyone else?"

"At two o'clock in the morning? No."

"Do you remember any of that?"

Christopher screwed up his eyes in concentration. "Nothing, not even my falling down. Do you?"

"No."

"I still can't believe we had that much to drink. You say he said we were staggering."

"That's what he said."

"Well it gives us one more reason not to go back to the police."

"Why?"

"If a taxi driver tells them he dropped us off at two o'clock in the morning in the centre of Zurich, and we woke up in a hotel in the centre of Zurich, you don't need to be Sherlock Holmes to put two and two together and get four."

"But the hotel will know if we checked in alone or not."

"You still think someone took us there."

"Don't you?"

Christopher took a deep breath and sighed.

Lisa shook her head. "Do you normally drink vodka?"

"Sorry?"

"There were empty vodka bottles in the room. I don't drink vodka, Christopher."

"Neither do I, normally, but if we'd drunk so much at Rudi's and we wanted more, maybe that's all we could get."

"From where, at two o'clock in the morning?"

"The hotel?"

"And what about the handcuffs? I don't carry them around in my handbag."

"Really?" Christopher could see that Lisa was being serious. "I suppose a hotel in that area of the city can supply anything."

"And the pink …"

"The what?"

"Nothing." Lisa remembered that it came from her hair. "We could go back to the hotel and ask them how we arrived."

"Do you want to go back and ask them for answers to some of these questions?"

"No … I suppose not."

Silence.

"What are you thinking?"

"Sorry."

"You seem deep in thought."

"No … I was … I was just thinking it was a bit strange the taxi driver remembering us so well."

"He probably doesn't get many customers who asked to dropped off in the centre of Zurich at two o'clock."

"And why was he still working at one thirty?"

"It's his own business, he's probably available almost any time."

"Hmm."

"Now what are you thinking?"

"Nothing."

"Something."

"Convenient, isn't it, having a taxi company so close to Affolter's house."

"So, what now, there's a conspiracy between Rudi and the taxi driver?"

"Could be."

"Lisa!"

"OK, OK. So what do you suggest we do now?"

"To be honest, I'm not sure."

"So, Christopher, did you talk to Wolfgang Zwindel?"

"Wolfgang …?"

"The man who owns the taxi company."

"Ah, yes, thanks for the information Rudi."

"Did it help?"

"Yes, and no."

Rudi smiled and shook his head. "Don't look so worried. You had a good evening, and night, just enjoy it; even if you can't remember it all."

Christopher didn't see much of Lisa over the next few days. He had planned a one-and-a half-day session with the new product development team. Lisa was busy helping Herr Muri prepare for a shareholders' meeting.

On Friday afternoon Herr Muri invited the senior management to listen to and critique his speech for the shareholders' meeting. Afterwards Lisa had arranged a cocktail. Although they were sure no one knew about what had happened, both Christopher and Lisa felt that people were watching them and expecting them to show signs of the liaison. They avoided each other until only a few people remained.

"Where's Rudi, Christopher?"

"Did you miss him?"

"You know I like to keep tabs on him."

Christopher was not sure how much she was joking. "He left for Germany; the exhibition starts tomorrow."

"Ah yes, he sent me a note. I thought you were also going."

"Next week."

Christopher stopped at Lisa's door on the way back to his office. "Have you got any plans for eating?"

"I was thinking about pizza delivery."

"I found a new, excellent pizzeria around the back of the Bahnhof last week, would you like to join me?"

"Can I trust you not to drag me off to your hotel again?"

"My hotel, I was wondering if I could trust you not to kidnap me again."

"As long as I pay, I owe you a bottle of brandy."

"Half a bottle. Are you ready now?"

"Give me five minutes."

"I agree, excellent pizza."

"Better than your delivery?"

"No contest."

Christopher sipped his wine, they were on the second carafe, and he had to drive. "Pretty good Chianti also." Another sip. "How have you been?"

"OK."

"I don't know about you, but although it's only one week ago, what happened seems somehow less … less dramatic, if that's the right word."

"Does it?"

"I'm not saying it wasn't frightening, but from what we've found out, less mysterious."

"Not for me. I still don't believe we decided to go to that hotel."

"I don't want to believe it either, but the evidence–"

"The 'evidence' comes from Rudi Affolter and his taxi driver."

"At least he's back to Rudi."

"Sorry?"

"Rudi's back to being 'Rudi' and not 'Affolter'."

"Yes, well I'm not a hundred per cent sure he was responsible any more."

"Good."

"But I'm not sure he's a hundred per cent innocent either."

"But you still think someone put us there."

"I just don't see us doing that." Are you sure of that, Lisa asked herself.

"I don't see who else can help us find any answers. We already agreed we don't want to go and ask at the hotel."

"The taxi driver mentioned that you said something about listening to jazz. Are there any places to listen to jazz on the Niederdorfstrasse?"

"One that I know of."

"You know one?"

"I've been a couple of times, it used to be a hobby of mine."

"Trad? Blues? Soul?"

"Big band jazz is what I like. You don't find that in a jazz club, so I go more for blues."

"Interesting."

"Why?

"My ex-husband liked trad jazz."

"You never went with him to a jazz club?"

"André went to such places with his friends, not me. So if you know these places perhaps we did go–"

"Perhaps."

"and something happened while we were there."

"Still looking for the villain?"

"I don't know what sort of people you get in jazz clubs."

"People like me."

"No, I mean other types of people."

"People who leave couples in compromising positions in hotel rooms?"

The image of the pink ribbon flashed through Lisa's mind. She blushed.

Christopher also started to feel a bit hot under the collar. "Well there's one way to find out if we were there."

"How?"

"Go and ask."

The next night Christopher took a look at the three places to listen to live jazz on the Niederdorfstrasse. One of them was out-and-out Dixieland jazz and he realised he had forgotten about it because Dixieland jazz was not his style. The Celler offered trad jazz and the one he had been to, Night Blues, was strictly blues. The signs on both their doors said open until 03.00. If they had gone anywhere at his suggestion it would have been Night Blues, so he tried there first.

The story he and Lisa concocted was that he had been there a week ago last Friday and thinks he may have left his scarf. He'd been out of town for a week and so had not been able to get back until now. The barman at Night Blues said Friday was always busy and he couldn't recall every customer. No, he didn't remember Christopher and they hadn't found a red scarf. Christopher had one beer and asked a couple of the waiters the same questions, but got the same answers.

He wondered if it was worth trying The Celler, but he knew Lisa would not be happy with half an answer, especially as it had been his idea to ask the questions.

"Gruetzi."

"Gruetzi, ein Bier bitte."

"Draft or bottled?" Typical! He tried his best German accent, but even simply ordering a beer people detected he was English, or even American. "Draft please."

"Zum Wohl."

"Danke. Were you here a week ago last Friday?"

"I'm always here on a Friday."

"Do you by any chance remember seeing me here?"

The barman studied his face and began to shake his head. "It's always packed on Friday nights."

"I'm sure."

"Is there a particular reason you ask?"

"I lost a scarf and thought I might have left it here."

"I don't think anyone found a scarf."

"Oh well, it was worth a try. Do you only have trad jazz here?"

"That's what our customers like."

"I'm more of a blues man myself."

"Everybody to their own tastes. Our customers like something a bit more lively. We often get people dancing. Excuse me." He waddled to the other end of the bar to serve one of the waiters.

"I've just been talking to one of my colleague. He recognises you, and now he's mentioned it so do I."

"I was here a week ago last Friday?"

"You and a young lady. I can't think how I didn't recognise you."

"Any particular reason?"

"Well you both put on quite a show for us. You took over the small dance floor."

"We did?"

"Yes. The lady even took off her shoes and got up on one of the tables. She's a real mover. We were a bit worried because she wasn't too steady on her feet."

"You mean drunk?"

"I think she'd had one or two."

"Well we enjoyed the evening."

"It looked like you were enjoying it."

"I must admit I don't remember leaving. What time was it?"

"We must close at three, polizei stunde. I think you would have danced all night if the music hadn't stopped. One of my colleagues helped you both up the stairs."

"So that's it. We went to The Celler, danced, you on the table–"

"On the table? Never."

"That's what he said."

"Who was this person?"

"The barman."

"What did he look like?"

"A big, big man. Why?"

"I just wondered."

"You're not thinking of going to talk to him, are you?"

"No."

"I wouldn't if I were you. He seemed sure. It might be embarrassing."

"It might."

"According to him we left when they closed, at three, and presumably went to the hotel, which is just across the Niederdorfstrasse."

"So, as far as you're concerned, everything is clear now?"

"I wouldn't say 'clear', but the various pieces do start to fit together. Don't you think?"

"I can just about accept we went to the jazz club, but not the dancing on the table. I still don't see why we went to a hotel."

"I agree that it's not the sort of thing either of us would do under normal circumstances, but the whole evening was hardly 'normal'."

"Hmm."

"So, can you stop giving Rudi the third degree?"

"I suppose so."

Lisa's 'I suppose so' about stopping giving Rudi the third degree had meant 'yes' at the time. But she was not happy with the 'explanation' of how they came to be in that hotel. She couldn't think of any other avenues to explore, except going to get the story direct from the barman, and looking into his eyes to see if he was lying. That might be embarrassing if she had been dancing on a table. And she hadn't given up on trying to prove that Rudi Affolter was the one who stole Christopher's briefcase.

Erna's job in the purchasing department gave her contact with many people. She could collect information, meaning gossip, about Rudi Affolter without appearing to be nosey. Erna reported what she heard, mostly with her opinion on top, and Lisa kept a record. All they'd got so far were snippets of information about Rudi buying new clothes in Basel. Lisa had never believed that Rudi had done it for the money. From the stories about his lifestyle she knew he was 'not short of a bob or two' as her father would have said. Her theory was that he'd done it to cause Christopher some difficulties after what happened at the Steering Committee. If she was right, information about what he bought wouldn't prove anything.

She convinced herself that a person who takes petty revenge for something that happens in a business context would probably keep a souvenir of it to remind himself of his triumph. She needed some physical evidence, something from the briefcase. She looked for opportunities to search his office.

The exhibition in Germany was the show of the year in the glass industry and most of ZFFM senior management were attending. This left Lisa with little to do. She just happened to be wandering past the marketing department late in the afternoon, and noticed that it was completely empty except for a junior secretary.

"All by yourself?"

The young girl jumped up. "Yes, Ms Stern."

Normally Lisa would have said immediately 'call me Lisa', but she wanted to retain some authority over the girl, which she did not have. "It gets a bit boring when everyone's away."

"The telephones been ringing, and I've got a report to type for Mr Affolter, and–"

"So, you've been busy."

"Oh yes, I've done–"

"Well, it's almost five o'clock, I should take the opportunity to go a bit early, you'll avoid the mad rush for the trams."

"Do you think I can?"

"Yes, of course, there's no one here to notice."

"If you think it's OK?"

"I'm sure it is. I'm going to leave myself. Have a good evening."

"You too, and thanks." The girl switched off her typewriter and started tidying the papers on her desk.

Lisa hovered by the display of a new advertising campaign, studying the text and pictures.

"Good night, Ms Stern."

"Good night, …?"

"Brigit."

"Good night, Brigit."

Lisa waited five long minutes to make sure Brigit hadn't forgotten anything, and then strode into Rudi Affolter's office. As she didn't know what she was looking for, she didn't know where to start. The desk rather than the cupboards would be the obvious place to hide something. The top right-hand draw wouldn't open. Lisa looked under the blotter for the key: nothing. All the other drawers yielded to her pull. Mostly they contained papers. Lisa knew there was no point in looking through them because she wouldn't be able to identify if any had come from Christopher's briefcase. In the bottom draw on the left was a collection of bric-a-brac that Rudi must have collected on his travels. She quickly rummaged through the items. Her eyes fell on a small pewter cup, which she picked up. The engraving was in English

Summer Squash Tournament
Winner 1988

She tried to recollect if Christopher had ever said anything about playing squash. Would he have such a thing in his briefcase? On the other hand why would Rudi have a cup engraved in English?

Lisa saw the desk was almost identical to one she'd had when she started at ZFFM. She'd once lost the key to her desk draw and had been able to release it from underneath by removing the draw below. She sank to her knees and started to feel along the lower edge of the locked draw. The sound of hurrying heels stopped her in mid search, and she looked up to see Brigit entering the department. There was no obvious reason why anyone coming through the door would look directly into Rudi's office, but Brigit did. Lisa's arm was still inside the space below the draw and her chin was level with the desk.

"I forgot my scarf," said Brigit, as though Lisa's position in her boss' office was the most natural thing in the world. "Good night again." She called as she ran out.

Lisa quickly withdrew her arm and replaced the second draw. She reasoned that Brigit might suddenly realise what she had seen and come back. She hurried to the entrance, but Brigit was gone. It'll probably come to her when she gets home, thought Lisa, I'll have to think up some excuse and make sure I see her first thing in the morning.

"Brigit, good morning."

"Ms Stern, good morning."

"Lisa, please. You must have thought it funny to see me kneeling on the floor in Mr Affolter's office last night."

"When?"

"When you came back for your scarf."

"I was in such a hurry to catch my tram, I didn't really notice anything."

"Oh, well that's OK then. Have a nice day." Lisa turned and expelled relieved air.

Brigit made a note on her dictation pad.

When Rudi returned from Germany a few days later, he asked Brigit if there had been any calls while he was away.

"I made a note of everything," said Birgit reaching for her pad.

Gazda

The Raid

16 September to 26 September 2008

Detective Sergeant Jochim Friedmann walked past The Celler for the third time. His slight stumbling suggested that he was just another drunk waiting for one of the Niederdorfstrasse prostitutes to become available. But the chances of that at two am on a cold September Tuesday were slim. He was alone on the street.

Everything was in place. Around the corner, out of sight, the uniform troops waited in the van. Friedmann's boss, Inspector Erich Kullmer, was with the troops, well away from the sharp end of the operation, as usual. If all went to plan, Constable Bernstein would emerge from The Celler with one of the women, immediately light a cigarette, and Friedmann would signal Kullmer.

Bernstein had been in the bar for half an hour, and Friedman was getting cold. As he turned to go past the bar again, the door opened, Bernstein came out and lit a cigarette.

From previous visits they had seen The Celler was not full on a Tuesday night. They'd estimated that a team of eight officers would be enough to contain the customers and detain the working girls. As it turned out, there were more customers than normal because the band had a strong following in Zurich. A few people escaped through the cordon while the officers concentrated on the targets of the raid.

Kullmer arrived at The Celler when all the action was over. He made a, 'I'm the officer in charge' speech to the bar customers about being careful in the future of 'some of the unfortunately, unsavoury elements of our fine city'. Friedmann doubted that many of them were listening: either concentrating on pretending to be sober or eager to get out of there as quickly as possible.

The van took three prostitutes to the station. Two received a caution and release. The one who approached Bernstein spent the night in a cell.

The next morning Kullmer and Friedmann briefed Chief Inspector Müller on the raid. Müller liked to-the-point summaries, so they kept it short. As they turned to leave Müller asked Kullmer to stay behind.

"This needs careful handling, Erich. The local newspapers will cooperate I'm sure, but we have to be watchful. So, no leaks. Restrict information to as tight a circle as possible. No one talks to the press. Friedmann's a good man, we can rely on him I think."

"Certainly, Sir."

"At the same time, I want this to be a full investigation."

Kullmer nodded. "Even as far as bringing charges?"

Chief Inspector Müller pondered the question. "Yes, even as far as bringing charges, if the crime is serious enough, and we have proof."

Inspector Kullmer guessed the Chief Inspector wouldn't want to define what 'serious enough' meant at this stage, so he didn't ask.

When he got back to his office Kullmer wondered if they could handle this 'carefully'. A clamp down on soliciting in bars was the message of the raid. At the same time they didn't want to suggest any interference with the 'normal' prostitution business. A knock on the door brought him out of his reverie. "Come in."

Although there was no need, Sergeant Friedmann ducked his head as he entered. Like many tall people, he'd learnt to live in a world designed for people of average height.

"Sit down Friedmann." Kullmer rarely asked his subordinates to sit in his office. It was his way of maintaining a position of authority. Friedmann's height however made Kullmer feel uncomfortable and gave him a crick in the neck. Kullmer liked working with Friedmann. They had similar, methodical approaches to investigation. Kullmer's more years of experience meant the young sergeant clearly deferred to him, which reduced the 30 centimetre height difference somewhat. "I've been thinking. Should we drop the charges against, what was her name?"

"Francesca Kardomah, Sir."

"Yes, Francesca. Perhaps we should drop the charges."

"But she did try to solicit Bernstein."

"Yes, I know, but charges mean court, which means press."

"I doubt if the press would report anything about a single prostitute. There's been nothing about the raid."

"That's because they probably don't know about it. We kept the raid low-key by choosing a quiet night like Tuesday. We didn't tell the press and I'm sure no one from The Celler 'phoned a newspaper. But they have reporters permanently in the court. It only needs some overeager, young reporter looking to make a name for himself to start digging around the ownership of The Celler"

"I thought the idea was to send a message—"

"Quite right Friedmann, but I think, although nothing has been in the newspapers, the word about the raid will have spread through the Zurich club owners and pimps."

"But dropping charges says you're not serious about the message. Are you serious?" Few sergeants in Kullmer's KRIPO team would have dared to speak to him like this. His reputation said he didn't like subordinates directly questioning his opinions. But Friedmann still hadn't acquired the caution that comes with age.

Friedmann's forthrightness reminded Kullmer of his younger self and his own rapid rise through the ranks. "Oh I'm serious, we're serious, but I'm not sure charging this Francesca makes the message any stronger or just gets us some unnecessary publicity."

"And we're trying to keep it quiet are we, because–"

"No, we're not trying to keep it quiet, Sergeant."

"Really? Not because of the footballer's involvement?"

Now Friedmann had stepped over the mark. "No, Sergeant Friedmann, we are not trying to keep it quiet because of the footballer's involvement. We will drop the charges against Ms Kardomah. As your superior officer let me remind you that whatever you may feel about this decision you're not to discuss it outside this room."

Friedmann was young, but he was smart. He got the message and nodded.

"You and I will carry out a full investigation into what has been happening at The Celler and other places. And I mean 'full'. Understood?"

Friedmann smiled. "Yes, Sir."

Friedmann eyed the woman through the cell door spyhole. She sat hugging her knees in the corner of the bed, which had not been slept in. Probably 24/25 years old, it was difficult to tell with some of these girls who'd been in the trade for a long time. Looked European, even Western European, which was getting more and more common these days. Zurich had come through a Far East phase a few years ago. Now, most of the girls were from Eastern Europe. Could this one even be Swiss?

"Open up please constable."

"Yes, Sarge."

Here Friedmann did need to duck his head.

"Grüezi Fräulein, wie gähts."

"What?"

He switched to English. "Good evening. How are you?"

She leapt off the bed. "How am I? How am I? Dragged out of a club where I was having a quiet drink and listening to the music. Bundled into a van. Manhandled down two flights of stairs, and left in this fucking cell for hours. How the fuck do you think I am?"

"It's called 'getting arrested'. It can't be the first time for you."

"I thought this was a civilised country, it's like being in Russia."

"Worked there have you?"

She turned her back on him. "It's got fuck all to do with you where I've worked."

"What's your name?"

Silence

"Where are you from?"

She raised two fingers.

"You'll have to talk later, in court."

"If you want to know my name and where I'm from you can go and ask that gorilla who locked me in here, he's got my papers." She turned and took a step towards Friedmann, which was a mistake because he towered more than a head and shoulders above her. "And speaking of papers, I'm registered, you can't arrest me."

"We have done."

"Fucking police state."

"You broke the rules."

"What fucking rules?"

"Your permit is for prostitution services offered on the street, in the designated zones."

"So?"

"Not in bars."

"Well I wasn't 'offering prostitution services' in a bar. I was having a drink and listening to the music. I just told you that, and I told that gorilla outside. What's wrong with you people, are you deaf?"

"Neither deaf, nor dumb nor blind. You approached several men in the bar."

"And there's a law against talking to people is there?"

"Talking, no, but asking if they might be looking for some 'fun company' is."

"'Asking if they might be looking for some 'fun company' who uses that old line?"

"You evidently, at least that's what you said to Detective Constable Bernstein."

"I was joking. I knew he was a copper."

"Really. Then you carried the joke too far. He asked you what you had in mind and you whispered 'fucking' in his ear. He asked how much, you said 100 francs. He slipped you the money, you said let's go."

71

"That was a special offer for coppers at two o'clock in the morning."

"Tell that to the judge."

"I'm saying nothing to any fucking judge."

"Up to you." Friedmann turned and ducked his head.

"What did you come down here for? Like to gloat do you?"

Friedmann stopped, but did not turn around. "I thought I might help you."

"You, help me?"

"Forget it."

"How could you help me?"

Friedmann turned. "You know what will happen later. There are no options. The judge will simply take away your permit. No more work in Zurich ... or any other city in Switzerland. End of career, if that's what it is." He could see from her reaction that she hadn't fully considered all the consequences. "Depending how the judge reacts he could also send you to prison, to send a clear message to any of your colleagues about not working in bars. Then with a prison record–"

"And what could you do?"

Friedmann shrugged.

"And how and why would you help me?"

"How, is not definite. Why? Maybe you could help me."

"Want a free one do you?"

Friedmann ran his eyes slowly over her body from head to toe, and grimaced. "No thanks.

"Then why?"

"Information."

"What, me give you information?"

Friedmann shrugged again, and turned to go. "Enjoy your time in prison."

"You said it depends on how the judge reacts."

"Influenced by statements from the police."

"Is that a threat?"

"More like a promise." He started to walk away.

"What if I agree? I'd still have my permit?"

"You'd be no good to me if you weren't on the street."

Her eyes flicked from Friedmann to her surroundings in the cell back to Friedmann. "OK, but you must handle anything I tell you carefully, I don't want people to know–"

"Oh, you don't need to worry, you wouldn't be any use if people found out."

72

"So, when can I get out of this hellhole?"

"It might take a few hours to sought out the paperwork."

"A few of hours!"

"Procedures." And, he thought, it will do you good to experience being in cell for a bit longer: make you even more willing to accept the 'offer'.

She plonked herself onto the bed.

"I look forward to a long and fruitful relationship, Francesca. Perhaps we can start by you telling me about why you were in The Celler."

"I told you, having a drink and listening to the music."

"Now, Francesca, that's no way to start a relationship, by lying. Who told you to go into The Celler?"

"No one tells me to do anything."

Friedmann shook his head. "If you're going to be like that every time I ask you for something, this is not going to work. See you in court." He strode to the door. "Open up Constable, we're finished in here."

"OK."

"Just a minute Constable." He waited with his back to her.

"There's a man."

"A man?"

"A man who we see every few days."

"Name?"

"We call him Felix, but I'm not sure that's his real name."

"Can you contact him?"

"No."

"When do you see him?"

"It's not regular, could be any night."

Friedmann decided not to push any more at the moment. "OK, I'll go and start the paperwork. Constable."

Friedmann put his head around Kullmer's door. "Just thought I'd let you know, Sir, we've released Francesca."

"OK. Did you make sure she understood that next time she'd be in real trouble?"

"Oh, I'm sure she understood about the future, Sir." That's all Kullmer needed to know. Francesca was Friedmann's informer. If she ever supplied any useful information it would be to his credit.

The next task on Friedmann's list was to talk to The Celler's owner, André Wissler. After the raid Friedman had interviewed the bar staff. Not surprisingly no one knew anything about the prostitutes. He gave his card to each of them, saying they could contact him on his direct number if they had any information. He didn't expect any calls. A big man, Mathias, seemed to be in charge. He told Friedmann the owner was not at the bar. He'd tried to call him during the raid, but there was no reply. Friedmann tried the number a couple of times, also without success.

Friedmann was not a big football fan. He'd watch the Swiss team in action, but his duty schedule didn't allow him to regularly attend club matches. André Wissler had made the headlines often enough for Friedmann to know his name. The morning after the raid he was still getting no reply from the number, so he called the FC Zurich club.

"Good morning, I'd like to speak with André Wissler please."

"The team is training at the moment."

"It's rather important I speak to him."

"May I ask who's calling?"

"It's a personal matter."

"I'm sorry, I cannot interrupt training."

Friedmann was trying to be discreet, but sometimes the only way was to use the hammer. "This is Sergeant Jochim Friedmann from KRIPO. I need to speak to André Wissler, please get him to the 'phone."

"Yes, Sergeant. Sorry, Sergeant."

Friedmann smiled.

"Thanks for coming down so quickly, Mr Wissler. I hope this doesn't disrupt your training too much."

"Missing training is not a problem for me."

"I tried to be discreet, but there was no way the lady was going to get you to the 'phone."

"They have strict instructions."

"You are the owner of The Celler, is that right?"

"Yes."

"Do you know what happened last night?"

"Where?"

"At The Celler."

"No."

"We raided your bar last night because there were prostitutes soliciting for business inside the bar. We brought three of them to the station."

"Nothing to do with me."

"We tried to call you last night and this morning."

"My 'phone's been out of action for two days, several people have told me they tried to contact me.

"Do you know anything about the prostitutes using your bar."

"No, of course not."

"But you do own the bar."

"Yes."

"So what goes on there is your responsibility."

"I can't be there all the time."

"Or most of the time I'm told."

"What does that mean?"

"Just that if you own the place, you are responsible for everything that happens there."

"Look, inspector–"

"Sergeant."

"Sergeant, I've told you I know nothing about these prostitutes. If you want to accuse me of something I need my lawyer here." Wissler pushed back his chair, jumped to his feet and leant both hands on Friedmann's desk

"I would suggest you sit down Mr Wissler. Nobody's accusing you of anything."

Wissler took a deep breath and sat down.

"How long have you owned The Celler?"

"Just over a year."

"Why did you buy it, may I ask?"

"I like jazz and someone told me The Celler would be a good investment."

"And is it?"

"Pretty good so far."

"Unusual for a footballer to own a bar, especially one in the Niederdorfstrasse."

"Is it?"

"You know the law about prostitutes soliciting in bars?"

"No, I would have assumed that on the Niederdorfstrasse it's OK."

"So, you OK'd it at The Celler.

Wissler started to rise again, but stopped halfway and sat. "I've told you, I know nothing about it."

"How often are you at the bar?"

"Not often."

"Once a week?"

"Something like that."

"Is that because you don't want people to know you own it ... might spoil your image?"

" My visits depend on our fixtures."

"So you don't manage it as such?"

"I wouldn't know how to, Sergeant."

"Who does?"

"The barman."

"Would that be the large gentleman I met last night?

"Mathias, yes."

You know that he's got a criminal record?"

"He was arrested couple of times for fighting."

"But you complete trust him to leave him to run the place."

"I do."

"Why?"

"Why what?

"Why do you trust him?"

"He came well recommended."

"From the same person who recommended you to buy The Celler?"

"Yes as a matter of fact."

"May I ask who that was?"

"You can ask, but I won't tell you. I don't see what that's got to do with what happened."

"Maybe. We'll see where our investigation goes."

"Investigation. I thought you said you'd arrested three girls."

"Not arrested, They received warnings this time. What interests us more is stopping this spreading. And that means finding out who's behind it. These girls don't do anything without checking with their pimps. So, someone told their pimps that it was OK to be in The Celler. I would say the only person who could give that OK would be the owner." Friedmann waited for another explosion. It didn't come.

"I told you, I know nothing about this," said through gritted teeth.

"Noted. OK, I have another appointment now."

"I can go?"

"Yes, of course, you're not accused of anything ... at the moment. But we will need to talk again. Please let me know your footballing commitments for being out of Zurich." Friedmann stood and offered his hand. "Goodbye, Mr Wissler."

Felix Braun never answered the 'phone. He kept the answer machine on permanently, and the ringtone muted, so he could choose who he wanted to talk to and when. This was especially important when he'd had a long night and needed to catch up on some sleep. Last night he'd been checking the performance of one of his new girls. It rarely happened that they were better than they claimed, but Erica had been one of those exceptions. It must have been six o'clock when he'd finally said enough. It was hard work, but someone had to do it.

The sound of his upstairs neighbour over-enthusiastically vacuuming woke him at eleven fifteen. Raising on one elbow to look at the clock he saw the 'Call received' light on the machine was blinking furiously. He tried to count the flashes, but lost his way at fifteen. What was going on?

He swung his legs out of bed and was halfway to standing when a dizziness swept over him: too much sex and whisky. He sat back down, held his head in his hands for a few moments and then pressed 'Playback'.

The first ten calls ended without a message. The beep, beep, beep grated on Felix and made his head sink deeper into his hands. The distorted voice of the eleventh call brought him fully to consciousness. "Felix, what the fuck's going on?"

The message didn't need a name.

He went to the bathroom and put his head under the cold tap. Quickly drying off most of the water he sat by the 'phone in the space he used as an office in the living room. He took a deep breath and dialled the number.

"Hello."

"You called."

"Start talking, Felix, and it had better be good. If not I shall arrange for the removal of the part of your body you were busy using when I tried to call you a hundred times during the night."

"About what?"

"Felix, Felix, you know better than to play games with me."

"Has something happened?"

"Have you heard from Mathias?"

"There were a lot of calls on my machine. As soon as I heard you'd called I stopped checking them."

"That's the right thing to do, Felix, but you're still going to lose your appendage if you don't come up with an acceptable explanation. Call Mathias."

The telephone call was the fastest hangover cure Felix had ever known. After his call to Mathias, a feeling of absolute terror replaced it. And the terror of having his cock removed was only a small part of what he imagined could happen to him.

It had seemed like such a good idea at the time. It couldn't fail to please the boss. He would put some of his girls into the places where the punters were drinking. They'd be more receptive to the girls' suggestions of continuing the good time. The Celler seemed the obvious place to start. He'd known Mathias for a long time, and Mathias knew Felix was an important person in the organisation. Mathias had pointed out that it was against the law and he would have to check with the owner. When Felix arrived with the three girls last night Mathias didn't say anything.

Felix had to grip his dialling hand to stop it from shaking. "It's me."

"Talk."

"You've always said we should look for new ways of doing business."

"So this is you being an entrepreneur is it, Felix?"

"Isn't it?"

"I always thought you were smart, Felix. Now I'm beginning to think you're too dumb to be part of this organisation."

Silence.

"So now we've got the police on our backs."

"Don't we– you have some contacts?"

"I do. Depends who's handling the investigation. Why The Celler?"

"I thought you have some connection with it."

"No! I'm not– The trouble is, Felix, you didn't think."

Silence.

"Tell everyone to keep a low profile for the next few weeks."

Friedmann leafed through the transcripts of the interviews with the two prostitutes. As expected he didn't find anything other than names, addresses, permit number. Plus denial that they were doing anything except 'having a quiet drink and listening to the music'. One of the interviewing detectives had extracted the name Felix - the same name Francesca had mentioned.

His memory bank hadn't come up with any connection between a 'Felix' and prostitution. The computer contained 54 Felix results, far too many to follow up at this stage. A quick survey of his colleagues also produced nothing useful. Time to make a call.

He'd taken the release papers for Francesca down to the cells himself: just to make sure she continued to believe that he personally was responsible for her not having to face the judge. There was no telephone registered to the address she'd given, so he'd told her he needed some way of contacting her. She remained reluctant to cooperate until pushed. Suggesting the only way might be to meet her on the street during 'working hours' changed her mind about giving him a mobile number.

The ringing continued for over a minute.

"Hello."

"Hello, Francesca, did I wake you?"

"What time is it?"

"Eight thirty."

"But it's still light."

"Eight thirty in the morning."

"What? Who is this?"

"Your friendly police sergeant."

"Friedmann, you bastard."

"Ah, you remembered me. And a very good morning to you too."

"What do you want?"

"Sorry I forgot, you've probably only just got to bed. Are you alone?"

"Fuck you."

"I told you I'm not interested."

Silence.

"You told me Felix is your pimp. I need a second name."

"I don't have one."

"And you can't contact him."

"I told you. We see him every few nights, not regular."

"And he told you The Celler was OK for picking up clients?"

"I was having a drink and listening—"

"Francesca."

Silence.

"When did you last see Felix?"

"I can't remember."

"Would another night in the cells help your memory?"

"You can't do that."

"Try me."

"Monday."

"The day before we met at The Celler."

Silence.

"Francesca are you still there? You haven't fallen to sleep have you?"

Silence.

"So, you'll probably see Felix again at the weekend."

Silence.

"Tell him you're not happy about what happened in The Celler. Tell him you want to be able to contact him when things like that happen."

"You don't tell Felix, he tells you."

"Try it."

Silence.

"How do you get the money to Felix?" Friedmann knew the pimps generally employed young people, pimps in training, to go around collecting money, but maybe Felix had a drop-off point.

"What money?"

"The hundred franc notes like the one you took from Constable Bernstein."

Silence.

"Francesca, if I have to force every piece of information out of you, our relationship won't work. You know what that means."

"A collector comes."

"When? Who?"

"Late. A different one each night."

"OK. Go back to bed, Francesca. You need your beauty sleep. I'll be in contact."

Inspector Kullmer wasn't a 'people person'. Except for interviews with suspects and witnesses where he could dominate, he was uncomfortable with one-to-one discussions, especially if they involved any conflict. From his subordinates he preferred brief, written reports.

81

Brief, so if anything went wrong he could claim he didn't know about something important. Friedmann personally would have preferred to have brainstorming sessions with his boss, but made sure he took advantage of Kullmer's preference for something in writing. He added his comments and observations to the reports, and sent copies to Chief Inspector Müller. At the end of his September 18 report he wrote:

```
Comments:
The combination of prostitution being legal in
Switzerland and a shortage of police resources,
means investigation of who controls the 'business'
is, mostly, superficial. As long as there is no
reported trouble, we assume the licensing system,
combined with periodic police checks, is enough to
regulate how many prostitutes work and where they
work.
   The increase in the targeting of bars, resulting
in the raid on The Celler, might suggest we need
to understand more about the organisation behind
the women on the street. From the current
investigation I suspect there may be one or two
key figures involved.
```

He deliberately left off the report his contact with Francesca. The only real purpose of the 'Comments' paragraph was to impress Müller.

A follow-up interview with André Wissler before the end of the week would have been preferable. FC Zurich had an away match on Saturday, which meant travelling on the Friday. André Wissler arrived at police headquarters at nine forty-five, thirty minutes late, on Monday morning.

"Sorry I'm a little late, Sergeant. We had a difficult journey yesterday and didn't arrive back until late."

"Did you win on Saturday?"

"You don't follow football, Sergeant?"

"No."

"What can I do for you, Sergeant? I have a team meeting in one hour. I told you last time I don't know anything about those prostitutes."

"And I said we would have to talk again. I still don't know who gave the OK for those women to be in The Celler."

"Well it wasn't me. Can I go now?"

"I suggest you sit down, Mr Wissler."

Silence.

"When was the last time you saw Felix?"

"Who?"

"Felix."

"I don't know Felix."

"You don't know Felix, or any Felix?"

"I have a teammate called Felix."

"But you just said you didn't know Felix."

"I assumed you meant someone connected to this prostitution business."

"Your teammate could be."

"Unlikely."

"Why?"

"He's a young lad from Brazil. He only arrived in Switzerland there months ago."

"But you know him."

"Of course."

"So, your answer 'I don't know Felix' was wrong."

"I haven't got time for these stupid games."

"I've suggested once that you sit down, Mr Wissler, now I'm telling you. Someone called Felix put those women in your bar. Did Felix ask you if it was OK?"

"No."

"So, that still leaves us with the question of who gave the green light to Felix."

Silence.

"Not me."

"Would your bar manager, Mathias, do something like that without your permission?"

"No."

"So, that leaves you."

"Maybe Felix, whoever he is, didn't need permission."

"Tell me about the person who recommended Mathias to you. The same person who recommended you to buy The Celler."

"I told you before, I don't see what that information has to do with what happened."

"That's me for me to decide."

"It's confidential."

"What's the big secret? Someone does you a favour and recommends you buy a bar, and you can't tell me their name."

"I don't see any reason to involve them."

"Was it Felix?"

"I've told you I—"

"OK, OK calm down. I don't want you jumping up to leave again."

Silence.

"Are you married, Mr Wissler?"

"No."

"Girlfriend?"

"Not at the moment. What's this got to do with anything?"

"Just ... interested. Fit, young man like yourself must need some female company."

"Are you implying that I pay—"

"I'm not implying anything."

Silence.

"So, you have no contacts in the prostitution business."

"I've told you, I don't know anything about prostitution."

"Not even as a customer?"

"I'm leaving."

Friedman simply pointed to the chair, as you might do with a child.

"FC Zurich won the Super League Championship last year didn't they?"

"I thought you didn't follow football?"

"I don't, but I know what happened after the cup final."

"I've no idea what you're talking about, again."

"Hotel Bernplatz, ring any bells?"

Silence

"Well?"

Silence.

"OK, I'll tell you. The team stayed there after the match. Celebration dinner in the restaurant with wives, girlfriends, friends. Jog any memories?"

Silence.

"After the 'official' party, the unattached members of the team continued in one of the rooms, your room. Still nothing?"

A deep breath, but silence.

"At four-thirty there were complaints about the noise. Hotel security found four drunken men in your room AND five girls. What happened did one of your colleagues decide he didn't want a hooker, or did someone like two?"

"How do you know this? Security didn't call the police."

"Hotel security in places like the Bernplatz automatically report such instances to the police, especially ones involving hookers."

"So, we had a party, we'd just won the Cup."

"Ah, so now you remember."

"That was over a year ago, has it got anything to do with The Celler?"

"You tell me."

"What?"

"How did those hookers get into your room?"

"Part of the hotel room service?"

"Not at the Hotel Bernplatz."

"I was jok–"

"It's not a joke. I think someone made a telephone call, someone who had contacts. Someone who knew how to get five hookers delivered to the hotel at four am. Unfortunately I can't check the telephone records. The hotel will not release the telephone records unless I have a court order: guest confidentiality. I can only get a court order if I have evidence that someone may have committed a crime. At the moment I don't have that."

"It could been anyone in the room. Maybe I just enjoyed the results of someone else's good connections."

"Maybe, but if it was you who made the arrangements, it would suggest you have connections with the world of hookers, which links you to what happened at The Celler."

"If you put two and two together and get five."

"Oh I do, Mr Wissler.

"Could lead to false assumptions, Inspec– Sergeant."

"Not if you have the one."

"The 'one'?"

"Two plus two plus one equals five."

"You've lost me again."

"Calling up the hookers was one thing. Getting them into the hotel was another. Someone went down to reception and had a piece of luck. A junior member of the concierge team was on duty. For a hefty bribe he arranged for the hookers to come in through the service entrance. Later, he either felt guilty or was afraid of losing his job, he told the hotel security."

Silence.

"That young man was a football fan, an FC Zurich fan. He'd have done anything to help the man who'd scored the goal that won the Cup, even without the bribe."

André Wissler slowly rose. "Still doesn't prove anything."

Friedmann didn't stop him leaving.

This time the telephone only rang twice.

"Hello."

"Thought I'd catch you before you went to work."

"Sergeant Friedmann."

"Ah, you recognise my voice, that's nice."

"What the fuck do you want this time?"

"Now that's not nice."

"I haven't got time for 'nice'. As you said, I have to go to work."

"Now, now, Francesca, it's only eight o'clock. I'm sure you have a few minutes for me. The punters won't be lining up yet."

Silence.

"Francesca, talk to me."

"What do you want me to say."

"Do you remember our last conversation?"

"How could I forget, you woke me up."

"Am I sorry about that? Let me think. No."

"You're a basta–"

"Language, Francesca."

"Fuck you, Friedmann."

"I've told you before. I'm not interested."

Silence.

"So, did you see Felix?"

"I might have."

"Did you see Felix?"

"Yes."

"And?"

"Did you tell him you need to be able to contact him?"

"Don't you listen? You don't tell Felix. Besides he was in a foul mood."

"Something must have upset him. What could it be? Oh, I know, some of his girls had a trip in a police van."

Silence.

"Did you ask?"

"I tried, but he got even more angry. He said he had enough trouble with Gazda on his bac–."

"Gazda?"

"What?"

"You just said Felix had trouble with Gazda."

"Did I?"

"Who's Gazda?"

"No idea."

"I'm sure I don't need to remind you, there's a prison cell with your name on the door."

Silence.

"I've never heard of Gazda. I'm not even sure I heard Felix right. I swear I don't know who Gazda is."

Friedmann believed her: the threat of prison was a strong motivator for Francesca to tell the truth. Who hell was Gazda? His attempts to identify Felix had come to nothing, which was unusual. With all the contacts he and his colleagues had in the Zurich crime world normally someone knew someone who knew someone. Felix was either new in town or had managed to keep a low profile. Now there was another name to add to the list, Gazda.

He could mount a night time watch on Francesca until Felix contacted her. But that would need Kullmer's permission, which would mean revealing his contact with Francesca. Not something he wanted to do at the moment.

Die Täglichen Nachtrichten
Daily Diary 23 September
Bernd Zolliker

Have you been down the Niederdorfstasse lately? I took a stroll last night. Something was missing, not completely, but certainly much less in evidence: the ladies of the night. Not, you understand, that I was looking for any 'company' (this note for my wife). And not that there's anything wrong with looking for 'company'. For the record, I was on the way to a rendezvous with the owner of a restaurant I am writing a review about. The number of working ladies was clearly fewer

Being an inquisitive journalist I asked myself 'why'. Was there a decrease in demand for the oldest trade in the world? Was money still tight after the recent recession? Was Monday a poor night for business? I talked to one of the ladies - purely for research purposes!

The relationship between the business management and the authorities, the pimps and the police, has changed. Last Tuesday, unbeknown to me and probably you also, Zurich police raided The Celler, a jazz bar on the Niederdorfstrasse. Permits allow the ladies to work on certain streets, but not in bars. Why didn't we hear about this raid? In some countries such an event would have made the inside pages if not the front pages of newspapers like Die Täglichen Nachtrichten

I asked my colleagues in the Crime Department. They knew about the raid, but did not think it worth reporting because of the release of all the ladies taken into custody. A police spokesperson told me the raid did not represent a clampdown on the legal prostitution business. However my contact on the street said that's not the way the ladies see it, and many have decided to keep a low profile for a while.

Most people agree that Switzerland's over 50 years open attitude to prostitution, through its licensing system, has largely kept the criminal element out of the business. If someone in the police hierarchy has decided to clampdown, the public needs to know why. Driving prostitution

underground may not be in Switzerland's best
interest.

Friedmann brought the Zolliker article to Inspector Kullmer's attention later in the day. Kullmer was not pleased. The idea of the raid on The Celler had been his, but not out of any thought of 'clampdown'. Impressing the higher-ups with some initiative might increase his chances of promotion. Prostitution was an easy target. But he knew his superiors would not like him stirring up a situation that they believed was under control.

"Who is this 'police spokesperson', Jochim?"

"No idea, Sir. Probably someone from the central press office."

"Müller doesn't want people talking to the press, but in this case the message is correct, this is not a clampdown on legal prostitution. We agree on that don't we?"

"Yes Sir."

"So pass the word to the team. How much time are you personally spending on this?"

"There's not a lot we can do. We haven't identified Felix–"

"Felix?"

"The man mentioned during the interviews. I put it in the report."

"Oh yes."

"And unless we lean heavily on some people I think it will be difficult."

"Which we don't want to do–"

"Because this is not a clampdown."

"Exactly. Low key is the way to play it."

Friedmann left Kullmer's office with a small smile on his face. Whatever happened to Kullmer's 'full investigation'. The mysterious Felix, the shadowy Gazda and his interviews with André had stimulated his police brain. He had to find the connection. He'd keep his investigation low key, of course. Low key until the results started to look good for his promotion prospects.

"Mr Althaus."

"Sergeant ..."

"Friedmann. Have you got a minute?"

"I'm expecting a deliver–"

"It'll only take a minute."

"Come into the office. Talking to you in the bar is bad for business."

Friedmann thought about insisting on staying where he was and putting Althaus under pressure, but decided on another form of pressure, one more 'low key'.

"I've told you everything I know."

"I doubt that's true. Has Felix been around since the raid?"

"Who?"

"Felix."

A shake of the head.

"Is that a no?"

"I know many Felixs."

"Well that's a good start. Any of them pimps?"

"Could be, who knows?"

"You. How about Felix the pimp of the girls we picked up in your bar."

"It's not my bar."

"You run it."

"But not own it."

"So the owner told Felix it would be OK for the girls to be in The Celler?"

"Could have been."

"André Wissler says he knows nothing about it."

A shrug.

"So if he didn't, who did?"

Another shrug.

"You?"

"I told you, I knew they were prostitutes and told them not to 'work' in the bar. I can't contro–"

"Perhaps it was Gazda, not Felix."

No head shake, no shrug, just an icy stare.

Silence. Sweat started to trickle down from Mathias' temples.

Friedmann put his face up close to Mathias'. "Surprised I know about Gazda?"

Silence. More sweat.

"I wonder what Gazda will say when he finds out you told me about him."

"I didn'—"

"You know that, I know that, but will Gazda believe it?"

Silence. More sweat. Twitching eyes.

"We'll talk again Mr Althaus."

Friedmann turned and walked slowly out of the office. He wished getting a wiretap on a telephone was easier. If he was right, Mathias would be dialling a number as soon as the door closed.

Sounded like the same lady answering the telephone at FC Zurich, so Friedmann didn't waste time introducing himself and asked for André Wissler immediately.

"You're a difficult person to reach Mr Wissler. Still no reply from your home or mobile 'phones. Don't tell me they're still out of action."

"I don't spend all of my time sitting at home waiting for the 'phone to ring and my mobile's switched off when we're in training."

"I would like to have a meeting with you."

"Again! I don't know how many times I've got to tell you, I don't know anything about—"

"Shall we say three o'clock this afternoon?"

"We've got a training session for the cup match tomorrow."

"Will you be at The Celler later? We could meet ther—"

"No. No, I won't be."

"So?"

"So? ... I could be at your office at four o'clock."

"OK, four o'clock." But I've got a better idea than my office thought Friedmann as he cut the line.

Unfortunately Friedmann's path into the centre of Zurich took him close to Letzigrund, FC Zurich's stadium. On the few occasions he hadn't be able to avoid going that way on a Saturday when there was a home game, he'd waited in traffic queues and navigated around the crowds, who seemed to think the road belonged to them for that afternoon.

Now, at three o'clock on a Wednesday afternoon, the area around Letzigrund seemed eerily quiet. Never having been to a match, Friedmann expected to find an imposing main entrance. Instead he saw many smaller entrances with signs for ground positions and seat numbers. Today all of them were locked. He knew the training session was going on inside because he heard the occasional whistle. Walking round the stadium he eventually found a small door that was not locked. He ducked his head and went in. No security. The club obviously thought the door, probably for players and officials, was inconspicuous enough. Friedmann smiled to himself. Making his entrance via this 'secret' door would be even more of a surprise for André Wissler than his just turning up at the club. Exactly the effect he was aiming for. Surprised people were often less guarded in their answers to questions, especially surprised people who were hot and sweaty and needed a shower.

"I had to change my appointments and as I knew you'd be here–"

"I have to–"

"Yes I can imagine you need to shower, but this will only take few minutes. I have to be back at the station." Friedmann deliberately kept his voice loud enough for the other players milling around to hear.

"I can't talk no–"

"Only a couple of questions. We have to get to the bottom of what happened at The Celle–"

"Yes ... OK ... OK ... let's sit down over there."

"You've told me you don't know how those prostitutes came to be in The Celle–"

"How many times do we ha–"

"I'm just confirming where we were in our last conversation. You also told me you didn't know anyone named Felix exce–"

"Except for my colleague."

"Exactly."

"So?"

Sweat ran down the sides of Wissler's face and dripped off his chin. Friedmann almost felt sorry for him having to sit answering questions. Almost.

"You see Mr Wissler, I know the prostitutes would not go into The Celler without their pimp telling them it was OK. The pimp was Felix. The question is, who told Felix it was OK?"

Silence, except for the drip, drip.

"I had another chat with Mathias. He still says he knows nothing. You know nothing. So who does?

Silence.

"Gazda?"

"Who?"

"Gazda."

"I don't know anyone called Gazda."

"No?"

"No."

A track-suited figure appeared at the end of the players' entrance tunnel. "Come on, André I need you in the shower and on the massage table."

"Coming boss. The manager. I have to go."

"Is Gazda the person who recommended you to buy The Celler and hire Mathias?"

"No, because I don't know any Gazda."

"André come on, now."

"Yes, OK, OK I'm coming."

"You're going to get into trouble."

"I have to go." He started to get up.

Friedmann put a restraining hand on his arm. It felt hot and wet. "You're going to have to tell me sometime you know."

Wissler shook his arm free. "A friend of my mother's." He raced off down the tunnel.

A couple of weeks after his visit to the jazz bars on the Niederdorfstrasse, Christopher was sitting in his office, after a sandwich lunch, reading TIME magazine. A name he recognised jumped off the page.

"Lisa, have you got a minute, I've just found something interesting in TIME?"

"Can it wait? I have to go out with Erna to buy a wedding present for Helga. I'll be back in about an hour."

"So, what's so interesting?"

Christopher reached for the magazine in his briefcase. "There's an article here on the increase of prostitution in Europe. Read the paragraph I've marked there."

Even in Switzerland, where prostitution is legal and regulated, there are signs the people who control it are pushing the boundaries. Recently police raided The Celler, a bar in the centre of the city. Groups of women have started using the bar to solicit clients, something not allowed even under the country's liberal laws.

Lisa's mouth fell open. "The Celler!"

"So it would seem. Quiet a coincidence."

"Too much of a coincidence."

"But a coincidence."

"I wonder."

"Now where's your Miss Marples' brain going?"

"I don't know, but it's worth asking a few questions."

"Of whom?"

"Erich."

"Erich?"

"My police connection."

"Lisa …"

"I know, I know, discreetly."

Christopher shook his head. He'd learnt it was a waste of time trying to dissuade Lisa once she was in her investigation mode.

Towards the end of the afternoon Lisa knocked on Christopher's door, entered and closed the door behind her without him saying anything.

"Was there something Lisa, I'm rather busy."

"I've spoken to Erich and—"

"I think you'd better sit down. I don't know if you look shocked or excited."

"Both probably. Erich says they had been watching The Celler for some time. They raided the place to send a message to other establishments. Erich said it was surprising this was happening in The Celler because of the ownership."

"Should he be telling you all this?"

"I called to say we hadn't unfortunately got any further with finding out who stole your briefcase. I may have hinted that I would like to buy him a drink sometime to say thank you for his help. I think he still fancies me. I mentioned The Celler raid almost in passing."

Christopher smiled and nodded his head. "Feminine guile."

"Sometimes it's useful."

"Well, it's interesting, but clearly nothing to do with us being in The Celler and then—"

"But I haven't finished the story."

Silence.

Christopher waited. "Are you going to?"

"Guess who owns The Celler?"

"I've no idea."

"Guess."

"Herr Muri."

"No! Try again."

94

"You're not going to tell me it's Rudi Affolter are you?"

Lisa laughed. "No, that would be too much of a coincidence. It would have made more than a few pieces drop into place though."

"Who then?"

"A player from FC Zurich."

"From the way you're smiling I gather that should mean something to me."

"Well, that's the reason the police were surprised it was happening there."

"I can understand that."

"But the really interesting part is the player is André."

"André?"

"André Wissler, my ex-husband."

"What would he be doing owning a jazz club?"

"I told you, André was a big jazz fan."

"So your ex-husband owns The Celler, another coincidence."

"Exactly yet another coincidence."

"Which means you see something more."

Lisa got up and slowly walked to the door and back. She remained standing in front of Christopher's desk.

"OK Ms Holmes, let's hear it."

"You're certain now that we went to The Celler?"

"Yes, aren't you?

"Y e s."

"Means No."

"No, it means yes. Maybe he was there that night."

"Who?"

"André. Maybe he saw us. Maybe he thinks I saw him. Maybe he was afraid I would go to the newspapers and expose him as the owner of a jazz club where prostitutes go. Maybe the kidnapping was a warning."

"Too many maybes."

"Maybe."

"Why would he think you would go to the newspapers?"

"To get back at him. Our divorce was not exactly amicable. Although we married in England, his clever, expensive lawyer told me the divorce was under Swiss law. They'd show that I came into the marriage with nothing, therefore I'd get nothing when it broke up. As we had no children and I was still young enough to earn a living, I would also not be able to claim financial support from him."

"Hmm, sounds like he won, but why would he think you'd go to the newspapers now, to get back at him after what, three years?"

"Because I wouldn't 'lie down and die'. His lawyer told me I had no chance and warned me not to pursue it, But I insisted on going to court, which was pretty much a waste of time. I got my costs and little else. However, the newspapers picked it up, and it got embarrassing for André."

Christopher held up his hand. "Incidentally, did you hear anyone, Erna for instance, mention a story about the raid on The Celler?"

"No, why?"

"Well, with a local footballer involved, the tabloid papers in England would have had a field day, pardon the pun."

"The Swiss newspapers are more discreet when it comes to well-known figures, that's why so many celebrities find refuge here. Stories might make the inside pages."

"So, you think to get back at you for embarrassing him he'd kidnap us and put us in that hotel?"

"You don't know him. He has quite a temper."

"Even so, it's a bit far-fetched."

"And there was something else. I heard through a friend that André blamed me for his absence from the Swiss team for the World Cup in 2006. He said all the hassle and worry of the divorce affected his playing. And that's why he might want to get back at me."

"But you think that night he saw you and decided to warn you off and get back at you? It takes time to arrange to kidnap two people and put them in a hotel."

"Does it?"

"I don't have any experience, but I would assume so."

"But if he's running a prostitution racket he probably has the connections to do it."

"We don't know he's running a 'prostitution racket' as you call it."

"The police think so."

"Is that what your friend said?"

"No he didn't actually say that."

"So"

"But a raid on the bar, prostitutes warned, and André the owner …"

"Two plus two equals five."

"Exactly."

"I still find it difficult to believe."

"I find it difficult to believe we were in that hotel, but we know that was true."

Gazda

The Second Abduction

27 September to 29 September 2008

In the three years she'd been at ZFFM, Lisa had not been on a 'girls' night out'. She remembered the ones in Birmingham with a mixture of pleasure, embarrassment and regret. When Erna's colleague, Helga, announced the date for her marriage, Lisa automatically asked what they normally did on the hen night.

The expression 'hen night' caused some confusion. Even after Lisa's toned-down description of what had gone on in Birmingham, most of the Swiss-German ladies were not sure of the reasons for such an evening. Erna of course caught on to the idea, and managed to persuade a group of eight to have a dinner together.

After they had eaten, excuses for leaving mushroomed: 'I have a babysitter', 'Sorry, I've got an early start in the morning', 'my fiancé kindly said he would collect me'. In a short while only Erna and Lisa were sitting at the table, as expected.

"Is this what happened in Birmingham?

"Not most times."

"Not any time I should think."

Lisa nodded.

"So, what shall we do?"

"You want to do something else?"

"Of course. It's Sunday tomorrow, I haven't 'got an early start'."

"Or a babysitter?" Lisa reached for the bottle of Chianti. "Well, I think the first thing to do is to finish this. Did you see some of the faces when I ordered a third bottle?"

"Shock I should think."

"Or maybe they didn't want to spend so much."

"They'd probably all had an allowance from their husbands."

"Half of them aren't married."

"No, but they all have boyfriends."

"And they already control what they spend?"

"Most probably."

"Cheers."

"Nothing more's happened on the Rudi Affolter front, Lisa?"

"Have you seen anything?"

"No. I heard him bragging about a new car, but I don't think he'll have bought that on Mr McLendi's credit card. By the way, how are you getting on with Mr McLendi, Christopher? I haven't seen much of you in the last few weeks."

"There's nothing to be 'getting on', as I've told you many times."

"So, I guess we'll never find out who stole the briefcase."

"Affolter's still guilty of something."

Erna looked puzzled. "What?"

"Never mind."

They discussed a few possibilities of what to do, but neither had enough experience of the centre of Zurich at eleven o'clock on a Saturday night to make any interesting, let alone exciting, suggestions.

"We should have asked Rudi Affolter for some recommendations. I bet he knows a few interesting places," said Erna.

"I'm not sure I'd want to go to the places he knows." Lisa refilled their glasses. "Unless …"

"What?"

"Do you like jazz?"

"I can't say I'm a great fan, but …"

"There's a place called The Celler not far from here. We could at least have a drink and see what it's like."

Erna drained her glass. "Let's go."

It was still early for The Celler and there were free tables. Lisa said if they sat at the bar they'd see more of the band on the small stage. Lisa chose two stools near the beer taps, "Quicker service." The barman was resting on the taps, Lisa gave a big smile. "What are you going to have, Erna?"

"I think after all that wine I'll have a beer."

"Is that OK?"

"Why?"

"You know, beer before wine makes you feel fine, wine before beer makes you feel queer."

"Never heard that."

The barman was listening and drumming his fingers on the taps. Lisa gave him another big smile. "Zwei bier, bitte." He grunted, topped up two glasses standing beneath the taps, and placed them none two gently in front of Erna and Lisa.

"I don't think you made much of an impression on him, Lisa."

"I'm not sure I'd want to. Have you seen the size of him? Imagine that on top of you."

"Shush, he'll hear you."

"So, cheers."

"Cheers."

"Did you hear about this place?"

"No. What happened?"

Lisa glanced at the barman, who was leaning on the beer taps again. "Raided by the police for being a den of iniquity."

"Iniquity?"

Another glance. "A place for prostitutes to pick up customers."

"Really! I hope they don't think that's what we are, sitting at the bar."

The four piece jazz band returned from their break and after a few minutes of tuning up exploded into 'When the saints go marching in'. Although the music was loud Lisa continued to talk. "We might be able to make a few francs if …"

Even though Lisa was almost shouting Erna couldn't hear her, and she saw the barman look in their direction several times. Erna shrugged and concentrated on the stage.

Two beers later the band announced 'whisky time'. Erna made a discrete scan of the room. "I don't see anybody who looks like a prostitute here," she whispered.

"Frightened off by the police," said Lisa almost as loud as when the band was playing.

"Noch ein bier?" asked the barman

Erna opened her mouth, but Lisa jumped in first. "Noch zwei, bitte."

Erna leant into Lisa. "Does he know you? He keeps looking at you."

"I've been here a couple of times before." Again said more loudly than Erna felt comfortable with.

The barman reached over and put the beer in front of them. Lisa nodded at him. "I once danced on the table."

The barman frowned.

"Lisa! You didn't."

"I did. I bet the owner remembers me." She waved to the barman. "Mathias" she said reading his name badge,"is André here tonight?" she said in English.

"André?"

"The owner."

"Weiss ich nicht."

Lisa shrugged. "Probably recruiting some more ladies," she said in stage whisper.

The barman moved to the opposite corner of the bar and busied himself with drying glasses, but Erna noticed him still glancing in their direction.

The Celler was now full, and when the band returned, the place started to pulse with music, singing and chatter. Lisa and Erna got "talking" to some people squashed up against them, and the beer flowed. The last time Lisa saw Mathias, he was taking on the telephone.

The 'polizei stunde' was well past, when the band decided they couldn't play 'one last number'. Erna and Lisa struggled up the stairs. At the entrance they let the cold, early morning air refresh their faces for a few moments. The cobblestones of the Niederdorfstrasse made walking difficult, at least that's what they agreed as they giggled and stumbled their way to a taxi rank.

Lisa insisted that Erna take the only taxi. "You've got further to go than me." Luckily almost as soon as Erna's taxi drove off another one arrived.

Christopher had tried several times to adjust the ringing volume of the bedside 'phone, and thought he had at last succeeded. As he surfaced from the depths of slumber to the shrill, insistent beep he knew he would have to try again. He looked at the illuminated digits: 7.30 on a Sunday, who?

"Hell–"

"Christopher, I nee– I need to see you."

"Lisa, what's wrong?"

"Please come."

"Yes, sure, later this morning or this afternoon?"

"Now."

"What's wrong?"

"I need to see you, now"

"I'll be as quick as I can."

He showered and dressed quickly, thought about breakfast, but the tremor in Lisa's voice made him just grab a piece of dry bread, which he ate as the lift descended to the garage.

The sound of the buzzer died away. Christopher could hear sounds of movement and frustration. Lisa opened the door, gripped Christopher's arm and pulled him in. She frantically locked the door.

Christopher stared at Lisa: dishevelled hair, smudged make-up, and clothes that looked as though she'd slept in them

Lisa continued gripping his arm and dragged him into the kitchen, slamming the door behind them.

"Lisa, what's wrong?"

She didn't answer immediately, but first pulled the edge of the closed curtains away from the window and peeked out. "Christopher check the other rooms?"

"For what?"

"To make sure there's no one there."

"Could there be?"

"Just check. Please."

Again the urgency in her voice persuaded Christopher to act rather than ask any more questions.

He found her still in the kitchen, perched on a stool nursing a glass containing what looked like cognac. "All-clear." The news had no effect on the fear in her eyes. "What happened?"

She let out a deep sigh, and stared at him in silence.

"Lisa, what's wrong?"

"I've … I've been … I don't know which word to use."

"Take it slowly."

She took a sip of her cognac, and coughed and spluttered. "Someone kidnapped me."

Christopher patted her gently on the back. "Kidnapped?"

"It's the only way I can describe it."

"Come into the living room, you'll be more comfortable there."

"I'd rather stay here, it feels safer because it's smaller."

Christopher pulled a stool opposite her. "OK, start from the beginning."

"Erna and I went out with some others for Helga's hen night."

"I shouldn't think they knew what a hen night was."

"They didn't, and now I'm not so sure I should have told them." The sound of footsteps caused her to stare wide-eyed at the door. "What was that?"

"Sounds like someone walking about in the apartment upstairs."

"Oh yes, she walks about in high heels all day, even on Sunday."

"Look, why don't we walk around the apartment together so you can see there's no one here, and we can check the doors? Maybe you'll feel a bit calmer then."

Lisa instinctively grasped Christopher's hand and he led her from room to room, like a child. Afterwards they sat in the living room. Christopher waited for her to decide when she wanted to continue the story.

"Erna and I decided we didn't want the evening to end so early, it was only eleven. So we went to– for a drink, and after we–"

"Where did you go at eleven o'clock?"

"The– a bar. Anyhow, after it finished we went to get a taxi. I remember getting to the taxi rank. After that it becomes a bit hazy for while."

"I don't want to be rude, but had you had a lot to drink?"

"A few I guess. I think there was someone else in the back of the taxi."

"Erna?"

"No, she'd taken the first taxi, I'm sure of that."

"Who then?"

"I don't know. I remember giving the driver my address, and that's it until I woke up."

"Open your eyes ... open your eyes."

The slap on her cheek sounded much stronger than it felt. She tried to do what the voice told her, but her lids were heavy.

The voice grew harsher. "Open your eyes ... open your eyes ... now."

With great effort, first the left then the right retinas lit up, but the room was in almost darkness. She blinked, and like a moth was drawn to the single bulb at head height straight ahead. She wanted to rub her eyes, but her arms were fastened to the chair she was sitting on. No, not fastened, gripped. She struggled, and the hands tightened.

"Stay still, Miss Stern."

The voice came from behind the bulb. Even though her eyes were adjusting to the darkness she could see nothing but the light. She made another attempt to move her arms.

"Still, Miss Stern. I don't want you to be hurt ... yet."

The voice was simultaneously gentle and threatening. It was distorted and bounced off unseen walls.

"Why are you asking so many questions, Miss Stern?"

"I don't understand."

"You are asking too many questions about things that shouldn't concern you."

"I don't know what you mean."

"People who outstay their welcome and ask questions about things that don't concern them get into trouble."

"I–"

"Trouble, Miss Stern, a lot of trouble."

Lisa tried to stand, but the vice-like grip tightened further and made her yelp. "Who–"

The malice part of the voice took control. "If you enjoy being hurt, Miss Stern, I can help you.

"You can't–"

"Oh I can. I can do what I want. Stegnuti."

The vice tightened even further and Lisa's yelp pitched higher.

"I don't think you understand what 'trouble' is Miss Stern."

"Let me go."

"I'll let you go, when I'm ready. When I'm sure you've understood. Do you understand Miss Stern?"

"Understood what, you basta–"

"Language, language Miss Stern. Understood you stop asking so many questions, or Zur–"

"Or what?"

106

"Or, the lake fish will have an English treat, and Zurich Flaschen Fullungs Machinen will need a new secretary."

"The next thing I remember is waking up on my bed."

"Fully clothed?"

"Fully clothed."

"Any idea where you were?"

Lisa took a deep breath. "No. It was cold, damp and had a musty smell. Probably a cellar."

"And that was all the discussion?"

"A discussion. It wasn't a discussion Christopher. You make it sound like a friendly chat."

"OK ... OK, sorry."

"I can still hear the icy threat in that voice."

Christopher waited. Lisa stared into her glass. "Was all this in German or English?"

"English."

"But why did he say you were asking too many questions?"

Lisa shrugged.

Christopher was silent as he looked questioningly at Lisa. "You said you went with Erna to a bar, which bar?"

"Just a bar."

"The Celler?"

Lisa looked up from her glass. "Yes."

Christopher nodded slowly.

"What am I going to do?" Tears were starting to form in Lisa's eyes.

"Do? I don't think there's anything to do. Have a shower and I'll take you for a good lunch."

Lisa's eyes widened. Her hand shook so much she almost dropped the glass. "Kidnapped and threatened, and your suggestion is to go for 'a good lunch'!"

"Lisa," Christopher placed his hand on her shoulder. "are you sure this all happened?"

She jumped up. "'Am I sure this all happened?' What are you suggesting now? That I made it up?"

"Not 'made it up', but ... dreamt it."

"Dreamt it!"

"Look, you'd had a few drinks. You got home and collapse– lay down on the bed and fell asleep. Going round in your head was the story about prostitution in The Celler, and the connection with us and that night in the hotel. You probably passed the hotel on your way to the taxi rank. Menacing, distorted voices echoing in a dimly lit, cold, damp, cellar sounds like a dream, or rather a nightmare."

Now it was Lisa's turn to nod slowly. She sat down. When she spoke her voice was monotone calm. "Sounds logical."

"I'm sure it–"

"Except for two things. When I woke up both my arms hurt and I thought I must have been lying awkwardly, but …" She pulled up the crumpled sleeves of her shirt.

Christopher didn't need close examination to see the bruises above both elbows. "Perhaps–"

"No, don't suggest I fell down. I know how I got these. These bruises are where I struggled against the vice grip holding me on a chair. Look, you can see the finger marks."

Christopher was silent.

"Still not convinced? While I was waiting for you I felt an irritation on my thigh." She pulled her skirt up. "As you can see there is a hole in my tights on both legs, and small red patches on my legs at those points."

Christopher let his eyes discretely examine the leg closest to him. In the centre of the red patch was a tiny, purple spot.

"Oh no, this was no dream or even a nightmare, this was real."

Christopher stood up. "I think I need one of those cognacs, even if it is only nine o'clock in the morning. May I?"

"Help yourself," said Lisa handing him her glass.

Again they sat in silence, both were staring into the amber liquid.

"So, what do you think happened."

"As soon as I got in the taxi, if it was a taxi, someone stuck a needle in me. Not only did it knock me out, but also nullified the alcohol. When I came round in that cellar, or wherever it was, I felt completely sober. After the interrogation I know they stuck a needle in my other leg. I woke up on the bed. That's why I felt so frightened. I thought they might be still here in the apartment."

"But why?"

"Because I went to The Celler?"

"Were you asking a lot of questions?"

"No … not really."

"Means yes."

"Well … OK, I did suggest we went there. Erna of course knows nothing about … I wanted to see what it was like, where I'm supposed to have danced on the table. The big barman that you talked to was there."

"And you started questioning him?"

"No, of course not. ... I did deliberately sit at the bar, close to where he was resting on the beer taps. He must have overheard some of the things I said to Erna."

"Surprise, surprise. And what things did you say to Erna?"

"About the prostitution story."

"And?"

"Dancing on the table. ... I asked if André was there."

"Lisa!"

"The barman said he didn't know him, but I think, I'm not sure, I think I saw André pass by the door at the back of the bar."

"Did he see you?"

"I'm sure not."

"We have to go to the police."

"The police?"

"Yes. You're sure what happened to you was real, and from the marks on your arms and legs I have to agree with you. There's no choice but to go to the police."

"They didn't do much last time."

"You're assuming there's a connection between the hotel episode and last night."

"There is."

"Let's not jump to any conclusions."

"It's not a very big jump."

"Perhaps or perhaps not. But unlike the hotel episode–"

"You keep saying 'hotel episode' as if it was something on the television."

"I'm not trying to minimise it, I just don't know what else to call it. I know it was frightening for both of us, but we've seen there is an explanation."

"If you believe what a taxi driver and a barman told us."

"Yes, if you believe what they said. We must report what happened to you last night."

"You're right. Let me shower and change. Will you come with me?"

"Of course, but I think it might be better to go immediately: let the police see the condition of your clothes.

Lisa recognised the reason behind Christopher's suggestion of not changing, but she felt uncomfortable still in the same clothes as last night. Not that anyone could see them because she'd covered herself with a voluminous raincoat.

The officer at the desk said someone would see them in 'fünf minuten'. After half an hour Christopher approached the desk and received a standard 'noch fünf minuten, mein Herr'. After a further twenty minutes the door into the inner station opened and a sergeant approached them. He extended his hand. "Good morning, Ms Stern, Mr McLendi."

Lisa and Christopher jumped up.

The policeman looked at them as if he was waiting for a response. "How are you?"

Christopher looked at him, puzzled. "That's what we've come to talk to someone about."

"Come this way please." He punched a code into the keypad and led the way down a corridor to a small room as bare as the reception. The policeman pressed a button on the wall and a young, tall policewoman entered. She looked slightly surprised. "Sergeant Grindel?"

"This is Constable Menna, Ms Stern and Mr McLendi. Would you like something to drink? Tea? Coffee?"

"Coffee please," said Lisa and Christopher together.

"Constable, would you mind helping me."

Christopher wondered if leaving them alone was a deliberate ploy. He'd noticed the red light on the camera high in the corner as they'd entered the room. He and Lisa sat in silence.

The constable stayed when they returned. Again the sergeant looked at them for several seconds before speaking. "I would like to say it is a pleasure to see you again, but I'm sure your visit here is not for something pleasant."

"Again? What do you mean 'again'?"

"I thought you didn't recognise me, Mr McLendi. Sergeant Grindel?"

"I'm sorry I still don't recall—"

Lisa spoke for the first time. "The hotel." She blushed.

Constable Menna hid a smile behind her hand.

"That's right, Ms Stern, the hotel."

Christopher lifted the cup. The steam told him the coffee would be too hot to drink, but two thoughts were competing in his mind. One, the same policeman, this will make it easier; two, the same policeman, this will make it harder. He waited as long as he felt he could, but neither thought won. He made a choice to use the situation as an advantage. "As you'll remember, what happened in the hotel was both mysterious and frightening. Now something–"

"Why didn't you come to the station to discuss more about what happened at the hotel, Mr McLendi."

Lisa looked quickly from Sergeant Grindel to Christopher and back. "We thought you didn't believe us."

"It was not a question of believing or not. We try to work only with facts. The facts as we saw them on that Saturday did not suggest anything, what shall I say, anything unusual had happened."

"Handcuffed to a bed is 'not unusual'?"

Constable Menna's training kept the smile off her face this time.

"Ms Stern, I told you at the time, it's not for me to judge."

"But I think you made a judg–"

Christopher put his hand on Lisa's arm. "The fact is, Sergeant, although we tried, we didn't remember anything about what happened, at least nothing that made sense. So we thought there was no point coming back to you." Christopher was about to say something about their investigations, but decided what they'd found out was not going to help their credibility with this sergeant. 'The same policeman, this will make it harder' now dominated.

The sergeant's nodding head and pursed lips suggested either disappointment or relief.

It was Constable Menna who broke the brief silence "Please tell us why you are here now, Mr McLendi."

"Ms Stern was abducted last night."

Menna frowned.

"Abducted" said Grindel. "That's very strong, Mr McLendi."

"What do you call being taken against her will, drugged, interrogated and threatened?"

"Abducted, if–"

"If what, Sergeant? If it happened?"

Constable Menna stepped in again. "Tell us what happened."

"Ms Stern was–"

"Perhaps it would be better if Ms Stern told us herself."

Lisa cleared her throat. "I went to get a taxi and the next–"

"Start from the beginning."

Grindel sat back in his chair and let his junior continue.

"The beginning?"

"When you left home yesterday evening."

Lisa described the Saturday evening, giving as much detail as she could remember. Or at least as much detail as she wanted to tell the two police.

Grindel let her finish and a few seconds silence elapse before leaning forward. "You said you went to a bar Ms Stern, which one?

"The Celler."

"Why?"

"Why what?"

"Any particular reason The Celler?" Grindel was looking Lisa direct in the eyes, so he saw the swift glance at Christopher.

"No ... no, it was close to the restaurant."

"And the questioning, was about w–"

"Interrogation."

"Interrogation, was about why you were in The Celler."

"Yes."

"Only about why you were there?"

This time the contact with Christopher was more than a glance.

"Is there something you're not telling me, Ms Stern?"

"I don't know what you mean."

"Mr McLendi?"

Christopher almost whispered to Lisa. "I think we should tell them what we know."

Lisa took a deep breath and reluctantly nodded.

Christopher also took a deep breath. "Sergeant, may I tell you about what has happened since– in the three weeks since we met?"

"Please."

"We did some investigation ourselves about that Friday night. We had an invitation to ..." Christopher talked about the dinner at Rudi Affolter's, the information from the taxi driver, and the discussion with the barman at The Celler. Much to Lisa's embarrassment, he included the part about her dancing on the table. He deliberately left out any mention of Lisa's suspicions about Rudi and her ex-husband's involvement in a prostitution organisation. "... so Lisa, Ms Stern, went to The Celler to see if she remembered being there that Friday night."

"And did you, Ms Stern?"

"No."

"But you asked a few questions."

"Yes."

"And someone abducted you because you were asking questions about whether you had been in the bar or not? Sounds a little, how do you say, far-fetched? Or unusual to say the least. How about you Mr

McLendi, do you have any recollections of being in The Celler before going to the hotel?"

"I must admit I don't."

"But we didn't go to the hotel, Sergeant."

"So how did you get there, Ms Stern?"

"Someone put us there."

"Ah, another abduction."

"There's a part of our investigation Christopher, Mr McLendi, left out.

This time it was Christopher's turn to look at Lisa, but his was more than a glance. He didn't try to hide shaking his head.

Lisa either didn't see him out of the corner of her eye or ignored him. "You know, of course, about The Celler and prostitution."

Christopher inwardly breathed a sigh of relief. He'd been afraid Lisa was going down her Rudi Affolter track.

Sergeant Grindel narrowed his eyes and waited for Lisa to continue.

"You also know an FC Zurich player owns the Celler. What—"

"Ms Stern, I don't see what this has to do with anything that did or did not happen last night."

"What you don't know is—"

"Ms Stern, do you have anything to add to your story about last night?"

"What I want to tell you does—"

"Please stick to the facts about last night."

Lisa took a deep breath. "The owner of The Celler—"

"Ms Stern, I've asked you to stick to the facts. Constable Menna, would you check if Constable Schmidt has arrived yet?"

"Constable Schmidt, Sergeant? As far as I know he's not on duty today. I thought you were normally also not on—"

"Just go check Constable."

Menna frowned and left the room.

"Was anyone with you last night, Ms Stern?"

"I want to tell you about—"

"The facts, Ms Stern, just the facts." Grindel's back was to the camera and therefore it wouldn't record the contrast between his softly spoken words and the threatening look on his face.

Christopher guessed Lisa wouldn't give up, and so he decided to step in. "She was with a colleague."

"Name and telephone number?"

This time Lisa caught Christopher's look and head movement. "Erna Sameli. She works at ZFFM with me."

"Had you had a lot to drink?"

"A few, but we were OK. Erna will confirm we walked to the taxi rank."

"I'm sure she will. And after the 'abduction' and 'interrogation', you escaped?"

Christopher could see the frustration building in Lisa with Grindel's insinuations. "She woke up at home."

"At home?"

"Yes, at home, and before you ask, no, I don't know how I got there."

"Another mystery."

"They injected me with–"

"Injected?"

"Drugged."

"Drugged?"

Lisa lent across the table. "Which part don't you understand, Sergeant? Drugged? Abducted? Interrogated? Threatened? Drugged again? And dumped on my own bed, means someone illegally entered my apartment. I'm fed up with you treating me as if I'm inventing the whole thing. I thought the police help people in trouble."

"If they're really in trouble, yes."

"This is fucking ridiculous."

"Lisa, calm down."

"Calm down, Christopher! How do you think I can calm down, when this … this …"

"I know, but it's not going to help by getting angry."

Lisa stood up, flung off her raincoat, and pulled up the sleeves of her shirt. "What do you think these are, Sergeant? Are these figments of my imagination?" She pulled her skirt up, way beyond the holes in her tights. "And what about these? Mosquito bites?"

Christopher pointed to her skirt. "Lisa."

She tugged the skirt to a more modest level. "I'm sure the sergeant has seen underwear before." She sat down.

There was a knock on the door and Constable Menna came in. "Constable Schmidt is not here, Sergeant."

The look on the sergeant's face now matched his voice. "OK. Ms Stern let me try to summarise the story so far for Constable Menna, you tell me if I get anything wrong. You go out for an evening with a colleague–"

"Colleagues, there were eight of us in the restaurant."

"But only you and Ms Erna Sameli, a work colleague, went to The Celler?"

"Yes."

"After The Celler you went to get a taxi. You claim you were drugged, abducted, interrogated, drugged again, and put back in your apartment. That's the story?

"And threatened. It's not a story, it's what happened."

"So, Constable Menna, what does your police training tell you to do next?"

"What was the threat Miss Stern?

"I should stop asking questions or I would be dumped in the lake."

Grindel smirked. "Sounds a bit heavy just because you went to The Celler and asked a few questions. So, Constable?"

"Do you have any evidence to prove this happened, Ms Stern?"

"I have bruises on–"

"She has bruises on her arms and legs, but they could have been–"

Lisa jumped up, and leant across the table, her face within centimetres of Grindel's. "What the fuck is wrong with you? Why don't you believe me?"

Constable Menna was round the table in a flash, but Christopher was already calming Lisa back into her chair. He persuaded her to take a few deep breaths.

Menna broke the silence. "Ms Stern, what would you suggest we do? We have what you've told us, but nothing that we can investigate. You are the only person involved at the moment. Do you remember the number of the taxi or what the driver looked like?"

Lisa's answer was almost inaudible. "No."

"Where were you taken?"

"I don't know."

"Then what can we do?"

Lisa shook her head.

"Couldn't you talk to the people at The Celler?" said Christopher.

"We could and they would presumably confirm that Ms Stern was there last night, but what happened was after that."

"How about I take a drug test?"

Menna shrugged. "If you were given anything it would have been something fast acting and equally fast disappearing. We can try, but the chances of finding anything are small."

"'If' I was given anything, so you don't believe me either?"

"I'm only looking at the facts that we have, Ms Stern."

Grindel had been staring at Lisa and hadn't spoken for some time. "And, there is the 'fact' that you have been in such a ... what shall we call it? ... such a situation before."

Lisa started to rise. "What's that supposed to mean?"

"He's talking about the hotel, Lisa."

"Yes, Mr McLendi, the hotel."

When she spoke, Lisa had regained control, her voice like ice. "If this didn't happen, why am I here at the police station."

"Perhaps you dreamt it and you believed it happened, or–"

"Or what, Sergeant?"

"Or when you've had too much to drink, you feel guilty, and telling the police something happened to you, makes you feel less guilty."

"That's the most fucking ridiculous thing I've ever heard."

"We get all sorts in here."

"Well, I'm not 'all sorts', I know what happened. If you don't believe me I'll–"

"I think we'd better go Lisa."

Constable Menna offered her hand, Christopher shook it. "We'll talk to The Celler and the taxi company, and be in contact if we find anything." She opened the door. "I'll see you out."

Lisa and Grindel glared at each other.

Lisa took a shower, a long shower.

Above the sound of the water Christopher could hear Lisa stamp her foot several times and sounds of exasperation.

She noisily made tea and they sat on the couch. Only her sighs broke the silence. "He must be part of it."

"Who must be part of what?"

"Grindel, he's involved with this somehow. The same policeman on the two occasions something happened to us?"

"Coincidence."

"You don't sound as though you believe that."

"I can't believe it's anything else."

"Can't or won't?"

"Do you think your friend ... what was he called ... Erich could help?"

"I don't want to contact him. Who knows how far the police corruption goes."

"Corruption might be—"

"What Christopher, correct?"

"No, I mean—"

"I'm pretty sure Constable Menna's not in on it. Did you see the way Grindel sent her out of the room when he didn't want me to mention André?"

"He did seem a bit angry."

"Angry? It's me who should be angry. He said I was lying."

"I don't think he used those words."

"Whose side are you on?"

"It's not a question of sides. He was just trying to understand exactly what happened."

"By telling me I was lying! Great way for the police to help the victim. Of course you would side with him, because you still don't believe me either."

"I wouldn't say I don't believe you—"

"But?"

"But what I still find difficult to understand is why they brought you back here. Why not put you in a hotel again?"

"'Again', so you think someone did put us in that hotel."

"No … I'm not sure."

"'I'm not sure' is different to 'No'. They wouldn't use the same method. Dumping me back here makes the idea of abduction less credible. You saw how Menna and Grindel reacted."

"There's no sign of a break-in."

"They used my key obviously … just a minute … just a minute, my key."

"What about it?"

"Don't you remember? When you arrived this morning I was slow unlocking the door."

"Yes."

"I couldn't find the key. It wasn't on my key ring. I had to use the spare, which I keep in the draw in the hallway."

"So?"

"They must have taken my key with them."

"Why?"

"Look at the lock." She jumped up off the couch and almost ran to the front door. Christopher followed.

"See, it's one of those old-fashioned locks with a big key. When leaving you have to lock the door from the outside. So, they had to either leave the key in the lock, on the outside, or take it with them."

"Why not leave the door unlocked?"

"Because ... because ... I'm not ... because they wanted to be able to come back and get in another time? Lisa recoiled from the door as if it was on fire. "Oh my god."

"Are you sure you can't find your key?"

"I told you, it's kept on my key ring." She picked up the bunch and sorted through them. "No, not here."

"And you don't have any bolts on the door. OK, so, the first thing to do tomorrow is to get the lock changed.

"Do you believe me now?"

"I can't imagine you would lock the door, remove the key from the key ring, and hide it, even if you had a lot to drink."

"Is that a 'yes'?"

"Yes."

They sat in silence for several minutes.

Despite the discovery that someone had her key, Lisa started to calm down. She had at least stopped sighing. "Would you like some lunch?"

"Where shall we go?"

"I rather stay here. I'd be afraid to come back in case someone had used my key to pay a visit."

"OK."

"I bought pâte, bread and salad for me, but I'm sure we can do a five-loaves and two-fishes act with it. I don't have any wine, but the Asian shop down the road is usually open on Sunday. Please hurry, I don't want to be alone for too long."

Lisa shut the door almost before Christopher was out.

Christopher felt some of Lisa's fear. It made him check up and down the stairwell and in both directions of the street before stepping out. A cool breeze sharpened his mind as he strode down the empty street and mulled over what had happened at the police station. He still wasn't sure he agreed with Lisa about Grindel.

The only red wine he could find in the shop was a cheap Dôle. It would have to do. Searching for something more suitable to go with pâte would mean leaving Lisa alone for too long. He bought two bottles and hurried back.

He rang the doorbell four times, as they'd agreed, but he was still aware of the scrutinisation through the spyhole.

"Yes?"

"It's me, Christopher."

He almost fell over the baseball bat propped up beside the door. "Where did you get that?"

"Another passion of André's. Surprisingly, he left it behind when he moved out."

"And what are you planning to do with it?"

"I don't know, but it makes me feel better."

"Something just occurred to me: does André have a key to this apartment?"

"Ah, so you think he's involved in this?"

"Does he?

"No, we never lived here together."

Lisa continued to lay the table. From the way she slammed the plates down Christopher guessed her anger had risen again and he decided to stay quiet for a while and let it subside. He found the drawer containing utensils by trial and error, and found an old-fashioned, slightly rusty corkscrew at the back. He struggled with the awkward instrument for several minutes and only succeeded in removing small pieces of cork from the top of the neck. Unusual for him, he swore several times and not exactly under his breath. He felt rather than saw Lisa standing in the doorway.

"It's enough one of us getting angry and frustrated without you taking it out on a bottle of wine."

"It's not the bottle of wine, it's this damned contraption."

"Having trouble with it?"

"How long have you been standing there?"

Her mood had lightened. "Long enough to see if you, being an engineer, could work out how to use it.

"Well, I can't, so perhaps you'd be good enough to show me."

"Oh I don't know, I never use that. It was at the back of the drawer when I moved in. I don't know why I didn't throw it away. I kept it for emergencies, couldn't live without a bottle opener. I use this." She handed him a pump-action opener from a stand on the worktop. It was the first time he'd seen anything like a smile on her face since he'd arrived.

They ate and drank mostly in silence. The first bottle of wine disappeared quickly and they were well into the second one before they'd finished eating.

"Coffee?"

"I'll finish my wine first, it's grown on me now."

"It wasn't all that bad."

"For an Asian shop on a Sunday, no."

"I'll just clear these away."

"I'll help."

"No, I know where things go. You finish the wine."

Christopher refilled his glass and went to stand in front of the window. Lisa's apartment was on the fifth floor with a view over the Limmat. On the far side of the river a police car raced by, blue light flashing. The triple glass insulation deadened the sound of the siren, but Lisa's hearing must have been on full sensitivity. She called from the kitchen, "I wonder if they'll believe whoever they're rushing to?"

By the time Lisa brought in coffee on a tray, Christopher had made three slow circuits of the living and dining area and was sitting back at the table.

"Table or couch? she asked.

"Table I think."

When they did speak it was together.

"What—"

"What—"

"You first."

"No, you, first."

She took a deep breath. "I was going to ask you what you really thought of Sergeant Grindel and what happened this morning?"

He pursed his lips and nodded slowly. "I've been thinking about that, obviously."

"And?"

"It could have been a coincidence that Grindel was at the police station. Or perhaps the officer at the front desk recognised our names and knew to contact Grindel if we appeared. When Grindel sent Menna to find Constable Schmidt she implied that neither Grindel nor Schmidt were normally on duty today. Or perhaps I misunderstood."

"I didn't pick that up at the time, but now you mention it I do remember him being abrupt with her and telling her to go."

"And he told her to go when you started to say something about André."

"That I did notice."

"On the other hand, why did Grindel have Menna in there with us at all, if he's involved?"

"Don't they have to have two present?"

"I don't know, but we were being filmed."

"Filmed?"

"Yes, there was a camera in the corner."

"Shouldn't he have told us that?"

Again, I don't know. But … but …"

"What?"

"Something struck me as odd. When he offered us coffee he went with Menna to get it. Wouldn't the sergeant send the constable to get it? Perhaps he wanted to tell her that this was the couple he'd dealt with before and his questioning would be more aggressive than 'normal'."

"So you think he wasn't there by accident?"

Christopher thought for a moment. In his mind he'd decided, but he wasn't sure he wanted to say it out loud. "The one thing that makes me think he's not acting in a way you'd normally expect the police to react is the look on his face while Constable Menna was out. You probably didn't notice because you were angry."

"What look?"

"Threatening, very threatening."

Lisa shuddered, sat in silence, angrily pushed back her chair and paced around the room. "I knew it, I knew it the first time I saw him. They're all in it together, Grindel, Rudi Affolter, the taxi driver, that creep in the hotel, the fat barman, André, the–"

"Whoa, slow down. Let's not extrapolate too far."

"'Extrapolate too far'! Kidnapped, in my case twice, drugged, and threatened. And now someone's got the key to my apartment–"

"OK, OK, but let's not start imagining a huge conspiracy. We don't know Rudi's involved for instance."

"Wake up, Christopher, of course he's involved, that's where it all started."

"No, it started after we'd been to his house."

"When we were at his house." Lisa quickened her pacing. "Why? Why? What's going on?"

"Lisa, please sit down, pacing around like that won't solve anything."

"I can't sit. Why? Why? Who are they? What have we done?"

Christopher went into the kitchen to get the bottle of cognac. The only glasses he could find were two, cheap tumblers.

Lisa was still pacing when he returned, but sat after he'd poured the cognac. Her compressed lips were white and her eyes blazed. "What shall we do?"

"Do?"

"Yes, do. We can't let this happen again."

121

"Go to the police I guess."

"Grindel's friends you mean?"

"There are other police stations."

"And tell them what? We've got no evidence, as Menna told us. Even if they're not in with Grindel they'd probably contact him once our names go in the computer."

"Do you have any better suggestions?"

"At the moment, no, but we can't just let it drop. Who knows what could happen next."

"Look, I'm away until next Thursday. Let's think about it. We'll see if there's any reaction from the police."

"There won't be."

"Let's see. Please don't do anything until I get back."

Silence.

"Lisa?"

"OK."

"Promise?"

Christopher hoped the slight nod of her head meant yes.

Sonntag
28 September 2008

André Wissler breaks club record.

The FC Zurich record for the most goals scored in a season has stood for 15 years, but yesterday saw a new record holder. With his twenty-fifth goal André Wissler beat Bernd Müller's long-standing achievement.

In the six years since his return to football in Switzerland Wissler has scored an average of 18 goals each season. It was only a matter of time before he broke Müller's record

The record-breaking goal also consolidated FC Zurich's position at the top of the Super League, and almost guarantees their finishing this season as champions.

After the match Wissler said "I'm very proud to have been able to follow in the footsteps of my hero Bernd Müller." Müller was at the match to see his record broken. He said "The record has stood for too long. I think André will go on to set the record even higher. He's a great player."

It's a pity that Wissler's talents temporarily deserted him in 2006, which prevented his selection for the World Cup.

"Hello."

"Congratulations."

"Thanks."

"I always knew you'd do it."

"Thanks eh ..."

"It's your favourite Uncle."

"Sorry I didn't recog– what time is it?"

"Eleven o'clock. Out on the town celebrating were you?"

"Yeh, something like that."

"Well you deserve it."

"I'm not so sure the manager will agree with you, I'm supposed to be at the post-match briefing in half an hour, and that's the last thing I feel like doing right now."

"Two raw eggs in a glass of tomato juice, that's the cure, put you right in half an hour."

"Thanks. Sounds revolting, but I might give it a try."

Gazda

The movement to put the telephone back on its cradle made André's head swim. He lay very still and held his eyes wide open to try to stop the room spinning. The events of last night drifted through his brain: champagne with the directors, more champagne with the committee of the supporters' club, dinner and more champagne at the Zünfthaus, and then ... then what? On the occasions he and his colleagues went out for a night of 'relaxation' they'd end up at his bar, The Celler. He remembered being there last night, as usual in the office behind the bar where they could drink and hear the music unseen by football fans. But the office was a bit crowded for seven people, and they didn't like the music. Plus this was a special celebration and several of his mates wanted something involving female company, preferably with few clothes on. So, after only one bottle of champagne, they headed for The Lipstick Club. The rest of the evening became a blur.

Now, it was decision time: call and say he was sick or try his Uncle's cure.

He managed the poison in two gulps and, with some difficulty, succeeded in stopping himself throwing it instantly back up.

As she stepped out of the lift she almost collided with Herr Muri.

"Good morning, Lisa."

"Oh, good morning, Herr Muri."

"Monday morning again."

"Yes, sorry, I was miles away."

"Still thinking about the weekend?"

"Yes … yes … something like that."

"I'm just going down to see Bernard Steinborn. He wants to show me a new machine we've got on loan. I should be only half an hour."

"Yes … yes … OK, Herr Muri."

"Get a cup of coffee, Lisa."

Lisa wondered if her decision to come into the office today was the correct one. She hadn't discussed it with Christopher, but had thought about it after he left. He'd offered to stay, but she said she would be OK, mainly because she knew he had to leave early on a business trip the next morning. Before he left he'd helped her move a heavy chest of drawers from the bedroom to near the front door. Even though it took some effort, she managed to push it across the door herself.

She lay awake for over an hour, going over and over what she knew had definitely happened, trying to drag anything new from her memory. Nothing came and this frightened her.

At 5am she decided that concentrating on work in ZFFM for a few hours might interrupt the thoughts swirl.

The double ring of the telephone, signalling an internal call, started even before she removed her coat.

"Good morning, Lisa."

"Erna … hi, … good morning."

"Are you OK?"

"Yes, fine."

"I really enjoyed Saturday night."

"Yes … me … me too."

"How about coffee later?"

"Yes … coffee … good idea … coffee later."

"You sound as though you need a strong one now. Don't tell me you were partying again last night."

"Yes … coffee."

"See you about ten."

Lisa stared at the dead 'phone in her hand. In all the happenings of yesterday she'd forgotten about Erna. What was she going to tell her?

Everything? Erna was like a match in tinder-dry landscape. The story would be round ZFFM in no time.

Nothing? That would be the safest choice. Even a hint that something unusual had happened would get Erna's curiosity juices flowing.

On the other hand, perhaps Erna saw something, something small. And of course she had given Erna's name to the police. What if the police interviewed Erna? How would she then explain it? But Grindel would not be conducting any inquiries she was sure.

She dialled Christopher's number. After five rings she realised he'd gone away.

For the next two hours Lisa concentrated on her work and made an effort to talk herself into a state of calmness. The process went well except for a brief encounter with Rudi Affolter in the corridor.

"Lisa, how are you? I haven't seen you for some time. Did you have a good weekend?"

"Fine ... thank you, Rudi, and you?"

"Good, sehr gut."

Back in her office Lisa analysed the expressions that had accompanied Rudi's words. Friendly? – yes. Over friendly? – perhaps. Any suggestion of 'I know what happened to you'? – to be honest ... not really. Except ... except ... for the hint of a smirk when she hesitated after 'fine'.

By ten o'clock she was ready to face Erna and made sure she arrived in the coffee lounge early.

"Hi, Erna, I ordered you a cappuccino, hope that's OK?"

"Yes, of course."

"So, you enjoyed Saturday night."

"Sure."

"Something different."

"Certainly for me. My first hen night."

The coffee arrived and they stirred together.

"Are you feeling OK now, Lisa?"

"No, I wasn't 'partying again last night'. And yes, I am feeling OK now, thank you. It was just Monday morning blues, I expect."

"So, you didn't have to wait long for a taxi."

"No ... there was one there almost immediately."

"I seemed to be home very quickly: either he took a short cut or I'd had more to drink than I realised."

Lisa saw the chance she'd been hoping for. "More than I was."

"Why, what happened?"

"My taxi driver must have thought I'd had too much to drink. He took the long route. I kept telling him we should turn left, turn right, but he took no notice, and tried to charge me a fortune."

"What did you do?"

"I refused to pay."

"And?"

"He said he'd call the police."

"So, what happened."

"I didn't want the hassle outside my apartment block, so I paid and said I would report him."

"And did you?"

"The taxi company didn't want to know, so I told the police."

"What did they say?"

"Not much they can do about it. They suggested I might have had too much to drink. I give them your name to confirm we were OK."

"So, I might be called as a witness."

"I doubt it will get anywhere near that, but they may contact you. These cases must happen every day, or night, for them."

"If they do, I'll tell them we were both completely sober."

Gazda

The Attack

29 September to 3 October 2008

"I have to go."

"Not yet."

"I'm late already."

"Hmm." He snuggled his head into her neck and draped one of his long legs over her.

"And I'm cold."

"You were the one who threw off the duvet saying you wanted me to see your face when you came."

"That was then. Now I'm cold."

"I'll get the duvet."

"No, stop. I'll get all cosy and be even more late."

"What time are you supposed to be back?"

"Four."

He pulled her towards him. "It's only quarter past three."

She made a token resistance. "I need a shower and–"

"We'll be quick."

"I don't want quick."

"I really have to go now."

He released his hold on her. "OK, leave me alone."

She rolled out of bed before he changed his mind. "I need a shower."

His eyes followed her to the bathroom. As she turned to close the door the curve of her sideways silhouette caused stirrings.

The fast-fading, late-afternoon light was just enough to make out the scattered clothes. He smiled, and added a slight shake of his head when he saw her uniform neatly folded on a hanger.

The passion had been there since the day they joined the police academy. Meeting someone who they didn't tower over was a relief for both. The chemistry took over from there. There'd been no talk of marriage because they were too young, and both had ambitious career plans.

Jochim Friedmann was well on the way to achieving his ambitions. He reached the rank of sergeant only a few years after graduating and joined KRIPO. Unfortunately career progress for women in the Zurich police was a slow process. Beatrice Menna was still a constable in uniform, although she'd graduated first in their class. Something she frequently, but playfully, reminded Jochim of.

As new graduates working in different parts of the city they quickly lost contact. After five years they had a connection through a case and the passion reignited. Meanwhile Beatrice had married another graduate who had chased her all through the academy. Jochim had married a childhood sweetheart. Both marriages were virtually over. Divorce would have put a black mark on their records. So they met at an apartment that had belonged to his mother and he had not sold when she died: sometimes once a month, sometimes several times a week, depending on their duty schedules.

Beatrice came back into the bedroom wrapped in a large white towel. Despite various suggestions from the bed when she removed the towel, she continued becoming Constable Menna again.

"We had a strange case yesterday. A woman claimed to have been abducted, drugged, interrogated, threatened, drugged again, and then dumped back in her apartment."

"Hmm."

"But apart from a few bruises and some marks on her legs she had nothing to support her story. Grindel handled the interview, although what he was doing there on his day off I don't know. He'd seen her before. She was the one who was in that hotel in the Niederdorfstrasse. Did you hear about that?"

"Vaguely."

"Jochim, are you listening to me?"

"Sure."

"Anyhow, this was the same woman. Grindel was sceptical, but I think he was more than a bit hard on her." Bea straightened her tunic and shook her head. One reason she'd changed her shoulder-length hair for a much shorter style was that it just fell into place, even after a couple of hours frantic activity in bed. "She'd been to The Celler."

Friedmann came out of his reverie. "Who had?"

"This woman who we interviewed yesterday. That's the place you raided isn't it?"

"Yes."

"Could there be a connection?"

"Why?"

"The Celler's not had any trouble in the past, as far as I know. Now you raid it, and it's involved in two abductions within a few weeks of one another."

"Two abductions?"

"Yes. You're not listening are you? I'll tell you some other time."

Jochim propped himself up on the pillow. "OK, you have my full attention."

"This woman, Ms Stern, and the man she was with, Mr McLendi, found out that they'd been in The Celler before the hotel."

"The hotel? Remind me of what happened."

"Grindel and Schmidt went to the Hotel zum Kirsch on Saturday 7 September. The report on file gives no details, but says they found no reason for police involvement and made no follow up. However Schmidt couldn't help telling people about what they'd found in the hotel room: Mr McLendi naked and handcuffed to the bed, Ms Stern dressed for–"

"Yes, I remember the story that went around. Probably exaggerated by Schmidt."

"Possibly."

"And the two people claimed they didn't know how they got there."

"Yes." Bea searched the floor for her shoes. "But now they say they've found out they were in The Celler before the hotel and Ms Stern was in The Celler last night."

"I'm still not sure what that's got to do with our raid on The Celler."

"Probably nothing. It's just the name coming up a few times. Coincidence?"

"Never ignore coincidences, constable. Can you send me a copy of the interview transcript?"

"Grindel didn't think it necessary to make one. He said he didn't believe either of the stories they'd told us."

"So, no transcript."

"No ... but, yes."

"I thought you said Grindel didn't want one."

"He didn't. I also asked him if I should follow up with The Celler, the taxi company and the person who had been with the Ms Stern in The Celler. He said that wasn't necessary either. In fact he ordered me not to follow up."

"Perhaps he's right."

"I'm not so sure. The woman sounded genuinely frightened and angry about what she claimed had happened. I tended to believe her, and, as I said, Grindel was more than a bit hard on her."

"What about the tape of the interview?"

"Grindel told the tech people to wipe the tape."

"That's against the rules."

"Not if the interviewing officer considers it a waste of police time."

"Never an easy decision to make. Did he ask you what you thought?"

"Grindel doesn't ask juniors, especially women, for their opinions."

"You just said no and implied yes to the question about a transcript."

"I made one. I think it would be worth at least having a discreet word with this other woman, who was with Ms Stern in The Celler."

"Bea, you'll get yourself in trouble. Grindel's a bas–"

"I'll bring you a copy of what I wrote next time we meet. Bye."

"Bea–"

After Beatrice had left, the sergeant in Friedmann re-emerged. Was what she told him anything to do with his investigation? He could hardly tell Kullmer where he got the information from.

Beatrice had to wait until the next day to call. "Good afternoon. Could I speak to Ms Sameli please?"

"Speaking."

"Ah, good afternoon, Ms Sameli. This is Constable Beatrice Menna, Zurich police.

"Good afternoon."

"I'd like to ask you a few questions if I may?"

"What have I done?"

"Nothing, as far as I know. It's in connection with your friend Lisa Stern."

"Ah, Lisa told me I might be getting a summons."

"Hardly a summons, just a few questions for clarification."

"OK, fire away."

"I'd prefer that we meet."

"Shall I come to the station?"

"No ... no that's not necessary. I could come to your office, sometime later this afternoon."

"I don't know ..."

"I'd not be in uniform."

"OK, four o'clock."

"Erna, there's a Beatrice Menna to see you, she wouldn't say which company."

"Thanks, Pam, put her in the small conference room please."

"That's occupied by Rudi Affolter at the moment. The big one's free."

"OK. I'll be right down."

"Thanks for agreeing to meet me."

"I've only got ten minutes before a meeting."

"This won't take that long. Did Lisa tell you what happened on Saturday night?"

"Yes. I'm sure those taxi drivers are cheating many people at that time of night. They chose the wrong person with Lisa."

"Yes ... yes, exactly. I've talked to The Celler and they say you and Ms Stern left about three o'clock, is that right?"

"The music had stopped and the place was closing, so I guess it must have been about then. Polizei stunde in Zurich isn't it?"

"Indeed. You walked together to the taxi rank at the end of the Niederdorfstrasse?"

"Yes."

"And what happened?"

"Lisa said I should take the first taxi because I had further to go."

"Which you did and left Ms Stern at the taxi rank?"

"Yes."

"Did you see another taxi arriving as you drove off?"

"No, but my taxi did a U-turn down the road, and as we passed the rank I saw another car pull up."

"Another car?"

"A taxi."

"You're sure it was a taxi?"

"Yes, it had a yellow sign on the top, I think."

"Did you see the taxi drive away?"

"No, we'd already past it."

"OK, thank you. Just one more—"

"I've just thought. Something did strike me as a bit odd. The driver was getting out of the taxi. They don't usually do that, do they, especially late at night."

"Can you describe him?"

"Tall, very tall, and obviously muscular from the tight, leather jacket he was wearing."

"Anything else?"

"No."

"Thank you. If you do think of anything please give me a call, here's my card. Just one more question, and sorry it's a bit personal. How much had you and Ms Stern had to drink?"

"Enough, but not too much. Not completely sober, not drunk. I made a sandwich and coffee when I got home."

"Thank you again."

"Does this happen a lot?"

"Sorry."

"Taxi drivers trying to cheat customers."

"Oh ... yes ... eh quite a lot."

Constable Menna wondered how she could tell Sergeant Grindel about what Erna Sameli had said without admitting she had disobeyed him and interviewed her. Her difficulty increased after she disobeyed further and telephoned the taxi company. They had a record of delivering someone to Ms Sameli's address, but not Ms Stern's address, and they had no tall and muscular drivers.

She decided a little white lie would be the best way. But she didn't believe she would get away with it face-to-face. She wrote a report saying that Ms Stern and Mr McLendi had contacted her with the information about what Erna Sameli had seen, and they had asked the taxi company to telephone her. She thought this sounded reasonable after Ms Stern and Mr McLendi had admitted during that Sunday interview of doing some investigation of their own after the hotel incident. She waited to see Grindel's reaction.

"Nothing, absolutely nothing."

Jochim stretched lazily. "What did you expect?"

"At least some reaction. Even if he'd bawled my out for disobeying his orders."

"So, let it drop now."

"Let it drop? Is that your professional opinion?"

"It's my personal opinion that you should not be pacing around the bedroom naked if you are not intending to come back to bed."

"That's got nothing to do with this case."

"Bea, there is no 'case'. Grindel is many things, but he's regarded as a thorough cop. He wouldn't let something like you're imagining go if there was a case."

"Imagining! What about all the coincidences and open questions?"

"And you think that Grindel doesn't see them?"

"Obviously not ... or ... or"

"Or what?"

"Or he sees them and ignores them."

"Why would he do that?"

"Perhaps he's involved."

"Bea, now you're getting into the land of conspiracy. Come back to bed."

"Perhaps."

"That's better than no." He pulled the duvet down past his navel.

"No. I mean, the conspiracy."

He threw back the duvet and sat on the edge of the bed. "Clearly you are not going to let this go."

"What would you do, Sergeant Friedmann?"

He breathed out loudly and strode to the bathroom, unusually grabbing his dressing gown on the way. When he came back, Bea was sitting in bed with the duvet pulled up to her chin. "I didn't want to make you angry," she said in a quiet voice.

He sat on the stool in front of the dressing table. "You didn't. It's just that we never talk about work when we meet; we have so little time together."

"I know. It's just ..."

"You're letting this get to you."

"I know, and I'm not sure why. It's just that what Ms Stern told us sounded so believable, and the other information confirms–"

"Careful Bea, you're forgetting all our training, avoid emotional involvement."

"I'm not emotionally involved."

"When you start talking about 'conspiracy' you are."

"OK, OK, help me to look at this rationally."

Between them they decided the only real lead, not evidence, Beatrice had, was Erna Sameli. She couldn't ask Grindel about her report without arousing suspicion she was showing too much interest and might have disobeyed him. She couldn't talk to Lisa Stern or Christopher McLendi because that might get back to Grindel.

"Ms Sameli?"

"Yes."

"This is Constable Beatrice Menna. We spoke yesterday."

"Oh ... yes ... Constable Menna."

"Sorry to call you at home. Are you OK?"

"OK ... yes ... I'm OK."

"I was wondering if you'd remembered anything else about the taxi driver."

"The taxi driver?"

"The one you saw get out of the taxi that was picking up Ms Stern."

"I think ... I think I got a bit ... confused when I was talking to you."

"Confused?"

"Yes ... I ... I didn't see Lisa, Ms Stern, with a taxi."

"But you said your taxi did a U-turn and you saw another taxi pull up at the rank."

"I was ... confused ... I ... we ... my taxi didn't do a U-turn."

"And the tall, muscular taxi driver you saw?"

"Tall ... muscular ... ah ... that was much further down the road ... outside the ... outside the 01 Bar."

"So, you didn't see a taxi near to Ms Stern?"

"No ... no, definitely not ... definitely not."

"Are you all right, Ms Sameli?"

"Why?"

"Your office said you were ill, that's why I'm calling you at home, and you sound nervous."

"No, I'm OK ... I'll have to go, goodbye."

Beatrice swivelled round and traced her finger along the street map of central Zurich on the wall. The 01 Bar and Ms Sameli's home were in the opposite direction to the way the taxis face at the end of the Niederdorfstrasse. Her taxi must have a made a U-turn at Central and passed Ms Stern at the rank.

They'd always said the only telephone calls at work they'd have would be to change the plans they'd made the last time they met. This happened rarely and usually only because of last-minute duty rescheduling. But Bea wanted to tell Jochim about Erna's reaction as soon as possible.

"Sergeant Friedmann?" Bea used his title because, although she knew no one else would answer his telephone, she didn't know if anyone might be near enough to hear.

"Yes."

She waited for him to say something to show it was OK to talk. When he didn't, she assumed it was not. "I'll call back later."

"What can I do for you, Constable Menna?"

Confusion. Was someone listening? Normally he would have just put down the receiver and pretended the line was dead. Mentioning her name meant she had to continue, didn't it?

"I have that information you asked for. I'll send it over to you."

"What information is that?"

What was he doing? He obviously recognised it was her. Why was he continuing it? "Hmm ... Hmm ... the information about ... about the bank robbery." Stupid thing to say, but it was all she could think of.

"Ah, the bank robbery, yes, why don't you bring it over yourself?"

For one of the few times in her life Beatrice Menna was struck dumb. "I ... I "

"I'd like to see you, especially if ..."

"Yes?"

"... especially if you're wearing those tiny red panties."

"Jochim, you bastar–"

"Language, Constable, language."

"You bastard Jochim. Don't you ever do that to me again. I thought I'd made a mistake by call–"

"Yes, sir, I'll be there right away."

"Don't start again. I'll kil–"

"I'll call you later."

The phone went dead in Bea's hand.

Since their last discussion she'd made a real effort to get back into 'police mode'. She'd looked at the facts and ignored any sympathy for Lisa Stern.

She read over the 'transcript' she'd made. It confirmed her original opinion that Grindel's questioning was harsh. From the beginning Grindel's facial expression said he didn't believe them.

Why did he send her out to look for Schmidt? With a woman involved he should have had a female officer in the interview room all the time. He must have known that Schmidt was not on duty.

Why was Grindel himself at the station that morning?

What had Grindel been asking while she was out of the room? Ms Stern almost attacked Grindel, she was so angry. The look Ms Stern gave Grindel when she and Mr McLendi left made Bea shudder.

She waited all day for Jochim to call her back. She knew it wouldn't be easy for him. At five o'clock her shift finished and it would look strange if she hung around, so she went home. At eight o'clock her 'phone rang.

"Bea, sorry I didn't call you."

"I didn't really think you would, or rather could."

"It was a surprise to hear from you."

"Which you recovered from quickly enough to play your little game."

"I would have loved to see your face."

"Don't be so smug. I haven't decide whether I've forgiven you or not yet.

"You will."

"Don't be so sure."

"Are you wearing those–"

"Stop."

"I'm only asking about those tiny–"

"Stop or I won't forgive you. Where are you?"

"Still in the office, unfortunately. We had some information late this afternoon that needs checking. Everyone else has gone. I'm waiting for someone to call me back. What did you call me about?"

"I talked to Erna."

"Erna?"

"Ms Sameli, the woman who was with Lisa Stern on the night of the abduction."

"OK, and?"

She told him about Erna Sameli's reaction on the telephone and her review of the interview of Lisa Stern by Sergeant Grindel. "There are too many pieces that don't fit together. There's something going on here."

"Remember what we said about getting emotionally involved? 'Pieces fitting together' sounds like on track to conspiracy theories again."

"I know, I know, but I have really looked at this objectively. How many coincidences can you have before they start to form a real picture?"

"That's a question we have to continuously ask ourselves, or we jump too quickly to conclusions, which, as you know, can be dangerous."

"Yes, but–"

"Bea, I believe you."

"You do."

"I believe you've tried to look at this rationally."

"So?"

"Look, I can't talk just now. As I said, I'm waiting for someone to call me. When can we meet?"

"I thought we decided the next two weeks were impossible."

"Almost, but I think we need to talk about this before you do anything else. Can you get away tomorrow?"

"Tomorrow?"

"Yes. I could meet you in the afternoon for an hour or so."

"OK."

"But not at the apartment. Thursday's market day, there are too many people around there. How about the park, you remember, where we once met?"

"Of course."

"Three o'clock."

"OK. Are you going to able to leave soon?"

"I think I will. Someone 'phoned in to report seeing a woman attacked. We've had no one making a complaint, so I've asked the casualty departments to check their records; I don't think I'll get an answer tonight. Normally I wouldn't bother, without a victim there's nothing to go on. But this was a bit strange. The person reporting it said it happened last night, but they didn't want to get involved. However, their conscience had pricked them. So much for the public helping the police to fight against crime."

Beatrice and Jochim circulated the park area. Satisfied there was no one among the few people exercising their dogs who knew them, they sat on a bench partially hidden from the main pathway.

"Thanks for finding the time for us to meet," she said.

"You sounded so involved with this situation, and, as I said, I didn't want you doing anything more until we'd had a chance to talk."

"Thanks."

"So, tell me, how would you lay it out for your boss if you were asking for permission to investigate further?"

Beatrice took a deep breath. "OK. Lisa Stern comes to the station on 28 September and—"

"Sorry to interrupt, Bea. I've only got about forty minutes. Forget the dates for the moment. Just outline what you know and what you deduce."

She was a bit disappointed because she'd made an effort yesterday to remember all the dates. "OK, first the facts. Lisa Stern comes to the station claiming abduction by a taxi driver. Grindel and I interview her. Grindel recognises Ms Stern and the man with her, Mr Christopher McLendi, as the two people involved in an incident at the Hotel zum Kirsch three weeks ago. Ms Stern and Mr McLendi say they were abducted after visiting The Celler and dumped in the hotel - there is no evidence to corroborate this.

"Ms Stern has bruises on her arms, and possible needle marks on her legs, but again nothing to prove how they got there. Ms Erna

Sameli was with Ms Stern that night at The Celler. She tells me she took the first taxi and saw another taxi pull up beside Ms Stern and a tall, muscular man get out. The taxi company delivered Ms Sameli to her home, but have no record of Ms Stern's address. Yesterday, Ms Sameli denied she saw the taxi and the driver.

Beatrice took another deep breath. "For me there are several important questions. Why go to the police with two claims of abduction? What do they gain by them, if they're not true? OK, the first time in the hotel could have been to cover up they were having an affair. But they're not married, as far as I know."

"You know that do you?"

"I made a few discreet inquiries.

"Discreet?"

"Yes, discreet. But why would they go to the police with the story of the second abduction? Why was Grindel so hard on Ms Stern? Why did he tell me, order me, not to follow up? Why has Ms Sameli changed her story? I thought she sounded nervous on the 'phone. And, The Celler is a link between the two stories."

Beatrice had kept her eyes on Jochim during her summary. He had scanned the park, but now he looked at her. "I see there are some questions, but we have to always remember that even for the most seemingly difficult questions there can be simple answers. So, where do you go from here, Bea?"

"I'm not sure. Obviously working for Grindel makes it difficult for me to do anything 'official'. Any suggestions?"

Jochim scanned the park again. "I have to get back. Let me think about it. Promise me you won't do anything until we've had another chance to talk."

"But when will that be?"

"We'll work out something. Promise me."

"OK, promise. But just tell me, do you think there's something going on here?"

Jochim nodded his head slightly and slowly. He got up, started to bend to kiss Bea, but stopped himself, smiled and gave a little wave. As he walked across the grass towards the main pathway his mind focused on Bea's words 'And, The Celler is a link between the two stories'.

Erna had called Lisa immediately after the first discussion with Constable Menna on Tuesday and told her what she'd said about the taxi driver. Lisa said she didn't remember the driver getting out of the taxi.

On Thursday afternoon one of Erna's colleagues told Lisa that Erna had called in sick on Wednesday.

"Erna, it's Lisa, are you OK?

"Yes ... yes."

"Are you sure?"

"Yes."

"Will you be at work tomorrow? I thought we could have lunch."

"I'm not sure."

Silence.

"Not sure?"

"If I'll be able to make lunch."

"OK, let me know tomorrow morning."

"Yes ... tomorrow morning."

"Erna, are you sure you're OK?"

More than a moment of silence. "I ... I ..."

"Erna, what's wrong?"

"Nothing. I'll call you tomorrow. Goodbye."

Lisa rang the doorbell and waited. She stood well back from the spyhole so Erna could get a good look.

The door stayed closed

"Erna, it's me, Lisa."

"What ... what are you doing here?"

"I wanted to make sure you're OK."

"I'm OK."

"Can I come in?"

"Not at the moment."

"Erna?"

"Go away. Leave me alone."

"Now I know there's something wrong."

"I told you, I'm OK."

"Open the door then."

"Can't you just leave me alone."

"Erna, open the door and prove you're OK, and then I'll go."

Silence.

"Erna, if you don't open the door I'll start banging on it. That should attract the attention of your neighbours."

Silence.

Lisa clenched her fist and hit the door solidly, twice, with edge of her palm. The door opened as much as the safety chain would allow. Lisa could see the right profile of Erna.

"See, I'm OK, now please go."

"I don't understand. I thought we were friends. I only want to make sure you're OK. You'd do the same for me. That's what friends do."

"I told you ... I'm OK."

Lisa saw the glint of moisture that started to appear in the corner of Erna's right eye. She waited until the drop was about to fall. Lisa spoke softly. "Erna, let me in."

The door closed and reopened without the chain. Erna was already walking away down the short hallway. Lisa closed the door and for a reason she was not sure of, fastened the safety chain. In the living room Erna stood facing the window, although well back from it.

"Sorry for forcing you to let me in. I just wanted to make sure you're OK."

"I know." Erna turned and Lisa let out a gasp. The bruise on Erna's left cheek was dark blue, with streaks of red and yellow.

"What ... what the hell happened?"

"Would you believe I walked into a door?"

"If you tell me that's what happened."

"Well I didn't." The tears that had been threatening now rolled down Erna's cheeks.

Lisa put her arm around Erna's shoulders and guided her to the couch. "Sit down. Can I get you something to drink? Tea? Coffee?"

"There's a bottle of whisky in the cupboard."

"Even better."

Lisa let Erna take two large sips before asking the obvious question. "So, what happened?"

Erna took a deep breath. "I was ... what would you call it? Attacked? Mugged? ..."

"What? When? Where? Why?"

"On Tuesday night."

The internal audit of the purchasing department had taken a lot longer than expected. It was 9:30 before Erna left the office. The trams were less frequent than rush hour, and it was after quarter past ten when she reached her stop. She decided to take the short cut through that passageway between the pizza restaurant and the dry-cleaners.

It was pitch-black, and her heals stumbled on the cobblestones: the reason she normally walked 50 metres down the street and round the corner into Molkerstrasse. She was about halfway along when she heard heavy footsteps walking quickly behind me. She increased her pace, but more stumbling slowed her. The footsteps came closer and closer. An arm encircled her body, pinning her arms to her side. A hand covered her mouth. A raspy voice whispered in English "Do not move or make a sound."

She could feel the hot breath on her cheek. There was a strong, sickly smell of cheap aftershave, mixed with second-hand smoke. The mouth was very close to her ear. "The information you give the police is wrong. You did not see taxi or man. You understand?"

Her 'yes' was lost in her throat.

The arm around her and the hand across her mouth tightened.

"You understand?"

She nodded as much as the restriction would allow.

"You telephone police, say you make a mistake. You understand?"

Again she managed a nod.

The hand left her mouth, slapped her on the cheek, and covered her mouth again in one swift movement. "You get more if you talk. Understand?"

She started to nod vigorously.

"Good." The hand patted her cheek.

Erna drained her glass. "He let go of me and walked, slowly away. Somehow I managed to stop myself collapsing and crying out. I stood rigid for a long time: I was so afraid he would come back."

Lisa poured more whisky. "Have you been to the doctor?"

"No. I'm sure there's nothing broken. It doesn't really hurt that much, just looks awful. He probably knew exactly what he was doing. He caused the maximum amount of surface effect without any permanent damage, this time."

"Have you told the police?"

"No."

"Don't you think you should?"

"I'm too scared. And what could I tell them? I can't describe him. And it was clear what will happen if I did talk to anyone."

"But you said he told you to telephone the police and say you made a mistake."

"I was planning to, but Menna called me yesterday. I wasn't ready with my story, but I think I managed to convince her I made a mistake."

"Damn! Damn!"

"Sorry, Lisa?"

"Nothing, I was talking to myself. I'm so angry that this has happened to you."

"It's not your fault."

"I took you to The Celler. I shouldn't have involved you in this."

"Involved me in what?"

"This ... this ... oh nothing."

"Come on tell me."

"Nothing, forget I said anything."

"Lisa tell me."

"There's nothing to tell."

"Really?"

"Really."

"You're not to blame. You only gave my name to the police to try to prove you hadn't had too much to drink."

"I took you to The Cell–"

"This taxi racket must be bigger than we, I thought."

"Taxi racket?"

"Yes, I wondered why the police were investigating so much."

"Ah, yes, the taxi racket."

"But how did they find out what I'd told the police?"

"Sorry?"

"How did they find out I'd given the police a description of the driver of your taxi?"

"Good question. Did you tell anyone besides me and the police?

"... No."

"No?"

"Well ... well it was exciting. It was my first police interview."

"So, you told one or two people what had happened to me and what you told the police?"

"Probably a few more than one or two."

"There's your answer–"

"My god, that means one of the people I told is part of the gang."

"Gang, might be a bit strong, but what you told the police got back to ... to whoever is running this ... this taxi racket. Do you remember who you told?"

"As I said, it was more than one or two. And you know how one talks to another, who talks–"

"Yes." Lisa sighed. "I wonder ... "

"What?"

"Nothing."

"You wonder if they might attack you?"

"No, they've already– "

"Already what?"

"Already ... already found out that I couldn't describe the driver, as I told you."

Lisa's anger at what had happened to Erna started to build as she rode the tram home. When she reached her apartment several plans had started to form inside her head, all of which involved confronting people - Grindel, Menna, André, Rudi. She picked up the telephone several times and started dialling their numbers, but always stopped halfway though because she realised she was still working out what she wanted to say. In the back of her mind she also knew that she should call Christopher. Wasn't he supposed to be back from his business trip today?

After the third time of letting the 'phone ring until the answer machine cut in, she decided to leave a message, 'Christopher, it's Lisa, please call me as soon as possible'. Not having received a return call, she went to bed at midnight. She was sure there were too many thoughts going round in her head to allow sleep to come. She was right.

"Lisa, it's Christopher. Sorry I–"

"Christopher, what time is it?"

"Sorry, did I wake you. It's seven o'clock I thought I'd catch you before you left for the office."

"Seven o'clock, I'm late, I should have been up 30 minutes ago."

"Sorry I didn't–"

"Christopher, I'll have to rush, Herr Murri's got a meeting at eight thirty. I'll call you later."

"Lisa, hello."

"How about I make something to eat tonight?"

"OK, I'll bring the wine."

"Eight o'clock?

"OK."

"Am I too early?"

"If I was Swiss I would say ten to eight is too early, but as I'm not, come in."

Christopher watched her turn the keys in the double-action bolt lock and secure the chain. "Sorry I didn't call you back last night. There was a delay at the airport, it was one o'clock when I got home."

"Dinner, well, spaghetti vongole, will be ready in twenty minutes."

"I guessed it might be pasta, so I brought Chianti."

Lisa took the bottle into the kitchen and Christopher went back to look at the new door lock. The chain was also new and at least twice as thick as the previous one. He stood at the entrance to the kitchen. Even though he and Lisa were still strictly work colleagues, the discussions they'd had in this apartment meant that he didn't feel like a first-time, dinner guest. "Your voice on the answerphone sounded a bit urgent I thought of calling you back even though it was late. Is something wrong?"

"Yes, you could say something is very wrong."

"What is it?"

"I was going to tell you after we've eaten, but I think it's best I tell you now so we can discuss while we're eating. This sauce could benefit from simmering for a few minutes. Let's go and sit down."

"Sounds serious." Christopher was already guessing and fearing that something more had happened about … about … what would they call it? The abductions?

Lisa told him what had happened to Erna. She tried hard to tell it verbatim, without any of her opinions. Christopher listened with the same attitude. In the short experience they'd had at talking about incredible things that had happened, they'd both learnt that mixing facts and opinions only resulted in confusion.

"I was fuming last night. I started several telephone calls–"

"Who to?"

"Grindel, Rudi, André–"

"But only 'started'?"

"Yes."

"Good."

"I've calmed down … a bit, but we've got to do something."

"We'll come to that. So, Erna thinks this is about a taxi racket?"

"Yes, based on the story I made up in case the police called her."

"Do you think she did see something?"

"When she told me she seemed to be sure."

"Did you think about telling her the truth? She might remember something important."

"Telling Erna what really happened would be like announcing it over the loudspeaker. Besides, I think because of what happened to her she will try to erase the whole episode from her head, not try to remember more."

"OK. So–"

"We'd better eat or my 'gourmet' vongole sauce will be spoilt."

Christopher stretched his legs under the table. "That was good, thank you."

"I thought you might be fed up with my spaghetti vongole."

"No way." Christopher could see Lisa itching to start talking. "So, what have we got? We talked to Grindel and Menna–"

"Grindel interrogated me."

"Yes, OK Lisa, I agree it was more of an interrogation than a discussion, but–"

"We should stick to the facts, I know. Carry on."

"Menna talked to Erna. Did Grindel know that? We don't know. Erna talked to half of ZFFM. Someone attacked Erna. We don't know who or how they found out what she'd told Menna. I can't believe anyone who Erna talked to at ZFFM could have passed on the information."

"Aren't you forgetting someone?"

"Who?"

"Rudi Affolter."

"When did you tell Erna?"

"Monday morning."

"Rudi's been away with me all week. We left on the eight o'clock flight on Monday morning. So that eliminates him."

"He could have heard from his secretary or someone."

"Unlikely."

"So, who then?

Christopher shrugged. "That only leaves Menna or Grindel?"

"I said on Sunday, I don't think Menna's involved."

"Why?"

"The way Grindel sent her out when I was mentioning André."

"But you said Menna wanted to talk to Erna at the office, not at the police station. Bit strange?"

"They're probably all involved."

"Let's not get carried away again, Lisa."

"You keep saying that, Christopher, but what are we going to do?"

Silence.

"You finish your wine. I'll make some coffee.

'What are we going to do?' The question bounced around Christopher's head. If someone had asked his advice in a situation like this he would have said immediately 'go to the police'. Why was he finding it so difficult to follow his own advice?

Lisa brought in the coffee and put the tray down heavily on the table. "I'm going to have a cognac. Do you want one?"

"You have a never-ending bottle. Is there enough for two?"

"You have a look. I'm going to make a telephone call."

"At ten-thirty? That's not very Swiss."

"Well I'm not Swiss, as I told you once tonight. I'm sure your friend Rudi will still be up."

"I thought you didn't have his number."

"I found it."

"I won't ask how. Why call Rudi?"

"I want to know if he knows about what happened to Erna."

"How will that help?"

"If he says yes, I'll ask him how he found out."

"Lisa, do you really think that's a good idea?"

"A good idea? I don't know what's a good idea ... I'll call Erna then, see if she's remembered anything else."

"What might be a good idea is to wait until tomorrow, when we've had time to think about it a bit more."

"'Think about it'? I've been thinking about nothing else since last Sunday morning. You remember last Sunday morning Christopher, when I told you about what happened on Saturday night? Kidnapped, drugged, interrogated, and dumped here by someone who took my door key?"

Christopher took a deep breath. "OK, I understand, I really do. Let me get the cognac and then let's talk."

"Talking is not going to get us anywhere."

"OK, just let me get the cognac."

Christopher went to the toilet before collecting the bottle of cognac and glasses from the kitchen. He wanted to give Lisa a few extra minutes to reflect. As he poured he saw some of the wildness had gone out of Lisa's eyes. He hoped his continued silence would aid the calming process. "I still think we should try some other way through the police. Perhaps through that contact you have."

"We've been through that before." The anger had gone out of Lisa's voice, now it was a cold monotone.

"I don't see an alternative, do you?"

"There must be something we can do."

"I don't know what."

"I don't know either, but I do know I do not want another kidnapping."

"I still think we should go to the police."

"They don't believe us."

"Grindel doesn't believe us."

Lisa shook her head. "Because he's involved somehow."

"But not all the Zurich police force."

"No, but word would get back to Grindel and then ..."

They sat in silence, both holding their glasses in front of their lips, not preparing to drink, but to give a reason for not saying anything.

Lisa nodded several times. "What ... what if ... what if we ... we try to find out what's going on?"

"We've already tried asking a few questions, the taxi company, the barman at The Celler, and it's not got us far, except another abduction, supposed–." He realised he'd said one too many words when the word was halfway out of his mouth."

"'Supposedly'?"

"Sorry, I meant abduction."

Lisa shook her head and fumed."You think I volunteered for the interrogation? The–"

"No. It was a slip of the tongue. Sounds stupid I know, but ... I do believe you, promise. We used to say that as kids, 'promise', to let someone know we were telling the truth.

"We did also."

The sipped their cognacs.

"The question is why? Why was I abducted? It can't be because I asked a few questions about being in The Celler. Grindel was right there. What did he say the idea was, 'far-fetched'?"

"You still think there's a connection between your abduction and our being in that hotel?"

"Yes, don't you?"

"They certainly have something in common: The Celler."

150

"Exactly, The Celler's a key part in all this. The Celler, where I supposedly danced on a table before drinking vast quantities of vodka, which I hate, and then handcuffed my boss to the bed in a seedy hotel. The Celler, where I asked a few questions and was drugged and interrogated for doing so. Yes, The Celler."

Silence.

"They must think we know something."

"Who? About what?"

"I don't know, Christopher. I don't bloody know." Lisa stood and paced in the restricted space between coffee table and couch. "You remember I told you the thug who interrogated me kept saying I was asking too many questions."

"Questions about what?"

"He didn't say, and, you know, Christopher, for some reason, I forgot to ask at the time."

"OK, OK."

Lisa paced vigorously a few more times, then slowed and sat. "Prostitution."

"What?"

"Prostitution at The Celler."

"But we don't know anything, about that, except what was in the TIME article."

"And what Erich told me."

"Which wasn't much more."

"No ... but it must be something to do with that."

"I don't see the connection between The Celler, prostitution and us."

"André."

"André, your ex-husband?

"André, my angry ex-husband."

"Ah, your theory about him getting back at you for the embarrassing divorce."

"And missing the World Cup. That must have made him really angry."

"Anger is one thing, abduction is quite another."

"Perhaps not if you're a local football hero. News about his involvement in prostitution would damage his image and ego. And if he thought his bitch of an ex-wife was going to be the one to tell the world, abduction as a way of warning her off might be attractive."

"OK, so?"

151

"So, let's stop concentrating on The Celler and find out more about prostitution in Zurich. Find out who runs it: André or someone else. It might lead us to whoever's responsible for what's happened to us."

"But what's happened to us might have nothing to do with prostitution."

"Might not, but I don't have anything else to link our abductions and The Celler, do you."

"No, but–"

"Christopher, please don't say again that we should go to the police. I feel the bruises on my arms and legs every time I shower. I showed then to the police and they did nothing."

"Lisa, if you're right–"

"'If I'm right', you still have doubts?"

"Let me finish. If you're right, these are criminals. We've obviously done something to annoy them. They've warned us off twice, three times if you count what happened to Erna. Next time might not be a warning."

She shrugged.

"It's dangerous, Lisa."

It might be more dangerous if we don't do something."

"How?"

"We don't know exactly what we've done to cause two abductions and an attack. So, we can't stop doing whatever we've done, which may mean more abductions. No, we have to try to find out ... find out at least what we've done."

"And you think trying to find out about prostitution in Zurich will tell us that?"

"Christopher, I keep asking you if you have any other suggestions?"

He took a deep breath and breathed out slowly. He looked at the expression on Lisa's face and saw steely, fierce determination. She was not going to give up. He had glimpsed some of this part of her nature when she was trying to find out who stole his briefcase. His approach in life had always been to walk away from trouble. He knew this meant he sometimes let people walk over him. Images slid through his mind of kids in his neighbourhood picking on him because he was the one who went to grammar school.

"So?"

"It's too risky, Lisa. We know nothing about this type of thing."

"For me there's no choice."

"How will we go about finding out? In disguise?"

"Yes, if necessary."

"I was joking."

"I'm not."

"I don't like it."

"I don't like what's been happening to us. I'm going to see what I can find out."

"But–"

"You don't have to be involved, but I need to find out."

Christopher looked into her eyes and she starred back at him. He saw hurt and anger, mixed with the determination. He took a deep breath. "I can't let you do this on your own, but we'll need to put a lot of thought into it before we do anything."

Gazda

The World of Prostitution Part I

8 October 2008

In front of the hotel a party of backpackers were loading enough rucksacks into a minivan for a team of twenty Sherpas on a trip up Mount Everest. After waiting for ten seconds the taxi driver sounded his horn.

"It's OK, we can get out here," said the passenger.

"Careful the traffic," said the driver

The trainee receptionist put on her corporate welcome smile as they approached the desk. "Welcome to the Hotel Excelsior."

The couple stood in silence as the young woman made a thousand keyboard strokes before handing them each a magnetic card key.

"Grüezi, was kann ich für Sie tun?" The absence of the crossed keys symbol on the lapels of his black jacket said the porter was not a member of Les Clefs d'Or, and therefore perhaps more open to his question.

The man looked left and right and leant in. "I wonder if you can help?"

The porter matched the man's low voice. "I'll try, Sir."

"I'm only here for one night and I'd like a bit of … company." The last word came out as almost a whisper.

"Company, Sir?"

"Yes, company. I've got the numbers of several places that provide … company for visitors, and I was wondering if you could tell me which is the … the best." He reached two fingers into the top pocket of his jacket and slipped out a 50 franc note.

The porter closed his hand around the note. "Depends what you mean by 'best', Sir." He winked.

The man's face started to flush. "Oh, em nothing … nothing unusual, just … well just more sophisticated."

"Could be expensive Sir."

"Oh that's not a problem."

An elderly lady tottered up to the porter's counter, and instead of waiting behind the man, stood beside him. "Now, porter, I'm going into the restaurant for dinner, and I need you to go and check on Timmy every half-hour."

"Excuse me, madam, I'm dealing with this gentlemen at the moment."

"I'm sure this gentleman won't mind. You have to make sure Timmy still has water in his bowl, and if he shows any sign of discomfort you'll have to take him for walkies."

"So just leave that with me, Sir. I'm sure I can arrange something. Your room number Sir."

"Four twenty-two."

"Did you hear what I said about Timmy?"

"And what time would be convenient?"

"Ten o'clock?"

"I'll see what I can do, Sir. Now, madam, tell me about Jimmy."

The bell of the Frauenmunster struck once, signalling the quarter past the hour. The man paced the floor and twirled the bottle in the ice bucket. He looked at his watch. "Five more minutes." His head swivelled towards the door at the sound; not so much a knocking as a gentle, but repeated tapping.

A long-legged, blonde-haired young woman glided into the room. The man knew he'd been right to trust the porter. She was mid to late twenties, and wore a red, silk dress that was short enough and tight enough to show off her legs and stunning figure, but was in no way tarty.

"Hello, I'm Sabina," she said as she did a three-hundred and sixty degree scan of the room. She saw nothing to alarm her. Her eyes came to rest on the man: fortyish, small beard and moustache, scar on right side of face, thick rimmed glasses, smartly dressed.

"I'm … John. Would you like a drink?"

"Yes, please."

The clinking of the bottle against the glass suggested nerves. "So, cheers."

"Cheers."

He gestured to one of the two chairs by the low table and she sat. A well practised crossing of legs made sure he thought he saw everything, but actually saw nothing. He remained standing.

She sipped the champagne. "Before we go any further we have to talk about business." This could have sounded cold and emotionless, but her eastern European accent made it sound like an invitation to bed, which in a way it was.

"Yes, of course."

"It's 400 Swiss francs for one hour or 1,500 to stay the night, paid in advance." Again cold words, but said in a way that was dripping with passion.

He reached into his inside jacket pocket and handed her three five hundred-franc notes.

"Thank you." She took another sip of champagne and recrossed her legs.

He looked at her, seeming unsure what to do. She smiled lightly, rose, stood in front of him, and ran a well-manicured, red fingernail lightly down the left side of his face and across his chin below the lip.

"I think ... I think I should explain something," he said.

"You don't have to explain anything, just relax."

He moved to his left. She'd missed the door in the wall on her survey scan. Interconnecting doors between adjoining rooms were unusual in hotels nowadays. As he turned the handle her mouth started to become dry and she had to lick her lips and swallow.

The woman who entered was smaller than the man. She had thick red lipstick, a mass of red/brown hair and heavy black mascara that almost hid her eyes,. Sabina relaxed a little, but was still on her guard. "I didn't realise there was going to be three of us."

Neither the man nor the woman spoke. The man closed the door.

"The price goes up if she would like to join in."

The man gestured to the chair where she had been sitting. "Please sit down."

She backed into the chair, keeping her eyes on the woman, who had remained near the door.

"Sabina I ... we ... we want ... we want ..."

The woman came forward. While the man looked friendly, the woman's face had a hard expression. "We wanna ask yeh a few questions."

Sabina had met many different types of clients. Some liked to talk, some not. If this couple wanted to talk first, OK.

"Where dya werk?" Like the man, the woman sounded English, but she was more difficult to understand because of her accent.

Sabina reached for her handbag and pulled out a card. "Discreet Escort Agency."

The woman handed the card to the man. "Who's the gaffer at Discreet Escort Agency?"

"Sorry?"

"She means who owns Discreet Escort Agency?" said the man, frowning at the woman.

"Why do you want to know that?"

The woman's voice became harder. "Luke, lady I'm asken questions, who's yer gaffer?"

"I don't know."

"Yeh don't know? Yeh must know."

158

"I don't."

"Luke lady, it's a simple question."

Sabina was starting to feel there was something strange here. She managed to stand even though the woman was almost leaning over her. "Look, I'm going to leave now. You can have your money back." She reached into her handbag.

The man now stepped forward, placed his hand under the red-haired woman's elbow and guided her to the other chair. "You can leave when you want to and you can keep the money. We want to know who owns Discreet Escort Agency because we have a similar organisation in England and we are looking at possibilities to have some exchange of escorts."

Sabina studied him. "Why didn't you just ask the agency?"

"We thought this might be an easier way to find out."

"An expensive way."

"Maybe."

"And I'm afraid I don't know."

"She's lying." The woman started to stand up, but the man signalled her to sit back down.

The man kept his friendly manner. "Have you never seen anyone from the organisation?"

"We make arrangements by telephone."

"And what about the money?"

"Paid into a bank account."

"After taking off your part."

"After taking off my part."

"Trusting!" The woman still looked as though she had a nasty smell under her nose.

"So, you have no idea who owns the agency. What about when you started to work for them, didn't you meet anyone then?"

"It's not a normal job you know, I didn't have an interview."

"Yeh don't have to tell us 'it's not a normal job' lady. There's gotta be a selection process. I do that in our organisation."

"I can only suggest that you contact the agency and ask. The number's on the card."

The man glanced at the card and nodded his head.

Sabina picked up her handbag, took a step closer to the man and said in a whisper that was loud enough for the woman to hear. "Are you sure I can't do something to make your visit to Zurich memorable?" Her eyes swivelled to the woman and back. "After all you have paid for it."

"Don't tell us you've gotta conscience about tekin the money. Get outta here you slut, he don't need to pay for any favours from the likesa you."

Sabina's eyes never moved from the man's face. "I just thought it might be better than 'favours' from anybody else." Now her eyes rested on the woman.

"Why you– "

The man reached out his arm to prevent the woman reaching Sabina, who stepped out of arms length. "I think you'd better go."

"If you're sure."

The woman struggled, but the arm held her.

Sabina glided towards the door in the same slow, sexy way she had entered.

"Just one thing," said the man. "We would appreciate it if you didn't tell anyone about this discussion."

She didn't turn round and the door closed behind her.

Confrontation

9 October to 16 October 2008

It was a week before Bea and Jochim were able to meet again. And it wasn't the apartment or the park. For the first time, they talked in Sergeant Jochim Friedmann's office. He'd requested some information about a case Sergeant Grindel had worked on and, because the information was confidential, Grindel asked Beatrice to deliver the file personally. When they'd finished the 'official' business, Jochim got up and closed his office door. He stroked Bea's hair as he passed her on his way back to behind his desk. "I've got something to tell you."

"Is it safe?"

"Safe?"

"What if someone comes in?"

"It's OK."

"It feels a bit strange."

"It's OK Bea. We've been continuing to investigate The Celler. Do you know who owns it?"

"Why should I?"

"A member of FC Zurich."

"The football club?"

"Yes. One of the players owns The Celler."

"And?"

"Do you know who the star player is?"

"No, you know I'm not all that interested in football."

"There was big news about him a couple of weeks ago."

"No, still don't know."

"André Wissler."

"Jochim, I'm getting more nervous being here, where is all this leading to?"

"André Wissler had a wife."

Bea fidgeted in the chair. "Jochim, please."

"André Wissler is the ex-husband of ... Lisa Stern."

"What?"

"I was going through my notes to see if there was anything we'd missed. I'd made a note to check on Wissler's marital status. I checked today. The divorce was in 2005."

"Lisa Stern. That joins a few pieces of the puzzle together."

"Now don't start jumping to conclusions too quickly."

"OK, but you must admit it connects your case to mine."

"Keep in mind that at the moment you don't have a case."

"Quite a few coincidences though."

"Coincidences, yes, but connections? I'm not so sure."

"So, now what?"

"I told André Wissler I would need to have another talk to him. Let me see if I can make any connections."

"What can I do?"

"Nothing at the moment."

"But."

"No buts."

"I feel I should—"

"Thanks for bringing this information over, Constable Menna." Friedmann stood, walked quickly to the door and opened it. "Thank you Constable."

Beatrice glared at him. If anyone had seen her storm down the corridor they might have suspected she'd received a reprimand from the detective sergeant.

When she got back to her desk most of the frustration had evaporated. Of course, Jochim was right. She couldn't do anything at the moment. Under normal circumstances she would have gone to her boss with the information she'd just obtained. Although telling him where she got it would be difficult. Lisa Stern's ex-husband owned the bar that she'd visited before two abductions. Good reason to talk to him, independent of the investigation into the prostitution. But with Grindel's attitude she doubted he would pursue it.

Bea brought up some information about André Wissler on her computer screen. Almost all of it was, of course, about his football career, which she didn't interest her. She entered Lisa Stern and found her name in an article about Wissler's career in England. And there was a small piece in the Neue Zürcher Zeitung about the divorce. She noticed his mother's name a few times in the football articles, but there was no father mentioned.

On closing the Internet, the default screen of all police computers appeared: the Incident Log. She'd scanned it before going to see Jochim. Now she read each line.

```
9 Oct - No progress on 02 Oct reported attack
on Kreuzweg;   file closed.
379
```

Why did 'Kreuzweg' catch her attention? What was the attack reported? She went back to the Incident Log for 3 October.

```
2 Oct - Telephone report of seeing attack on
woman two days  ago; no police or hospital
report.
379
```

What was it about Kruezweg? She took the Zurich street map book out of the top draw of her desk. Kruezweg was a small passageway between Schusterstrasse and Molkerstrasse. "Molkerstrasse ... Molkerstrasse ... that's where Erna Sameli lives." She looked again at the date of the attack: 30 September.

"When did I talk to Ms Sameli?" She opened her notebook. "September 30 and October 1." Beatrice leant back in her chair. Another coincidence? No, not this time. Dates and place fit. She needed to talk to the incident reporting officer, Officer 379, asap, certainly before their next planned tryst.

Jochim Friedmann was also tapping his computer keyboard. There was no obvious connection between prostitution and the abductions. Unless this Ms Stern, had a night job. He brought up the Prostitute Register on his screen. Not surprisingly, no mention of the name 'Stern'. He typed 'lisa' and 'stern' into the search box of the Incident Log. Three hits:

```
06 Sept - Call from Hotel zum Kirsch; customer,
Mr  Christopher  McLendi,  asked  for  police.
Couple  in  compromising  situation.  No  police
action required.
472, 514

28 Sept - Front desk visitors; Mr Christopher
McLendi, Ms Lisa Stern.
271

28 Sept - Interview Mr Christopher McLendi, Ms
Lisa Stern.  Claim of abduction  (Ms  Stern).
Nothing to support story.     WOPT.
472
```

The Incident Log was always brief, but these entries were exceptionally short. Usually 'N' or 'T' for notes or transcript appeared if more information was available. There were no additions to these entries. 514 was Schmidt and 271 a young constable on desk duty.

There was no mention of 384. Constable Beatrice Manna on 28 September. Time for a word with 472, Sergeant Grindel.

The stood facing each other, close, but not touching. Bea spoke first.

"Was it difficult to get away?"

"I said I was 'going for a very long walk'. That's code for talking to an informer. Nobody will look at how long it takes and will not call me unless there's a real emergency. We have a couple of hours. And you?"

"Monday's my day off."

"I forgot."

They knew they both had things they were dying to tell, that's why they'd hurriedly arranged this meeting. Talk first and make love after, or … Jochim reaching out and touching Bea's cheek made passion win, not that there was ever any real contest.

Time was too short to think about a second excursion into sexual ecstasy or lingering in bed. After showering they sat at the kitchen table in their dressing gowns with mugs of tea.

"OK, you first," said Jochim.

Bea told him about seeing his notes on the Incident Log and linking Kreuzweg with Erna Sameli's address. "So, there was no report of anyone going to the hospital."

"Nothing."

"What about the person who reported the attack?"

"The woman wouldn't give a name."

"Did you speak to her."

"Yes, I happened to take the original call. That's why I was still in the office so late."

"Do you remember what she sounded like?"

"Not particularly. Why?"

"I wondered if it could be Erna Sameli trying to report the attack anonymously."

"Assuming the attack was on Ms Sameli."

"Dates and place fit."

"True. Does she have a distinctive voice?"

"Not really. Quite deep I suppose for a woman."

"I don't remember."

"I'm wondering if I should have another discreet word with her or even try to see her."

"You're thinking there could be a connection between the attack on Ms Sameli and the abduction of Ms Stern."

Bea looked at him with surprise. "Is that what you're thinking?"

"After my discussion with Grindel I–"

"You spoke to Grindel?"

"Yes, that's what I wanted to tell you about."

"When? Where? What did he say?"

"Whoa, slow down. Last Friday. I would have preferred to be on home territory, but he said he was waiting for a telephone call, so I went to his office."

"Jochim, come in, thanks for coming over."

"No problem, Walter."

"What can I do for you, it sounded urgent."

"Not urgent, just following up some peripheral information on The Celler investigation."

Jochim noticed a slight stiffening of Grindel's body. "How's that going? You didn't charge anyone."

"No, we decided we'd sent a strong enough message to the bars with the raid, without clogging up the courts."

"You said something about 'peripheral' information."

"Yes. André Wissler ..."

Grindel sat more upright.

"... the FC Zurich star player owns The Celler. His ex-wife is a lady called Lisa Stern, who you interviewed recently, twice."

Now Grindel's upper body jerked forward and his eyes widened. "Lisa Stern is ... Lisa Stern is ... was André Wissler's ex-wife?"

"Yes, didn't you know? Are you OK, Walter?"

"Know? Why ... why should I know?"

"I thought you might have checked on Ms Stern."

"Checked? No, I didn't check on her." A deep, deep breath held in for couple of seconds steadied Grindel's mind and body.

"According to the brief information on the 28 September Incident Log, Lisa Stern claimed she'd been abducted."

"It wasn't the first time she'd made such a claim. We found her and a Mr McLendi in the Hotel zum Kirsch. It looked as though they'd had a wild night of drinking and sex, including handcuffing him to the bed–"

"Ah, that's the September 6 incident."

"Yes."

"You remember a lot of detail."

"It's not something that happens every day."

"Why were we involved?"

"McLendi told the hotel to call the police."

"What do you think it was about?"

"They shouldn't have been doing what they were doing. Probably they're both married and wanted to cover themselves in case their partners found out."

"Sounds a bit extreme."

"It takes all sorts, as I'm sure you've found out, even in your short career."

"Do you know where they had been before the hotel?"

Only Friedmann's close observation detected Grindel's shoulders jerk. "I didn't ask."

"Must have been one of the bars in the Niederdorfstrasse I suppose."

"I suppose."

"Could have been The Celler?"

A more pronounced jerk. "I don't know."

"So, there was no follow up?"

"I told them to come to the station if they wanted to talk about it. They never came.

"And no notes."

"I asked Schmidt to make some, but he forgot. We've all got more important things to do."

"Sergeants don't usually answer routine calls for police help?"

"What do mean?"

"Well, it just seems a bit odd. The hotel calls and says a customer has asked for the police and Schmidt AND you go to the hotel."

"There must have been some reason."

"You can't remember?"

"Look I'm busy. Does it matter?"

"No, probably not. So, Ms Stern turns up at the station on 28 September claiming she's been abducted–

"For the second time."

"Quite a coincidence that you were on duty."

"My bad luck, having to deal with her again."

"What did she say had happened?"

"Something about a taxi driver drugging her and dumping her in her apartment."

"Any sexual assault?"

"That she didn't claim."

"Did she say where she'd been earlier?"

Grindel's shoulders jerked again. "Not as far as I remember."

Jochim gave a little laugh. "Probably The Celler."

Grindel remained silent, but Jochim could see the anger building.

"So, you thought the whole thing was a 'waste of police time' as you wrote in the Log? Nothing worth following up?"

"No."

"No notes or transcript again."

"No."

"Tape?"

The anger almost boiled over. "Why are you so interested?

"As I said, peripheral information concerning the raid."

"The technicians accidentally wiped it."

Jochim stood. "Thanks Walter, sorry for disturbing you." He turned towards the door. "Oh, by the way, the Log didn't show who else was at the interview."

"Who else?"

"The female officer you have to have when interviewing a woman."

Silence.

"Menna."

Without turning round Jochim could tell from the way the word came out that Grindel was struggling to control himself.

Bea listened without interrupting, which was unusual for her. When he'd finished they sat in silence for several minutes.

Jochim spoke first. "So, what do you think?

"Do you think he didn't know about André Wissler and Lisa Stern?"

"From his physical reaction I would say it came as a shock to him."

"He certainly didn't show he knew who she was at the interview."

"Hmm. If I ignore what you told me–"

"Remember I wrote down what took place at the interview immediately afterwards. I gave you a copy. You think I made that up?"

"Calm down constable. I didn't say anything about the truth of what you wrote. If you'd let me finish. If I ignore what you told me, for a moment, and look at my discussion with Grindel in an objective way, I would say ... I would say there are some real question marks about his handling of these situations. First, not explaining why there are no notes or transcripts or follow up. Second, not including you as being present at the interview on the Log. They could be just mistakes, but not ones that I would expect an experienced officer like Grindel to make–"

"Unless he has something to hide."

Jochim bowed and shook his head, and pursed his lips.

"OK, OK, I'll just listen."

"And I find it odd that he avoided any mention of The Celler. It figured strongly in both situations involving Ms Stern and Mr McLendi."

Bea opened her mouth to speak, but changed her mind.

"Plus, there's no explanation why he made the visit to the hotel. That's a constable's job."

Bea took a deep breath. Only Jochim planting his lips on hers prevented her protest.

"And why was he at the station on the morning of the 28 September? I checked the duty roster and he had Saturday and Sunday off."

"Can I speak now?"

"No!"

"I think ... what? No?"

"Joke."

"There's something to joke about? I–"

Jochim held up both hands.

"OK, OK I'll calm down. ... I think you're right about him avoiding mentioning The Celler, that is strange. And the way he handled Lisa Stern was not standard procedure. But you sergeants always think you can handle things in your own way."

In her anger and frustration Bea had allowed her dressing gown to open. Jochim reached for the appearing breast. "I like to handle some things."

Bea pulled the robe tightly around her. "How was Grindel during your discussion with him?"

"There was certainly a reaction when I mentioned The Celler and ex-wife Lisa. He was holding back his anger, especially when I asked why he hadn't included you in the Incident Log. Have you seen him since Friday?"

"No. He wasn't there at the weekend and I'm off today."

"You said that during the interview on 28 September he was unfriendly towards Ms Stern. What did you mean exactly?"

"Hard on her, as though he didn't believe her from the start."

"If he thought the hotel incident was–"

"I've just remembered something. At the beginning he asked them if they wanted a drink. Normally, as you know, the slave labour, the constable, has to go and be the waitress, but Grindel came with me. While we were out he said something like 'I've met these two before. This'll probably be another waste of time, so be prepared'."

"Unusual, I'll admit."

"And ... and ... when Ms Stern started to talk about The Celler and her husband, Grindel sent me to find Schmidt."

"Did he continue the interview while you were out."

"From the conversation when I came back, I would say yes."

"Against the rules again, but as there is no tape–"

"Conveniently wiped."

Jochim looked at his watch. "I have to get back."

"So what now?"

Bea washed the beakers. After a few minutes a sharply dressed Detective Sergeant came into the kitchen. "I need to find out more. Something solid."

"Can you go to your boss, make it more official?

"What do we have? Some coincidences, strong coincidences I agree, but still coincidences. Grindel not following procedure. No link between what happened to Ms Stern and what I'm supposed to be investigating, except mention of The Celler. Certainly not enough for Kullmer to stick his neck out and start any investigation of Grindel. Plus, if Grindel is part of the story, who knows who else in the police might be? Although I can't imagine Kullmer would be."

"The link between the two parts is key. Perhaps I can see if I can get any more out of Erna Sameli."

"I don't like it, but I can't think of anything else at the moment. Be careful. Grindel might be more sensitive to you doing something behind his back."

"I'll be the height of discretion."

"I want to talk to André Wissler again."

Their parting kiss lasted its usual several minutes.

The next morning Bea passed Grindel, twice, in the corridor. He was his usual dour-faced self, not acknowledging her or anyone else. Just before her lunch he asked her to come to his office.

Grindel treated the constables under him, especially the female officers, with an air of reluctant, tolerated, contempt. They were obviously far inferior to him, but he had to put up with them to get the job done. No constable had ever sat down in his office.

"Come in, Beatrice. Sit down."

Bea swallowed hard. This was going to be difficult.

"Did you have a good weekend?"

Another swallow. "Yes, thank you, Sarge."

"Good, good."

Silence. He looked at her over the top of his glasses, with what he must have thought was a smile.

"I've just been going through some old paperwork, trying to clear space. You know how it is."

"Yes, Sarge."

"I came across the report you wrote."

"Which report was that, Sarge?" She knew perfectly well which report, but didn't want him to think that it was uppermost in her mind.

"The one about the crazies, Ms Stern and Mr McLendi. I don't think I replied to you, did I?"

"I'm not sure, Sarge."

"Well, I saw what the taxi company said, but you know they don't log each trip, especially late at night. Did you do anything after the report?"

"No, of course not. Not without your approval."

"Good girl."

Condescending bastard thought Bea, but said nothing.

"You saw what I wrote on the Incident Log - WOPT, waste of police time."

"Yes, I saw that, Sarge."

"And I owe you an apology, because I didn't include you on the Incident Log. As I said at the time, I've seen people like Stern and McLendi many times before. They get a kick out of it."

"You have a lot of experience, Sarge."

Grindel smiled and nodded his head. "OK, thanks Beatrice. You're doing a good job, keep it up."

"Thanks, Sarge."

As she walked down the corridor Bea wanted to cry out in frustration. Instead she muttered to herself. "With a performance like that I should be on the stage."

After the raid on The Celler there were no more reports of prostitutes in bars in the Niederdorfstrasse. So, job done, case file officially closed. Chief Inspector Müller was happy, which meant Inspector Kullmer was happy. But the policeman in Sergeant Friedmann was not happy. Too many open questions: Felix? Gazda? The mysterious person behind Wissler's ownership of The Celler? The connection between Wissler, The Celler and the abductions of Lisa Stern? When Friedmann cautiously suggested some follow-up, Kullmer told him to 'put it on the back burner'. Friedmann's interpretation of this was 'don't drop it, but use a low-key approach'. He would have fit it in with his many other investigations, under the radar of Kullmer. In his head he made a 'The Celler to do list'.

The easiest part was taking a look at the 54 Felixes in the database. Normally he'd give the job to a junior constable, but the low-key approach meant Friedmann did it himself. He quickly crossed 23 names off the list. They'd been arrested for one-off, minor offences some years ago, and unless they'd turned to a life of crime and escaped arrest they could be eliminated. Ten people were dead. Eight were foreigners who had left Switzerland. Which left 13. Ten were small-time career thieves who'd been in and out of prison all their lives and unlikely to have moved up to pimping. Two were serving lengthy prison sentences for breaking bank secrecy laws. Leaving Felix Braun.

```
Braun, Felix, Born 1982, Swiss, white, male,
180cm, 76kg.
Arrest record:
2 July 2000 - possession of Class C drugs;
police caution
3 May 2001 - drunk, fighting outside bar;
damages + 7 days jail (suspended)
18 November 2001 - fighting outside bar;
damages + 14 days jail
12 August 2003 - observed selling drugs;
customer (tourist) refused to give evidence,
case dropped
5 February 2005 - causing a disturbance in
licensed brothel; police caution
24 January 2006 - selling Class B drugs in
Niederdorfstrasse; two years jail; released
with remission early 2008
Address: unknown
```

Theory said it was better to interview 'suspects' at a police station than in their home or place of work. The surroundings made them more nervous and therefore more likely to be less cautious in their answers and/or make mistakes. But not immediately following his teammates off the training pitch, three weeks ago, must have been embarrassing for André Wissler. He'd probably faced questions from the manager about the intruder. Going to see him again after training would be a good tactic.

The training planned for 15 October was a public session. Friedmann sat as close to the pitch as possible and hoped that Wissler would see him. It worked. For the last fifteen minutes Wissler suffered the frustration of colleagues and manager for missing tackles and being out of position. While other players signed autographs, Wissler signalled Friedmann to follow him down the tunnel and though some corridors to a small room full of boots and cleaning material.

"This could be police harassment, Sergeant."

" I just wanted a word and I thought this was the easiest way. Of course if you'd rather not help with the inquiries I could go, and we could do it more formal–"

"No, it's OK."

"If you're sure?"

"Yes, but I can only take a few minutes. First, members of the public shouldn't be down here, and second, I got a bollocking from the manager last time."

Friedmann shrugged. "Last time we talked, you said a friend of your mother's advised you to buy The Celler. Who was that friend?"

Wissler slowly shook his head. "I can't tell you that."

"Can't or won't?"

"Won't. It's got nothing to do with what happened at The Celler."

"I'll be the judge of that."

Again the shake of the head. "No."

"I could ask your mother."

Up to now Wissler had been surprisingly calm considering how he had reacted at previous interviews. Now he exploded. "Leave my mother alone."

"or your father."

Wissler took a step forward. Yes, hit me, thought Friedmann, please hit me, then I'll have you in a cell for questioning. Wissler took two deep breaths and backed off. "Go near my mother and you'll hear from my lawyer."

173

Friedmann knew he was on thin ice. Harassing Wissler, and talk of lawyers was not something he wanted to get back to Kullmer. He pulled out his notebook. "In our meeting on 22 September you told me you aren't married."

"That's right, I'm not."

"But you have an ex-wife."

Wissler's victory in forcing Friedmann to back off had restored him to full calm "Perhaps."

"Yes or no?"

"Yes, and what's that got to d–"

"Are you still in contact with your her?"

Silence.

"Do you see her?"

A cold stare.

"Lisa isn't it?"

Wissler's chest rose and fell.

"Lisa Stern isn't it."

Wissler's lips tightened, his eyes narrowed and a heavy breath escaped his nose.

"Perhaps I should have a talk with her."

"You can talk to that bitch all you want. She knows nothing about The Celler. I bought it after I dumped the bitch."

"Sounds like you don't have happy memories of your ex."

"The bitch spoilt my chances–"

"Your chances of what?"

Another deep breath. "Never mind."

"But I do."

Silence.

"So, you don't mind if I talk to Lisa."

"Fuck off, Friedmann."

"I'll take that as a no."

Silence.

"And you could be wrong. Your ex may know more about The Celler than you think."

Wissler got up and walked away. It took Friedman more than a few minutes to find his way back through the maze of corridors.

Item two on Friedmann's 'The Celler to-do list' was the meaning or origin of the word 'Gazda'.

He entered Gazda into Google. Nothing. He hoped he would find something in the University of Zurich library

He was sure that 'Gazda' did not originate from one of the three languages he spoke, Schwyzerdütsch, Hochdeutsch and English. He asked one of the library assistants, who entered it into the library's own database. ""Nothing, I'm afraid

"Any other suggestions?"

"The linguistics faculty?"

"Any idea who to contact?"

"I'm afraid not, I've only been here a few months."

"Thanks anyway." Friedmann turned.

"Just a minute. I think someone from linguistics is in the library now." The assistant started searching through some cards in front of her. "Yes, I remembered checking her in earlier, she'd booked a microfiche reader. She must be still here because she's not checked out. Professor Bisset, Gabrielle, reader number 6, down the corridor on the left.

"Professor Bisset?"

"Oui."

"I'm Sergeant Jochim Friedmann from KRIPO." Friedmann held out his card. "I hope I'm not disturbing you. The assistant at the desk told me you were in the library."

"I am rather busy, young man. And you will have to keep you voice down, this is a library. What can I do for you?"

"Help me I hope. As part of an investigation, I've come across a name of a person, and I was wondering if your could help me identify where it might originate from?"

"I can try. My speciality is Oriental languages."

"I'm pretty sure this is not Oriental."

"What is the name?"

"Gazda. I don't know how it's spelt, I've only heard it spoken once."

"You're right, it is not oriental. Sounds eastern European to me." She pronounced it with a heavy nasal accent.

"Interesting. Any chance of narrowing it down?"

"Not by me. You need a specialist."

"Do you know someone I can contact?"

"There are several people in the department."

"Could you give me any nam–" Professor Bisset's look over the top of her glasses, raised eyebrows and fingers rapid drumming on the table signalled that this discussion was over. "Well thank you for your help. Sorry to have interrupted your work."

"Sergeant Friedmann?"

"Speaking."

"Gabrielle Bisset."

"Professor Bisset, good afternoon."

"I talked to some of my colleagues. They agree the word 'Gazda' probably comes from a Slavic language. There is a word in Serbo-Croatian that means 'master' or 'host'. You said that you had heard it as the name of a person."

"Yes, that's right."

"If it is Serbo-Croatian maybe someone is using it to mean 'chief' or 'boss'."

"Thank you very much, Professor. I appreciate you taking the time."

"My colleague, Professor Zsaky, would like to know if you find out any more about its use,.

Friedmann thought he had pushed André Wissler as far as he could on the topic of who recommended him to buy The Celler. He switched to another track. What had been the reputation of The Celler in the past? Who was the previous owner? Those questions should be easier to answer.

The entry in the Zurich Commercial Register showed the owner was André Wissler since May 2007. Between April 2002 and May 2007 the Register named H. Zubke, Obfelden, Zurich. Who was H Zubke originally from Obfelden and living in Zurich? Friedmann could have made an official request for the address, but that meant paperwork and signatures. He pulled out the Zurich telephone directory. There was only one entry for Zubke: Baumgartner Zubke and Zubke, Rechtsanwälte. Lawyers? Why would a firm of lawyers own a jazz bar? More likely they were acting on behalf of someone.

"Good afternoon, could I speak to Mr Zubke please."

"Mr Herman Zubke or Mr Djordje Zubke?"

"Mr Herman Zubke please."

"Can I say who's call?"

"Sergeant Jochim Friedmann from KRIPO." The full title usually increased the chances of getting through.

"Good afternoon, Sergeant, Herman Zubke. How may I help you?"

"Good afternoon, Sir. According to the Commercial Register you were the owner of The Celler from 2002 to 2007."

A noticeable pause. "Yes, that is right."

"Were you the owner or were you acting for a client? If I may ask?"

"As you said Sergeant, my name is in the Commercial Register as the owner."

Friedmann knew client-lawyer confidentiality would prevent him getting further with that line of inquiry. "And you sold it to André Wissler last year."

"Yes."

The slightest of pauses, only obvious to Friedmann's trained ear. "Do you know André Wissler?"

"Only from the newspapers."

"How did he know The Celler was for sale?"

"Perhaps I mentioned to some people that I was thinking of selling."

"Did you?"

"I must have done. He found out and approach me."

"And you decided it was time to sell."

"Yes ... Why all the questions, Sergeant? Is there something wrong?"

Now Friedmann made a slight pause, to see if Zubke knew about the raid and connected it to the call.

"Is it anything to do with the raid?"

"Only in general terms. I'm trying to build a complete picture of The Celler."

"I understand."

"Are you a jazz fan, Mr Zubke?"

"No. Why?"

"I just wondered why you bought The Celler in the first place.

"Ah ... well ... when I say I'm not a fan ... I mean I'm not a fanatic. I like jazz and The Celler had a good reputation."

"For blues jazz."

"Exactly."

"Thank you for your time, Mr Zubke."

"Pleasure, Sergeant."

"Oh, sorry, just one more question. Do you happen to know André Wissler's mother?"

Longer pause, and, if Friedmann's hearing was good, swallowing. "His mother ... why ... how would I know his mother?"

"Just thought you might know her. Goodbye, and thank you again."

Friedmann wrote in his notebook:

Zubke is Wissler's mother's friend
How does she know him?
Who is Zubke's client?

Friedmann wanted to follow up the information about Felix Braun. The record of possession of drugs, violence, and selling drugs meant that Braun had certainly shown up on the criminal world's radar. He would be a target for 'promotion', especially while in prison: go in as small-time hustler, come out with a new job as a pimp. It would help to know who he associated with in prison.

Friedmann and his friend from school, Ralf Baracluf, had planned to join the police force together, but Ralf had chosen a career in the prison service. They'd kept in touch through the squash club. Once upon a time they played every week, now it was more like once a month.

"So, ready for another beating?"

"Jochim, you haven't even come close to beating me the last three times we've played. I thought the police dealt in facts."

"You always were lucky, Ralf."

"Was that luck again?"

"I let you win because I want some information."

"Yeah, yeah."

"And I injured my hand in the second game."

"Really? It didn't show."

"I suffered through so you could win."

"What information are you prepared to suffer so much for?"

"You were at Gefängnis Affoltern am Albis until you became Assistant Director of Prisons last year weren't you?

"That's right."

"Do you remember Felix Braun?

"Felix Braun?"

"Two years for selling drugs."

"Yeah, he thought he was a real hard case when he arrived."

"And when he left?"

"Don't know, I wasn't there, but he'd already, what shall I say, quietened down after one year."

"Seen the error of his ways had he?"

"I suspect not. We think he'd come under the influence of one of the barons."

"The Swiss gang boss presumably?"

"No, strangely, the Serbo-Croat Mafioso."

"How come? Those groups are usually pretty tight aren't they? They don't let foreigners in."

"Usually, yes. There was an attack on one of the Serbo-Croat group. Minor injuries, but of course no one knew anything about it. We assumed revenge would be coming. The Serbo-Croat group were all small guys, so no one could take-on the job. We guessed Felix Braun 'volunteered' his services, probably for a few cigarettes. He turned up in the medical wing with a badly damaged right hand. He said he'd scraped it in the wall when he fell. Once again no one had seen anything, so we had no evidence to accuse him."

"Seems a bit unusual for the Serbo-Croats to take him in just for hitting someone."

"Oh he didn't just hit someone. He put the bloke in hospital for a week. The other groups got the message: mess with the Serbo-Croats and revenge will be severe. Braun became an honorary member, or associate as the Italians call it."

"Do you remember the names of the Serbo-Groats?"

"No, but I can get them. Why?"

"I've got a feeling that Felix Braun may have a connection with something I'm working on."

"OK, I'll send you an email."

"No. How about meeting for beer after work on Friday? You can bring it with you."

Ralf pursed his lips and inclined his head.

"Don't worry, it's all kosher. I'm just supposed to keep this one on the back-burner."

Beatrice Menna drummed her fingers on the desk. How were the raid, the attack in Kreuzweg, and the abductions connected? The Celler was the common element.

Contacting Ms Stern 'off the record' would not be a good idea: word could easily get back to Grindel. Could Erna Sameli provide any more information? She'd changed her story last time, and then been unwilling to talk. Presumably she knew more about Lisa Stern and her ex-husband.

It had been raining all day, but thankfully it had stopped when Beatrice got to Schusterstrasse at six o'clock. She stood on the opposite side of the street to the pizza restaurant and looked towards the tram stop. If Erna Sameli had left work at the normal time, if she was coming straight home, if Beatrice had calculated correctly, Erna should be getting off one of the next three trams. The No 4 arrived, no Erna. The No 9 came and went, as did the No 12. Too many 'ifs'? Beatrice went to the tram stop on her side of the street to go back into town. Five minutes later, as she was about to step onto the tram she glanced down the street and saw Erna approaching carry a plastic shopping bag.

Beatrice hurried back to her observation position. She timed her crossing of the street so she came into Erna's view when she was about twenty metres from the restaurant. Erna showed no signs of slowing down; either she didn't recognise Beatrice or didn't want to.

"Ms Sameli, what a surprise."

Erna turned her head, smiled and continued walking.

"It is, Ms Erna Sameli, isn't it?"

Erna stopped. "Yes, who–"

"Beatrice Menna, we spoke a couple of weeks ago."

"Did we?"

"About Ms Stern."

"Ah, Consta–" She looked nervously around. "Ms Menna."

"I was just going to the restaurant for a pizza. I heard this is one of the best in Zurich."

"I don't know."

"Do you live around here?"

"No ... eh yes."

"What a coincidence meeting like this."

"Yes."

Beatrice tried to looked for signs of any injury on Erna's face. "Are you feeling better?"

"Better?"

"When I spoke to you last you were at home. Your office said you were ill."

"Oh, it was nothing ... just a cold."

Beatrice thought the make-up on Erna's cheeks was a little higher than one would normally expect. Was there some discoloration on the left side? It was impossible to be sure without staring. "How is Ms Stern?"

"Lisa? Oh she's ... fine."

"She's got over her experience with the cheating taxi driver?"

"Cheating tax– Oh, yes, the taxi driver ... yes ... she's got over that."

"And you didn't remember any more about the taxi Ms Stern took?"

"No ... no ... definitely not."

"Or the driver?"

"The driver?"

"The tall, muscular man you saw."

"No ... look I ... I have to go."

"Of course, get your shopping home."

"Yes."

Beatrice had slowly moved around so she was standing in front of Erna, blocking her path. "So, have you and Ms Stern been out for any more nights at The Celler?" Beatrice kept her voice light and friendly. She knew she was pushing the limits with these questions, but that's why she'd risked coming here.

"No, we don't go out much together. In fact I haven't seen much of her recently." Erna took a deep breath.

"I've never been there, is it good?"

"I've only been once, on the night ..." Erna stiffened again.

"I might give it a try. I'm not a big jazz fan, but it's something different for a night out."

"Well I must be ..."

"Yes. Me too. Get my pizza. Have you eaten here?"

"A few times."

"And it is good?"

"Yes." Erna stepped sideways to go around Beatrice. "Goodbye."

Without physically holding her back Beatrice could not think of anything else to stop Erna moving away. "Goodbye. Nice to see you again."

As Erna moved past the restaurant and started to turn the corner, an idea that Beatrice had had at her desk came back into her head. "Oh, Ms Sameli be careful going down there."

"Down where?"

"That's Kreuzweg isn't it."

"Yes ... I think so, why?"

Beatrice approached Erna and spoke in a low voice. "There was an attack on a woman down there a couple of weeks ago."

Erna's left hand flew instinctively to her left cheek. She pulled it away immediately, but she saw from Beatrice's pursed lips that it was too late. "An attack ... when? ... where? ... how? ... I ..."

"We had an anonymous telephone call."

"Did you catch anyone?"

"Nothing to go on I'm afraid. There may not even have been an attack. Too many people love to get the police chasing ghosts. Cranks I call them."

"I'm not a cran–" A tear formed in Erna's left eye

"Sorry?"

"I mean ..." The tear spilt over.

"Shall we get a cup of coffee?"

Erna said she knew too many people in the area and would feel more comfortable at home. Beatrice would have preferred a more public place. Nervous people say more.

Erna described the attack in detail. After Lisa's visit she'd written down everything she could remember, sights, smells, sounds, accent. When she saw what she had on the paper, she'd decided to telephone the police. The threat was still strong enough in her mind to do it anonymously. On the telephone she lost her nerve and just said she'd seen an attack. She could not describe her attacker.

"You told Ms Stern about the attack?"

"Yes, of course."

"What did she say?"

"She was angry."

"Angry?"

"She blamed herself."

"Why?"

"I told her it was nothing to do with her."

"Perhaps she felt guilty about persuading you to go out that night."

"I don't think she did. We were having what the English call a 'hen night'."

"Was it Ms Stern's idea to go to The Celler?"

"Probably. I didn't know it existed before that night."

"So that's why she felt guilty." Despite the excitement she was starting to feel, Beatrice kept her voice sympathetically friendly.

"Perhaps. She did say something about The Celler."

"Do you remember what?"

"Something like ... yes, 'I took you to The Celler, you're not involved' ... I can't remember exactly."

"What did she mean by 'you're not involved'?"

"I don't know. I asked her, but she wouldn't say any more."

Beatrice allowed a silence. "Did anything unusual happen when you were are at The Celler?"

"What do you mean by 'unusual'?"

"Something you didn't expect."

"I'm not sure what you mean ... you think something that happened there may have something to do with what happened later with the taxi?"

"The taxi?"

"The taxi that tried to overcharge Lisa."

"Ah, yes, the taxi."

"You think they could have spotted us as being vulnerable?"

"Could have."

"We drank some beer, listened to the music, talked to some people, nothing 'unusual'."

"Just thought there might—"

"Lisa told me about the raid on The Celler. She was talking quite loud, over the music. The barman kept looking at her. I thought he might ask us to leave, not that we were disturbing anybody."

Bea let the silence hang.

"I asked her if the barman recognised her. She told me she'd been there before. And ... and ... yes, that's right, she said she'd once danced on a table. I didn't believe her, but she said she was sure the owner would remember her. She asked the barman if the owner was there. What was his name?"

"André?"

"Yes, André. How did you know?"

"That's the owner of The Celler. What happened?"

"I think the barman ignored her. She said, quite loudly, that he was probably out finding more ladies."

"She actually said that to the barman?"

"Not directly to him, but I would think he heard. Do you think there might be a connection?"

"Connection?"

"To the taxi."

"Probably not."

"Do you think it has anything to do with my attack?"

"No. The attack on you was probably because of what you told me about the taxi and driver that picked up Ms Stern. That was true what you told me wasn't it?"

"Yes, but the attack scared me."

"I understand that. What I don't understand is how someone found out what you'd told me." In her head Bea thought she already knew the answer.

"Lisa, Ms Stern, asked me the same question. I must admit that I told a few people what had happened to Lisa and what I told you. It was exciting ... sorry. Would it help if I try to remember who I told?"

"Probably not at this stage."

"So, this taxi racket must be really big."

"Big enough." Bea's brain was already working overtime on scenarios.

"Do you think I'm in any danger."

"I wouldn't think so. We're not following up on the information you gave me, so—"

"Oh, I thought that's why you'd come to see me."

"No ... I told you, I came to get a pizza."

As soon as she got on the tram Bea pulled out her notebook and started frantically writing. Her notes would normally have been almost complete at the end of an interview, but she'd not wanted her talk with Erna to seem like an interview. When she reached her stop in the centre of the city she'd come to a conclusion, preliminary as her police training taught her, but still a conclusion.

The World of Prostitution Part II

17 October to 18 October 2008

It was unusually quiet for a Friday night. Francesca had paced the fifty metres of her territory more times tonight than she could ever remember. Now she stood under the street lamp that marked one of her borders. Her 'neighbour', approached and they exchanged 'poor night' expressions.

"It's cold tonight."

Francesca looked up and down the street. "Sorry?" she said in English to match what she'd heard.

"I said, it's cold tonight."

"Yes." So now she was breaking two 'rules', standing still under the street lamp, and talking to one of the other girls.

"I don't think I'll be staying here for the winter."

Francesca tried to recall if she'd seen the girl before. She must be new. She didn't know the 'rules'. "No?"

"No. I prefer somewhere warmer, and I don't just mean the weather."

"How then?"

"The cold-hearted men around here."

Again Francesca looked up and down the street.

"What's your name?"

"My name?"

"Yes, what are you called?"

"Francesca."

"You don't say much, Francesca. I'm Naomi."

"You know that we're not supposed to talk to each other."

"Is that one of the 'rules'. Yeh, he told me about the 'rules'. Who cares as long as I earn some money, which on a night like this, is impossible."

The sound of footsteps made them both turn their heads. "Female," said Naomi.

"So?"

"I'm not into that, she's all yours."

They went back to their territories. Francesca watched out of the corner of her eye as the figure approached on the opposite side of the street. Clearly the woman was not just passing through. Several of the girls returned her stare with come on gestures or sounds, but the woman kept on walking. Francesca decided on a demure stance, and although she bowed her head it would be obvious to anyone looking from across the road that she had her eyes on them.

The woman stopped and crossed the road towards Francesca. "Grüetzi, Fräulein."

Not Swiss thought Francesca. She replied in English. "Good evening."

They stood looking at each other, Francesca's head tilted down, the woman's up. Their chests started to rise and fall in unison. A moment spread to seconds. The woman spoke first. "I was wondering if–"

"If I could be of service to you."

"If you could do something for me."

"Did you have something particular in mind?"

The woman's eyes never left Francesca's, but she remained silent.

"Why don't you come with me and we can see what happens?"

"No … it's not that kind of something."

Francesca did her scan of the street. "What is it then?"

"I want some information about–"

"I'm not in the information business. Now please move on." Again the anxious glance around.

"Don't worry, I'm not the police or anything."

"I'm not worried about the police, I'm registered."

"That's what I wanted to ask you, how do I register here in Zurich?"

"You mean–"

"Yes, register."

Francesca took half a step back for a fresh look at the woman. She was a little older than most of the girls, but some of the johns liked older women. A nose that was a little too big for her face must have stopped anyone ever saying she was beautiful. She already had the 'uniform': four-inch-high, red heels; a skirt only just long enough to qualify; and beneath an open, fur jacket a white sweater filled to bursting point. There was already enough competition thought Francesca. "I can't help you."

"Can't or won't."

"Please move away."

"Why, is your pimp watching? Perhaps I should talk to him or her."

"Just move away."

"What if I take you up on your offer? Might be interesting, for both of us."

Francesca shook her head and started to walk, hoping the woman would not follow her. When she reached the far end of her patch she stole a look over her shoulder. The woman had gone.

Saturday the busiest night of the week, as usual. Francesca thought she saw the woman once, but one of her 'regulars' approached just at that moment.

After two o'clock things quietened down. Francesca saw Naomi approaching. She knew there were still too many people in the street to be able to see if anyone was watching them. She turned away.

"Psst, Francesca."

"What?"

"Come here."

Francesca approached her, but would not step within two arm lengths, despite encouragement to do so.

"I think you talked to that woman looking for a job last night."

"Yes."

"Well, she approached me and one or two of the others tonight. I think she got the same no answer from everyone."

"Where is she now?"

"I called Felix–"

"You have a 'phone number for Felix?"

"Yes, of course. I insisted at the beginning."

"And you called him?"

"Yes, that's his job isn't it, to protect us."

"Yes, but–"

"But nothing."

"Nobody calls Felix. He decides when we need protection."

"Well I called him."

"What happened?"

"When I told him she was looking for work he came quickly. I don't think he's ever far away anyway."

"And?"

"He found the woman and they went off together."

He called it 'my office': a small, cramped space behind what had been the check-in desk before the girls rented the rooms by the hour.

"Sprechen Sie Deutsch or you want English?"

"English."

"Sit down. What's your name?"

The woman looked around. There was only one, low chair. "Betty."

We'll have to change that, thought Felix, too English. He perched on the edge of the table, his knee inches away from her face. "So, Betty, you're looking for a job."

"Yes."

"Any experience?"

"I've been around."

"Around where?"

"Around."

He smiled. Not the usual type he would think of employing. Nice legs though. He thought that when he first saw her and was even more convinced now he'd seen more of them as her skirt rode up when she sat down. He'd always been a leg man, leg and arse; not that he was against something to suck on, and she obviously had plenty up there. "In Switzerland?"

"As I said, around."

"Any specialities?"

"Specialities?"

"Something different on the menu. Man? Woman?"

"Either."

"Or both?"

"Or both."

He smiled and let his hand rest on his crutch.

Her eyes fixed on his hand. She smiled.

He stood in front of her. The bulge in his trousers on level with her face.

She adjusted her position in the chair, making her skirt ride up further. She stared straight ahead. "I am going to work for you, aren't I?"

His hand moved towards his zip. "I'm sure we can come to an arrangement."

"You can arrange it?"

His face contorted as he struggled with the zip. "Yes, yes."

She looked up into his face. "What do I have to do to guarantee a job?"

"There's never any guarantees, but I'll talk to the right people."

Her eyes slid down to the bulge. It had grown. "It's not your decision?"

"Yes … yes." The zip finally started to move.

A loud bell made them both jump. He looked angrily at the telephone and pulled the zip back up.

He spoke into the mouthpiece in a low, husky whisper. His body language suggested the person on the other end of the line was someone who demanded respect. The conversation lasted no more than three minutes, and at the end he said loudly, "Yes, yes. OK, immediately" and almost bowed.

"Now, where were we?" he said reaching for the zip.

"Was that your boss?"

"What?"

"Was that your boss on the telephone?"

"Yes … I mean no. What's it got to do with you?"

"Is it he, or she, who decides whether I get a job or not?"

"As far as you're concerned I decide. Now get down on this." But the zip wouldn't move, and the more he struggled with it the more it jammed.

"Perhaps it's your boss I should be showing what I can do."

"You're not his type."

"Perhaps he should decide if I'm his type or not?"

The zip pull-tab came off in his hand. "Look lady, you're not going to meet my bo– my associate."

"Not even if I do something for you." She ran her tongue over her lips.

"I've lost interest. I have to go out."

He was still holding the pull-tab and threw it across the room when he realised. "There are no jobs, especially for you. You're not the right type."

"Your associate might think otherwise. What's his name and where can I find him?"

"Who are you lady? You ask too many questions. Get out of here."

"All I want is a name."

"Get out of here, and don't let me see you talking to any of my girls, or there'll be trouble.

Action Plan

19 October 2008

As usual, Bea arrived at the apartment before Jochim to make sure she had enough time to make the bed with the fresh sheets. Jochim had removed all the things his mother had left and replaced them with basic furnishings. Except for the bed and bedlinen. Bea was not so keen on taking the expensive silk sheets to the cleaners, but there was no other way to get them washed and ironed ready for collection next time they could meet. Did the people at the cleaners think it strange that sometimes they were not collected for two weeks or more?

Jochim was not surprised to see Bea sitting in the kitchen with coffee rather than smiling over the edge of the sheets. She kissed his cheek. "How long have you got?"

"Most of the evening." He smiled and raised his eyebrows. "And you?"

"Until at least nine."

"OK, you, first, I can see you're bursting".

Bea took a deep breath. She couldn't let the excitement of what she'd found out distract her from presenting it as Constable Menna.

She outlined her plan for meeting Erna Sameli, their initial chat, Erna's reaction at the mention of the anonymous telephone call, and their discussion at Ms Sameli's apartment. Jochim listened without interrupting. Bea wished he would break eye contact with her now and again. She kept losing her formal voice and wanting to go and press her mouth to his.

He recognised her 'difficulty' every time she stumbled, but held back a smile. "So, Constable, what's your conclusion?"

Now Bea made absolutely sure she had her reporting voice. "Well, Sarge, Lisa, Ms Stern, blames herself for what happened to Ms Sameli. Why? Because she believes it's connected to what happened to her after the visit to The Celler."

Jochim nodded.

"It certainly makes Ms Stern's story more believable–"

"'Could' make it more believable."

"OK 'could' make it more believable. Which could make the story about Ms Stern and Mr McLendi in the hotel more believable."

"A lot of 'coulds', but carry on Constable. I must say, you look very sexy when you're reporting like this."

"Thanks Sarge, but if you interrupt me again I'll have to come over there and lick your ear."

"Is that a threat or a promise?"

"Both. Now, where was I." Bea composed herself. "Ms Stern told Grindel that she went to The Celler to see if she remembered being there before the hotel. Ms Sameli said Ms Stern spoke loud enough for the barman to hear, and asked if the owner was there."

"You think she knows her ex-husband is the owner of The Celler?"

"Yes. Remember Grindel sent me out to find Schmidt when Ms Stern started talking about FC Zurich and ownership of The Celler."

Jochim nodded.

"Ms Sameli said she'd told a few people about what had happened to her. She thinks that whoever attacked her found out through one of those people, but I–"

"But you don't agree."

"How did you guess? I thin–"

"You think it was Grindel, from the report you wrote."

"Well done Sergeant, you're not a just a pretty face."

"I've got more to offer than just a pretty face."

"I know, and I want some of it."

He started to stand up.

"Do you agree with me?"

He sat down. "My first thought is, yes–"

Bea cheered.

"But we have to put the thought into the complete picture."

"OK."

In one motion Jochim rose, took Bea's hand and pulled her to her feet. "And now it's time–"

"I want to hear what you've found out."

"Afterwards."

On this occasion, there was no Hollywood style lying on their backs and sharing a cigarette: neither of them smoked anyway. Soon they were in the shower and back at the kitchen table.

Jochim sketched what he learned from Professor Bisset, Herman Zubke and Ralf Baracluf. Bea listened intently and made some notes. When Jochim finished they sat in silence, concentrating on drinking their coffee.

"Can we draw the complete picture you talked about?"

"I'm not sure, Bea. If this was part of an investigation we'd have a lot more different input and opinions. There's only you and me, and it's easy to get into that self-fulfilling prophecy situation, as you know."

"Let's try Jochim. It won't be complete, but at least we'll see what we have."

"And don't have."

"Exactly."

"We need a blackboard."

"That we don't have. How about a big piece of paper?"

"You have one?"

"No, but I could cut a carrier bag and flatten it out."

"Very creative. It'll have to do."

The makeshift planning sheet covered most of the kitchen table. Jochim moved his chair to Bea's side of the table. Their pens hovered over the paper. They wrote the names of all the people involved, and for each one listed some facts.

Lisa Stern
English
Works for ZFFM
6 Sept found in hotel room, Grindel interview
27 Sept went to The Celler with Erna Sameli
28 Sept went to police; Grindel/Menna interview

Erna Sameli
Swiss
Works for ZFFM
27 Sept went to The Celler with Lisa Stern
30 Sept Menna interview, describes taxi driver
1 Oct attacked
2 Oct Menna interview, changes story
3 Oct telephoned police
16 Oct Menna interview

Walter Grindel
Swiss
Police sergeant
6 Sept interviewed Lisa Stern and Christopher McLendi at hotel, no record
28 Sept interviewed Stern and McLendi, Menna sent out, no record, tape wiped

194

30 Sept Menna writes report on Erna Sameli description,
   Grindel ignores
10 Oct discussion with Friedmann

Christopher McLendi
English
Works for ZFFM
6 Sept found in hotel room, Grindel interview
28 Sept went to police, Grindel/Menna interview

André Wissler
Swiss
Footballer
Owns The Celler
Ex-husband Lisa Stern
17 Sept Friedmann interview
22 Sept Friedmann interview
26 Sept Friedmann interview
15 Oct Friedmann interview

Mathias Althaus
Swiss
Barman The Celler
25 Sept Friedmann interview

Herman Zubke
Swiss
Lawyer
Previous owner The Celler
16 Oct Friedmann interview

Felix Braun
Swiss
Criminal
Honorary member of Serbo-Croat gang
Pimp

Gazda

Gazda
Name Serbo-Croatian
Boss of Felix

The Celler
16/9 Raided
27/9 Visited by Lisa Stern and Erna Sameli

Bea and Jochim stared in silence at the unfolded carrier bag.

Bea spoke first. "Is that the complete picture?

"No, but it's a start. We have to be careful now. The temptation is to start reaching conclusions too early."

"So, what do we do, Sarge?"

"You mean other than going back to bed?"

"Now there is a temptation."

"So?"

"Let's try putting some things together, subconsciously mull them over while we do what you said, then come back to them."

"Well done Constable: combining your police training with your passion. Let's start with Stern and McLendi in the hotel. Can you write some notes?"

Bea gave him a quizzical look. "So, I'm the secretary now?"

"No, your writing's so much better than mine."

"Flatterer."

"Lisa Stern and Christopher McLendi wake up in a hotel, with McLendi handcuffed to the bed. They ask the hotel to call the police. Sergeant Grindel and Constable Schmidt attend. Stern and McLendi say they can't remember how they got there. Grindel suggests they go to see him at the station to discuss further. They don't go. First question, is it true that they can't remember how they got there?"

"I asked before, why would they call the police if it's not true?"

"According to Grindel, to cover themselves if their partners found out they'd had a night of drinking and sex games."

"But they don't have partners."

"So, we assume they didn't go to the station because they can't remember how they got there and were embarrassed. Agreed, Constable."

"Agreed, Sarge. The second question for me is, where had they been before the hotel?"

"We know Grindel didn't ask, but–"

"But according to what Stern and McLendi found out they'd been at The Celler."

If this had been taking place at the station Jochim would have told the junior officer not to interrupt him. "What Stern and McLendi say they've found out."

"True, but, again, why would they lie?"

Jochim nodded. "And then Stern goes back to The Celler and we get the story about abduction."

"Jochim you've had some contact with The Celler during your prostitution investigation. Is there any way you could check if Stern and McLendi were there on that night?"

"Maybe, but ..."

"What?"

"We'll come back to it."

"What?"

"I said, we'll come back to it."

Bea looked at him, puzzled.

The sat in silence, staring at the words on the sheet.

"I know you said about reaching conclusions too early, and I agree with you–"

"But?"

"But let me pull a few pieces together and see if you agree."

"OK, Bea, but–"

"No buts. Just let me completely finish with no comments or interruptions."

"That's another thing that makes you sexy."

"What?"

"Being bossy."

"Promise? No interruptions?"

"Yes, constable."

"Ms Stern and Mr McLendi's story is true. They did visit The Celler, and afterwards found themselves in a compromising position in the hotel. Why? There is a connection between Ms Stern and The Celler: her ex-husband, the footballer André Wissler. Ms Stern goes back to The Celler to try to find out more. Because she asks too many questions, she is drugged, abducted, questioned, drugged again and put back in her apartment. Why? Because by this time the raid on The Celler has taken place. Ms Stern asking questions about André Wissler might mean she's looking for information to give to the police to get back at her ex-husband."

Jochim opened his mouth, but Bea shook her head.

"Ms Sameli tells me what she saw at the taxi rank. I write a report to Grindel hoping to get an investigation started. The attack on Ms Sameli is the next day. Grindel must have told someone about what Ms Sameli said. If you put together Grindel's appearance at the hotel, his reaction to Ms Stern's story, and his nervousness when talking to you, it points to his involvement with The Celler and the owner André Wissler."

Silence.

"Finished?"

"For now, yes ... Sergeant Friedmann ... Sir."

"OK."

"What does that mean? You agree with me?"

"It's an interesting ... story, with obviously more than a few assumptions–"

"Isn't that what we have to do sometimes?"

"Yes, but–"

"And then we have to test those assumptions."

"Exactly. That's what I was going to say. You took the words out of my mouth."

"A very kissable mouth."

"Later, Constable."

"Yes, Sarge."

"Let's see if any of that fits with the pieces I've put together."

Bea's eyes widened. "You've put some pieces together."

"Yes, Bea, I've put–"

She patted his cheek.

Jochim smiled and gently shook his head. "Same rules: no interruptions."

Bea saluted.

"We raid The Celler on 17 September to send a warning about not allowing soliciting in bars. I recruit one of the 'ladies', Francesca, as my informer." Jochim saw Bea's mouth start to open. He held up his hand. "Yes, I know I didn't tell you that. I didn't tell anyone, including my boss."

Bea smiled. She knew how ambitious Jochim was.

"No one knows who gave permission for the prostitutes to be in The Celler. From Francesca I get the name of her pimp, Felix, and the name of his boss, Gazda. During several interviews with André Wissler he claims not to know anything about the prostitutes, Felix or Gazda. He bought The Celler on the recommendation of a friend of his mother's. I've found out the previous owner of The Celler was

Herman Zubke, a lawyer who was certainly acting on behalf of a client. Wissler gets angry during all the interviews, suggesting he has something to hide. He clearly feels anger towards his ex-wife: 'the bitch spoilt my chances', of what I don't know.

"The name 'Gazda' means 'chief' or 'boss' in Serbo-Croatian. The pimp, Felix Braun, is a petty criminal. During a spell in jail he helped someone from a Serbo-Croat gang and became an honorary member. I got the names of the members of the gang from a contact. I haven't had chance to follow up. When he comes out of jail Gazda gives Felix a job as a pimp."

Silence.

"Don't tell me there are some assumptions."

"I wasn't going to. You're also quite sexy when you're bossy."

"I'll show you just how much in a few moments."

"What, how bossy or sexy you are?"

"Both."

"Time to mull over?"

"Yes."

Back at the table in the kitchen they both took time to reread the notes.

"André Wissler," said Bea.

"The common thread."

"Yes."

"If our assumptions are correct."

"You keep calling them 'assumptions', but aren't our conclusions logical from the facts we have?"

"As I said earlier, it's easy to get into that self-fulfilling prophecy frame of mind."

"How about going to your boss; see what he thinks?"

Jochim slowly nodded his head. "Possibility."

"But?"

"But if Grindel's involved–"

"So you agree with me about Grindel?"

"Ninety-nine per cent. We don't know the involvement of our other colleagues."

"So, it's just you and me? Friedmann and Menna or Menna and Friedmann." Bea smiled. "Sounds good."

"I think that should be Friedmann and Menna. Rank, male before female, age before beauty and all that."

"Only the last reason, Sergeant Friedmann, has saved you from a month-long moratorium on having the pleasure of my body. Now, a team would try to find out more facts to support the conclusions, the preliminary conclusions."

"OK, what do we need to know?"

"Before we start that, can you clarify something you said earlier. I asked you if you could use your contacts at The Celler to find out if Ms Stern and Mr McLendi had been there before the hotel. You said 'maybe, but'."

Jochim didn't reply immediately. "If ... if there is a connection between what happened to Ms Stern and Ms Sameli and The Celler–" He saw that Bea was ready to jump into his thought process, and held up his hand. "Would my asking questions at The Celler put them in any danger?"

Bea nodded. "Possibly."

"Another thought occurred to me ..."

"Well? I can't read your mind."

"You can sometimes."

Bea smiled.

"I was wondering if we could involve Ms Stern and Mr McLendi?"

"How?"

"Unofficially, of course."

"They obviously know more about what happened on 6 and 27 September. Small details are often important."

"Separating what they know from what they assume would be difficult. Might lead us down wrong paths .... No. It's too early."

"Later perhaps."

For the next hour they looked at what they'd written and highlighted parts where they could try to get more information.

Bea used the kitchen scissors to cut a strip from the flattened carrier bag and divide it in two. She folded the rest of the carrier bag and left it in a drawer in the apartment. The two action lists left with the owners, but not before one more coupling of bodies.

Actions

Bea	Jochim
Check the divorce papers of Ms Stern and Mr Wissler - reasons for split?	Look up André Wissler's history
	- birth certificate
	- anything to explain 'the bitch spoilt my chances'?
New follow-up with taxi company who picked up Ms Sameli after The Celler	Review Grindel's police history

Put pressure on Francesca
- Felix

Put pressure on André
- his mother?

Find Felix Braun
- contacts he had in prison

Check on Herman Zubke
- visit from Bea as client?

Run name of Gazda though police informers

Gazda

The World of Prostitution Part III

21 October 2008

One person, English, shy, that's what the signal meant.

Jürgen, the waiter, and Georg, the gorilla doorman, had worked out a system of characterising the Lipstick Club customers. Georg would stand under a lighted area just inside the entrance and give three quick signals based on his efforts outside to persuade someone passing by to enter the club. The number of fingers signalled how many were in the party; fingers pointing up for German speaking, horizontal for French and down for English; hand waving for lively, fist clenched for shy. On some occasions, like tonight, if he felt no one was looking, George blew a small kiss to Jürgen.

Jürgen went into full Uriah Heep mode. "How are you this evening, Sir? Welcome to the Lipstick Club, Sir. Would this be all right for you, Sir? You'll be able to have a good view of the show from here, Sir. You can always move to a table later if you would prefer, Sir."

"Thank you."

"Tony, our wizard of the drinks will get you anything you want, Sir. Tony."

Tony continued taking the glasses out of the dishwasher. He'd seen the kiss blown by Georg.

"Tony, this gentleman would like a drink."

Tony glided over. "I'm sorry, Sir, I usually come quickly when Jürgen wants me."

The man perched on the edge of the stool, with one foot on the floor.

"So, what'll it be, Sir?"

"Sorry?"

"What would you like to drink?"

"I'm not sure."

"Let me guess. After all these years, I'm usually good at guessing what people's favourite tipple is." Tony leant back in an exaggerated gesture, held a limp hand in front of him, and looked the man up and down. "I'd say you were a Campari soda, man."

"A beer please."

"I still think you're a Campari soda, but one beer coming up."

The man sat further back on the stool and scanned the room. People occupied only about a third of the tables. He glanced at his watch, eleven thirty, probably still too early, especially for a Tuesday.

Tony flipped a beer mat in the air and brought it to land directly in front of the man. The draught beer followed quickly. "One beer."

"Thanks."

"Is this your first visit to the Lipstick Club, Sir?"

"Yes."

"Are you here on business?"

"Yes."

"Just the one night?"

"Two."

"Which part of the USA are you from, Sir?" Tony thought he had worked out Georg's signals to Jürgen. He was sure about fingers pointing up and horizontal, German and French, but had assumed fingers pointing down meant American.

"London."

"Oh, I'm sorry, I thought I detected an American accent."

"English."

Tony and the other bartenders tried to find out about the customers placed at the bar by Jürgen. They used this information to select a suitable girl from those available. Sometimes, like now, this was not easy. The monosyllabic answers said this man was shy. He caught the eye of Manuala.

"Would you like some company?"

She had approached from behind him, so the man had not seen her. He jumped slightly, sliding forward on the stool. "Sorry?"

She stood in front of him, her leg just touching his. "Would you like some company?"

"Yes."

She thought that was unusual. Tony had signalled shy, and the shy ones usually said no at first. "Shall we sit here or would you prefer a table?"

"A table."

Again, very decisive for a shy one.

Jürgen appeared, as if by magic, and humbled them to a table in a small alcove. The man tried to take his beer, which he had only sipped twice, but Jürgen said he would take care of it.

Jürgen looked at the man. "What can I get madam to drink?".

At this point the shy ones always mumbled something about seeing a menu or asked about prices. The man said, "champagne, and forget the beer."

Jürgen didn't bother to ask his usual question of 'large or small bottle'.

"My name's Manuala."

"Pleased to meet you, Manuala," he said without taking the hand she held out.

She realised this was someone with experience of places like the Lipstick Club, and knew not to ask further if he didn't give his name automatically.

The champagne arrived with great flurry, presumably to let the other customers know that someone had ordered a full bottle of champagne; two waiters with ice bucket and stand, and Jürgen flourishing the bottle.

"Cheers."

"Cheers."

They chatted, or rather Manuala asked questions from the same list as Tony. He answered with the same monosyllables, and she kept revising her opinion of him; it varied from self-assured to nervous.

"I've been to London twice."

"Working?"

She smiled. "No, holiday."

"Where are you from originally?"

"Rio, Brazil."

Jürgen materialised again to pour champagne, even though they had hardly drunk anything since the last time he was there.

"What's it going to cost me to go somewhere private with you?"

"That's a very direct question."

"What's the answer?"

She looked at him. Was this a sign of nerves or confidence? "Three hundred francs."

"What if I pay you double?"

"For what?"

"To interview you."

She'd had some strange, some very strange, requests but ... She took a long look at him. Over the years, her judgement of the character of the punters had reached a high level of accuracy. His face didn't look old, but the greying hair suggested more advanced years. A ponytail hung down the back of his casual leather jacket - artistic she thought. The small gold earring that caught the light when he turned his head was confirmation for her. "To interview me?"

"I'm a reporter."

Her instinct was to get up and walk away, but she knew she couldn't obey it. The Club 'rule' was you could only leave totally drunk or dangerous customers. It happened rarely. Georg's' team of heavies removed the customer.

"I'm a reporter, from England, and I'm doing a feature on the sex trade in Europe. I just have a few questions. Nothing difficult. Easy money for you."

"Why me?"

"I didn't choose you."

They both took longer than normal drinks from the champagne glasses.

"Six hundred francs?"

"Cash, up front."

"How long will it take?"

"A few minutes."

"OK."

He lent towards her, slipping his hand into the inside pocket of his jacket. She thought of backing away, but it would have looked unnatural to anyone watching, and there was always someone watching. She felt something drop into her cleavage.

"Do you want to go to the toilet and count it?"

"How do you know I'll come back?"

"I trust you."

She looked hard into his eyes. "Then I'll trust you."

"Perhaps we should finish the champagne before we go."

"It would be better to do it here. I'm never sure if the rooms have hidden cameras. We could make it look as though we were having a good time." She put her hand on his leg.

"Should I order more champagne?"

"It might be better."

"Better?"

"If you leave alone after buying two bottles it will look better for me."

He started to raise is arm to attract a waiter. Jürgen was at the table before it was half way up.

Whoever was watching them over the next fifteen minutes would have seen a lot of whispering in ears, smiles, nodding heads, stroking of arms and legs, and drinking champagne. Manuala led the way and he followed.

"How long have you been doing this?"

"Doing what?"

"Working in a bar like this."

"Four nearly five years."

"How old are you?"

"You should never ask a lady that question."

"I was just curious. Have you always worked in this country?"

"We move around."

"Voluntarily or ... "

"It's never a good idea to stay in one place for too long."

"What do you?"

"Get the customers to buy drinks, preferably champagne."

"And?"

"And?"

"How far do you have to go?"

"That's up to me."

"Really?"

"Really."

"Tell me."

"There are rooms behind the bar. I pay a 'rent' for the room, charge the customer what I want and keep the difference."

"But you're not forced to ... entertain so many customers a night?"

"For drinks yes, for anything else, no."

"And all the girls here do the same?"

"Most. Perhaps they don't make as much as being out on the street or with an escort agency, but they're protected here."

"Who's the boss?"

The sudden change of direction surprised her. "Why?"

"I would like to talk to him, or her."

"I can't tell you that."

"I'd keep your name out of it."

"No."

"Please."

"No."

"How much more would you want to tell me?"

"You've already paid me six hundred francs, and you haven't paid for the champagne yet. I think it's cost you enough."

"That's for me to decide."

"No, me now." She got up slowly, bent down and kissed his cheek, and gave him a little wave as she walked towards the bar.

Building a Picture

23 October 2008

They placed their action lists on the table.

"Ladies first."

"A gentleman."

"There's not many of us left."

Bea nodded. "Rather than make an official, written request for information, I decided to visit the Zurich Court Records Office myself. When both parties agree about a divorce, the record gives no details of the reasons. But I found that Lisa Stern had contested André Wissler's petition and so there is a full record of the court process. I got a copy of the summary."

```
Date of marriage: 14 February 2003
Both parties agree the marriage has irrecoverably
broken down and should be terminated.
Mr André Wissler (the petitioner) claims he was an
international footballer when the marriage took
place, and as such had amassed a considerable sum
of money (details on record). His wife had little
or no financial assets when they married, had not
made any financial contribution during the
marriage, and therefore had no entitlement to any
share of the couples' current assets.
Mrs Lisa Wissler (the respondent) contends that as
the marriage took place in UK, the divorce
settlement should be according to UK law, and as
such she is entitled to a share of the couples'
assets.
The court found in favour of the petitioner on the
grounds that the divorce was taking place in
Switzerland. However the court ordered the
petitioner to pay the legal costs of the
respondent, and make a settlement payment of CHF
5,000.
Date of divorce: 18 August 2005
```

"I should imagine it was very embarrassing for André Wissler. Was it embarrassing enough for him to want revenge after three years? Did such a small settlement make Lisa Stern hold a grudge?"

Jochim nodded. "Perhaps we can answer one of those in a minute."

"Next I contacted the taxi company again."

"LATE Taxi."

"Good morning, could I speak to Mr König please?"

"Speaking."

"Good morning Mr König, this is Constable Beatrice Menna. We spoke about three weeks ago."

"I've spoken to a lot of people in the last three weeks, Miss."

"Constable. This was about one of your taxis picking up someone at the end of Niederdorfstrasse in the early hours of 28 September."

"The early hours can be a busy time for us, Miss–.

"Constable."

"Where was the drop-off?"

"Drop-off was Molkerstrasse."

"28 September, Molkerstrasse ... yep, you're in luck Mi– constable. Three thirty am."

"OK. You told me last time that you had no other drop-offs around that time."

"Correct. Looks like an unusually quiet night."

"I described one of your drivers to you as being tall, very tall and muscular, and you said no one like that worked for your company."

"That's right."

"Would any other taxi company have picked up a passenger at that time of night in the Niederdorf area?"

"There'd be trouble if they did. That's our area."

"What about a car posing as a taxi?"

"It'd need a yellow taxi sign on the roof."

"Would the driver get out of the taxi?"

"At that time of night, near the Niederdorfstasse? No way, constable. Not unless some of your colleagues, no offence, but male colleagues, were around."

"Thank you Mr König. Offence taken."

"And your conclusion, Constable?"

"The car Erna Sameli saw Lisa Stern getting to was not a taxi, which gives the abduction story some credibility."

"Assuming Ms Sameli's original story is the correct one."

"She told me it was."

"OK."

Silence.

"OK, Sergeant, your turn."

"I went to the Births, Deaths and Marriages Records Office. Here's a copy of André Wissler's birth certificate."

```
Name: André Drago Wissler
Born: 15 July 1981
```

```
Place: Zurich
Mother: Krystal Wissler
Father: Not declared
```

According to the database, Krystal Wissler had a prostitution licence from 1979 to 1981, but no criminal record. So, that explains the 'not declared' father entry."

"Could also mean she had contact with the Zurich criminal world."

"Could. Through various sources, mainly newspaper articles, I followed Wissler's football career. The start was luck. A part-time talent scout for Grasshopper Club Zurich happened to be at the school football match where André Wissler scored five goals. The Club signed Wissler at the age of seventeen, and he played a big part in Grasshopper winning the National League two years later. The start may have been luck, but the rest of the success was because of talent. A transfer to the English Premier League club Aston Villa did not work out. He could not settle in the English Midland city and FC Zurich brought him back to Switzerland. He became an automatic selection for the Swiss national team."

"A total success story?"

"So, I wondered what he meant by 'the bitch spoilt my chances'. I assumed it must have something to do with football."

"And does it?"

"Yes."

Silence.

"Are you going to tell me, Sarge, or is it a secret?

"You don't seem all that interested Bea."

"It's all this talk about grasshoppers and villas. You know my interest in football is pretty low."

"OK, so here comes the interesting, part–"

"Good." She stroked his cheek.

"I was looking at his goal scoring. Wissler was, is, a prolific scorer. He even broke the club record this year. Switzerland played in the 2006 World Cup, but there are no goals against his name for the tournament."

"Perhaps he didn't play. Injured? A stubbed their toe is a major injury for these prima donna football players. Not that I know anything about it."

"No, not injured, not selected for the Swiss team."

"Sounds strange even to me not to select the star player."

"And that's what's interesting, the reason why."

Silence.

"Are you waiting for a roll on the drums?"

"How can you be so annoying and still so sexy?"

"It's a special talent."

"He had a huge loss of form during the months leading up to the tournament."

"Okay, but I don't see—"

"When were Wissler and Ms Stern divorced?

"The final court judgement was in August 2005."

"And the World Cup started in June 2006."

A smile spread from the corners of Bea's mouth. 'the bitch spoilt my chances'."

"Exactly."

"Who's a clever detective then?"

"Do I get my reward now?"

"Well ... I'll have to think about that."

Jochim planted his mouth on hers and probed with his tongue.

Bea pulled away. "OK."

Bea called from the kitchen. "Coffee Jochim?"

"I'd rather have tea."

"Tea? When did you start drinking tea?"

"That new WPC introduced me to it."

"Did she now?"

"Yes. She said it was more refreshing, especially after exertion."

"Hmm."

Jochim came into the kitchen drying his hair. "What does 'hmm' mean?"

"Just hmm. Do we have any tea?"

"I bought some on the way over."

"Recommended by your WPC?"

"So, where were we?" Jochim looked at his action list. "Grindel's history. Not much to tell. He joined the police force immediately after high school, took 15 years to reach sergeant and progressed no further. Most of his work has been in community policing and traffic. It's generally recognised that all his work on the streets of Zurich has given him good contact with the criminal world. A colleague in the vice squad told me that Grindel was sometimes a good source of names. I had a chance to 'test' Grindel's knowledge of names, and at the same time put him under a bit of pressure."

"Tut, tut, Sergeant."

"I nodded as I passed him in the corridor, then turned around and asked if the names Felix Braun and Gazda meant anything to him."

"And he turned bright red and stammered 'No'?"

"Not exactly. He waited two seconds, slowly turned, gave me a stare to turn ethylene glycol solid, and said in a loud, cheery voice 'sorry, can't help you there, Sergeant Friedmann'.

"There's always been some talk about why he's never married, and that he'd taken bribes at one time. The most consistent rumour is that he'd fathered a child many years ago."

"So, nothing to help us?"

"We've still got how he reacted when interviewing Ms Stern and Mr McLendi, and when I talked to him. There must be some reason for that. I know he can be unfriendly, demanding, and not above displaying his power by belittling junior officers–"

"Especially WPCs."

"Especially WPCs. But with a member of the public? There must be a connection."

"Another cup of tea?"

"No ... Yes please."

"Did your WPC tell you to drink two cups?"

Jochim looked at his list again. "Francesca."

"Ah yes, your street lady friend."

"My street lady informer. I talked to her.

"Good morning."

"Who? What?..."

"Time to wake up Francesca."

"Who is this?"

"Don't say you've forgotten me already."

"Is this some kind of joke? What time is it?"

"I know it's been a month, bu–"

"Friedmann."

"Ah, you do remember me."

"Who else would call me at ... seven o'clock."

"Last night was Sunday, I thought you might have had an early night."

"You're a bastard, do you know that Friedmann."

"You've told me before."

"What do you want?"

"I'm disappointed not to have heard from you Francesca."

"I've got nothing to say."

"You're not doing very well as my informer."

"I'm not your–"

"You're right there because you're not giving me any information, but you are my stool pigeon and that means I should be getting some information from you. So, come on, give."

"Fuck–"

"Tut, tut, Francesca at this time in the morning. Found out any more about Gazda?"

"Gazda?"

"Felix's boss."

"No idea who that is."

"Any news on how to contact Felix?"

"I told you, Felix contacts us, we don't have–"

"You don't have what?"

Silence.

"Francesca speak to me."

"OK here's something for you. A couple of nights ago ... last Saturday one of the other ... one of my colleagues said she had a telephone number to contact Felix. She told me–"

"Who was it?"

"Don't get all excited Friedmann, she's disappeared. There's a new girl on that ..."

"Beat? So, why are you telling me?"

"If you'd let me finish. You wanted me to talk and when I do you interrupt me."

Silence.

"So, no 'I'm very, very sorry for interrupting you, Francesca'."

"Just get on with it."

"My colleague told me she'd called Felix about a woman who'd been hanging around. I'd talked to her the night before. She said she was looking for registration."

"And what happened when your 'colleague' called Felix?"

"She said he went off with the woman."

"And I don't suppose you asked your 'colleague' for Felix's telephone number."

"No."

"Well done, Francesca. What did this women look like, perhaps you can tell me that?"

"Nice legs ... big tits–"

"I don't want your assessment of her as a competitor Francesca. Anything that would help me to identify her?"

So, did she tell you anything else about her, this woman?"

"Late twenties, early thirties, not tall, nice figure. The only distinguishing feature, if you like, is that she has 'a nose too large for her face' as Francesca put it."

"Not very useful then."

"Not unless someone like that applies for a prostitute's licence."

"Probably wouldn't help to get to Felix anyway."

"No, probably not. Francesca did say the woman had the trace of an accent from an area where she once worked."

"Which was?"

"Birmingham, England."

"You have been a busy detective. What's next?"

"I told you I had the names of the Serbo-Croat gang Felix met in jail. All three had criminal records, mainly small-time crime, housebreaking, selling illegal cigarettes, and passing forged banknotes. Two of three reportedly left Switzerland in 2007. There're no further arrests of a third person, Anto Dedeić, since his release in mid 2007, roughly the same time as Felix Braun's release. My prison contact identified him as the leader of the gang. He lives in Wallisellen, near Zurich airport. I could have asked the local police to check on him, but the less I do officially, the less chance of Kullmer finding out that I'm doing a bit more than 'playing it low key'. Dedeić is a small man in his late sixties."

"Mr Dedeić?"

"Yes."

"Sergeant Jochim Friedmann, KRIPO."

"I've done nothing."

"I'm not saying you have. I just want to ask you a few questions."

"What about?"

"May I come in?"

"I've got visitors."

Friedmann stepped into the hallway. "It'll only take a few minutes.

"But–"

"Is this the way to the living room?" Friedmann didn't wait for an answer. As he stepped into the room a figure was hurrying into the kitchen. Even though he only caught a brief glimpse, Friedmann registered a description: 180/190 cm, heavy, grey hair.

Anto Dedeić positioned himself between Friedmann and the kitchen.

"Do you remember Felix Braun?"

"No."

"That's strange because you were big friends in prison."

"That's all behind me."

"Good. So, you've no idea where Felix is now?"

"No."

"Anto Dedeić is an unusual name."

"I'm Yugoslavian."

"Does the name 'Gazda' mean anything to you, Mr Dedeić?"

"No."

"Strange because I understood it meant 'master' in Serbo-Croatian."

"I have not used the language for a long time."

"So, a gentle interrogation compared with your usual style, from what I've heard."

"It wasn't an 'interrogation'. I was trying to obey my boss, and playing it low key."

"I never thought you were so obedient, Sergeant Friedmann."

"We'll see how obedient you are in a moment, Constable Menna." He reached for her.

She spun away. "Do you think Anto Dedeić is Gazda?"

"Possibly." He feinted to the left and caught her as she tried to get around him to the right.

Bea propped herself on the pillow and pulled the duvet up to her chin. "So, who else was on our action list?"

Jochim lay on his back. "Herman Zubke."

"Ah yes, the lawyer."

"I'm sure he's acting on behalf of a client. Someone who wants to keep his ownership of The Celler secret."

"What did you find out about Zubke?"

"Not much. Born in Obfelden in 1948, married with one son. He's a partner in Baumgartner, Zubke and Zubke. The second Zubke is probably his son, Djordje. Nothing unusual there, except perhaps the name 'Djordje'. Could it be Serbo-Croatian? Or is that me making five?"

"Sounds a bit too much like a coincidence, I have to say Jochim."

"You think so constable?"

"I do, Sarge."

"If this was an official investigation I could try to force him to give me the name of his client, the real owner of The Celler."

"What about client confidentiality?"

"When I say force, I mean put him into a position where he has to tell me."

"Strong-arm stuff?"

"Nothing physical, just find a weak spot. Everybody has one."

"Maybe I should try using my charms on him."

"Hmm."

"What?"

"What if ... what if Zubke owns other bars?"

"You mean if his client owns other bars."

"Exactly. I can enter a few names of other bars into the Commercial Register and see what comes out."

"And then?"

"If Zubke does or did have other bars it might give us a leverage point with him."

"Maybe his client is this Gazda."

"Now that would too much to hope for."

"I still doubt he would reveal who his client or clients are."

"Not even if you use your charms on him? Speaking of which ... "

What's Next?

24 October 2008

Christopher pressed the doorbell. One long, two short was the code now. They kept it simple, but changed it every few days. He saw something move in the spyhole, and heard the locks click.

"Hi." Lisa could have left him to secure the door, but she felt happier doing it herself.

The odour of thyme drifted through the apartment and Christopher noticed the flicker of candles as he passed the dining area.

"Lamb chops and rösti, OK?"

"One of your specialities."

"Other than spaghetti vongole, my only speciality, as you know."

"Better one or two good specialities than many mediocre ones."

"Flattery now! It'll be about twenty minutes. Glass of white wine?"

They deliberately avoided the topic they were dying to discuss until they sat on the couch with their coffee.

"Disappointed?" said Christopher.

Lisa shook her head and breathed out more noisily than she intended. "To say the least. And you?"

"I didn't like the idea from the start."

"But you went along with it."

"I wasn't going to let you do it on your own."

"Did we find out anything?"

"Perhaps some things about what happens in the world of Zurich prostitution, but not about who runs it."

"Maybe we did the wrong things."

"Maybe, but I still think they were the best options."

"Not the cheapest options."

Christopher shrugged. "It would have been easier and cost less if, what was her name, had given us a name."

"Sabina."

"Yes, Sabina."

"Perhaps we, I, didn't push her enough."

"Did I hold you back?"

Lisa pursed her lips. "I don't think she knew anyway." She unfolded her legs from under her and stood. "I think I'd like a cognac, how about you?"

"Your cognac bottle is never-ending."

"I bought a new one, a good one. My small contribution."

Christopher also rose and went to the window. He'd picked up Lisa's habit of peeking out of the curtains from time to time, 'just to check' she said.

Lisa returned with two English-pub triples of golden liquid. She couldn't suppress a giggle.

"What?"

"I was just thinking of you in that beard and moustache, it didn't suit you."

"What about you in that large red and brown wig?"

"It was bit over the top I admit. And what about your scar?" Another giggle escaped.

"I kept thinking it was falling off." Now Christopher laughed. "I thought you were going to lapse into a full Birmingham accent at one stage."

"I know, I realised it was sounding comical and that's why I stopped."

"I suppose we were more subtle with our disguises after that."

"Except for my heavy falsies."

"And my earring."

"Yes, where is your earring? I thought it suited you. And your ponytail."

This time they both had big smiles.

Christopher sipped his cognac. "I can't help feeling we put ourselves in danger, especially you."

"That's what makes me even more disappointed that we didn't find out anything. But I wasn't in so much danger."

"I'm not sure that's true. What would you have done if this Felix had been the boss? How could you have avoided doing ... doing whatever he wanted."

Lisa took a deep breath. "I'm not sure. I expected to meet him on the street, not in that cramped space. When he started tugging at the zip I just stared. I think he interpreted my smile as a come-on, when it was actually a nervous reaction to stop the shock and fear appearing. My only thought was to suggest we went somewhere more comfortable so I could really show him what I could do, and hope that would give me a chance run. I guess I was saved by the bell, the telephone bell. The caller obviously ordered him to do something immediately. In his hurry not to miss out on what he thought I was promising he broke the tab off his zip."

"You were lucky he didn't get angry. That would have been dangerous."

"I certainly didn't need any second telling when he said 'get out of here'. What about your hostess?"

"Manuala? Oh, there was no danger there. I'm sure she won't say anything. She'd want to keep the money and her job."

Lisa got up and paced behind the couch. "So, what now?"

"Now?"

"What shall we do now?"

Christopher inhaled, pressed his lips together, raised his eyebrows, and slightly shook his head.

"We can't give up, Christopher."

"I don't see what else we can do. Do you?"

"No, but–"

"It's been a month since your abduction. Nothing–."

"And my bruises have disappeared, so I suppose we just forget about two kidnappings?"

Christopher had learnt not to respond when Lisa asked one of her rhetorical questions.

"No, we can't let André get away with this: let him win."

"So, you're convinced it's André now, are you?"

"As opposed to?"

"Ru– anyone else.

"I've been doing a lot of thinking. It has to be André. Affolter's most probably a customer, and a briefcase thief, but I can't imagine him running a prostitution business."

Christopher wanted to ask why, but held back.

"No, it has to be André. He must have been so mad that he missed the World Cup. When we turned up at The Celler, already, what shall I say, a bit worse for wear is the polite English expression, he saw it as the opportunity he'd been waiting for to take revenge. He spiked our drinks, and had us dumped in that hotel."

Again Christopher held back from saying anything.

"Then the police raided The Celler, and I started asking questions. Perhaps he thought I'd guessed he'd put us in that hotel, and that I might go to the police or the newspapers. From what I've read, he's the star of FC Zurich and is a cert for the Swiss team for World Cup 2010."

"If they qualify."

"Whatever that means. Any exposure would probably spoil his chances of selection and he'd do anything to stop that happening, again."

"Still seems extreme to me: abducting you and threatening Erna."

"You don't know how ruthless ambition makes these footballers. I saw a little of it when I worked at the Aston Villa club. Playing for your country in the World Cup is their dream. It's what they train so hard for. Left out of the selection is devastating for them. It's as though they've wasted their lives."

"OK."

"So, back to my question, what do we do now?"

"What conclusion have you reached about Grindel?"

"Oh, he's obviously the prostitution organisation's police insider: André's police mole."

"Obviously."

"So, next step?"

"I guess that's not 'let sleeping dogs lie'?"

Now it was Lisa's turn to shake her head.

"How about arranging a meeting with André?"

"And?"

"And telling him you're not going to the police or the newspapers."

Again the shake of the head, this time slowly. "Who says I'm not?"

"Why would you?"

"After what he's done to us, me, Erna?"

'What you think he's done' formed in Christopher's mind but the words did not come out.

"I could go back and see what I can get out of Felix."

"No way."

"Why not? He's the only direct link to the prostitution we have."

"Why not? Precisely because he is a direct link with the prostitution. You already know what he wants from you before going any further. If you start pushing him to meet his boss he'll demand more and then what will you do?"

"Hmm."

"No, Lisa, not 'hmm'. No."

"So, what else do you suggest?"

"I don't have a suggestion. We tried to find out who's involved. Although what we would have done with information I don't know. Gone to the—"

"Don't say 'gone to the police'."

"Lisa, I said before, these are criminals. There's no choice but to go to the police."

"They don't believe us, Christopher, they don't believe us."

"Grind– "

"It's not only Grindel. How do we know Menna wasn't the one who told them what Erna saw?"

"You said you didn't think Menna was involved."

"Who knows who's involved. We haven't heard anything from Menna have we."

"No, but–"

"No, but. No, but."

"Think about what I said. Nothing's happened in the last month."

"André's not getting away with this. He's not getting away with this. Do you hear me, Christopher? He's not getting away with this."

Christopher took a deep breath and slowly shook his head. "Let's think about what we've discussed, then decide what to do next."

"I've had plenty of time to think about it. We've got to–"

"Just a couple of days. Please."

Undercover

27 October to 28 October 2008

Bea was nervous. She had no experience of undercover work. There was no real danger, but she was afraid she wouldn't be able to stay in character. Jochim had rehearsed her.

"Mrs Fischer, please come in and take a seat."

Bea glided slowly to the large desk on the far side of the room, giving plenty of time for the scan that was surely taking place. The man rose and they shook hands across the desk. The eyes behind the heavy glasses were on level with her breasts, but he looked her in the face during the contact. As she sat, the eyes slid across the tightness of her shirt to an expanse of leg as her skirt rose.

"Can I offer you something to drink, Mrs Fischer?"

"Thank you, Mr Zubke."

"Tea? Coffee?"

"I'd probably prefer a whisky right at the moment, but coffee would be fine."

He transmitted the request to his secretary. "Did you have trouble finding us?"

"No."

"I thought you seem a little stressed."

"Yes, but it's nothing to do with difficulty in finding your office."

He waited for her to elaborate, but she just smiled. "So, what can I do for you? You told my secretary you are looking to buy a property."

"A bar."

"A bar?"

"You look shocked, Mr Zubke."

"Not shocked, a little surprised perhaps."

Bea uncrossed and recrossed her legs. Something that she planned to do regularly. Something that had come out of their rehearsals. She also pushed the chair slightly further away from the desk.

"What sort of bar may I ask? A cocktail—"

Zubke's secretary brought in the drinks on a silver tray.

"A cocktail bar or a bar as part of a restaurant?"

"A bar in the Niederdorfstrasse or the Langstrasse."

Zubke choked on his coffee. "Sorry?"

"I'd better explain."

"Please."

"My father died last year and left me his bar. I've been running it for several years because he's been ill."

226

"This was in Zurich?"

"No, Hamburg, on the Reeperbahn."

Zubke's eyes had been having a sly wander from her face to her legs and back. Now they widened and rested on the lower view for a couple of seconds. He recovered quickly. "I see."

Not yet you don't thought Bea. "I have to move to Zurich as soon as possible. My daughter will receive treatment only available at the Universitätsspital. I've just come from there, that's why I seem a bit stressed. I can't keep going back and forth to Hamburg, I need to be here with her. And I need to earn some money. Running a bar, a Niederdorfstrasse or Langstasse type bar, is all that I know how to do."

Zubke shifted uneasily in his chair. "How do you think I can help you?"

"Until recently you owned The Celler and you currently own The Lipstick Club."

The eyes blinked twice and the faintest smile appeared at the corners of Zubke's mouth. "You are very well informed, Mrs Fischer."

"It's public information in the Commercial Register."

"My name is there, but not an address."

"There's only one Zubke in the Zurich telephone book."

"So, I ask again, how do you think I can help you?"

"I took a look at the Lipstick Club. Seems ideal for me."

"It's not for sale."

"Even to me?" Bea's leg movement was much more deliberate.

"Sorry."

"I usually get what I want, Mr Zubke." More movement. Bea could see Zubke was having great difficulty keeping his eyes where he knew they should be: on her face. "Who owns the Lipstick Club, Mr Zubke?"

"You've seen my name in the Commercial Register."

"Yes, but you're a lawyer, a very good one from what I hear. Lawyers don't own bars like The Lipstick Club, at least not in Germany. Perhaps Switzerland is different."

"I really don't think I can help you, Mrs Fischer." He started to rise.

"Just put me in contact with the real owner."

"He has no interest in selling."

"So, it's a man. I'm sure you, and he, would not regret it." This time no leg movement, just an eye movement from breasts to legs.

When she looked up he had obviously copied her movement, but had stayed in the lower position.

Zubke plopped onto his chair.

For a moment Bea thought he was trying to decide.

"I really can't help you, Mrs Fischer, as much as I would like to."

"What about the new owner of The Celler, perhaps he can help me? André Wissler, the footballer, isn't it?"

"I'm sure Mr Wissler couldn't help you."

"Do you know him?"

"I've met him one time, in connection with the sale."

Bea angled her legs so the exposed thigh faced Zubke.

Zubke's shirt collar seemed to have got tighter. "I think you must leave now Mrs Fischer, I have another appointment."

"Just one more question. Why did you sell The Celler? It looks like a successful bar."

"My cli–, I decided ... I decided it was time to cash in my investment."

"So, you can't put me in contact with the owner of The Lipstick Club."

"Not can't, won't. And now I really must get ready for my next appointment."

As Bea rose she made sure she exposed as much leg as she dare. She expected Zubke to get up and escort her to the door, but he remained seated, and held out his hand. Bea smiled. Her display must have had an effect on more than his eyes and neck. Ignoring Jochim's warnings about overplaying the cover, Bea sashayed to the door. She heard the low moan and rustling behind her.

In the outer office Zubke's secretary retrieved Bea's coat from the wardrobe and helped her into it.

"Did you meet the famous footballer when he visited Mr Zubke?"

"Yes. I asked him for his autograph for my nephew, who's a big fan."

"Did he sign? I heard he's a bit arrogant."

"Oh, no, not at all. He's a very nice man, and his mother, who was always with him. He brought me a different souvenir for my nephew each time he came."

"I waited until I got down the street and round the corner before I relaxed, just in case he was watching. Then I was shaking, partly with nerves and partly with laughter at how comical it had been."

"I'm not so sure he found it so comical, especially being too embarrassed to stand up."

"I was almost tempted to try to force him to see me out."

"I think you'd done enough tempting for one day, Constable Menna. Poor man."

"That's not what you say when I tempt you."

"No, but I don't have to hide the effect you have on me behind a desk."

"So, we can be sure Zubke's ownership of The Celler and The Lipstick Club is a front for his clients. Is it the same client? Could be. Not knowing André Wissler is a lie. Wissler visited Zubke's office several times."

"Each time with his mother."

"Yes, I thought about that. A bit strange."

Jochim nodded. "Unless, Zubke is the friend of Wissler's mother who recommended him to buy The Celler."

"A bit of a leap?"

"Maybe, but why would he take his mother to meet Zubke, and several times from what you say?"

"How would a top lawyer like Zubke know an ex-prostitute like Wissler's mother?"

Jochim shrugged. "Ex-customer?"

"OK, but a friend? Didn't Wissler's mother 'retire' in 1981? That's 27 years ago."

"What if ... what if ..."

"What?"

"Nothing."

"Come on, Sarge, spit it out."

"No, it's nothing."

Silence, both in deep thought.

Bea took his hand when he reached for her. She kissed him on the lips and sashayed towards the bedroom. She stood still in the doorway and slowly turned. "Zubke is André Wissler's father."

"Add the words 'could be' and you've got my 'what if'."

Friedmann wanted to confront André Wissler about Zubke as soon as possible. He decided this discussion would be on his home ground: the station. Interviewing Wissler after the training sessions may have been embarrassing for him, but it had been too easy for him to walk away when he chose. Friedmann would apply some pressure by not contacting him direct, but by leaving a message with the club secretariat.

"Hello, this is Sergeant Jochim Friedmann, KRIPO. Please tell André Wissler he must come to the central police station at nine o'clock tomorrow, Tuesday, morning."

Wissler arrived at nine thirty. Friedmann kept him waiting in the reception for thirty minutes.

"Did you have to telephone the secretariat and let the whole club know?"

"Good morning, Mr Wissler. Please sit down."

"You could have called me."

"It's never possible to reach you."

"You could have left a message."

"I did."

"On my 'phone."

"It must have been a huge disappointment not going with the Swiss team to the World Cup in 2006."

"What?"

"A shock, not going to Germany."

"What the fuck are you talking about?"

"I think you know."

"What's that got to do with ... with anything. I thought I was here for you to badger me again about The Celler."

"Oh you are here to talk about The Celler. I was just curious to know what you meant when last time we met for one of our little chats you said 'the bitch spoilt my chances'. Now I know."

"You know nothing."

"True. I don't 'know', but it's a fair assumption the divorce process from Lisa didn't help your football playing."

"So, you've been talking to the bitch."

"No, should I?"

Wissler shrugged.

Friedmann opened the folder in front of him and pretended to read.

"Can we get on with this, I'm already late for training."

"You arrived late."

"I can't just arrange my schedule to be available when you want me to be."

Friedmann's look suggested this was not true. "So, Mr Wissler, have you had any thoughts about who gave the prostitutes permission to be in your bar?"

"I've, told you once, twice, I don't know how many times, it wasn't me. Haven't you got anything better to do than keep asking me the same question and getting the same answer. Why don't you go and hand out a few parking tickets?"

"You've had a few of those in your time."

"What? Am I under investigation? If so, I want my lawyer here." Wissler pushed back his chair and stood.

"Sit down André. May I call you André? You're not under investigation. I'm just trying to understand why you don't want to cooperate."

"I am cooperating. I can't answer your question any other way. It was not me who told the prostitutes they could go into The Celler, and I don't know who did."

"Herman Zubke perhaps."

André Wissler's whole body twitched and he rapidly closed and opened his eyes. "Who?"

"Herman Zubke, the lawyer you bought The Celler from."

"I ... I ... I don't know him. I never met him. My lawyer dealt with it."

"Never?"

"No."

"Maybe he was the one who gave the permission, before he sold it to you."

Wissler nodded his head and breathed out through pursed lips. "Yes, yes that could be it."

"And you don't know him?"

"No."

"So, he's not the friend of your mother who recommended The Celler to you?"

Wissler's roller coaster of emotions reached new heights of shock.

Bea shook her head. "What did he say to that?"

"He mumbled what I took to be no, and said he had to leave."

"And you let him go?"

"I thought I'd done enough for the moment to 'put the cat among the pigeons'".

They sat in silence, staring at the remains of the pizza Jochim had collected on his way to the apartment.

Jochim stood and started to clear away the plates. "So."

Bea leant back on a her chair. "So."

"Next step constable?"

"Draw some conclusions, Sarge."

"Or at least draw a better picture than the one we had before."

"A coloured picture, not black and white."

"Good thinking."

They discussed for over two hours, unbelievably without any visits to the bedroom. Bea held back her tendency for leaps that she could not support easily, and Jochim tried to be less cautious. They were in total agreement with the conclusion. "We need to contact Ms Stern and Mr McLendi."

A meeting of Minds

30 October to 31 October 2008

Bea held out her hand and smiled "Mr McLendi, Beatrice Menna. Thank you for meeting us."

"You made it sound so mysterious, 'developments that could be significant'. Come in."

Lisa came out of the kitchen. "And then when you suggested meeting here at my apartment, even more mysterious."

"This is Sergeant Jochim Friedmann."

Lisa led the way into the lounge. "Can I offer you something to drink? Tea? Coffee? A glass of wine? Or are you on duty?"

"A glass of wine please."

"For me also, thank you."

Lisa and Christopher must have expected the answer because they quickly returned from the kitchen with four glasses and an open bottle in a cooler.

"Cheers."

The four raised their glasses, but didn't clink, it felt too familiar. Jochim winced as he sipped.

"Is the wine OK?"

"Yes, Mr McLendi, it's my wrist that's not. I damaged it playing squash a couple of weeks ago and it's not improving."

"I did that once. It took three months before it was right

"I'm sorry if my telephone call sounded mysterious, Ms Stern. I hoped you'd remember my name, but I wasn't sure how you would react. The situation at the end of our meeting in September wasn't exactly cordial."

"Oh I remembered you. That Saturday night and Sunday morning is not something I can easily forget."

"I can understand that."

"But you were not the problem, it was your boss, Grindel. He was a real bast—"

Christopher tried to pat Lisa's arm, but she pulled it away.

Bea nodded.

Lisa fumed.

Christopher looked anxious.

Jochim decided to jump ahead of what they'd tentatively planned. "Can I tell you why we are here?"

Silence.

"We believe you about the abductions: the two of you on 5 September, and you, Ms Stern, on 27 September."

"So, the same as that bastard Grindel told us."

Christopher did manage to pat Lisa's arm this time.

"No, I'm sorry, Christopher ... no I'm not sorry ... Grindel's a bastard, and that's the polite term."

"But you didn't hear what Mr Friedmann said."

"What?"

"Ms Stern, Jochim and I are here to tell you we believe you about the abductions."

"What? ... Why? ... How?"

Lisa and Christopher stared at Bea.

Bea looked at Jochim, who gave a small nod.

"Ms Stern, what we're about to tell you is strictly confidential. This is not an official meeting. That's why we asked to come here. Are you OK with that?

Lisa and Christopher exchanged glances and simultaneously, slowly said "Yes."

"Jochim and I have been doing some investigating on our own. I couldn't forget what happened on Sunday 28 September and Jochim is following up on the raid of The Celler. We've found some things that seem to connect the two. We'd like to get your input. At the moment it's all unofficial."

"But why?"

"As Ms Stern just pointed out, Mr McLendi, not all our colleagues agree with us about the abductions."

"You mean Sergeant Grindel, Mr Friedmann?"

"Yes. Sergeant Grindel's reactions at various stages were strange, which might, and I stress might, mean that he's somehow involved–"

,"I knew it."

"I stress, Ms Stern, the word 'might'. But, if he is then we don't know how many other of our colleagues could also be. That's why this is unofficial at the moment."

Lisa and Christopher looked shocked, but both nodded with a certain satisfaction.

"Perhaps we can start by you telling us what's happened so far. All we know is from a brief note on the computer, and what happened at the meeting when Beatrice was there. Build the picture from the beginning."

Lisa took a deep breath. "It started when Christopher's briefcase was–"

Christopher frowned in Lisa's direction and stood. "This wine tastes a bit strange. Lisa will you help me?"

In the kitchen, Christopher closed the door and spoke in a low voice. "I think they're here to help us, so let's stay with the facts."

"Of course, what else?"

"I mean no assumptions, guesses or theories."

"OK."

"That means not starting with the theft of my briefcase."

"But–"

"No, please, Lisa, let's stay away from the Rudi Affolter track ... for now."

"But–"

"Please. Anyway you told me you're sure André is behind all this."

"OK, but we can't ignore that it all started after us being at Affolter's house."

"Exactly, after being at his house."

"OK ... why don't you tell them?"

"Please support what I say, and only add facts that I miss out."

Christopher opened the kitchen door and picked up the tray.

"Just a minute." Lisa closed the door. "I've just thought of something. I didn't know you played squash. Then again why would I."

"I used to play a lot. I even won a small cup once. I found it when I finally unpacked all my things from England. It had never been engraved with my name so I thought I'd get it done. Unfortunately it was in my stolen briefcase. Why?"

Lisa's eyes grew wide. "The talk of squash before and the mention of your briefcase and Rudi Affolter just now made a connection in my head for some reason I didn't understand. The cup you won explains it."

"Explains what?"

Lisa nodded.

"Explains what Lisa?"

"Your cup wasn't in your briefcase when Erna found it was it?"

"No."

"Rudi Affolter's got a cup in his desk draw."

"So, he has a cup."

"A cup for squash." Again the knowing nod.

"Are you putting two and two together and getting five again?"

"It proves that he stole your briefcase."

"It doesn't prove anything of the sort.

"No?"

"No. Did he show you this cup?"

"Not exactly."

"What does that mean, 'not exactly'?"

"It was part of my investigation."

"You searched his desk?"

Lisa's silence answered.

"Did this cup have anything written on it?

"Something, but I don't remember what."

"So it doesn't prove anything. We still–"

"I've remembered."

"What?"

"What was on the cup. 'Summer Squash Tournament Winner 1988'."

"I won my cup in 1998."

"Could have been 1998."

"Lisa, we still stay away from the Rudi Affolter track, agreed."

Christopher was not sure Lisa was nodding.   "Agreed?"

"OK, agreed."

Christopher carried the glasses on a tray. "Sorry it took so long. This is a new wine, we didn't think the first one was so good. And, of course, the cork in this bottle was difficult to get out."

Christopher talked in some detail through the events of the past two months. He frequently glanced towards Lisa. The first time, her face was expressionless, but she got the message of his nod, and afterwards also nodded. He made no mention of the theft, Lisa's investigation of Rudi Affolter, or their ventures into the Zurich prostitution world.

Bea made notes. Jochim took up the questioning. "If I understood you correctly Mr McLendi, you remember very little between arriving at the dinner party and waking in the hotel?

"That's ... correct."

"I detect from your tone that it's not 100% correct."

"We think we've remembered certain things, but they're not facts, some are even the result of images in dreams."

"Thank you for sticking to facts at the moment. We'll come back to the dreams later. Do you remember who else was at the dinner party?"

"Again vague recollections, but we did get some names from Rudi Affolter."

"So you talked to him about what happened."

"Not exactly. We did thank him, of course, and he said something about what happened when we left."

"And that was?"

Christopher coughed and began to flush. "He said I fell down and needed help to get into a taxi."

"And you'd never met any of the people before?"

"No."

"You didn't tell Mr Affolter about waking up in the hotel?"

"No."

"May I ask why, he's a friend I presume?"

"A work colleague." Christopher glanced at Lisa. "It could have been embarrassing. At that stage we didn't know if we made the decision to go to the hotel. If we had–" Christopher felt rather than saw Lisa stir. "If, and we're sure now we didn't, if we had gone we wouldn't have wanted our colleagues to know."

"I can understand that," said Bea.

"Plus, Rudi suggested he thought we might not have ended the evening when we left his house."

"Oh."

"He ... he said 'Lisa said she was going to look after you' and winked."

"Ah, the English all-knowing wink."

"Jochim I just want to make sure I've got my notes right. Mr McLendi, you said a taxi company told you they dropped you in the centre of Zurich. How did you know which taxi company to contact if you couldn't remember anything?"

"Rudi Affolter gave me the name of the company."

"And where in the centre of Zurich?"

"On the Limmatquai ... just after the Rudolf-Brun Brücke. The driver said we walked ... staggered ... towards the Niederdorfstrasse."

Now Bea and Jochim looked at each other.

Bea continued. "And The Celler said you were there until three?"

"Yes ... the barman said he remembered us because we did a lot of dancing and Lis–"

Lisa's head jerked up and towards Christopher.

"and Lisa was enjoying herself."

Jochim let the silence hang for a few seconds. "But you're not convinced you went to the hotel afterwards?"

Now Lisa spoke. "We're sure we didn't."

Bea nodded. "Tell us why."

Christopher nodded at Lisa. She took a sip of wine. "We're neither of us what you would call drinkers." She put down her glass.

"Except for a glass of wine or two, or even three, but not a mixture of champagne and vodka."

Bea looked up from her notepad. "Why do you say champagne and vodka?"

"Because they were the bottles in the hotel room when we woke up. I hate vodka. So, that's the first reason. Second, we are work colleagues, Christopher is one of my bosses. I, we, don't believe we would end up in a hotel like that no matter how much we'd drunk." Lisa waited for a comment from Bea or Jochim. Bea was still writing. Jochim was looking directly at Lisa. "Third, neither of us are trad jazz fans we wouldn't know about The Celler."

Jochim smiled. "But if you'd had a few dr– a good evening at your colleague's house you could have gone to the nearest place open, which just happened to be The Celler. What time was it?"

"According to Lisa's discussion with the taxi driver it was about two o'clock."

"Not many places open in Zurich at that time of night."

Bea looked up. "Ms Stern is there anything else that makes you believe you didn't go to that hotel."

Lisa thought for a few moments. "No. But just going back to all that alcohol we're supposed to have drunk. The next morning when we got back here we both needed a couple of nerve-steadying cognacs. If we'd drunk all that champagne and vodka we wouldn't have been able to do that, would we?"

Jochim broke the silence. "Why don't you tell us what you think happened?"

Christopher expected Lisa to start talking immediately about André and his involvement in what had happened, but she pressed her lips tightly together. "Lisa, you want to say what you ... we think?"

"It would be better coming from you."

Bea and Jochim exchanged a glance.

Christopher noticed their reaction. "OK. You'll understand why Lisa said that when I tell you that we think there's an involvement of Lisa's ex-husband in this."

"That would be André Wissler?"

Christopher couldn't hide the surprise. "Yes, Sergeant Friedmann, André Wissler."

Christopher took a deep breath. "It seems we did go to The Celler after leaving Rudi Affolter's. Quite why, we don't know, maybe we just didn't want a good evening to end. Wissler owns The Celler.

We think he saw us there and decided it was an opportunity to take revenge on Lisa. He drugged us and put us in that hotel."

Christopher outlined the divorce process Lisa and André went through and why they thought André would be looking for revenge. He glanced at Lisa several times, expecting her to add some comments, but she just nodded. The two police officers exchanged nods and little smiles several times.

"We think–"

Jochim interrupted. "Before you go on Mr McLendi, could I ask you a couple of questions? Did you go back to the hotel and ask them how you got there?"

Lisa and Christopher exchanged looks. "We thought about it, but we were too embarrassed because of ... how they found us in the room."

Jochim nodded. Lisa wondered if he knew. "Was anything missing?"

"No. My wallet was on the floor, with all my credit cards, and Lisa's handbag was on the chair."

"Do you know how you paid for the hotel?"

Christopher looked puzzled. "That's a good question. I've not seen it on any credit card bill."

"Cash?"

"Could be ... the receptionist, if that's what he was, said I paid for one night. I remember I'd been to the cash machine that afternoon. I had two, 200-franc notes ... we took a taxi to Rudi Affolter's–"

"And you apologised to the taxi driver for only having two hundred francs."

"That's right, Lisa, and he give me the change in 20-franc notes."

"Do you remember what was in the wallet when you found it in the hotel?"

"No ... but ... but when I bought the raincoats and sneakers–"

Bea looked up. "Did you say 'raincoats and sneakers'?"

"Our clothes stunk of alcohol, so I had to find us something to wear to get us out of the hotel. When I paid for them I remember seeing many 20-franc notes in my wallet, and handing over a 200-franc note."

"Which suggests–"

"Which suggests, Mr Friedmann, that I didn't pay for a lot of drinks at The Celler, and didn't pay for one night at the hotel."

"Which means someone put us there."

"It's called circumstantial evidence, Ms Stern, but yes that would seem to be one possible conclusion."

"I knew it."

"As Mr Friedmann said, Lisa, it's one possible conclusion."

"It's André, I knew it was André."

"Lisa, let's just—"

"Perhaps you can go on telling us what you think has been happening since then, Mr McLendi, I interrupted you."

Christopher didn't look at Lisa, but he could feel her breathing fire. He concentrated on quickly organising floating thoughts into a coherent, factual summary of the conclusions they'd come to. "If André Wissler was responsible for our abduction," he saw four police eyes swivel to Lisa and back, "then what happened afterwards makes some sense ... well not sense, but can at least there's an explanation. I went to The Celler and found out we had been there. So Wissler knew that we knew, if you see what I mean. Lisa went to The Celler and asked some questions. Between our two visits you raided The Celler. We think Wissler knew we'd worked out he was responsible for our spending the night in that hotel. If we made it known he owned The Celler, to get back at him, the publicity would not be good for his image. Especially as, we found out later, he'd just become a football hero by beating the goal scoring record at FC Zurich. Considering what had happened in 2006 he decided to warn us off by abducting Lisa."

Once again Bea and Jochim exchanged nods.

Bea was still writing.

"That happened on 27 September, is that right, Ms Stern?"

"Yes, Sergeant."

"And since then nothing's happened?"

Lisa and Christopher answered together. "No."

Bea looked up from her pad. "You know, of course, about what happened to Ms Sameli."

"Erna, Ms Sameli, told Lisa."

"You also know that I talked to her. She thinks the attack was because she'd told me she could identify the taxi driver who cheated you."

"I made up the story about the taxi driver because I didn't want to tell her about the abduction. Erna's a good friend, but she likes to talk. We think she was attacked as another warning to us." Lisa took a deep breath. "What I don't understand is how they found out about Erna's contact with you, Constable Menna."

Bea started to answer, but Jochim interrupted. "We'll come back to that later, if we may. We have some questions, mostly for you, Ms Stern. I'll let Beatrice lead the way."

"Ms Stern, during your marriage, did you ever meet André Wissler's father?

"No, why?"

"Because there's no father mentioned on his birth certificate."

"Really. When he was taking me to meet his mother for the first time, I asked him where his father was. He told me his father was nothing to do with me and I was not to mention him again, so I didn't."

"I've talked to André Wissler several times. He claims not to know anything about why the prostitutes were in The Celler—"

"And I bet he said it with his best, baby-innocent face on. He was always good at lying."

"Let the sergeant finish, Lisa."

"Sorry, I'm just so angry with him for causing all—" A shake of the head from Christopher stopped Lisa's outburst. "Sorry, Sergeant."

"That's OK, I understand how you feel. As I said, he claims not to know anything about the prostitutes."

"Do you believe him?"

"As a policeman I have to be careful about saying I believe or don't believe someone. Those ladies would not have been in The Celler unless someone gave them permission."

Bea changed topics. "The taxi that picked you up at the end of the Neiderdorfstrasse—"

"Abducted me."

"Do you remember anything about it or the driver?"

"No ... I have a vague recollection there was someone already in the back when I got in, but after saying goodbye to Erna everything's hazy."

"So, it can't have been long between Ms Sameli's taxi leaving and yours arriving."

"No, immediately I would say. After that I don't remember anything until being in that cellar held down on a chair."

"Mr McLendi said the person who interrogated you spoke English."

"Yes, but it was a distorted voice."

"Distorted?"

"As though he was talking through a cloth."

Bea looked at the notes she and Jochim had made in preparation for this discussion. "Jochim, you wanted to ask Ms Stern about André Wissler's character.

"Yes. Ms Stern, in my meetings with André Wissler I've found it difficult to form an opinion of what type of person he really is. Not surprisingly perhaps, he was very defensive with me. Tell me about him from your point of view."

"When I met him he was shy, certainly compared with some of the other footballers. He was fanatical about fitness and keeping his body in shape." Lisa felt herself starting to blush, remembering one of the first times she'd seen André, through the open door of the team changing room, naked except for a towel draped around his shoulders.

"Ambitious?"

"Certainly. When I met him he'd just been picked for the Swiss team. He was only twenty."

"Could he have anything to do with prostitution?"

"When I knew him I couldn't imagine him using the services at the back of Rackhams."

"'At the back of Rackhams'?"

"Rackhams is a large department store. To 'go round the back of Rackhams' meant to work as a prostitute, don't ask me why, it's an expression we use in Birmingham."

"Is that where you come from, Birmingham?"

"Yes. André played for Aston Villa, a team in Birmingham."

Jochim looked towards Bea. When he caught her eye, his titled head and raised eyebrows received a puzzled look.

Although they'd only been sipping their wine, the bottle was eventually empty. Lisa offered more, but Bea and Jochim suggested coffee.

In the kitchen Lisa and Christopher spoke in whispers.

Lisa poured coffee beans into the grinder. "Why do you think they're doing this? In this non-official way I mean."

Christopher pressed the start button, which meant he had to speak a little louder. "I'm not sure. It's a bit unusual."

"What if they're only here to find out what we know?"

"Your police conspiracy theory."

Lisa spooned coffee into the filter. "Menna does work for Grindel."

"But Friedmann suggested there might be an involvement of Grindel and others."

"Could be a trick. Have we said too much?"

Christopher poured water on the coffee. "I don't think so. If, and I stress if, they are part of some conspiracy, all we've told them is what we know happened. I don't–"

"We've told them a lot more: being at The Celler, suspicions about Wissler." Lisa arranged the cups and saucers on a tray.

"Don't ask me why, but I think, feel, they're here to help us." He poured the coffee.

"If you're right, then I ask why?"

Christopher picked up the tray. "Let's ask them."

"You didn't say anything about our ventures into the seedy underworld."

Christopher smiled. "Seedy underworld might be a bit strong. Let's see if we're convinced they're here to help us."

In the living room Bea finished her notes. "Well?" she whispered.

"Yes, well." said Jochim in a normal voice. "The questions is, do we believe them?"

"Shh, they'll hear you."

"Probably better if they do."

"What do you mean?"

Jochim lowered his voice. "They have to know that we need convincing."

"You think they don't know that already?"

Jochim thought. "Yes, probably."

"But you still have doubts?"

"No, not really. I'm just being a policeman. This is going to be a difficult mess to sort out: two abductions, prostitution racket, police corruption, a football hero."

"Here we are, coffee."

They sat in silence while Christopher distributed the cups, cream and sugar.

"Ms Stern, clearly you've had–"

"Sergeant, before we go further, could I ask you a question?"

"Of course, Mr McLendi."

"Constable Menna, you said at the beginning that this was not an official meeting, that what you would tell us was strictly confidential. Could you tell us why the two of you are doing this?"

Bea glanced at Jochim. He smiled. "Good question. I think it's best if we explain our separate motivations. Bea."

She talked through her disappointment at how Grindel had treated Lisa on the Sunday after her abduction, and her surprise there was no to follow-up. The attack on Erna Sameli had convinced her that something serious was happening. She suspected the attack on Ms Sameli was because of a report she wrote to Grindel giving details of what Ms Sameli had seen at the taxi stand.

Jochim started with the raid on The Celler and the need to find out who gave permission for the prostitutes to be in the bar. André Wissler was the main suspect. "So, if you're right and he abducted you the first time to take revenge and the second time to warn you off, that gives us a link between my prostitution investigation and what happened to you. Add in the attack on Ms Sameli and possible police involvement and we might have a good reason to thoroughly investigate Mr Wissler. I say 'might' because the links are very tentative and certainly not enough to go to my superiors and justify an official investigation."

When Bea and Jochim had finished, Christopher tried to get some idea of what Lisa was thinking about what they'd said. She was frowning and biting her lower lip.

Silence.

"Is something not clear, Mr McLendi?

Silence.

"Jochim, I think Ms Stern is uncertain about something. Ms Stern?"

Lisa took a deep breath.

"Ms Stern, do you think we might be here to find out what you know? That we're on the side of the people who've been harassing you?"

Lisa's look changed from frown to surprise.

"Bea, I'm sure Ms Stern doesn't think that for the moment."

"Ms Stern?"

Lisa was back to frown.

"Mr McLendi?

"Lisa ... we, thought ... as you're a colleague of Sergeant Grindel ..."

Bea nodded. "That's correct, but I can assure you I ... we are not part of any police conspiracy. We're here for the reasons we just outlined. I was more than disappointed at the way Grindel treated you Ms Stern, I was angry. It went against all the reasons I joined the police."

Lisa and Christopher looked for confirmation in each other.

245

"Mr McLendi, Ms Stern, could Jochim and I have a word together?"

"Of course, Lisa and I will go into the kitchen."

"We have to do something, Jochim, to get their confidence."

He nodded. "What do you suggest?"

"What about telling them some of the things we've found out?"

He grimaced. "I'm not sure we can do that. We don't want to get into how we got the information."

"Of course not. Just some facts that are relevant to what we've discussed. Things that we wouldn't tell if we were part of some police conspiracy."

"OK. I think there might be more belief in you than me at this stage, you lead, but stick with facts."

Lisa leant against the kitchen worktop, arms folded across her chest.

Christopher liked to pace when he was thinking. The small kitchen limited his range. "So?"

Lisa tightened her arms. "I want to trust them, but ..."

"But?"

"But ... I don't know."

"What do you think they're talking about?"

"Either how to convince us they want to help or how they can get more information out of us."

"Thanks for giving us a few moments. You've told us what you think has been happening. It's about time for us to tell you what we've found out. Bea."

"There may not be a connection between the prostitutes in The Celler and what happened to you. What they have in common is André Wissler. Wissler bought the bar from a lawyer, Herman Zubke. Zubke was almost certainly acting on behalf of a client whose name we don't know. Wissler says he bought The Celler on the recommendation of a friend of his mother's. Again we don't know the name of this person. Zubke says he met Wissler only once, but we know several meetings took place at Zubke's office. Wissler's mother was also at those meetings. Why? Could Zubke be André's mother's 'friend'? Does it matter? No, until we add that Mrs Wissler was a prostitute in Zurich. Long since retired, but obviously with contacts.

"We know—"

The shock on Lisa's face halted Bea's explanation. "I'd no idea André's mother was a prostitute."

"How could you, it was a long time ago. Over twenty years."

"Almost thirty, Jochim."

Lisa recovered her composure. "You think there's a connection between this lawyer and the prostitution business?"

"We have to be careful about jumping to conclusions, Ms Stern, but there are some connections we need to look at. So, André never gave any sign he knew about his mother's past?"

"No. To André his mother was an angel and a hero for dedicating her life to giving him the best upbringing possible. Did you talk to Mrs Wissler, Sergeant Friedmann?"

"No. It's one of those situations where we suspect a connection, but if we start questioning Mrs Wissler his lawyer would immediately start yelling harassment."

"Sorry, Constable Menna I interrupted you."

"That's OK. Where was I? Oh yes. We know who the local pimp is and who his boss is."

"When Bea says we know who they are, we have their first names, but, surprisingly, have not been able to find them yet."

"Yes, thank you, Sarge, I was going to say that. Gazda, an unusual name, is the boss, and the pimp is Felix."

Lisa and Christopher could not have synchronised their eyebrows rising better if they'd spent weeks rehearsing.

"Ms Stern? Mr McLendi? does the name Gazda mean something to you?"

Christopher looked and got the nod he wanted from Lisa. "Not Gazda, but Felix, Constable Menna."

Now it was Bea and Jochim's turn to exchange looks, and Jochim to nod.

"Mr McLendi?"

"We haven't told you everything we've done in our 'investigation'."

Bea and Jochim looked puzzled.

"We tried to find out more about prostitution in Zurich and who runs it."

"Why?"

"We thought, Sergeant, that it might lead to André Wissler and what had been happening to us."

"What did you do?"

"We went into that world."

247

"You–"

"Perhaps I'd better explain."

"I think that would be a good idea, Mr McLendi."

Christopher described in detail their first two ventures into the Zurich prostitution world. If Bea and Jochim had not been the police they would have sat wide-eyed at the revelations. But Jochim could not help reacting and interrupting when Christopher said that Lisa had talked to Felix. "Do you know where he took you, Ms Stern?"

"It was a small, backstreet hotel."

"Do you know the name?"

"No."

"On which street?"

"I don't know. I'd never been in that area before. Felix hurried me along. It was less than five minutes away."

"Could you find it again?

"I'm not sure. I could try."

"It could have been dangerous, Ms Stern."

"That's what I told her."

"OK, we'll set something up. Now–"

"Excuse me, Sergeant, I haven't finished telling you about what we've been doing."

"There's more?"

"Yes." Christopher decided to shorten the description of his visit to the Lipstick Club. It hadn't resulted in any information, and Lisa's meeting with Felix had taken on a new significance.

Bea looked up from her notes. "Why did you chose the Lipstick Club?

"I'm not sure ... I think it looked the least sleazy."

"It's 'owned' by Herman Zubke, the previous 'owner' of The Celler."

Jochim smiled and shook his head. "So, Ms Stern and Mr McLendi, did your amateur detective work give you any answers?"

Lisa and Christopher sheepishly shook their heads.

"Don't get me wrong, I understand why you did it after the reaction you got from the police, or rather from Sergeant Grindel. But you were putting yourselves in vulnerable situations."

"It never felt like that, Sergeant."

"I don't just mean in the hotel, on the street or in the bar, Ms Stern. It seems likely that your abductions and the attack on Ms Sameli were because of you asking too many questions. It only needed someone to recognise you and ..."

Lisa and Christopher took deep breaths.

"But it gives us a lead on Felix."

Four people stared into their coffee-cups.

Christopher broke the silence. "So, now what?"

Jochim glanced at Bea. "I think the four of us agree about what might have happened, but I have to stress 'might'. There's no real evidence for any of our ideas. As I said, I couldn't even to go to my boss with this and get an official investigation started."

"But we can't just let Wissler get away with it."

"No, Ms Stern, you're right we can't do that."

"What if he had me abducted again?"

"Unlikely. Nothing's happened for over a month. He probably thinks the message got through to you."

"And if I show him it hasn't?"

"How?"

"By going back to The Celler and asking questions."

"No. If we're right that would be very dangerous."

"Sergeant Friedmann's right, Lisa. We've already taken big risks by venturing into the Zurich prostitution world."

"But this time we would have police backup."

"With you wearing a hidden microphone perhaps, Ms Stern?"

"See, Christopher, Sergeant Friedmann understands."

"I'm afraid I was joking, Ms Stern. Situations like that are dangerous and don't always have endings like in the movies."

"But–"

Jochim's and Bea's heads shook in unison, and Christopher joined them.

"Let's try something less ... something less dramatic first, Ms Stern. Let's see if we can find the hotel Felix took you to."

Lisa said she would have to try retracing the path Felix used to take her to the hotel. There was no chance she could remember which turns she made in her blind panic to escape.

She thought the best chance would be if she searched when it was dark: the same condition as when Felix took her there. But Jochim insisted on daytime because there was less chance of someone recognising Lisa. He also chose Friday because there was a fruit and vegetable market in 'prostitute allee'. The few ladies about were shopping not soliciting.

Jochim's face was too well known to some people in the area, so Bea carried a shopping bag, bought some produce and shadowed Lisa.

Although the street looked different with the market stalls, Lisa could start from roughly the place where Felix had met her. She recognised the church tower at the end of the street and headed in that direction. When she reached the tower she knew she'd gone too far, but she'd not seen the turning she'd expected on the left. Backtracking, she saw that a fruiterer's van hid the entrance to the narrow passageway. Now she had to rely on her senses because when Felix led her down the passageway it was pitch-black and she hadn't seen the many ways that led off to the left and right.

Counting steps was not going to work because she'd been stumbling along behind Felix's hurried strides, on heals not normal for her. She was sure they turned left and then immediately right, but after how long? She tried the first and second lefts. Neither had an immediate right. Could it have been right and then immediate left? They'd been a few other things on her mind than remembering the direction on that night.

The third left was a short dead end with only a door on the left. Lisa peered round the corner of the fourth opening and saw another passageway immediately to the right. A sign above a door about 20 metres down read 'Hotel Stein'. Lisa hadn't seen the name before, but she remembered the creaking as the sign swung in the breeze. She heard movement behind her and turned to see Bea. She pointed to the sign. Bea nodded and signalled for Lisa to follow her.

That had been Jochim's instruction, "If you find the place, leave with Bea and we'll handle it from there." Except in work, Lisa had never been good at following instructions. She waited until Bea had turned the corner and then strode towards the creaking sign.

The door was open and the small entrance hall was empty. The curtain behind the reception desk confirmed to Lisa that this was the place. She could see there was no one in the 'office'. She stepped around the desk so she could see into the space beyond the curtain. The sight of the chair close up against the table flooded her mind with the events of that night two weeks ago. She shuddered at the thought of how dangerous it seemed now compared to then.

"Guten tag."

Lisa's head spun round followed too quickly by her body and she almost lost her balance. Her brain somehow convinced her she would be facing André or Felix.

A small, thin man in black, leather trousers and tight-fitting T-shirt lent against the door frame. "Was machen Sie?"

Lisa decided for English. "I was ... I was looking for a man."

"Aren't we all, dear."

"No I mean ... I was looking for Felix."

"You one of his ladies? You don't look like one of his regulars."

"No ... yes ... I mean ... is he here?"

"Haven't seen him today."

"Does he come here often?"

"Hmm, now that's a question I wouldn't like to answer, dear."

"So, you don't know when he will be here?"

"'fraid not. Shall I tell him you were looking for him?"

"No ... No don't–"

"Lisa, I thought I'd lost you."

"Constab– Bea there you are."

"Come on we'll have to hurry or we'll miss the train."

"The train? ... oh, yes, the train."

"Bye you two. I hope you find a man ... I'm still looking."

"Ms Stern, what were you thinking of? What if Felix had been there? What if he'd recognised you?"

"Well he wasn't, and last time he saw me I looked a lot different."

"But what were you hoping to find by snooping around the office?"

"I don't know. Something to link Felix to André perhaps."

"Well, please don't go anywhere near that place again. We'll talk to Felix."

Lisa took a deep breath.

"Ms Stern?"

"What?"

"Please promise me you'll not go near Hotel Stein again ... or try to contact Felix Braun."

"Lisa?"

"OK ... OK."

Jochim checked Hotel Stein with the uniform team - rooms rented by prostitutes; ownership difficult to establish; run by Clive Pritt, described as 'queer as a twelve-franc note'.

Three Murders

1 November to 9 November 2008

"Mr Braun, Felix Braun."

"Who wants to know?

"Detective Sergeant Friedmann, KRIPO."

"I've got nothing to say to cops."

"I'll decide that, Felix."

Felix shrugged.

"How's business?"

"What business?"

"The business of supplying opportunities for carnal pleasure."

"What are you talking about copper?

"Prostitution Felix, prostitution."

"I don't know anything about that."

"No? Perhaps I should pull in a few of your ladies and see if they can tell me anything."

"It's not illegal."

"Prostitution, no, but putting your girls in bars is."

"I've no idea what you're talking about."

"The Celler, does that jog your memory, Felix?"

"Yeah, I heard your lot raided it. Nothing to do with me."

"No? Someone gave the girls permission to be in there. As their pimp that makes you the number one suspect."

Another shrug. "Nothing to do with me."

"Must have been your boss then."

This time a shudder more than a shrug. "My boss?"

"Gazda."

Felix managed to stop his mouth opening fully. "Who the hell is Gazerdia?"

"Gazda, Felix, Gazda."

"Gazerdia, Gazda I've no idea what you're talking about."

"Not 'what', Felix, 'who'."

"Have you finished, I've got a meeting to go to."

"With Gazda?"

A shake of the head and a threatening stare.

"Do you know André Wissler?"

"Plays for FC Zurich."

"And owns The Celler."

"So?"

"Do you know him?"

"No."

"How about Mathias Althaus?

"Never heard of him."

"You don't know many people do you, Felix?"

"Not the same people you know."

"Pity, because if one of those people had given the permission it would have put you in the clear. As it is you're still prime suspect."

"So, arrest me."

"I just might do that. Perhaps a visit to the station would improve your memory. Not now though. I'll send a couple of squad cars with sirens blasting. Wouldn't be good for your image would it? Gazda's lackey arrested."

Felix's face turned red and he began to ball his hands into fists. "I'm nobody's lackey.

Jochim took half a step towards him. "Oh please use those fists, then we can have a real discussion."

Felix took two deep breaths.

"Pity, I would have enjoyed having you in a cell charged with assaulting a police officer. Perhaps there'll be another chance in the future."

"Have we finished copper?"

"Soon."

"I have a meeting."

"And I have a pimp who put girls in a bar to catch."

Felix stared and gave a small shake of his head.

"Are you still in contact with Anto Dedeić?

"Who?"

"Are you hard of hearing Felix or do you just want to pretend you don't understand any of my questions? Anto Dedeić."

Another shrug from Felix.

"OK, I'll call up the squad cars." Friedmann turned.

"I knew him in prison."

"That much I already know Felix. I asked if you were still in contact with him."

"No."

"But he did give you the name of someone to contact when you came out of prison."

"Why would he do that?"

"Because of what you did for his Serbo-Croat group."

"I don't like to see people bullied."

"But you don't mind bullying people yourself."

"You don't know that."

"No, good guess though isn't it?"

"Can I go now?"

"No. Quite a change for you. Going into prison as a small-time drug dealer and thug, and coming out as pimp. Someone must have helped you. Anto Dedeić? Did he tell you to contact Gazda?"

"I've told you, I don't know Gazda."

"So, who then? Come on Felix I need a name."

Felix's narrowed his eyes and bit his lower lip: a decision process.

Friedmann knew he was near the end of how far he could push Felix. Squad cars with wailing sirens would not fit well with Kullmer's low-key approach.

A playful grin spread across Felix's face. "Georg Herzog."

"Otherwise known as Gazda?"

Felix shook his head.

Jochim ran the name though his police memory: nothing. "And he set you up as a pimp?"

"He offered me a job."

"And where do I find this Georg Herzog?"

"Don't know."

"You don't know?"

"He contacts me."

"Who owns this 'hotel'?"

"Geor–"

"Georg Herzog."

"Very good inspector."

"Sergeant."

"Oh I'm sure you'll be an inspector soon."

"Don't get smart with me Felix. Where do you live?"

"Here."

"Why aren't you registered with the City?"

"I keep forgetting."

"Well start remembering. I'll want to talk to you again."

Georg Herzog was dead. He had no criminal record, and was unknown to the police. The only reason Jochim found out he was dead was the police report. On 25 October his neighbours in the Dietlikon area of Zurich called the local police when the smell became overpowering. He'd been dead for more than a week. Surrounding the body were the paraphernalia of a heroin addict. Herzog's body had received a massive overdose. The police report concluded accident or suicide.

Jochim assumed Felix must have known about the death, that's why he gave the name so 'easily'. Interviewing the neighbours was a possibility, but Jochim didn't think he would get anything useful, and it risked disclosing his investigations to Kullmer.

"Is Felix here?"

"No."

"Will he be back later?"

"I don't know. He doesn't tell me what he's doing. Nobody tells me anything. I don't want to know anything. If I don't know anything I can't give away any secrets. I just run the place. They can all come and go as they please."

"You must be, Clive."

"Ooo fame at last."

"Detective Sergeant Friedmann."

"Hmm you're tall boy. I'm getting a crick in my neck looking up at you."

"So, you haven't seen Felix?"

"Not for a couple of days."

"Is that unusual?"

"He's usually here at some time most days."

"Is he your boss?"

"Him! He might think he is."

"What about Georg Herzog, is he the boss?"

"Juraj's a friend."

"Juraj?"

"Georg's name before he became Georg. It's what his friends, his intimate friends, still call him."

"Juraj Herzog?"

"Juraj Herceg. I think it's Croatian."

The options raced through Jochim's brain. Should he tell him or not tell him about Georg? He needed him to be cooperative, not to break down.

"So, Clive, you run this place?"

"I keep it tidy."

"And Juraj owns it?"

"Georg to you."

"Georg owns it?"

"Owns? I'm not so sure he owns it."

"So, he has a boss?"

"I don't know. I told you I don't know anything."

"I'm sure you know a lot Clive. Do Felix and Georg have the same boss?"

"I know nothing."

"Do you mind if I have a look around?"

"Help yourself. Most of the rooms are empty during the day."

"I'll just have look in the room behind the desk."

The room contained a desk, two chairs and a filing cabinet. Jochim had the impression the room had been abandoned. There was nothing on the desk and the filing cabinet drawers were partially open. Felix was not coming back. That left Clive, who hovered in the doorway. Jochim decided to try his other option.

"When was the last time you saw Georg?"

"I don't know. I don't see him all that often, he has other friends. It must have been over a week ago."

"Was he well?"

"Why all the questions?"

"He's dead."

"What? ... What? ... Dead?"

"Yes."

"How? ... Why didn't you tell me before?"

"I needed you to answer some questions."

"Oh how cruel ... how cruel. Juraj dead! Poor luv." The tears and sobs sounded false at the beginning, but, as the reality sunk in, quickly became real and intense.

Jochim stood in silence, letting the emotion deepen. "Any idea who could have done it?"

"You mean ... you mean ... he was ... murdered."

"Looks that way. So, any ideas?"

Clive took two deep breaths. "He knew he was vulnerable because of his sexuality and addiction, but he told me protection was not far away."

"What do you think he meant by that?"

"He didn't say and I didn't ask. Oh, poor, poor Juraj." The sobbing started again.

Clive Pritt was not going to be any use. He was probably right, he didn't know anything. But Georg Herzog might be the link to something. Juraj Herceg's name didn't show up in a search of European police records. Wikipedia confirmed that Juraj was Croatian or Slovak. If Felix did get his job because of providing some muscle for the Serbo-Croat gang in prison, then there must be a link between Georg Herzog and Anto Dedeić, which could suggest a heavy involvement of the Serbo-Croats in prostitution. Another visit to Mr Dedeić.

Jochim went to the map of Zurich that almost covered one wall of his office. Parking had been difficult last time he visited Anto Dedeić, he wanted to see which tram went past the Dietlikonerstrasse apartment block. When he found Dedeić's address he noticed it was close to the point where Dietlikonerstrasse became Riedenerstrasse. Why did that name ring bells? He clicked on the report of Georg Herzogs death - 2a Riedenerstrasse. That's what he meant by 'protection was not far away'.

"Mr Dedeić."

"I answered your questions last time."

"Answered yes, but you didn't tell me anything. Besides that was two weeks ago. A lot happens in two weeks."

"I've got nothing more to say."

"There's a lot of that about."

"What?"

"People who've got nothing to say. Can I come in? Thank you."

Dedeić made a token attempt to stand in Friedmann's way.

"No visitors this time?"

"What do you want?"

"Information, Anto, information."

"I don–"

"Don't tell me you don't have any, Anto. Please don't tell me that. Have you remembered Felix yet?"

" Who?"

"Felix Braun. He remembers you from your time in prison together."

"His memory must be better than mine."

"Where is Felix now?"

Anto's neutral expression changed to puzzlement.

"I spoke to him a couple of days ago and now he's disappeared."

"I don't know anything–"

"about it. That's what people keep saying to me." Jochim walked around the small living room. He ran his finger over the spines of books on a shelf, picked up a newspaper lying on the floor and put his head around the frame of the kitchen door. "Too bad about Georg."

Surprise replaced puzzlement.

"You probably know him better as Juraj."

Surprise became shock. "How do–"

259

"How do I know about Juraj? I told you Anto a lot happens in two weeks."

Dedeić struggled to get the neutral expression back on to his face. "I heard about him, but I didn't know him."

"No? You don't seem to know anyone, Anto."

"I met him a couple of times at weddings in the Serbian community."

"Did he talk about Hotel Stein?"

"I said I met him, not had a conversation with him."

"Who owns the Hotel Stein?"

"I've no idea."

"Gazda?"

"Who?"

"Now Anto you must remember that I name, it's an unusual name. I asked you about it at our last little discussion. Was Georg Gazda? Are you Gazda?"

"Who is this Gazda?"

"Your friend Felix's boss. The one who puts prostitutes in bars."

"Means nothing to me."

"According to your police record, prison was a revolving door for you. You're one of the big names in the Zurich drugs world."

"Big names? A minor player, Sergeant. But not any more"

"And you've never heard of Gazda?"

Dedeić pursed his lips and shook his head.

"OK." Friedmann strode towards the door.

"Thanks for calling, Sergeant."

"Oh, we're not finished, Anto, but we're not getting anywhere here. I find that a visit to the station usually jogs people's memories. I'll send a patrol car."

"You're arresting me?"

"Why have you done something I could arrest you for? No, I want some answers and I think you can help me much more than you're doing at the moment."

"And if I refuse to come to the station?"

"Then I'll find something to charge you with."

"I've been clean since I came out of prison."

"Doesn't mean I can't find something."

"You would wouldn't you, you bastar–"

"Careful Anto, careful."

"OK, I knew Felix in prison."

Jochim stopped, but didn't turn or speak.

"Felix did me, us, a good turn inside and I wanted to help him. I put him in contact with Juraj, who started as a customer and became one of my dealers."

"And Juraj set Felix up as a pimp."

"I don't know anything about that. I'm not spending any more time in prison, I've avoided all contact with my previous ... associates."

"So, if Georg didn't work for you any more who would he be dealing for?"

"No idea."

Jochim turned to face him. "Anto, Anto I thought you were starting to be a bit cooperative. You must know everybody in the drug business in Zurich. Who's also got a string of girls?"

Rapid eye movement again. "I don't know."

"OK, don't go anywhere, the patrol car will here later."

"Look, Sergeant ... I ... The only person I can think of is Heinrich Sommers."

"And where would I find Heinrich Sommers?"

"He runs the Lipstick Club."

"Don't think I'm finished with you Anto, just because you've given me a name."

Dedeić took a deep breath and nodded.

"What did you do with all the money you made from drug dealing? This flat's not exactly a penthouse suite."

"Gave it all to charity."

"To atone for your sins?"

"Something like that."

"Hello."

"What did you tell Friedmann?"

"Nothing."

"What did he want to know, Felix?"

"Who put the girls in The Celler."

"We know who that was don't we, Felix. What did you say to him?"

"I said I don't know anything about it."

"If you're as good at lying as you are at some other things, Felix, we're in trouble. How does he know the name Gazda?"

"Who told you he does?"

"I'll ask you again, Felix. How does he know the name Gazda?"

"I don't know."

"If you say one more time 'I don't know' I'll make sure you don't remember anything ever again. Now, how does Friedmann know the name Gazda?"

"I'll find out."

"That's better, Felix. I think it must have come from that girl they arrested after the raid."

"Arrested, but not charged."

"Still, she must have talked to Friedmann. Maybe she's still talking to him."

"I don't think so. I know my girls."

"Felix, what you think doesn't interest me. Get to her and stop her talking, permanently."

Conflicting duty rosters meant they'd only been able to meet for a couple of hours a week ago. Today they had the whole afternoon, so they'd taken time to reach the peak of satisfaction. At the highest point Jochim's mobile rang. For both of them it was too late to stop, but the insistent repetition of the melody brought them to normality without going through the floating, dreamlike state.

Jochim got his breathing back to normal by taking two deep breaths. "Hello."

"Sorry to trouble you, Sarge, there's something I thought you'd want to know about."

"Yes, what is it, Weber?"

"A young woman was admitted to the University Hospital in the early hours of this morning with life-threatening injuries. She's just regained some degree of consciousness and is asking for you."

"What's her name?"

"Francesca."

Jochim sat bolt upright, pulling the duvet, which she had just snuggled into, off Bea. "Jochim!"

"Meet me there, Weber." Jochim threw the 'phone onto the bed and in three strides was in the bathroom.

The young doctor looked tired, harassed and anxious. "Admission was at four thirty. She'd had several heavy punches to the stomach, probably an hour or so before. There was already damage to several organs and a lot of internal bleeding. Since admission there has been compete kidney and liver failure, and the blood loss has had an effect on her brain. We didn't expect her to regain consciousness. She had only her ID card on her, so we couldn't contact anyone. Forty-five minutes ago she suddenly very clearly said 'Sergeant Friedmann' without opening her eyes."

"Can we see her?"

"This way."

Jochim had, unfortunately, had to go into many hospital rooms where people lay critically injured or dying, but he had never seen a bed surrounded by so many machines. A guilty feeling tightened his stomach.

"We're controlling all her functions externally."

"What are her chances?"

The doctor took a deep breath. "We're waiting for some scan results, but from what we've seen I'd say only the machines will keep her alive. Do you know how we can contact any relatives?"

"I'm afraid not. I only know her 'professionally'."

"Hmm."

"We can try to find out."

"We might have to make a decision about switching off the machines."

"Do you think she can hear?"

"Difficult to say, and even if she can hear, can she understand? All I can say is that with the machines' help she's what we call 'stable'."

One of the nurses moved to allow Jochim to approach the bedside. He put his hand on her arm and found a place among all the tubes to touch the skin. "Francesca, can you hear me?"

No sign of response.

"Francesca, who did this to you?"

No sign of response.

Jochim looked at the doctor. She shook her head.

"Francesca, who did this to you?"

No response.

Jochim moved away from the bed. "We'll see what we can do about finding any relatives, doctor." He moved towards the door, then stopped and went back to the bed. "Francesca, this is the bastard Friedmann. Did Felix do this to you?"

The pulse monitor beeped as a small peak appeared. The little finger on the hand closest to Jochim moved, no more than a couple of millimetres, but moved.

"Well done, Francesca. We'll get the bastard."

The pulse monitor beeped again.

Once in the corridor Jochim spoke quickly to DC Weber. "OK, get a description of Felix Braun out to all units."

"Priority level?"

"One."

"Won't we need to run it by Kullmer to do that?"

"Leave Kullmer to me. I want Braun in custody before the end of the day. Use all the contacts."

"You think the reaction in there is enough to go all out after Braun?

"Just do it."

"This seems to be a bit personal, Sarge."

"Just do—"

The sound of an alarm made everybody in the corridor freeze, except the people rushing to Francesca's room.

The alarm faded. The doctor slowly emerged from the room, eyes downcast. She shook her head.

"Just do it, Peter. This is a murder inquiry now."

"What's going on, Jochim?" Inspector Kullmer never came to the offices of his subordinates, he summoned them to his.

"A murder."

"Müller's not pleased, which means I'm not pleased."

"I needed to move fast. The first forty-eight–"

"You don't need to remind me about the importance of the first forty-eight hours, Sergeant Friedmann."

"I'm sure I don't, Sir."

"A priority level one because some prostitute is beaten up?"

"She was the woman we took in after the raid on The Celler. Her pimp was Felix Braun. He killed her."

"How do we know that?"

Jochim had expected this conversation. "She told me just before she died."

"Where?"

"At the hospital. She must have remem–"

"What were you doing at the hospital?"

"She asked for me. She must have remembered my name from the raid. I can only guess that Braun thought she must have talked to me and beat her up so badly she died."

"But the raid was six weeks ago, why now?"

"Perhaps–"

"You have been keeping the investigation low key, as we agreed?"

Friedmann had not reported any of his discussions with André Wissler, Felix Braun or Anto Dedeić. "Of course."

"Good. So, do we know where this Felix Braun is?"

"No, but with a priority level one I'm sure we'll find him."

"You'd better, because if you don't Chief Inspector Müller's going to be asking some awkward questions, and you're going to have to answer them. You've got twenty-four hours."

"Priority level one is normally for forty-eight hours, Sir."

"Twenty-four hours, Friedmann, and you've already had four."

It had been a quiet day. In fact every day was a quiet day these days. Sergeant Walter Grindel stared at the blinking cursor. He'd hoped that his selection earlier in the year as one of the three sergeants leading the newly created teams of Kriminalpolizei First Response, KFR, was his promotion at last. But KRIPO had not supported forming the new units and had made little use of them so far.

The cursor moved off its rest position at the left of the screen. 'Priority level one alert. Felix Braun wanted in connection with the murder of Francesca Kardomah. 180 cm, 76 kg ...' Grindel scanned through the detailed description that followed and Braun's police record. He was about to go back to the magazine he'd been reading when the name of Braun's last known address stopped his eye movement: Hotel Stein - a place that had a special place in his memory.

Grindel knew who owned Hotel Stein. He shouldn't know that, but he did. The name Felix Braun meant nothing to him, but then he hadn't been anywhere near the Hotel Stein for a long time. Should he call the owner? You didn't call him: he called you when he wanted something. But surely he'd want to know about a priority level one alert about someone who probably worked for him. Grindel peeked over the partition to make sure the room was empty.

"Yes."

"Sorry to trouble you. There's a priority level one alert for Felix Braun."

Silence.

"Hello?"

"Yes, I'm here. Do you know why?"

"The murder of ..." Grindel checked the screen "Francesca Kardomah."

Silence. "I'll find where he is. Send someone to silence him, permanently."

"Send someone to ... to silence him?"

"Permanently."

"But ... I ... couldn't ... wouldn't ... can't ... be involved in–."

"In making sure someone doesn't start talking to your colleagues Walter? Once someone starts talking, Walter, you never know what they might reveal."

"But ... but ... ."

"Think of it as a favour for me Walter. In return for all the money I've paid you."

"But I ... I wouldn't know how to– ."

"Silence someone permanently? You don't have to do it yourself Walter. You must know plenty of people who can."

Now Grindel was glad he had no work. Thinking about anything other than the three words 'silence him permanently' would have been impossible. He'd done a few jobs, but an accessary to … murder was something else. But could he refus–. His direct line rang.

"Hello."

"The Lipstick Club."

"I don't–"

"Don't let me down, Walter."

Detective Sergeant Jochim Friedmann stared out of the window of his third floor office. The minute hand of the large wall clock ticked over to twelve: eleven o'clock, eight hours of Kullmer's twenty-four gone. Where was Felix Braun? It can't be that difficult to find him, not with a priority level one out.

Bea saw the priority level one and called Jochim on the number only she had. "Do you think Lisa Stern is in any danger?"

"Why?"

"If this Felix finds out she led you to the Hotel Stein, he might be in the mood to take some revenge on her."

"I'm sure Felix doesn't know who Lisa Stern is and–"

"No, but the person she spoke to at the hotel might give him a description."

"Unlikely, besides I think Felix will be lying low."

"I hope you find him."

"Oh, I'll find the bastard, I'll find him."

He started pacing. The shrill of the telephone stopped him in midstride.   "Friedmann."

"We've got him."

Jochim tucked the 'phone between ear and shoulder and reached for his jacket. "Where are you Weber?"

"A & E at University hospital."

For the second time in the day Jochim found himself looking into a room full of machines beeping and humming. But Francesca's room had an air of tranquillity compared to the frantic activity happening around Felix Braun. He could see there was no chance to talk to any of the medical personnel.

Weber joined him at the window. "He was in the toilets of The Lipstick Club. The paramedics didn't expect to find a pulse, there was so much blood coming from wounds all over the body. Whoever did this had a sadistic streak. It looks like bare-knuckle punches followed by attack with a knife. The knife wounds were positioned to cause a slow, agonising death. They reckon he had less than fifteen minutes to live."

"Will he live?"

"I ... they don't know Bea. None of the knife wounds are life-threatening by themselves, it's just there are so many of them. There's been no improvement in his condition in the last twenty-four hours."

Bea poured wine into Jochim's glass, but not her own: she'd only taken two small sips in the ten minutes since they sat down at the kitchen table.

"Kullmer agreed to putting a round-the-clock guard on him."

"You think they might come after him."

"I think he's supposed to be dead. They might think he'd talk if he survives."

"What's Kullmer's reaction to all this, he likes a quiet life doesn't he?"

"Yes, but he and Müller both see the connection with prostitution in Zurich, and don't want this getting out of control. Kullmer knows about Felix's involvement in the raid on The Celler. He told me to clear this up asap. I've got a couple of extra DCs. Fortunately the press haven't picked up on it, yet."

"I assume you haven't said anything about Lisa Stern and Christopher McLendi."

"No."

"Lisa's called me several times, asking if you've found Felix–."

"What did you tell her? She knew we were looking for Felix? She knew about Francesca?"

"No, no of course not. She was just following up on the last discussion we had with them. I said we were still looking. What if she, they, find out about what's happened?"

Jochim poured more wine into his glass; Bea put her hand over the top of hers. "As I said, the press haven't picked this up. Perhaps you should call her. Tell her about Felix, but don't mention Francesca." He took a large swallow of wine. "I'm angry about Francesca. Maybe if I'd have done more to find Felix ..."

"You did what you could. What about this Anto Dedieć character?"

"He gave me a name. Dedieć put Felix in contact with Georg or Juraj Herzog as a 'reward' for services carried out for the Serbo-Croat gang in prison. Herzog worked for Dedieć as a drug dealer and set up Felix as a pimp. Georg Herzog died of an overdose. According to Dedieć he was working for a Heinrich Sommers, drug dealer and pimp. What's interesting is that Sommers runs The Lipstick Club."

"The same Lipstick Club owned by a client of Herman Zubke; visited by Christopher McLendi, by accident; and where Felix Braun is almost beaten to death."

"Exactly."

"Did anyone see what happened to Felix?"

"I'm sure someone saw something, but the usual wall of silence."

"Did you talk to this Heinrich Sommers?

"Not yet. He wasn't at the club, and surprise, surprise, no one knows how to contact him, even though everyone calls him the boss."

"He could be Zubke's client ... or Gazda."

"Clients like that usually stay hidden. Gazda?"

"He might give you a name."

"If he knows."

"Or ... or could we use what's happened to pressure Zubke?"

"Now there's a thought. I can't imagine Zubke would be happy having his name associated with a place where a brutal attack took place. You're pretty smart when you want to be, constable."

"Is that pretty and smart, Sarge?"

"Well ..."

Bea pouted.

"Well ..."

She undid the top button on her blouse.

"Pretty, smart and sexy."

Bea rebuttoned her blouse. "You said the press haven't pick this up yet."

"They probably won't. We asked the hospital not to release any information. The presence of the guard convinced them this was a good idea. I shouldn't think anyone from The Lipstick Club will call a press conference."

"But Zubke will hear about it."

"Certainly."

"Are you going to talk to him?"

"I'm sure I wouldn't get anything from him. I want to talk to this Sommers first and I hope to Felix soon. They might give me something to pressure Zubke with."

Constable Beatrice Menna stared at the telephone. Jochim had suggested she should call Lisa, but would it be better to visit her? She felt they had established a good relationship when the four of them met, and she wanted to keep Lisa informed about what was happening. The telephone would make it easier not to reveal too much about the violence.

Was Grindel in his office? He called it his office, but in reality it was just a part of the room he'd insisted on partitioning off. Her three colleagues wouldn't be back for a couple of hours, so it was a good time to make a 'private' call. She hadn't seen Grindel come in, or heard him, so assumed he was out.   She reached for the 'phone. The sound of Grindel's 'phone ringing stopped her hand in mid-air. Grindel's 'Hello' brought her hand back to her desk, quietly.

"Can I call you back?"

Bea assumed he knew she was there.

"Yes. Yes, but–. Just give me a minute and I'll call you back."

Grindel's head appeared above the partition: something he did rather than come out to talk to people. "Ah, Constable Menna, Beatrice, could you ... could you do something for me ... please."

"Tell me, sar–"

"Go over to the photo library and see if you can find a picture of ... a picture of ...."

"A pict–"

"Yes, a picture of ... of Felix Braun."

"Felix Braun, Sarge?"

"Yes, Felix Braun, the person we had the priority level one alert about."

"Is it urgent, sar–"

"If you could go now."

"I'm on my way." Bea was halfway down the corridor when she realised she'd left her mobile 'phone on her desk.

Their 'absolutely necessary to meet immediately' place was the small cafe in the University library. That'd only needed to use it once before.

"Are you OK Bea? You sounded desperate on the 'phone and now you look flustered."

"Desperate? Flustered? No, not flustered. Excited."

"At seeing me."

"Of course, but there's something else."

Gazda

Bea took the mobile 'phone out of her handbag, placed it between them on the table, plugged in the audio splitter and handed one of the two earpieces to Jochim

```
Beep, beep, beep.
Hello, hello. Sorry I couldn't talk before,
there was som-.
```

"Sergeant Walter Grindel?"
"The very man."

```
Yes, yes I know, and I di-.
... ...
But Gazda, I did as you asked.
... ...
To stop Felix Braun being arrested.
... ...
Yes, to silence him permanently, I know.
... ...
Still alive? He can't be Gazd-
... ...
I sent The Mad Frog.
... ...
Yes, he can be a bit sadistic sometimes, but he
gets the job done.
... ...
You told me Felix was at the Club.
... ...
Ah, I didn't realise you have a connection to
The Lipstick Club.
... ...
There are a lot of things I don't want to
realise Gazda.
... ...
Where is Felix?
... ...
I'll find out which hospital they took him to.
... ...
I will Gazda.
... ...
I'll make sure he doesn't talk.
... ...
Ever.
... ...
```

    No, I wouldn't like a visit from The Mad Frog.
I'll take care of it Gazda.
    ... ...
    I will Gazda, I promise.
    ... ...
    Gazda? Gazda?
    Jesus Christ.

"How on earth did you get this Bea?"

"I accidentally left my mobile on record when Grindel sent me on a wild goose chase."

"When?"

"About two hours ago."

"I have to get Kullmer to increase the protection of Braun. He must be an important figure to Gazda if he wants him out of the way so urgently."

"Can Grindel find out where he is?"

"After what we've just heard, who knows what can Grindel can do?"

"What should we do about him?"

"Maybe if we ask him nicely he'll give us Gazda's telephone number."

"Phone records?"

"Is your recording enough evidence to officially request them?

"Probably not. Redial on his telephone?"

"Even though I don't like the guy, I think he might be just smart enough to have deleted the number."

"I'll go back to the station. See if I can keep an eye on him."

"I'll call Kullmer and go to the hospital. Be careful, Bea."

When Bea got back two of her three colleagues were at their desks. Before sitting down she pointed towards Grindel's partition and nodded. Her colleagues nodded back.

Unusually Grindel walked around the partition and approached Bea's desk. "You're back, Constab– Bea."

"Yes, I took my break outside, Sarge. It's a beautiful day."

"Is it? ... Yes, it is. I was asking Constables Schmi– Johann and Bruno if they'd heard anything more about that POA we had."

"POA, Sarge?"

"Yes, that one from the day before yesterday."

"Which one, Sarge?"

"Felix Braun or whatever his name was."

272

"Ah, that one."

"Did you hear what happened?"

"No, what?"

"That's what I'm asking you, constab– Bea."

"No, I didn't hear anything. Isn't there something on the computer?"

"No! You don't think I've already looked, Constab– Bea."

"If you're interested, I could try to find out, Sarge."

"No. I'm not particularly interested. I just ... I just wondered what had happened."

"Who ordered the POA, Sarge?"

"I can't remem–"

"Sergeant Friedmann, Sarge."

"Thank you, constab– Johann."

"Why don't you ask him, Sarge?"

"I ... I ... I don't think it's necessary, Bea."

"Should I ask him, Sarge?"

"If you want, Bea, it's not that important. Just let me know if you find out anything."

Thirty minutes later Grindel's head appeared above the partition. "Any news, constab– Bea?"

"News, Sarge?"

"About that POA."

"I didn't think it was urgent, Sarge."

"No ... no, not urgent." The head disappeared.

"Excuse me, Sarge."

"Yes, constab– Bea, what is it?"

"I just met one the DCs working with Sergeant Friedmann in the canteen. He s–."

"Yes, what did he say?"

"He said they were looking for someone called Henri."

Grindel's voice went up at least an octave. "Henri?"

"Yes, in connection with what happened to this Felix Braun, the target of the POA."

"What ... what happened to him?"

"Beaten up apparently."

"Did the DC say where they'd taken him?"

"He wouldn't tell me."

"I told you to be careful, Bea."

"I was."

"Grindel could be dangerous, especially if cornered."

"I wasn't cornering him. I just gave him some information."

"Still."

"He did look very angry, no not angry, flustered. He started sweating and mumbling, what, I couldn't make out."

"And?"

"He grabbed his coat and nearly fell as he rushed out."

"Please don't tell me you followed him."

"No. But I did check his phone memory. He's never made a single call."

Jochim entered his password. At the top of his home page was a message from DC Weber, `Felix Braun, no improvement.`

Jochim typed the name Henri Cousteau, alias The Mad Frog. Three arrests for brutal assault. All three charges dropped because witnesses changed their minds. He typed a message to Weber, `Bring in Henri Cousteau.`

He entered Anto Dedeić's name. Information from numerous sources appeared with references. Jochim scrolled through the information and pulled together the parts that gave him an outline of Dedeić's life.

- born in Yugoslavia about 1940.

- arrived in Switzerland in 1941 as a war refugee, with his nine-year-old sister

- several arrests and three terms in prison for drug offences.

"I'm sure he knows more than he's saying," said Jochim out loud. Worth having another talk to him, he thought.

Bea didn't 'phone Lisa until the next evening. The attack on Felix Braun and Grindel's involvement, made the situation much more complex. She wanted to keep the confidence of Lisa and Christopher by telling them what was happening, but didn't want to alarm them.

"Ms Stern?"

"Yes."

"Beatrice Menna. How are you?"

"Constable Menna, I'm OK, and you?"

"OK."

"Any news?"

Bea held the 'phone away from her mouth and took a deep breath. "Yes, we've found Felix Braun."

"Good. What did he have to say?"

Another deep breath. "He's in the hospital."

"The hospital?"

"He was attacked."

"Attacked?"

"It's not unusual in the world he moves in."

"You don't think it's got anything to do with what happened to me."

"No." Bea immediately realised her reply was a bit too quick. "No, certainly not."

"Have you interviewed him?"

"No, it's better to wait until he's at the station. We'll stand a better chance of getting something out of him."

"What about Wissler, have you spoken to him?"

"Not yet. Jochim, Sergeant Friedmann, is going to see him today."

"So you haven't forgotten about Christopher and I?"

"Certainly not. We want to get to the bottom of this, but as Jochim, Sergeant Friedmann, said we have to get some real evidence before we can start an official investigation."

"You think Felix Braun can help you get that evidence?"

"We don't know, but he is our link to prostitution in Zurich."

"Are you still working for Grindel?"

"Yes ... Sergeant Grindel is still my boss."

"That can't be easy, especially when you think he's involved somehow."

"We didn't say that Ms Stern. We onl–"

"Our conversation last week brought it all back to me. The way he treated me, us, the basta–"

"We're keeping an eye on him. I'll let you get on with your Saturday, Ms Stern. We'll keep in touch."

"Thanks for the call, Constable Menna. Goodbye."

"Goodbye."

"André come in. Good to see you. How you've been in the last two weeks? How's the football?"

"I thought we'd finished with all this, Friedmann."

"You hoped, Wissler."

Wissler took his 'phone out and flipped through a few pages. Jochim moved the cursor around on his screen. This cat and mouse continued for more than five minutes. Wissler was the one to blink. "Can I go now?"

"No."

The icy stare would've made most people shudder. "So, why am I here?"

"I thought you'd never ask."

Silence.

"I haven't got time for this, Friedmann. What do you want?"

"Some information."

"Not the same old question 'who gave the prostitutes permission to be in The Celler'."

"You remembered."

"I've told you, it was not me."

"Same old answer."

"It can't be anything else, because it's the truth."

Jochim shrugged.

"Well?"

Jochim smiled.

"If you're not going to say anything I'm going."

"Sit down, André."

"When does this become police harassment, Friedmann? I going to ask my lawyer."

"I think you and I got off to a bad start, André. I don't want to harass you, André. I've got a job to do. I want to keep these prostitutes from going into bars and hustling. It's not good for anyone: for the bars like yours where people want to have a drink and listen to jazz; for tourists; for football fans who come to watch you. We already have prostitutes on the streets, but it's controlled. One day you and I may have children. I wouldn't want mine growing up in a city with prostitution out of control. Would you?"

"I'm not planning to have children."

"OK, but what about all your young football fans?"

André took a deep breath, nodded and adjusted his position in the chair.

Jochim mirrored his movement.

"I asked you about the football earlier. I meant it. I've started taking an interest."

"Really."

"Yes, I'm not yet what you'd call a fan, but I've started reading a bit about what's going on."

"Good."

"You've done well."

"Thank you."

"Your father must be very proud of you."

"I don't know my—"

"Sorry?"

"My father's not involved."

"Oh, sorry."

"My mother's very proud."

"I'm sure she is."

"And my uncles."

"That's important."

Silence

"Uncle Walter is my biggest fan."

"Really. My Uncle Walter died last year."

"I'm sorry."

Jochim let the silence hang again. "And now my Uncle Herman is ill."

"What a coincidence, I also have an Uncle Herman."

"Yes?"

André stood. "You know Sergeant, it wasn't me who invited those women into The Celler."

Jochim stood and held out his hand. "Thanks for coming in, André."

Bea stroked Jochim's face. "The good-cop trick."

"It works sometimes."

"Pity about poor Uncle Herman."

"Not planned, flash of inspiration."

"You're thinking Uncle Herman Zubke?"

"Could be."

"I suppose it would too much to hope that Uncle Walter was our Walter?"

"As you say, too much to hope."

"Do you believe Wissler?"

"No."

"Sarge there's a Heinrich Sommers at the front desk. Says he wants to see you."

"Bring him up, Roth, interview room three. Try to find DC Weber. If you can't find him you stay with me while I talk to him."

"Them, Sarge, he's with his lawyer."

"Mr Sommers, what can I do for you?"

"Sergeant Friedmann, a pleasure to meet you. I assumed you'd want to talk to me." Sommers' smile was a false as his hairpiece.

"Why?"

"Come, come, Sergeant, I'm sure you know I manage The Lipstick Club."

"Ah, the elusive Mr Sommers."

"I've been away. I only got back last night and heard the terrible news.

"It must have come as a shock to you."

"Most distressing, Sergeant."

"So you thought you'd come and tell me how distressed you were ... with your lawyer."

"Merely a precaution, Sergeant."

"Based on previous experience of talking to the police, Mr Sommers?"

"A precaution, Sergeant, merely a precaution."

"No one at the Club knew how to get in contact with you. Strange that. Usually the owners of such establishments want to know what's going on."

"I'm the manager, not the owner, Sergeant, and I have a private life."

"Convenient, to be away when someone is almost beaten to death in the club."

"Pure coincidence, Sergeant, pure coincidence."

"So, who owns The Lipstick Club?"

"Oh Sergeant, come now, I'm sure you don't need me to answer that."

"You said you've been away, do you mind telling where you've been?"

"No I–"

"Sergeant ... Friedmann, my client came here of his own free will. I don't think he needs to answer questions about his personal life."

"Mr ..."

The lawyer placed a business card on the table.

"Mr Baumgartner, your client came here of his own free will, but now that he's here he'll answer my questions."

"Sergeant Friedmann, my client is not under arrest and–"

"Not at the moment."

"not under arrest and does not have to answer any questions."

"Good. OK, you're free to leave ... but as soon as you step out of the door I'll have your client detained for questioning in connection with the attempted murder of Felix Braun."

"I can assure you, Sergeant, I'd have nothing to do with an attack on a scumbag like that." Sommers looked at his lawyer, who was slowly shaking his head.

"So, you know Felix."

Silence.

"OK, let's start with a few basic questions. If you don't own The Lipstick Club, who does?"

Sommers glanced towards his lawyer again. Another shake of the head.

"Perhaps you know the answer, Mr Baumgartner?"

"I don't see the relevance of–"

"How's Herman Zubke?"

"Who?"

"Herman Zubke, your partner."

"Partner? I don't have a partner Sergeant, as you can see from my card."

"Oh I can read that your card says Arnold Baumgartner, Rechtsanwalt, but could you be the same Baumgartner as in Baumgartner, Zubke and Zubke?"

Now it was the lawyer's turn to look anxiously towards his client. "I ... I." Sommers expression had changed from confident smile to shark eyes stare.

"So, is this another coincidence, Mr Sommers?"

Sommers' stare hardened. "What does that mean, Friedmann?"

"You manage The Lipstick Club, but you're away when someone tries to murder Felix Braun at the Club. Mr Herman Zubke is the registered owner of The Lipstick Club and is therefore your boss. You turn up at the police station protesting all innocence about the attack, accompanied by Mr Baumgartner, law firm partner of Zubke. No, that's not a coincidence, that's planned."

"But I came here of my own free will."

"Knowing that if you didn't you'd have arrived here in a police car."

Baumgartner had recovered some of his lawyerly composure. "My client–"

"Your client, Mr Baumgartner, had better start answering some questions or–"

"Or what, Sergeant? You can't blame him for what happened to this Felix ... Braun."

"Let's put the word 'blame' to one side for the moment. I can hold him and Mr Zubke responsible for what happens at the club. Incidentally you can tell your partner Herman Zubke I'll want to talk to him."

"I'm sure Mr Zubke will have nothing to add about this ... incident."

"The man in hospital will probably not survive this 'incident', Mr Baumgartner. Now, Mr Sommers, what do you know about Felix Braun?"

"A low life. I've seen him hanging around the Club a few times."

"Trying to recruit some of your ladies?"

The stare was back, more icy. "My ladies?"

Friedmann met his stare. "What do you call them? Hostesses?"

"They only sit with customers who want a little company while they drink and watch the show."

"And the rooms behind the bar?"

"Some of the girls rent a room so they have somewhere to go during their break. We're not slave drivers. They have regular breaks."

"Depending if they have a customer who wants to go with them."

"That's up to them."

"Nothing to do with you?"

"Correct, Sergeant."

"What's not 'correct', Mr Sommers is that you're operating a brothel without a licence."

"I've just explained to you the arrangement. All the girls have proper contracts for the rooms. Mr Baumgartner can corroborate that."

Baumgartner had the look of someone who didn't want to corroborate anything.

"If you did have a licence you'd be subject to all the standards and inspections of course."

"But we're just a cabaret bar."

"I think the police have turned a blind eye to The Lipstick Club so far, as long as there was no trouble, but this 'incident', as Mr Baumgartner puts it, changes that."

"Meaning?"

"A lot more scrutiny of what really goes on."

"I'm sure the police have more important things to do than hassle a simple place of entertainment for gentlemen." Sommers' artificial smile was back. "Some of our customers are ... what shall we say ... well known in Zurich: councillors, footballers, even your colleagues."

"I'll have to come along and try it some time."

"You'll be most welcome. I'm sure we can arrange something special for you."

"Special?"

"Blond? Brunette? European? Asian? All four? Whatever you want."

"On the house?"

"We wouldn't want it to be bribery, Sergeant."

"We wouldn't. ... So, whatever I want?"

"Whatever you want."

Friedmann rapid rise from his chair put his face a few centimetres from Sommers'. "What I want, Mr Sommers ... what I really want ... is for you to stop fucking me around and tell me who owns The Lipstick Club, or I'm going to close The Club and put you away for running an illicit brothel."

Both Sommers and Baumgartner pushed back in their seats.

Sommers recovered remarkably quickly. "Sergeant, could we have a private word?"

Baumgartner put his hand on Sommers' arm. "I don't think—"

"I think your client is suggesting you leave."

Baumgartner shook his head so hard it almost came off.

Sommers nodded.

Friedmann signalled to Roth to open the door.

Baumgartner rose and walked slowly out, still shaking his head.

Sommers waited until the door closed. "Sergeant I—"

"Mr Sommers, are you expecting this conversation to be 'off the record'?"

"Sergeant, I really can't tell you much, but what I do tell you could be dangerous for me if certain people found out."

"OK. Constable Roth, please go and see if Mr Baumgartner wants a coffee."

"So?"

"I don't know who owns The Lipstick Club. I am employed by Baumgartner. He said he was acting for a client who wished to remain in the background. It's not the first time I've been in that situation, that's probably why they approached me a couple of years ago. I'm left to run the place as I want. On a couple of occasions I've received 'suggestions' through Baumgartner about decor or how we handle customers."

"And you have no clue of who the owner is?"

"No, but from the suggestions that came through Baumgartner, I'm sure he, or she, must have been to the club sometimes, or have someone working there."

"Do you know The Celler?"

"I've heard of it, but I've never been there, I'm not a fan of jazz."

"Does the name Gazda mean anything to you?"

"No."

"So, that's it?

"Well there was one thing. I don't know if it's important, but it's something that's stuck in my mind. As I said I got a few suggestions through Baumgartner, but there was one time, and only one time, when he told me to reserve the best table for a party of four and they were to be guests of The Club."

"When was this?"

"Early in September, a Monday night, not usually the busiest, so I arranged for a few friends to come along to create an atmosphere."

"Do you think the owner was with them?"

"I don't think so, but I'm not sure. I remember it because we noticed how rowdy they were with the Club not being so full. They did a lot of shouting about 'Munich, the best football team in Europe'".

DC Weber understood 'bring in' was different to 'arrest'. For arrest he would have arrived with several uniformed branch and a van. 'Bring in' usually meant a request to 'accompany me to the station'. However, Weber knew from personal experience Cousteau's reputation for violent reaction to the police, having been one of four uniformed officers sent to arrest him three years ago.

Cousteau was not difficult to find. He had three regular bars. Weber told Schwartz, one of the temporary DCs, who didn't know Cousteau, to go with him. He also persuaded the duty Inspector, his old boss, who knew Cousteau, to have a van round the corner from the bar, which turned out to be a wise precaution.

Cousteau was smiling as Weber approached him. "You have come to arrest me, no?"

"Why what have you done?"

"Rien."

"Sergeant Friedmann thinks you might be able to help us. He'd like a word."

"Friedmann! Il essaie toujours de me mettre des choses. Here is two words for Friedmann, 'fuck off'."

"Henri, Henri that's no way to answer a polite request."

"Bon. I finish my drink and we go." In one swift movement he lifted the glass, poured the whisky down his throat, replaced the glass on the bar, swung his fist into Schwartz's face, and ran out of the bar.

Weber pressed the panic button on his radio.

As Cousteau turned left out of the bar he came face to face with four uniforms carrying batons. It took fifteen minutes to get him handcuffed and into the van. Two officers sat on the ground nursing bruised faces and arms.

"Did you charge him Weber?"

"No, Sarge, thought you might want a word with him before he calls his lawyer."

"Good man."

"Henri, welcome to police headquarters. Oh but you've been here so many times before, so it must be like coming home."

Cousteau struggled against the handcuffs holding his hands and arms around the back of the chair. He pushed with both powerful legs, but the chair didn't move.

"Stop struggling, Henri. Perhaps you've not been in this interview room before. This is our special guest suite, with chair and table fastened to the floor. Reserved for violent guests, And it's been a long time since we had someone as violent as you."

"Va te faire enculer, Friedmann."

"Now, Henri we're not going to get anywhere if you're going to be like that."

"Va te faire foutre."

"Now you know that's physically impossible."

"Nique ta mère." Cousteau tuned his head and spit in three directions, but Friedmann, Weber and the constable were well out of range.

"You know, Henri, I only wanted to ask you a few questions, but now it's assaulting police officers."

"Je veux que mon avocat."

"Can you translate that, DC Weber?"

"No, Sarge."

"Sorry, we don't understand."

"Connard. I want my lawyer."

"But there are no charges ... yet. And your lawyer won't be much good to you this time. You're going to jail because there are no witnesses to intimidate. It's just a question of how much we charge you with. Assaulting two police officers, and GBH for breaking DC Schwartz's nose, are obvious, but who knows what else we could add to the list. Yes, I'm sure we could find some things to add to the charge sheet, don't you think, DC Weber?

"We did remove a knife from him."

"Nothing wrong with a penknife, Weber."

"A 20 cm hunting knife, Sarge."

"An offensive weapon."

"That was in a ... a gaine on my belt. There is no law against."

"Did he threaten you with the knife?"

"Yes, Sarge."

"That is a lie."

"We haven't searched him yet, Sarge, perhaps he's carrying drugs."

"Salaud ... miststück ... bastard."

"Merci, dankeschön, thank you. So, assault, GBH, threatening with an offensive weapon, possession of drugs - should be enough to put you away for few years."

"Coup monté."

"Is it? Sounds like all solid evidence to me, doesn't it to you, DC Weber."

"Yes, sir."

"And, once you're charged I can keep you here while I investigate another incident."

"Coup monté encore. Flics, vous êtes tous corrompus."

"Oh this is not a frame up, I know you did this, I just have to get the evidence."

Cousteau looked wary

"Find some witnesses."

"Cousteau smiled and shook his head."

"I hope I'll be able to talk to Felix in a few days.

"Cousteau jerked back in the chair as if he'd had a heavy slap across the face.

"And you'd better hope I can talk to him, because if I can't the charge will be murder. So, who put you up to this, Henri?"

"I want my lawyer."

"You'll go down for this Henri and whoever ordered it will go scot free."

"I want my lawyer."

"Was it Gazda?"

"I don't know–"

"any Gazda, of course not. Charge him, DC Weber, search him and let him call his lawyer. Be careful, we've already seen what he can do."

"Yes, Sarge."

"Get ... get some help, get ... KFR, it's about time they did something for us. Ask Sergeant Grindel to join us and, Weber, don't tell him who we've got in custody, it might frighten him off."

"Are you OK, Sarge."

"Yes ... yes thank you, Weber."

"You look as though you've seen a ghost."

"Not a ghost, Weber. Someone from Sergeant Grindel's past. You made the first arrest of Mr Cousteau didn't you, Walter?"

"What? ... eh ... yes, the first arrest."

"Come back and see me Walter, once you've got Mr Cousteau nicely tucked up in a cell?"

"Was he any trouble?"

"Struggled a bit, but we kept the cuffs on him until he was in the cell. His lawyer's calmed him down.

"Good. Walter, would you personally take charge of Cousteau? I'm–"

"Me?"

"Let me explain. I'm going to charge him with the attack on Felix Braun, but–"

"How is–""

"but I need time to assemble the evidence. In particular I need to talk to Braun."

"Where is Braun?"

"Weber and I are the only two people who know and I want to keep it that way at the moment. I think we might have a mole. And that's why I would like you to take charge of Cousteau. I want as few people as possible to come into contact with him, preferably no one else but you for the next few hours."

Jochim stared at the words on the screen Braun died 22:15.

"Walter, get Cousteau up here."

"Has something happened?"

"Just get him up here, please."

"Any suggestions of how we handle this Peter?"

DC Weber knew when his boss asked for suggestions it was a genuine request. "I don't think we'll get anything out him with softly, softly."

Jochim nodded.

"Good cop, bad cop?"

"Let's see how it goes. Keep an eye on Grindel."

"Any particular reason?"

"Just a gut feeling."

Grindel pushed Cousteau into the room. He'd added a chain between the Frenchman's ankles, but Cousteau was still struggling as much as he could. Grindel plonked him onto the chair and fastened the handcuffs to the restraint already there.

"Welcome back, Henri."

"My lawyer should be always with me after charges. I know my rights."

"Glad to see you've dropped the French. You should know your rights you've been our guest often enough. But this interview is not about the charges. This is something new."

"Another fit up."

"Felix Braun died 30 minutes ago." Jochim kept his eyes on Cousteau, but had positioned himself so he had Grindel in his peripheral vision.

Cousteau looked pleased. Grindel struggled to hide absolute fear.

"Now the charge is murder."

"Prove it, nique ta mère."

"Oh, I'll prove it."

"Connard."

"Who put you up to this, Henri?"

"Va te faire enculer."

"I know you're a thug Henri, but I didn't think you were stupid also. They're going to be free and enjoying life, while you're inside. And, after what you did to Felix Braun, I'm going to make sure you're there for a long, long time."

"Va te faire foutre." Lower quality restraints would have given way against Cousteau's massive struggle.

Weber patted Cousteau's shoulder. "Henri, look, we know this was not your idea. If you tell us who gave the orders it could have an influence when it comes to sentencing. Why should you carry all the can?"

Silence.

Jochim saw Grindel was about to say something and he motioned him to be quiet.

"So, Henri, what about it?"

Cousteau stared at Weber "You don't understand French? I just told your boss to go fuck himself. You can do the same." Another futile struggle.

Jochim drummed his fingers on the desk. "You'd better calm down Henri or you'll do yourself an injury and we wouldn't want that, would we, Sergeant Grindel?"

"No." Grindel's voice was barely audible.

"Besides you don't have to give us a name. We already know who gives the orders."

Cousteau slowly shook his head. Grindel blinked rapidly twice and bit his bottom lip.

Jochim let the silence hang. The only sound was the constant rattling of chains as Cousteau continued to struggle. "I want my lawyer, connard."

"All in good time, Henri, all in good time."

"Now, connard."

"I think we'd better let him cool off downstairs for a while. We'll charge him later. Take him away, Sergeant Grindel."

"I'll come with you."

"That's OK Weber, He won't give any trouble with these chains round his ankles."

"What the hell happened, Walter?" Jochim was having to hold himself back from grabbing Grindel by the lapels.

"We got to the top of the stairs and he stopped, as he had done before, to adjust his position to be able to take each step with the restricted movement he had. He stumbled forward. I reached out to pull him back, but it was too late. He hit his head on the wall on the way down. The blood pooled around his head as soon as he hit the bottom. He was dead before I reached him."

"Shit."

"Probably what he deserved after what he did to Braun."

"I think he might have talked eventually."

"But you said you already know who gave him the orders."

"But I can't prove it at the moment." Jochim sighed and shook his head. "Go sort out the paperwork, Walter, we'll talk later."

As soon as Grindel closed the door Jochim spoke urgently to Weber. "Peter, get me the CCTV tape."

"I'll have technical send it up."

"No, go down there yourself and get it now."

The CCTV system within Zurich Police Headquarters was state of the art. Friedmann and Weber watched at normal speed. Grindel's description of what happened seemed accurate.

"OK, half speed and close-in on waist up."

Weber adjusted the controls.

They stared at the screen.

"There."

Weber pressed STOP.

"Is Cousteau saying something to Grindel?"

"I can't see anything on the sound track."

"OK, go on."

The picture jerked forward.

"What's that?

Again Webber hit STOP.

"Go back a couple of frames ... Grindel nudges Cousteau."

"Let me zoom in and slow it down ... the picture quality gets worse, but there is certainly contact."

"Go on ... Cousteau stumbles ... Grindel reaches out ... but not to save him, there's another push, harder this time. Do you agree?"

"Let's have another look ... yes, definitely."

"Cousteau bounces from side to side down the stairs, like a pinball. With his hands handcuffed behind his back he can't stop himself ... and look there, he hits his head twice on the way down and lands on it at the bottom."

"Grindel killed him?"

Friedmann nodded.

"You said before that you had a gut feeling about Grindel."

"About something else. I'll tell you later. Run this again at normal speed and then ask Sergeant Walter Grindel to join us. Oh, and get the technical boys to see if they can do anything with the sound, I'm sure Cousteau said something to Grindel just before he pushed him."

"Walter, I thought you'd like to see the CCTV of what happened with Cousteau."

Grindel sat bolt upright and stared at the screen, his face void of any emotion. "Exactly as I told you. He stumbled, I reached out to stop him, he fell down the stairs."

"That's certainly the way it looks. Did Cousteau say anything to you?"

"He isn't, wasn't, exactly the talkative type."

"True. Run the slower version of the tape Peter."

This time Grindel could not hold back a twitch at some points.

"A different picture?"

"Not really."

"I think you pushed him."

"You can think what you like, Friedmann. Can you prove it?"

"The tape proves it."

"Tapes can be doctored."

"This one wasn't."

"Cousteau was a scumbag, there won't be too many people weeping at his death. Was there anything else, Friedmann, I've got things to do."

"Sit down, Walter."

"I haven't got time for this."

"I said sit down. I know you did this and I know why."

"Tell me."

"No, you'll tell me and a lot more."

"Just who do you think you are, Fried–"

A single knock and a head appearing round the door halted the conversation. "Sergeant Friedmann, you asked me to interrupt you if I had any information."

"Wait there, Constable. Excuse me Walter. Peter, make sure Sergeant Grindel remains our guest."

Friedmann went out, closing the door behind him. He returned within one minute holding a piece of paper.

"Do you know who that was, Walter?"

Silence.

"Constable Schneider, one of our technical whizz kids. He's been able to enhance the sound on the tape: don't ask me how. It seems that Cousteau did say something to you. Funny you don't remember. It was just before he 'accidently' fell down the stairs. These are the exact words." Friedmann unfolded the paper and read. "'Tu ferais mieux de faire quelque chose ou tu vas avec moi'. Excuse my French. Schneider speaks French, so he's provided a translation, 'You'd better do something or you're going down with me'. I wonder what he meant."

Grindel moved quickly for a man of fifty and managed to get his hand on the doorknob before DC Weber placed his large frame in front of him. "Going somewhere Sergeant?"

Not surprisingly news of the death of someone in custody, spread quickly through police HQ. News, that is, of Cousteau falling down the stairs. Only Friedmann and Weber knew what the slow motion version of the CCTV tape and the translated, enhanced voice recording 'suggested'. Instructions of how to handle it came to Friedmann from Chief Inspector Müller via Inspector Kullmer: put a lid on it.

With Felix Braun and Henri Cousteau dead, Grindel was the last real lead Friedmann had to Gazda, and tying up the prostitution and abduction 'cases'. So, 'put a lid on it' was not what he told Grindel. "My bosses, your ex-bosses, want to show how they handle police corruption. The CCTV footage means you'll be going away for a very long time."

Grindel hadn't forgotten about the CCTV, but judged, or misjudged, the camera and microphone were too far away.

So, what now? He was well aware what happened to police officers in prison. Would Gazda be able to do something to help him? Why would he even try? Grindel was sure he was a useful, but a disposable cog in Gazda's organisation. The obvious thing to do was to try swopping what he knew for some leniency. But Gazda's world didn't treat informers lightly. He decided the chances of escaping Gazda's revenge were higher than finding somewhere to hide in prison.

Confession

9 November to 13 November 2008

"You wanted to talk to me, Mr Grindel."

Grindel noted the 'Mr', and that Friedmann was alone. "Yes Sergeant Friedmann."

Silence.

"So, talk."

"A trial could get messy."

"Very messy for you."

"Embarrassing for the force."

Silence.

"No, one's going to miss those low lives Braun and Cousteau, so why should the force cause itself trouble?"

Silence.

Friedmann switched off the interview recording system.

"I could give you a name."

"A name?"

"Someone ordered the attack on Braun."

"You?"

"No, I arranged it, not ordered it."

"You want to swap what you know for ... for what?"

"That'll be up to you and our– your bosses to decide."

"Full confession with no promises?"

Grindel stared at Friedmann and took a couple of deep breaths. "Full confession with no promises."

Now Friedmann stared. He tried and succeeded to keep a smile from appearing. "OK, Walter, let's see what you've got. You killed Henri Cousteau."

"He was threatening to expose me and–"

"And now you're fully exposed, ironic."

"The attack on Braun was–"

"Ordered by Gazda."

Grindel's eyes widened. He smiled and nodded. "How much do you know Jochim?"

"Quite a bit, but with details missing. You can fill those in Walter. Who is Gazda?"

"I only know him as Gazda."

"You've met him?"

"No."

"How do you contact him?"

"Telephone."

"Number?"

"0795241892."

Friedmann dialled.

Grindel's eyes were wide again, not with surprise, but fear. "Don't call him now."

"Why?"

"Because ... because ..."

"Don't worry you won't have to talk to him."

The ringing stopped, 'The number you are calling is no longer in service'.

Grindel's face and body relaxed. "He does that regularly. Next time he calls me he gives me a new number."

"I believe you. You'd better check your trousers."

"You can get a name and address from the telephone company."

Friedmann shook his head. "Walter, reengage your police brain. They're not allowed to give me the information without a court order, and I'd only get that if I've arrested someone. You aren't arrested ... yet."

Silence.

"So, is that all you're offering, Gazda's telephone number?"

"Tell me what else you want."

"I want Gazda. Tell me about him. How did you start working for him? Why? When?"

"Why is easy, money. I have ... had commitments. When? A few years ago. I got a call in the office giving me a number to call in the evening. That number is also no longer in operation. He said he needed ears in police HQ, just ears. To pass on any information that might affect his business interests. I'd get 500 francs a week, even if I didn't have anything to tell him."

"Did he say what those business interests were?"

"Not specifically, but he said anything about Niederdorfstrasse or Langstrasse would be interesting."

"And that's all you've done for him, pass on information?"

Grindel tried to avoid the pause, but failed. "Yes."

"Yes?"

"A few times there were some little extra things, always a few hundred extra francs in the envelope. But there was nothing involving violence."

"Until now."

"Until now."

"So, what else do you do for him?"

Grindel shrugged. "Using the uniform to frighten people."

"Any specific examples?"

"None that would be relevant to finding Gazda."

"'Full confession' remember Walter."

"I haven't forgotten."

"What about Lisa Stern?"

"Lisa? ... Lisa Stern? I don't—"

Friedmann slowly shook his head.

"I got a call. There would two people waking up in the Hotel zum Kirsch that had to be stopped ... no, not stopped, discouraged from finding out how they got there."

"Who was the call from? Gazda?"

"Yes."

"How do you know it was him each time? Did you have a password?"

"No. His voice always sounded ... strange."

"Strange?"

"Distorted, as though he was speaking through something ... a cloth perhaps."

"So, you went to the hotel, with DC Schmidt I think. Is he one of Gazda's also?"

"No. I took him along in case it went further, so I could show we acted correctly."

"And you succeeded in 'discouraging' them?"

"We didn't hear any more from them."

"Until Ms Stern's claim of abduction."

Grindel studied Friedmann. "I didn't know about that until they turned up at the station."

"And you did a good job, a very good job, in 'discouraging' them again. Did you tell Gazda?"

"Yes."

"Did you also tell him about Ms Sameli?"

"Who?"

"Erna Sameli."

"I don't know any Erna Sameli."

She was with Lisa Stern on the night of the second abduction."

"How do you know so much about what happened with Ms Stern? It's not on the record."

"And now I understand why. Ms Stern told you she'd been to The Celler?"

"Yes."

"You know that André Wissler, the footballer, owns The Celler, and that Lisa Stern is his ex-wife."

"I didn't know about her being his ex-wife when I interviewed her. You told me when you came to my office."

"Ah, yes, I remember you being a bit shocked."

"Could Wissler be Gazda?"

"No ... no, impossible."

"Why 'impossible'? You know him?"

"No ... I ..."

"So what have we got? On–"

"I've just remembered, Erna Sameli claimed she'd seen something about the taxi or the taxi driver that picked up Ms Stern. It was in a report ... a report by Constable Menna. Gazda just happened to call me that day. I told him about the report because of the connection with Ms Stern and Mr McLendi's visit to the station."

"Did you give him any contact details for Ms Sameli?"

"I didn't have any contact details."

"Do you know about the attack on Ms Sameli?"

"What? ... I'd ... I'd no idea."

" OK, where was I? ... On ..." Friedmann looked at his notes. "On 6 September you get a call from Gazda telling you about Lisa Stern and Christopher McLendi in the hotel. You manage to dissuade them from continuing their claims of abduction. On 28 September Ms Stern and Mr McLendi make more claims of abduction. You didn't know about this second abduction?"

"No. I'd left a note on the file that I should be contacted if these two turned up at the station. I wasn't on duty, but fortunately the front desk constable called me before getting someone to talk to them. Just after they left I got a call from Gazda telling me to expect them."

"Conclusion from all this?"

"What happened to Ms Stern and Mr McLendi involves Gazda."

"And Wissler is Gazda."

"No ... no ... he can't be."

"You seem sure, which I don't understand. We'll come back to it. So, where does that leave us?"

Grindel shrugged.

"If I'm going to persuade Müller to make a deal I'm going to need more than we've got at the moment."

"I don't know much more."

"Much more?"

"Any more."

"So you don't have any other contact with Gazda except through the telephone calls?"

"Correct."

"You know anyone else in Gazda's organisation?"

"I assume this Felix Braun, but I know nothing about him."

"What about Heinrich Sommers, the manager of The Lipstick Club?"

"I don't know him. Roth told me you interviewed him."

"He claims not to know who owns The Lipstick Club and has never heard the name Gazda."

Grindel shook his head.

"What about the telephone calls? Was there anything in the background to give a clue where he could be?"

Grindel thought. "No, not that I remember. There was always no background noise ... except ... except when he called about the raid."

"That would be on the morning of 17 September?"

"Yes. I could hardly hear him. There was the clinking of glass. I thought he might be in a bar."

"Any voices?"

"No, except there was a loudspeaker announcement ... in German."

Friedmann surveyed his notes once again. "So, no sound of a football crowd?"

Grindel shook his head.

"I still think it's Wissler. It all fits."

Grindel sighed. "It can't be ... can't be ... can't be."

"That sounded like a little doubt creeping in."

An even bigger sigh. "There's something I should tell you ... I ..."

"Spit it out, Walter."

"I'm André Wissler's father."

Friedmann looked up from his notes and blinked, twice. "You're what?"

"André Wissler's father."

"Does he know?"

"No."

"How? Well I know 'how', but ..."

"I was very shy when I was growing up, still am. When it came to girls I never got past the first meeting. I sweated and mumbled; they must have thought I was an idiot. But I had urges, of course. Discovering prostitution was like a dream come true. There was no need to find the right words and spend time meeting before getting anywhere near sex, and possible rejection. I decided quiet early that was the best life for me. That's why I've never married. I know there are rumours about me being queer, but it's not true. It was a bit cold at first of course, paying the money before the pleasure. But after a while I had my 'regular' ladies and there was a certain ... what shall I call it? ... friendliness.

"Twenty-seven years ago I met Krystal, André's mother. She was only 19 and I fell in love with her, or as much as I've ever thought I've fallen in love. We sometimes met at least once a week at the Hotel Stein. She always insisted that all her clients wore a condom. I was no exception. When she became pregnant I counted back because I was late putting it on one time. The dates matched exactly. She told me I was not the father, but I knew I was. She gave up prostitution and I sent her what I could afford until André got his first job. Extra money from Gazda came in useful."

"So, you're Uncle Walter."

"You know a lot, Friedmann."

"Oh, I didn't know that. Wissler told me his uncle Walter was his biggest fan.

"And I didn't know about André's marriage to Lisa Stern. How could I have missed that? Oh, I knew he married in England, but when he came back my occasional visits ended. I could only telephone him."

"You know that he missed the 2006 World Cup?"

"Yes, he was devastated."

"Did he tell you why?"

"No, I don't think so."

"He blamed the loss of form resulting from the stress caused by the divorce from Lisa Stern."

"And you think he told me to go to the hotel and frighten Lisa Stern and ..."

"Mr McLendi,"."

"Mr McLendi because he missed the World Cup?"

"Pretty important to someone like André Wissler, don't you think?"

"Not after two years."

"So, you don't believe your son is Gazda?"

"No."

"There seemed to be some doubt creeping in a few minutes ago"

A shake of the head. "No ... no."

"Let's try this. Supposing Wissler found out you are his father, recruiting you would have been an obvious choice. He could always have blackmailed you if you didn't cooperate."

"His voice is not the same."

"You said it was distorted."

"Yes, but–"

"What I don't understand is why Gazda got you to organise the attack on Braun. You supplied him with information, not arranged attacks on people. Why didn't Gazda do it himself, he must have the contacts? Probably Henri Cousteau has done jobs for him before."

"I told Gazda I didn't want to do it."

"He doesn't sound like the sort of person you say no to."

"He said it was a special favour for him, with the threat of disclosing my involvement with him. My guess is that he wanted to distance himself as much as possible. He probably knew you talked to Braun, and I told him there was a POA out."

Friedmann nodded. "So, you told Henri Cousteau to go after Braun. How did you know to contact The Mad Frog?"

"I arrested him, twice. Both times I got messages to him in the cells that Gazda would take care of things."

"Cousteau didn't complete the job, and we arrested him. You stopped him disclosing your involvement. Gazda will find out we arrested Cousteau. What will he do?"

"Call me?"

"Yes, if I were him I'd like to hear what you have to say. It's four days since he told you to have Felix Braun killed. He must be getting anxious. Where will he call you?"

"At home."

"OK, I have to talk to Müller and Kullmer."

In fact, Jochim didn't need to talk to Müller or Kullmer. He simply told the technical people that Sergeant Grindel was working on a confidential case and needed calls to his home telephone transferred to a new mobile.

"So, do I go home and wait for a call from Gazda?"

"Not quite. You'll be safer here. You'll have a mobile 'phone linked to your home number. When Gazda calls keep him talking and we'll try to trace his location."

"You don't keep Gazda talking."

"Do your best. Here's how we'll play it ..."

The mobile 'phone was in Grindel's hand for five minutes when it rang. Friedmann counted down from ten and signalled Grindel to answer.

"Hello."

"Walter, Walter so good to hear you, at last. Where the fuck have you been?"

"Gazda ... I ... I ..."

Silence.

"Felix Braun is dead."

"Good. That's just what I wanted to hear."

"They arrested Henri Cousteau."

Silence.

"Gazda, are you still there?"

"Tell me something I don't know Walter."

"He's dead."

"Can you do anything to stop him talki– What did you say?"

"He had a little accident."

"Did you see him?"

Grindel turned his back on Friedmann: it was easier to sound like the Walter Grindel Gazda knew. "I ... I was with him when the accident happened."

"Walter, you didn't do anything unfriendly, did you?"

"I think he was ready to give Friedmann some names."

"Well done Walter, I didn't think you had it in you. Does anyone suspect you?"

"As I said, it was an accident."

"OK, I'll be in contact."

Friedmann rushed round the desk and urged Grindel to keep talking.

"Gazda ... there's something else."

"What?"

Grindel hesitated.

Friedmann nodded.

"Friedmann knows your name."

Silence.

"What else does he know?"

"He told Cousteau he knew you'd ordered the attack on Felix Braun."

Silence.

"Anything else?

"No."

"Does Friedmann have any idea you're in contact with me?"

"I'm sure not."

"OK, keep your ear to the ground."

The line went dead.

Friedmann spoke into the 'phone' connected to the technicians. "Did we get a trace?" He nodded.

"Well?"

"Not long enough to be accurate. Somewhere in the region north-east of Zurich.

Jochim played the tape of the conversation between Grindel and Gazda. Müller and Kullmer looked puzzled, confused, shocked and angry all at the same time.

The tape finished, Müller was silent for 30 seconds. "I think you have some explaining to do, Sergeant Friedmann."

"Yes, sir." Jochim reviewed the raid on The Celler, Felix Braun's involvement and the name Gazda coming up."

"This raid on The Celler was some time ago wasn't it?"

"Sixteenth of September, sir."

"And it's taken all this time to find out who this Gazda is? Did you know about this, Kullmer?"

"Of course, sir." Kullmer's stare at Jochim said 'contradict me at your peril'. "but I did not consider this case to be high priority."

"And following Inspector Kullmer's orders sir, we've been picking up small pieces of information. We still don't know the identity of Gazda, but we've had a breakthrough." Jochim told them about the deaths of Francesca Kardomah and Felix Braun, and his suspicion that Gazda was responsible.

"It sounds that way from the tape, but who is the other person?"

Kullmer saw an opportunity to involve himself. "If I'm not mistaken, that's Sergeant Walter Grindel."

"Our Sergeant Grindel?"

Kullmer looked to Jochim. "Yes, sir our Sergeant Grindel. That's the breakthrough I mentioned.

"You're telling me one of our officers has been supplying information to this Gazda?"

"Yes, sir."

"And where is he now?"

"We have him in custody sir. The conversation you just heard took place with us listening."

"So, he's confessed and now he's helping us?"

"The information he'd given Gazda until now was insignificant. He told Gazda that we were going to arrest Felix Braun for the murder of Francesca Kardomah, and Gazda said Braun must be silenced, permanently. I think Grindel was so disgusted by what happened to Felix Braun, and Francesca Kardomah that he didn't want to have anything more to do with Gazda."

"And we arrested Cousteau for the murder of Braun."

"As Inspector Kullmer says, sir, we arrested Henri Cousteau."

"Who was the person who died in custody."

"Yes, sir."

"Well your tape seems to confirm Gazda's involvement in the murder of Felix Braun, but why would Grindel imply that he had caused Cousteau's 'accident'?

"My idea, sir. So Grindel keeps Gazda's confidence."

"But it was an accident?"

"Yes, sir."

They agreed the arrest of Gazda should now be their number one priority.

Müller asked Friedmann how he wanted to proceed.

"We keep Grindel in custody and wait for Gazda to call, which, now he knows we suspect his involvement, I'm sure he will."

"I suggest we get Grindel out of HQ ... put him in the witness protection programme. He'll be more comfortable and perhaps more cooperative. There'll also be fewer people know what's going on. I'll talk to the WPP squad."

"OK, Sir if you think that's the best way to handle it." Friedmann smiled to himself: that's exactly what he wanted.

After the attack on Felix, interviewing Herman Zubke should have been high on Friedmann's list. He'd hoped that Sommers and Braun would have given him something to pressure Zubke into revealing the name of the owner of the Lipstick Club. The death of Felix Bruhn meant the interview was high priority. The confession of Walter Grindel to killing Henri Cousteau, and getting Grindel in the WPP delayed it by 36 hours.

"Mr Zubke, Sergeant Jochim Friedmann, we spoke on the telephone last month."

"Did we, Sergeant?"

"Yes, about The Celler."

"Ah yes, I remember. As you know, I sold The Celler over a year ago."

"Yes I know, but I'm calling about another club you own, The Lipstick Club."

"The Lipstick Club ... what ... what about it?"

"Come, come, Mr Zubke. You know what happened."

"I heard there'd been some trouble. I'm not involved with the day-to-day running of the Club and what happens there."

"Well you'd better start getting involved, Mr Zubke. I want you to come to KRIPO at three o'clock this afternoon."

"I'm afraid that's impossible, Sergeant, I have client meetin–"

"Mr Zubke, I'm conducting a murder inquiry. A murder that happened in your club. Now, you either come to the station as requested, or I send some blue flashing lights to collect you."

"Please take a seat, Mr Zubke."

"I hope this is not going to take long, Sergeant Friedmann. I've had to postpone meetings with some very important clients."

"Do you also 'own' brothels on their behalf, Mr Zubke?"

"Sergeant, I really must protes–"

"Save your breath, Mr Zubke." Jochim steepled his fingers and stared at Zubke.

"You can't treat me like this. I'm not a criminal."

"The murder of Felix Braun was in the toilet of The Lipstick Club. As long as you insist on telling me you're the owner of the club, that puts you high on my list of people I want to talk to."

"I don't know any Felix Braun."

"That's possible. It's also possible you don't know the club's a brothel. What's not possible is that you're the real owner of The

Lipstick Club, but it's possible the real owner does or did know Felix Braun. So ..."

"You know I can't break client confidentiality."

"Unless we suspect the client of committing a crime."

"You have to present the evidence to a jud–"

"I know what I have to do, Mr Zubke."

Zubke sat back in his chair, rested his elbows on the arms and interlaced his fingers.

Jochim gave two short pushes on the doorbell. Out of the corner of his eye he saw the curtains flutter. He waited thirty seconds. Now his finger attached itself to the bell push.

"All right, all right, don't wake up the whole block."

"Anto. Good morning. Did I get you out of bed?"

"What do you want, Friedmann?"

"Ah, you remembered my name. Good start. Let's hope the return of your memory continues. Can I come in?"

Anto pulled the belt of his dressing gown tighter and glanced up and down the corridor.

"Heard from Gazda recently?"

"I told you I–"

"Yes I know, you don't know any Gazda. Unless you're Gazda. Did you hear about your friend Felix?"

"He is not my friend."

"Not any more he isn't, he died after been beaten up."

Even Anto's practised, tough-guy scowl could not hide his shock. "Beaten up?"

"More than beaten up, somebody tried to kill him. He finally died six days ago."

"You don't think I had anything to–"

"Somebody ordered it. Probably Gazda."

Anto shook his head.

"The attack happened at a place run by another friend of yours, The Lipstick Club."

"I never said Heinrich Sommers was a friend of mine."

"You don't seem to have many friends Anto. What about Henri Cousteau?"

"Who?"

"Perhaps you know him as the mad frog?"

"I've no idea–"

"Of course not, but somebody hired Henri to kill Felix."

"Where is this Cousteau now?"

"Worried Anto? Thinking you could be next if you talk?"

"I've got nothing to worry about."

"If you're Gazda, no. If you're not, then as long as Gazda thinks you haven't told me anything you don't have anything to worry about, but if he heard you had. On the other hand if you don't know Gazda now, but he gets to hear about our conversation, you might become acquainted with him or one of his associates, like the mad frog."

"You live in a complicated world, Sergeant."

"Help me simplify it."

"I'm not this Gazda and I don't know any Gazda."

Friedmann's face was expressionless. He slowly started to shake his head.

Anto returned the look and movement.

Thirty seconds ticked by. Friedmann turned and took two paces. "See you at the station."

Anto's voice was barely above a whisper. "I can't see the inside of a prison cell again."

Friedmann halted.

"If I knew anything I would tell you, believe me, I would tell you. I've had enough of prison cells."

Friedmann turned. Only the hint of movement at the corners of his mouth betrayed the smile in his head. He stepped towards Dedeić, who seemed to have shrunk. "Let's talk about your Serbo-Croatian contacts."

"I don't–"

Friedmann's smile was full. "No? You and your sister arrived in Switzerland from Yugoslavia?"

"We fled from the Nazis. Not that I remember anything about it, I was only six months old at the time. An air raid killed our parents and grandparents."

"And your sister later married."

"Yes."

"Did you have contacts with people from Yugoslavia?"

"No. My sister's husband wanted the four us to be Swiss. He–"

"Four?"

"My sister had baby a year after they married. Her husband wouldn't even allow us to speak Serbo-Croatian at home. It was only after he died that we had contact with the Serbo-Croatian community in Zurich."

"And in prison."

"Yes, and in prison."

"And you never heard the name Gazda in that community? It means chief or boss in Serbo-Croatian as far as I understand."

"I never heard it."

"Why don't you ask around? Someone may have heard it. You'd be doing me a favour."

Dedeić's expression suggested that this prospect did not fill him with joy.

"I don't forget people who do me favours. ... And you don't need to worry about the mad frog, he had a little accident, a fatal one. ... Here's my direct number, just say you want to meet."

"I can't promise anything."

"Of course not." Friedmann turned to go. "Oh, by the way do you know Herman Zubke?"

Dedeić's need to appear cooperative made the words start to come out before the brain called a halt. "I met him– no, I don't know the name."

"You don't know the name, but you met him?"

"No, I've never met him."

Friedman went back to expressionless staring and head shaking.

"I ... I don't know him. I remember the unusual name. I met him at a party some years ago."

"I wouldn't have expected you to be at the same party as an expensive lawyer. Whose party was it?"

"I don't remember."

"Anto, Anto, just as I was beginning to think we were getting along you lose your memory again. Perhaps that visit to the stat–"

"OK, OK it was a party at my lawyer's house."

"And who is your lawyer?"

"'Was' my lawyer, Arnold Baumgartner."

The call from Gazda came two days after Grindel entered the witness protection programme. Friedmann had the tape 30 minutes after the call.

```
"Walter?"
"Yes."
"Any news?"
"Friedmann's continuing his investigation."
"Who's he talking to?"
"I don't know, I'm not directly involved."
"I'm paying you to find out, Walter."
```

307

"I know Gazda, but Friedmann's playing it close. He's an ambitious bastard."

Friedmann smiled. That wasn't part of the script he'd agreed with Grindel, but it added some credibility to what he was telling Gazda.

"So, nothing?"

"I know from one of his DCs that Friedmann has linked the murder of Felix Braun to the raid on The Celler."

"Keep listening Walter."

Pooling Information

16 November to 19 November 2008

Jochim wanted to meet with Ms Stern and Mr McLendi again. Bea pointed out that they would have to separate facts and opinions for a discussion with them. They decided that Jochim would go through the interviews and events with Bea, and she would question him when something was not clear.

As before, they met at Lisa's apartment. Bea 'phoned Lisa the day before and suggested she would order a pizza delivery. Lisa and Christopher took this to mean it would be another 'unofficial' meeting.

Before the pizza arrived Jochim outlined what they wanted to do. "Ms Stern, I know you've been calling Constable Menna to find out what's going on. I can imagine hearing each time 'we are still investigating' was frustrating."

Lisa smiled and nodded.

"Many things have happened since we met. We want to bring you up to date. As you can imagine, when you're involved with something like this the brain takes in lots of information, and it's easy to start joining pieces that don't belong together and drawing conclusions. That's particularly true for me and for Bea also. We–"

"So Constable Menna's involved with the case also."

"Not directly Ms Stern, but ... but ..."

Bea could see Jochim's embarrassment creeping up his neck. "What Jochim is trying to say is that we are ... now I'm lost for words. What do you call it? Involved with each other? Sounds old-fashioned."

"A couple?" A smile and a nod passed between Lisa and Christopher.

"Thank you Ms Stern."

"Yes, we're a 'couple' as you put it, but that must also remain confidential. Could I also suggest that we think it might help our discussion if we were on first name terms. I'm Jochim."

"Bea."

"Lisa."

"Christopher."

They raised their glasses.

"OK, good. As I said–"

The door buzzer sounded. Lisa started to get up. Christopher waved her down "That'll be the pizza. I suggest we eat while it's hot."

Jochim could see from the speed with which Lisa ate her pizza that she was eager to hear what had been happening. "OK, as I said, we want to bring you up to date. This is not in chronological order. So if anything is not clear, please ask.

Lisa and Christopher nodded.

"The next step after we talked last was to follow up on Felix Braun. Braun was a local thug always getting into fights. While in prison for small-time drug dealing, he endeared himself to a Serbo-Croatian gang by beating up someone who had attacked one of their number. On Braun's release, the leader of the gang, Anto Dedeić, put him in contact with Juraj Herceg. Herceg set Braun up as a pimp working for this person Gazda, who I mentioned to you before."

"Not Swiss names."

"No, Christopher, Herceg was Croatian, Dedeić originally came from Yugoslavia, and Gazda means 'boss' or chief in Serbo-Croatian. In the area north-east of Zurich, Oerlikon, Wallisellen, Dietikon there's quite a concentration of people from the Balkan states. Dedeić and Herceg were almost neighbours. Unfortunately—"

Lisa raised her hand before she realised what she was doing. "Excuse me."

The other three gave little laughs and Lisa smiled. "I was just going to ask if you've talked to these people."

"Braun and Dedeić yes, but Herceg died, a week before Braun gave me his name. I'll come back to Dedeić in a moment. I'll let Bea tell you what happened next."

"One of the prostitutes taken in after the raid on The Celler, Francesca Kardomah, died. She—"

"Brutally murdered." Jochim took a deep breath.

"Jochim ... Jochim feels bad about it because someone must have found out she'd given him the names of Felix and Gazda."

"I should have done something to protect her."

"Jochim we talked about it. There's nothing you could have done."

Christopher was a little surprised to see the detective sergeant showing so much emotion. "So, this put the case in a different category."

"Yes ... it certainly did, especially when she told me with almost her last breath who'd attacked her."

Silence.

Jochim looked from Lisa to Christopher. "Felix Braun."

"So, you've arrested him."

311

"We didn't get the chance Lisa. Seems someone didn't want Braun arrested. He was found, barely alive, in The Lipstick Club eight hours after Francesca died."

"What? In the Lipstick Club."

"Yes, the same Club you went to' Christopher. Now you see why I said your venture into their world was not a good idea. These are not nice people."

"But it gets worse."

"As Bea says 'it gets worse'. Braun died six days later, without regaining consciousness. He was our big chance to get to Gazda, who we still believe is behind all this."

"Any idea who killed him?

"Oh we know who killed him, Christopher."

"There were witnesses?"

"You don't get witnesses when something like this happens."

"Then how?"

"An intuitive, clever piece of police work by Constable Beatrice Menna. Tell them, Bea."

"I managed to record one end of an interesting telephone conversation. Have a listen." She placed her 'phone on the table between them. Lisa and Christopher leant-in to hear.

Beep, beep, beep

Hello, hello. Sorry I couldn't talk before there was som–

Lisa and Christopher spoke together. "Sergeant Grindel?"

Bea and Jochim nodded.

As Lisa and Christopher listened they could not stop their eyebrows rising and their mouths opening. When the recording finished there was silence: Bea and Jochim smiling; Lisa and Christopher taking deep breaths and shaking their heads.

Lisa 'recovered' first. "Grindel, I knew–"

Quickly followed by Christopher. "That links Grindel, Felix and Gazda."

"I think they're impressed Bea, and rightly so. And don't forget Henri Cousteau, who tried to kill Felix Braun."

"I knew ... I knew Grindel was part of this. What did you do about him?"

"Nothing immediately."

"Nothing? But–"

"Just hold back on that for a moment, Lisa. You'll see why in just a moment."

Lisa didn't look pleased about 'holding back'.

"Henri Cousteau is a nasty piece of work. I haven't conducted many interviews with the person handcuffed to a bolted-down chair. We weren't getting anywhere with him so I sent him back to the cells to cool off, and I put Sergeant Grindel in charge of looking after him."

Lisa's outburst took everyone by surprise. "Grindel? Why? That sounds like the most stupid thing I've ever heard. I suppose he helped this Cousteau to escape. How stupid."

Christopher touched Lisa's arm. "I'm sure Jochim's going to explain.

"Bea's recording meant Grindel was the only person we definitely knew had direct contact with Gazda. I could have questioned him about it, but I don't imagine I'd have got very far. I thought it better to see how he reacted when he came face to face with Cousteau."

"Besides, the recording is not evidence of anyone committing a crime."

"Bea's right. As for Grindel helping Cousteau escape, the arrangement of the interview rooms and the cells makes it almost impossible."

Everyone looked towards Lisa. She was still fuming, but silent.

"So, how did he react?"

"You know the expression, Christopher, about a deer caught in the headlights, well this was the deer seconds before impact."

"I hope he had a heart attack."

"As you'll see, fortunately no."

Christopher shook his head. "I need a break. Who'd like some coffee?"

"Thanks Christopher, that would good."

"Jochim?"

"Yes, thanks."

"Shall I make it Lisa?"

"It's my kitchen, I'll make it."

"OK, I'll help."

"I got the news Braun had died, so I interviewed Cousteau again. Even though he was now facing a murder charge he still wasn't telling us anything. I sent him back to the cells to cool off."

"And did he?"

"He didn't have a chance to Christopher. He fell down the stairs, hit his head several times on the way down and was probably dead before he reached the bottom."

"So, another chance gone to get to this Gazda."

"Well ... yes ... and n–"

Bea jumped in. She had seen Jochim in this frame of mind on a couple of occasions before: dragging out a story for effect. "Cousteau's fall wasn't an accident."

"Grindel?"

"Yes, Lisa, well done. Grindel pushed him."

"How do you know?"

Jochim stared at Bea. He didn't like interruptions, but he recognised he was starting to get a bit carried away with the story. "We have the CCTV. Grindel knew about it, of course, but didn't realise how much we could zoom in and see the push, two pushes in fact. A bit of technical wizardry allowed us to hear Cousteau say to Grindel 'you'd better do something or you're going down with me'."

"Got him." Lisa's smile couldn't have been wider if she'd won the Lottery.

"Is the CCTV evidence good enough to charge him with murder?"

"Yes Christopher, but ... w–"

Bea knew he wouldn't like it, but she jumped in again. "Grindel realised he had the choice between prison and treatment as an ex-police officer, or cooperating with us, and running the risk of revenge by Gazda. He–"

"He chose cooperation." Jochim's nod and smile towards Bea surprised her by being warm.

Lisa was still beaming. "More coffee? I think I could also do with something a little stronger. Bea? Jochim?"

"We're not driving and no duty until tomorrow, so ... what do you think Bea?"

"OK with me."

"Cognac, cognac or cognac."

Bea and Jochim smiled. "Cognac please, Lisa."

Jochim described in detail his talks with Grindel. Lisa and Christopher sat in silence, sometimes with widening eyes at the revelations.

"He's never met Gazda and doesn't know how to contact him: Gazda telephones him. For example he got a call telling him to go to the Hotel zum Kirsch and 'discourage' the two people from following up how they got there."

Lisa and Christopher exchanged small nods and head shakes.

"He didn't know about your abduction, Lisa, until you turned up at the station. He just assumed he should do the same discouraging job. As far as—"

"What about Erna, Ms Sameli? Did he have anything to do with what happened to her?"

"I was just coming to that, Lisa. The answer is, not directly. Bea wrote a report after talking to Ms Sameli. Grindel told Gazda, but he didn't know about the attack."

"You believe him?"

"Yes.

Christopher refilled the glasses.

"Grindel knows that André Wissler owns The Celler, of course. It was a big shock to him, Lisa, to hear about your marriage to Wissler."

"Why? He wouldn't necessarily know us, unless he was a football fan."

"I'll come to an explanation for that in just a minute." Jochim paused. "You find yourselves in the hotel after visiting The Celler. Wissler owns The Celler. Gazda sends Grindel to The Celler. Is there a connection between Gazda and Wissler?"

"Or are Wissler and Gazda the same person?"

"A question we also asked Christopher."

Lisa and Christopher stared at Jochim.

"Let's just say it's a possibility. We'll be coming back to that later. Wissler buys The Celler from Lawyer Zubke, who is acting for a client. Zubke also 'owns' the Lipstick Club where the attack on Felix Braun took place. Gazda ordered the attack on Braun."

"Have you talked to Zubke, Jochim?"

"I talked to him. You know, Lisa, lawyer and client confidentiality is watertight in Switzerland. If we suspect the client has committed a crime the court can force the lawyer to reveal the name. Felix Braun is dead and there are no witnesses. There's nothing to link Zubke or the real owner to the murder. We don't have enough to go before a judge at the moment." He glanced at Bea again. "We haven't given up on getting something out of him."

Sips of cognac all round.

"I told you about Grindel's shock on hearing about Lisa and Wissler's marriage. He thought he knew a lot, everything, about Wissler ... his son."

Lisa slowly shook her head. Christopher frowned.

Jochim nodded towards Bea. She explained. "According to Grindel he was one of Krystal Wissler's clients. He's convinced himself he must be André's father. He sent money to her until André started work."

Lisa's head was still moving. "Does André know?"

"That Grindel's his father? Probably not. He knows him as Uncle Walter. Wissler told me Uncle Walter is his biggest fan. By the way Wissler also told me he has an Uncle Herman."

Lisa and Christopher looked puzzled.

"Herman Zubke?"

"I wonder, does this make the chances of Wissler and Gazda being the same person higher or lower?"

"You have lots of good questions Christopher. In my discussions with Grindel he dismissed the idea, as you might expect. Personally I think it's still more than possible."

"Where's Grindel now?"

"We're looking after him. He gives us a contact with Gazda." Jochim described the telephone call and their attempts to trace it."

Christopher looked puzzled. "What did you hope to achieve by telling Gazda you know he ordered the attacks on Felix Braun?"

"I want him to know we're getting close to him, and that he's no longer in the background."

Lisa felt the hair lifting in the nape of her neck. "Bea, do you think we, I'm, in any danger?"

"I don't think so. Jochim?"

"No. You've got nothing to do with Felix Braun, Cousteau or Grindel for that matter. And, as far as Gazda knows you have no knowledge of him."

Lisa looked far from convinced.

"I'm sure what happened with you was a minor irritation for him, not for you of course. Grindel's the only one to link him with the Felix Braun murder, so he's probably the one in real danger."

Lisa smiled.

"As long as he's in custody he'll be OK, but he might be good ... you never heard me say this ... good bait."

Lisa nodded. Christopher smiled and shook his head.

"So."

"So."

"So."

"So."

Silence.

"Last time we spoke, Jochim you said the links between the raid on The Celler and what happened to Lisa and me were tentative. Surely now there's a definite connection through Grindel and Gazda."

Bea nodded. "We agree. The question is how does that help us to get to the person responsible."

"Gazda you mean?"

"Yes, Lisa, Gazda."

"Wissler must be Gazda."

Three heads nodded. Jochim was the one who spoke. "OK, a possible conclusion. Can you talk us through it?"

Lisa looked slightly puzzled.

"Jochim means explain how you reason that out."

Lisa wanted to say 'intuition', but didn't think that would be acceptable to Jochim. She thought for a moment. "OK. For whatever reason Christopher and I ended up at The Celler on 5 September. Wissler, my ex-husband, saw us there and took the opportunity to take revenge for what he thinks I did to him during our divorce. He drugged us and put us in that hotel. That's the part I always found a bit difficult to believe: how would footballer André Wissler know how to do that? But if he's Gazda then ... . Gazda tells Grindel to go to the hotel. Who else but Wissler knew we were in the hotel? Wissler must be Gazda." Lisa sat back and folded her arms.

Three heads nodded.

Bea looked towards Jochim. He gestured for her to continue. "That's a conclusion we came to. The key is what you said Lisa. If Wissler did have you put there no one else knew you were in the hotel. If Wissler didn't do it, how did you get into the hotel? Assuming it wasn't voluntarily. Gazda, who is completely unknown to you, has you kidnapped and then tells Grindel to scare you off. Why? No, it doesn't make sense. Wissler must be Gazda."

Jochim cleared his throat. "Hmm."

Christopher frowned. "You don't seem a hundred per cent convinced."

"Ninety-nine per cent."

"And the one per cent?"

"I have difficulty seeing Wissler as someone who orders the killing of people, unless he's a real Jekyll and Hyde, but ... From what happened to Felix Braun we might assume that Gazda is the real owner of The Lipstick Club. If Wissler is Gazda why would he openly buy The Celler? Did he own it before, through Zubke, and bought it from himself for some reason? Tax? There has to be link between what happened to you two and Gazda. Otherwise, I agree with Bea, it doesn't make sense for Gazda to be suddenly involved. So, we conclude that Wissler is Gazda, but ... but what if Gazda is not Wissler, but someone Wissler knows?"

Frowns and silence.

Lisa took a deep breath. "Grindel?"

Jochim pressed his lips together. "From what he's told me so far, I think not."

Bea also took a deep breath. She stopped herself from saying 'aha'. "Zubke."

"Tell us Bea."

"Give me moment to work out why I said that."

Lisa and Christopher looked from Bea to Jochim and back to Bea.

"OK. We know Wissler bought The Celler from Zubke on a recommendation from a friend of his mothers. We know Wissler's mother was with him at Zubke's office. Wissler has an Uncle Herman. Could Zubke be Wissler's mother's friend and Uncle Herman?" Bea paused. She wasn't waiting for an answer, she was still collecting her thoughts. "Wissler saw Lisa and Christopher in The Celler. He saw they were a little drunk and having a good time. All the deep feelings of anger against Lisa resurfaced. Even though it was late he called Uncle Herman, who he looked on as a father-figure. Zubke knew about Lisa and thought it was about time she suffered some embarrassment. He arranged the Hotel zum Kirsch episode."

"So, Zubke is Gazda?"

"That's my conclusion Lisa. Jochim?"

"Could be. When I said 'someone Wissler knows' I wasn't thinking of Zubke, but it could be."

"Sorry, I have a couple of questions."

"Fire away Christopher."

"Does Wissler know what happened?"

"Possibly not. After Uncle Herman calmed him down he may have left The Celler."

"Does Wissler know Zubke is Gazda."

"Perhaps I can answer that, Bea. If this is the right scenario, and I stress if, I wouldn't think Wissler knows anything about Gazda."

"So, my ex-husband goes from someone who orders killings to a total innocent."

Christopher still looked puzzled. "Bea, is Zubke a prominent lawyer in Zurich or backstreet?"

"Prominent I would say."

"A prominent Swiss lawyer involved in prostitution and murder?"

"Well, his name's registered as the owner of The Lipstick Club."

"How does Wissler's mother know him?"

"Remember she was a prostitute."

"But even—"

"Perhaps ... no, that would be too much."

"Please, go ahead Lisa."

"No, I'm letting my imagination run away with me, Bea."

"Please."

"Could Zubke, Gazda, be Wissler's father?"

Three heads turned to Jochim. "Could be, he's the right age."

"So, when he heard I'd been asking questions at The Celler he had me kidnapped to protect Wissler, his son."

Christopher broke the silence. "So, now there are two suspects for Gazda, and two fathers for André Wissler. Are there any more candidates?"

"I don't know about candidates, but there is someone else who fits in somewhere. I mentioned before, Anto Dedeić, who arranged a job for Felix Braun when he came out of prison. As I've said several times, we have to be careful about fitting facts together to give us the conclusions we want, but Dedeić has the criminal connections."

"Is there any connection between Wissler and Dedeić?"

"Only a very tentative one, Christopher. Dedeić's lawyer is an associate of Herman Zubke."

Bea leafed through her pages of notes. "Jochim, what about what Heinrich Sommers told you, is that more significant now?"

"How?"

"Heinrich Sommers manages The Lipstick Club. He doesn't know who owns the club. He gets all his instructions through a lawyer. He was once, and only once, asked to reserve a table for four people who were to be guests of the club. He presumed the instruction came from the owner. The lawyer is the same lawyer who worked with Dedeić, and is an associate of Zubke."

Lisa looked puzzled. "Except for the lawyer I don't see the connection."

"The four 'gentlemen' were rowdy. They told one of the club's hostesses they were from 'the city with the best football team in Europe, Munich'."

Lisa clapped her hands. "Wissler's friends."

Silence. All four deep in thought.

Christopher stood up to stretch his legs. "Anyone a gambler?"

"No."

"No."

"No."

"Me neither. But if I were, of the three I'd put—"

"Three?"

"You just put Dedeić on the list as well as Wissler and Zubke."

"I don't think he's Gazda, or Wissler's father, but I do feel, and I wouldn't put it any stronger than that, he's involved."

"OK. I'd put my money on Wissler."

Silence.

"Anyone else want to place a bet?

Jochim stood, walked to the window and looked out. He turned and nodded. "All in, that's the expression they use in poker, on Wissler."

"I still can't believe my ex-husband's someone who gives orders to kill people, but I'd say Wissler."

Three pairs of eyes turned towards Bea.

"I'm going to stick with my flash of inspiration, Zubke, but I wouldn't go all in on that."

Jochim stopped pacing. "So, three and a half for Wissler."

"Now what?"

"That's obvious Christopher, Jochim arrests him."

"Would it be OK if I did it tomorrow, it's getting a bit late now, Lisa."

"I was joking."

"I know."

They all sat.

"Put some pressure on?"

"Yes, but how Christopher?"

"Intensive interrogation?"

"If he's the hardened criminal we're saying he is I doubt he would confess. And we're not allowed to use the thumbscrews anymore."

"In a situation like this we need some leverage, some evidence we can confront him with."

"Bea's right. We don't have that at the moment."

Silence.

Silence.

"Look, it's our job to find how to solve this. I'm sure Jochim would agree that you've been more than helpful in talking it through with us."

"Glad we could help." Christopher glanced at Lisa and saw narrow, hooded eyes and pursed lips. "I think you might have stirred the amateur detective in Lisa."

Jochim and Bea turned to Lisa. "Lisa?"

"Look, I know André Wissler better than anyone here. Maybe I can think of a way to ... I don't know what you'd call it."

"Identify a potential weak point."

"Something like that Bea."

"OK, let's all sleep on it. If you don't mind still being involved, why don't we meet again in a couple of days and see what we can come up with?"

Christopher looked at Lisa. She nodded. "OK."

"They could come to us Jochim?"

"Could do."

"We could cook something."

"No, that's not necessary."

"It'd be a pleasure Lisa. Jochim and I enjoy cooking together on the few occasions we get the chance."

"We do a mean spaghetti Bolognese."

"OK."

"Neither of us has duty on Wednesday night, would that be OK"

"OK with mc. Lisa?"

"OK."

Christopher placed his fork in the bowl and dabbed his lips with the napkin. "You were right, Jochim, you do a mean spaghetti Bolognese."

"It's Bea really, I'm just the kitchen hand."

"He's being unusually modest. He's at least the sous chef."

By unspoken agreement they'd eaten without mentioning Gazda. After Bea poured the second cup of coffee Christopher got them on the track they all wanted to be on. "Lisa and I had a discussion yesterday."

"Bea and I also."

"We've had second thoughts about André Wissler being Gazda."

Bea and Jochim exchanged glances.

"We, especially Lisa, don't think it can be him. Lisa?"

"I said before, I know André Wissler better than any of us. I just can't see him running prostitutes, and ordering killings. Unless he hid a side of his character from me for three years."

Bea fully expected Jochim to say something. She could see Lisa and Christopher looking uneasy. "So, who do you think is Gazda?"

This time it was Lisa and Christopher's turn to exchange glances. Christopher nodded.

"With what you've told us, we think it must be Zubke.'

Bea tried to minimise the smile starting to spread the corners of her mouth. "Jochim?"

Jochim slowly shook his head. "I agree."

Now Bea didn't try to hide the smile. "What? You were ... what was the expression you used ... 'all in on Wissler'."

"Men can change their minds also Bea."

"Yes, but—"

"I said before I had difficulty seeing Wissler in the role."

"But there's still something bothering me."

"What's that Christopher?"

"A prominent lawyer like Zubke openly owning places like The Celler and The Lipstick Club."

"What better way to disguise the truth than by hiding behind lawyer/client confidentiality."

"Bea's right. And, as we discussed before, even though someone tried to kill Felix Braun at The Lipstick Club, we don't have any evidence to link the owner to the murder."

"But you could still interview him as a suspect?"

"Yes Lisa I will be doing that. Without the thumbscrews of course."

Closing in

20 November to 22 November 2008

Being ordered back to police headquarters one week after his first visit did not please Herman Zubke. He hadn't consciously planned to arrive five minutes late, but finding a place to park in the centre of Zurich was difficult, as usual. Waiting in the reception for half an hour did not help his mood. Following the young WPC down the corridor to Friedmann's office calmed him in one way and excited him in another.

As they rounded a corner another uniformed WPC approached them. Bea smiled as she passed close to Zubke. He stopped, swallowed hard and felt his jaw drop. Images "Was ... was ..."

"Are you OK?" said his escort.

"I'm ... yes ... I'm ... who ... " He took a very deep breath and shook his head.

His escort knocked on the door labelled Sergeant J Friedmann, KRIPO.

"Come in."

Zubke was still shaking his head.

"Thank you constable. Sit down Herman. You don't mind me calling you Herman do you?"

"What ... I ..."

"Are you OK Herman? You look as though you've seen a ghost."

"OK? ... Yes ... yes ... OK."

Friedmann let Zubke see his smile. "Good. I asked you here–"

"Ordered Sergeant."

Zubke was recovering his composure, so Friedmann decided to plunge ahead. "The murder of Felix Braun–"

"Which as I told you, I know noth–"

Friedmann held up his hand. "Shut up and listen Zubke."

The lawyer flinched.

"There's a connection between the murder of Felix Braun in The Lipstick Club, and finding prostitutes in The Celler during the raid two months ago. That makes you, as the previous owner of The Celler and the current owner of The Lipstick Club, the link in the two cases I'm investigating. So, let's cut all the 'I don't know anything' crap and start helping me." Friedmann stood, rested his hands on the desk and leant towards Zubke. "Otherwise Herman, or is it Gazda, I'm going to make life more than difficult for you."

Friedmann was close enough to see any telltale signs in Zubke's eyes, nostrils or mouth. He saw some, but could not be sure they were because of Gazda's name or reaction to his aggressive approach. It would have been better to separate the two.

Zubke was silent.

"Well?"

Zubke shook his head. "I can't help you. I don't know anything." Zubke stopped expecting to Friedmann to say something.

Friedmann sat and starred.

"I don't know anything about prostitutes in The Celler, this Gazda, or the death of Felix Braun."

"The murder of Felix Braun."

"The murder–"

"We have the murderer."

"Good."

"Might not be so good for you when he starts talking."

"I can only repeat that I know nothing about the murder."

"OK, let's assume that's correct for the moment. Who did give the orders? The real owner of The Lipstick Club? You know who that is. So, if that's who the person we have in custody fingers, that makes you an accessory to murder by withholding the name. Or perhaps ... perhaps Andrè Wissler is at the centre of all this."

Zubke did a good job of controlling his face muscles, but his eyes gave Friedmann the reaction he was looking for. "Why ... why should he be?"

"Do you care."

"No, of course not." Zubke's eyes betrayed him again

"But you remember who Andrè Wissler is?"

"He's a footballer."

"You're a football fan, Herman?"

"Not particularly. His name's always in the papers."

"And ... "

"And?"

"Think, Herman, think."

Zubke squeezed his eyebrows together and wet his lips. "Wasn't he the one who bought The Celler?"

"Well done, Herman. Have you ever thought of acting? OK, Wissler doesn't want Braun saying who gave him permission to put the prostitutes in The Celler. He decides to warn him off. With me so far?"

"By killing him? Sounds a bit extreme."

"Perhaps the attack went wrong and Braun died."

Zubke shrugged. "Still nothing to do with me."

Friedmann pursed his lips. "No ... no ... unless ... unless ..."

Zubke was beginning to perspire. "Unless what, Sergeant? I really must be going be goi–" He started to rise.

"Unless Uncle Herman was the one who organised the attack on Braun for Wissler. Uncle Herman, known to all his friends as Gazda."

Friedmann wasn't sure how to interpret Zubke's shrug and sceptical look. Was it because he, Gazda, knew from Grindel that Henri Cousteau was dead. Or, because he knew that without any evidence Friedmann was on shaky ground. "I think another talk with Mr André Wissler would be interesting. What do you think, Herman?"

Silence.

"Oh well, goodbye, Herman or Gazda or whatever your name is, thank you for coming. We'll be seeing each other again."

"So, you've got Zubke on the ropes and you back off. Doesn't sound like the KRIPO sergeant I know."

"I just felt I'd stretched the elastic of 'what if' and 'suppose' far enough. If I went further and it snapped he would see there was nothing behind it, no evidence. He would retreat, composed, behind 'I don't know anything'. Letting him go leaves him wondering. As he runs what I said through in his head, he'll be trying to decide how much I really know. This will make him nervous. Nervous people make mistakes, and we need him to make a mistake. Being friendly at the end will only add to his confusion."

"How do you expect him to react?"

"If he's Gazda, he knows Henri Cousteau is dead so we won't be getting any information from him. If he's not, then he'll be warning Gazda, if he knows who he is. Either way I would expect Gazda to be calling Grindel. If Zubke doesn't know who Gazda is, he'll be wondering what this person might do next if he's already had one person killed. Whatever the situation what I said about André Wissler's involvement disturbed him."

"Who's a clever little policeman? You deserve a reward." Bea undid the belt of her flimsy wrap.

"Hmm, I'm afraid I'll have to put it in the bank. FC Zurich have a practice session tonight and I want to put some pressure on André Wissler, which, I hope, will make Zubke even more nervous."

Bea pouted and sighed. "A football widow. OK. I'll save your reward. It may even gather interest."

Jochim decided on another practice ground interview: maximum surprise and embarrassment.

Jochim worked his way to the front of the small group of spectators. After about twenty minutes André Wissler came to the touchline to retrieve the ball. He looked up expecting to see the smiling faces of his fans and saw the police sergeant's stony expression. Wissler dropped the ball and stood transfixed.

"Come on André, get the ball."

Jochim mouthed 'later', nodded, and turned away.

Jochim put himself in pole position at the exit from the pitch. "Hello André, you remember me? Detective Sergeant Friedmann." Too loud, considering Wissler was standing next to him.

"What do you want?" Whispered, so only Jochim could hear.

"Just a little chat." Whispered also.

"I've got nothing more to say to you Friedmann."

"I've got news about Felix."

"Felix?"

Jochim looked around to make sure there were people in hearing distance. "The pimp who put the prostitutes in The Celler."

Wissler looked anxiously around. "Shush! OK, wait here while I change."

"You won't forget me will you André?"

Jochim expected André would to keep him waiting, but in ten minutes he'd showered and changed. The practice ground had a small bar. André led them to a table in the far corner.

"Did I tell you about Felix being at–"

"I told I don't kn–"

"'You don't know a Felix', yes, you told me. Well you'll never know this one because he was attacked and now he's dead." Wissler should no signs of pleasure at the news.

"Who don't you know André? Whenever we've talked there's always been someone who you don't know. What about your Uncle Herman, you know him. Could he be the Herman who sold you The Celle–"

"Which I wish I'd never bought."

"Herman Zubke. You claim you've never met him, which is strange if he's your uncle. Even more strange if he's your mother's friend who recommended The Celler to you."

Friedmann's voice was getting louder as he spoke. Wissler looked anxiously around.

"Nothing to say?"

Wissler stared at his feet.

"OK, let's try this."

If Wissler was anxious before, now he looked frightened.

"Last time we spoke I mentioned your father. I think you started to say that you don't know who your father is."

"My father's got nothi–"

"Nothing to do with this? Perhaps, but aren't you curious to know who he is?"

Now Wissler stared into Friedmann's eyes.

"Could it be Uncle Walter?"

Wissler's eyes grew wider.

"You must have thought about it."

Silence.

"Or ... or ... here's a thought, could it be ..." Friedmann looked around and lowered his voice. "Uncle Herman? Certainly a friend of your mother's, once upon a time."

Fright changed to anger. "Leave my mother out of this."

"I'd be only to pleased to do so, André, if I was getting any cooperation from you. However ..."

"Go near my mother and you'll–"

"Yes, I know, you told me before, I'll hear from your lawyer." Friedmann stood, looked down at Wissler and shook his head. He turned, took three steps and said, in a voice that everyone in the room could hear, "Think about it, André, this may be the chance to find out who your father is."

Previous discussions with Sergeant Jochim Friedmann had left André Wissler feeling annoyed, but this time he was furious.

"Mum?"

"André, how ni–"

"Where have you been? I've been trying to call you."

"Out, if that's OK. It's nice to hear from you. I thought you'd lost my number."

"I've been busy. We've got an important cup game tomorrow."

"You'll be here for lunch on Sunday?"

"Yes."

"Good."

"Has anybody from the police been in contact with you?"

"The police? Why? What's happened?"

"Nothing's happened. Nothing new. They're still going on about that incident at The Celler over two months ago."

"You mean about those women being in the bar. I don't know anything about that. Why would they want to talk to me?"

"I don't know. There's this one sergeant who probably thinks he can get at me though you."

"Why would he think that?"

"I don't–"

"I told you it was a bad idea buying that bar."

"But–"

"You're not involved with allowing those women in to your bar are you?"

"Don't be stupid."

"André. I will not have you talking to me like that."

"But–"

"No buts, I'm your mother."

"So, if the police contact you just say you don't know anything."

"I don't know anything about those women."

"No, I mean about anything ... anything."

"OK, OK. Calm down."

"There's something else."

"André, I have to go out."

"Listen. I–"

"Sorry?"

"Just listen."

"Do I need to remind you again that you're taking to your mother?"

"OK ... OK, sorry. This Sergeant Friedmann suggested Uncle Walter might be my father and ..."

Except for sporadic calls from his lady friends, Grindel's 'phone had been quiet. Eight days since Gazda had called. Two days since the meeting with Zubke. Did this mean Zubke was not Gazda? Was Gazda feeling safe because he knew Henri Cousteau was dead? Did Zubke have no contact with Gazda?

Friedmann wondered how much longer they could keep Grindel in the witness protection programme. Most people in police HQ knew. At first there had been nothing on the corridor telegraph, but after a week and a half DC Peter Weber picked up talk about Henri Cousteau's death and Sergeant Grindel.

"New tape, Sarge."

"Thanks, Peter. Another one of Walter's women short of money? He must spend a fortune." Gazda must be paying him well thought Jochim.

"No, I think you'll want to listen to this one."

```
"Walter?"
    "Krystal? How are you?"
    "OK, and you?"
    "How's our boy."
    "That's what I want to talk to you about."
    "Has something happened?"
    "Is it OK to talk just now?"
    Slight pause. "Yes."
    "This Sergeant Friedmann is still questioning
André about that raid on his club. Can you do
anything?"
    "No ... not easily, I'm ... I'm not involved
with the case."
    "But-"
    "I'll do what I can, Krystal, but it won't be
much."
    "There's something else. Friedmann told André
you might be his father."
    "He what? What did you say to André?"
    "I told him it's not true."
    Silence.
    "Walter? Are you still there?"
    "I wonder ... I wonder Krystal if it's time to
tell André the truth."
    "No! No, Walter, it's not the time. No. No,
definitely not."
    "OK Krystal, OK."
```

"Get Friedmann off André's back Walter, get him off his back. ... If you want to have any more contact with 'your boy' Walter, get him off his back."

Friedmann pressed rewind and smiled.

"Is it true, Sarge, Walter Grindel is André Wissler's father?"

"True or not Peter it's ruffled a few feathers, which is exactly what we want. What's the time of this recording?"

"About a half an hour ago."

"Who's on WPP duty at the moment?"

"DC Klein."

After the call from Krystal, Jochim assumed Grindel would have a few choice to say to him. But his orders were not to contact anyone including Friedmann. His 'phone was for incoming calls only. Jochim waited an hour before picking up his 'phone.

"Hello, DC Klein?"

"Yes, Sarge."

"Let me speak to Grindel."

"Sergeant Fried–"

"What the f–"

"Good morning, Walter. Ho–"

"What the f–"

"How are you?"

"What the fuck's going on, Friedmann? Why did you tell André I was his father? I thought you want–"

"Calm down, Walter."

"Calm down! I thought we were trying to get Gazda, not you screwing up my life."

"Nothing's happening, Walter. It's over a week since Gazda called you. We need to stir someone into action, otherwise it'll all go cold and we'll never get to Gazda."

"But not by ruining the one good thing in my life."

"Oh, Walter, I'm sure there've been other good things in your life in addition to fathering André Wissler. He doesn't even look like you. I also asked him if Herman Zubke could be his father."

"Who?"

"Herman Zubke, he's a lawyer and friend of Krystal Wissler."

"Never heard of him."

"André calls him 'uncle'."

"I'm André's father."

"If you say so. It's all the same to me. Perhaps there are a few others who could lay claim to that honour."

"I know I'm André's father, Friedmann."

"OK, OK, calm down. All I want is to stop Gazda before he orders the killing of someone else."

Jochim could hear Grindel breathing heavily.

"Who else will Krystal call?"

"I don't know. I've no idea who she knows."

"Think Walter."

"Your Herman Zubke probably."

"Yes, definitely I would say. If you weren't where you are, how would you go about getting me off André's back?"

Silence.

"Well?"

"As I told Krystal, there's not much I could do."

"Oh I'm sure you'd think of something Walter, to help 'your boy'. Politely ask me to back off?"

"You're a bastard, Friedmann."

"So I'm told."

Silence.

"So, Walter what's going to happen now?"

"How should I know?"

Silence.

"I would think you'll be getting a call from Gazda soon. I now have a line connected to your telephone so I'll be able to hear what goes on. When he calls this is the way we'll play it—"

"Are you listening Walter?"

Silence.

"Walter?"

"Yes."

"I want your full cooperation Walter. I'm sure I don't need to remind you that's there's still the matter of the murder of Henri Cousteau."

"You don't need to remind me."

"Good. So when Gazda calls ..."

The new 'phone on Jochim's desk buzzed. He'd told Grindel to count slowly to ten before answering. The technical people had some new equipment and a better chance to trace the call. Jochim picked up when the buzzing stopped.

"Hello?"

"Walter."

"Gazda, hello."

"How are you, Walter?"

"I'm ... I'm OK thank you."

"It's been over a week since we spoke. Sorry I haven't called you."

Jochim shook his head: Gazda apologising!

"I don't think I thanked you enough for taking care of that situation with the mad frog. If that had got out of hand we could have all been in trouble."

Silence.

This was not the conversation they'd planned.

"Walter, are you there?"

"Yes ... yes I'm here."

"Well I want you to know that I don't forget people who do favours for me."

"Thank you ... thank you, Gazda."

"Is there any news?"

"News?"

"About Friedmann and his investigation."

"I told you Friedmann had linked the murder of Felix Braun to the raid on The Celler?"

Silence.

"Gazda?"

"Yes, you told me."

"And I told you he knows your name."

Silence.

"Yes, Walter, yes you told me. Now get on with it ... please."

"From what I hear, and it's second or third-hand information, because as you know I'm not directly involved in the Friedmann's investigation, but I've done my best to find out as—"

"Yes, yes, Walter, please tell me what you've been able to find out. I'm sure you've done your best,"

"Well, it seems that Friedmann thinks you're André Wissler."

Silence.

"What's he going to do next?"

"I can't know that, Gazda."

"Guess Walter, you know about these things."

"I can't read his mind."

"I'm not asking you to read his mind, Walter. What would you do in this situation?"

"I'm not sure."

"Give me an answer, Walter. I respect your opinion."

Silence.

"I'd ... I'd probably arrest André Wissler."

Silence.

Silence.

Silence.

"OK. The main reason I called you is I want to ask you for another favour, Walter, and from what you've just told me it's even more important."

"What is it?"

"I think we should meet."

Jochim sat bolt upright.

"Meet?"

"Yes, I have something to ask you and I would rather do it directly."

"But ... but I'm not sure that's a good idea Gazda."

'Don't miss the opportunity' mouthed Jochim.

"Also I some information about André Wissler that I'm sure you will find interesting."

"About André?"

"Yes."

"OK."

Jochim let out the breath he'd been holding.

"Where and when?"

"Excuse me, Sarge."

"Ah, yes, Winters, we must have given you plenty of time."

"More time certainly, Sarge."

"I feel there's a but coming."

"It was a mobile, a mobile on the move. So, we know it's been in various places in the centre of Zurich and where it started and finished, but th–"

"But that doesn't help me get to the person making the call."

Thoughts, ideas, questions collided in the grey matter as Jochim Friedmann started to form a plan.

Platzspitz at two o'clock tomorrow - neither the place nor the time pleased him: the place was too open, making it difficult to approach unseen; less than 24 hours to plan, put a team together and get approval was far too short.

The plan would have to be simple - simple plans stood the best chance of success. Details would have to be kept within a very limited group - who knew if there were others in the employ of Gazda.

He was sure Gazda himself would be putting in an appearance - this couldn't be a ploy to send a hitman to silence Grindel: that could easily be done 'discretely'.

Why does Gazda choose the park? - he could have arranged to meet Grindel at The Lipstick Club, for example: but after what happened to Felix, Grindel would be 'suspicious'. Gazda was unusually friendly on the 'phone - did he want Grindel to do something very special.

Could Gazda have any suspicions about Grindel? - if he did it's unlikely he'd be suggesting meeting in broad daylight: too easy to walk into a trap.

Should they arrest Gazda as soon as he appeared? - they didn't know what he looked like: how would they know it was him? He would certainly not arrive alone.

Could Grindel meet Gazda wearing a wire? - wires could be detected.

Jochim outlined his plan to Bea.

Unusually she made no comments until he'd finished. "Remember it's Sunday tomorrow. Depending on the weather, the park could be quite busy in the afternoon.

We'll ha–"

"Probably why Gazda chose it."

"We'll have to be careful about involving members of the public."

"Let's hope for rain."

"As for th– "

"Just a minute, what do you mean 'we'? I don't see how I could get approval for your involvement."

"If you'll just listen for a moment I was going to say, as for the team, it's obvious. Use KFR."

"KFR? Why?"

"That's Grindel's team. I can tell you there's been a lot of speculation about what's happened to him. I've had to be very careful about what I say. Use them. Tell them Grindel's been undercover and now we're moving in."

Jochim thought for a moment and then nodded. "OK, good, thanks."

"You can reward me later."

"I've asked, told, Müller and Kullmer I need to talk to them."

"So, you'll have Weber, Schmidt, Ericsson, Brandt, me and you. What about that young DC you've got working with you temporarily?"

"Schwartz? He's still recovering from the broken nose Henri Cousteau gave him."

"Six should be enough. Plus the heavy mob round the corner in a van."

Friedmann had expected getting approval for the operation would be the most difficult part. From the look on the faces of Inspector Kullmer and Chief Inspector Müller when he walked into Müller's office at half past nine he knew he was right. His message had reached them at the Mayor of Zurich's annual reception. 'Meet Friedmann, priority 1' demanded their presence.

Müller stood with his hands behind his back, and rocked on the balls of his feet. "This had better be good Friedmann."

Jochim outlined what had happened and what the plan was. Müller, stared with hooded eyes and listened in silence, so Kullmer also said nothing. "By tomorrow night, Sir, we'll have a major figure in the Zurich criminal world in custody."

"OK. I want no member of the public involved. I don't even want them to know what's happening. Is that clear?"

"Completely."

"We should still be in time for the main course Erich."

"You're back quickly. Does that mean they simply said no?"

"No, Bea, exactly the opposite. No discussion, just a simple OK. Either I was very persuasive, or the menu at City Hall was so exciting, or they knew what to expect from their abandoned wives if they didn't return quickly."

"I'm sure you were very persuasive.

The Arrest

23 November 2008

A cloudless, crisp November day greeted Jochim's team when they arrived in the park at one-thirty. They'd spent the morning locked in one of the situation rooms. Grindel was not present. Jochim's brief description of Grindel's undercover work in Gazda's organisation made it sound like a planned, police operation. He knew several of the officers would have questions, but they didn't ask, and he didn't volunteer any more information than he thought he needed to.

The meeting with Gazda was to take place 'in the area near the bandstand in Platzspitz'. On an enlarged map of the park they staked out six interlocking areas in which they could casually walk or sit, keeping the bandstand in view. The support would be in the courtyard at the back of the Swiss National Museum.

Everyone was in place by quarter to two. There were enough people in the park not to make the team look out of place, but not so many people that observation became difficult.

Grindel slowly circled the bandstand, quietly counting. Only Friedman could hear him. In spite of the transmitter being the size of, and looking like, a small, box of matches, which was sewn into his underwear, there was good reception three hundred and sixty degrees. It was too risky for Grindel to be wearing an earpiece, so Friedmann took out the white handkerchief and blew his nose. Grindel said "OK." He flicked the switch in his coat pocket to turn the transmitter off.

Friedmann switched his radio to channel 2 and spoke to the team. "We're ready." He'd decided on separate channels for Grindel and the team because of what Gazda might say that would incriminate Grindel.

The bell of the Grossmünster boomed twice. Grindel did one more round of the bandstand, walked 50 meters away from it and back again. Friedmann strolled to the edge of his area, doing a 180 degree scan as he did. No sign of anyone approaching the bandstand.

Bea stole a glance at her watch: five past two. The bise, the cold, north wind, had died down somewhat, but still made her regret not adding a scarf to her turned up collar.

The quarter-hour bell sounded. Friedmann wondered how much longer he could wait. He could see Grindel's pacing getting more erratic, and his team starting to stamp feet and rub hands: they'd become conspicuous soon.

Bea worried that more people were strolling around. The bandstand was a feature of the park and a few people stood reading the information board, and going up the steps onto the stand.

Now Friedmann looked at his watch: two-twenty. Five more minutes. He was looking towards where he knew Bea would be walking, and did not immediately see the small, rotund figure approaching Grindel from the other side of the bandstand. The man stopped close to Grindel and took a small box out of his pocket. No words were exchanged and the man walked quickly away, muttering to himself. Friedmann smiled. They'd expected there might be an RF check to see if Grindel was carrying a wire. Did it mean Gazda suspected something, or was he being extra cautious? The click in his earpiece told him Grindel had switched the transmitter back on.

From her position Bea also saw what had happened. Now, despite the numbness in her feet, she was on full alert. She saw the figure approaching from the Limmat side of the park. She assumed it was Gazda because following him was over six feet of muscle wearing dark glasses. Gazda's face was swathed in wool, his collar turned up and his hat pulled down over his forehead. He approached Grindel and the 'muscle, went up onto the bandstand.

"Walter."

Grindel automatically offered his hand, but withdrew it as Gazda's hand remained firmly plunged into his coat pocket. "Gazda."

"Let's walk."

Gazda led the way around the bandstand.

"Have you been talking to Friedmann Walter?"

"Talking to Friedmann? No."

"Then why does he think you're André Wissler's father?"

"I ... I don't know."

"You don't know. You don't know. I know. You've been talking to him."

Gazda was speaking so softly, Friedmann could hardly hear him. However, the menace in the voice was clear.

"I haven't, Gazda, I swear."

"Do you think you're André Wissler's father, Walter?"

"I know I am."

Silence,

"But you're not Walter."

"I am, I know I am."

"You're not, Walter I promise you, you're not. I know who André Wissler's father is."

"I know I am."

"You can't be Walter, because I am."

Silence.

Silence.

"Ironic isn't it, that Friedmann thinks I'm André Wissler."

"But ... but ..."

"Did you boast to Friedmann about being André's father, Walter? Did you tell him about me? Did Friedmann somehow make a connection between the death of Felix Braun, the raid on The Celler, André Wissler and me? Did you help him? ... No, that can't be true, you wouldn't steer him towards what you thought was your son."

"I haven't talked to Friedmann, I swea–"

"Friedmann's pushing too much, far too much. I don't want him going after my son."

Silence.

"We need to do something about him."

"We?"

"Yes, we, Walter."

"I told you I'm n–"

"Yes, I know, you're not involved in the case, but you have access to Friedmann."

"But I–"

"Shut up and listen Walter. I want Friedmann removed, I wan–"

"Removed? Ho–"

"I told you once to shut up Walter. I want you to arrange a little accident for Friedmann, as you did for Coustaeu, and I want you to do it quickly. I don't want him to probe any further."

"But–"

"No buts, Walter. Just do it. There are plenty of other people I know who can do to you what the mad frog did to Felix Braun."

Friedmann wasn't sure how much pressure Grindel could take. He switched to channel two. "OK, go. Quietly does it. "

Jochim, Bea and Weber waited until the 'muscle's' scan was in the direction away from Grindel and Gazda, then moved swiftly to three sides of Gazda. Weber's gun pressed against Gazda. Schmidt, Ericsson and Brandt arrived at the foot of the bandstand steps. The 'muscle' reached inside his coat. In two huge strides Hans Brandt was up the steps and beside the 'muscle'. The vice like grip of the schwingen champion clamped the 'muscle's' wrist, trapping the hand. Under Brandt's full control the hand slowly emerged holding a walkie-talkie. The power light was on. Brandt continued a tight grip.

Gazda

Friedmann stared at Gazda. Out of the corner of his eye he saw the small, rotund figure racing in from the right. Something glinted in his hand. Ericsson saw him, withdrew his gun, and walked slowly towards him. A young girl on the bandstand with Brandt and the 'muscle' saw Ericsson's gun and screamed. All eyes within 20 meters swivelled in her direction. The team had agreed they wanted to avoid a public panic. Schmidt made a decision. "Police. Everybody go to the park entrance as quickly as possible, please."

The small, rotund man stopped. He waved the gun in front of him. "Checkmate, copper."

A high-powered motorbike raced towards the bandstand from the left and stopped 5 meters away. The rider started to dismount. Schmidt grabbed him round the waist before he completed the manoeuvre. The still revving bike fell to the ground. The two men rolled over several times, arms flailing. Schmidt's knuckles made heavy contact with the shiny, silver, crash helmet. He cried out and tried to escape from under the black, leather-glad figure. A leather-gloved hand reached behind and pulled a knife from a belt.

Friedmann drew his gun and plunged it into Gazda's ribs alongside Webber's. "Peter." Weber raced towards the motorbike. From two meters in front of the men on the ground he saw how close the knife was to Schmidt's throat.

The scene froze. Except for a lone bird, eerie silence.

Gazda smiled.

The crash helmet, that had been instrumental in bringing about the bike rider's advantage over Schmidt, restricted peripheral vision. Weber inched forward on the opposite side to the knife. A perfectly aimed edge-of-the-hand chop to the brachial plexus, just below the helmet line, caused immediate paralysis of the arm. The falling knife missed Schmidt's ear by millimetres. He drove his knee between the man's legs.

The small, rotund man's eyes flicked to the commotion. Ericsson dived to his right and fired. The shot hit the man's upper left arm. The natural reaction to grab the arm with the right hand caused the gun to fire. The bullet went skyward.

The chief inspector of the support team had watched everything over the wall of the Swiss National Museum. He shouted into his helmet microphone. "Go, go"

Jochim took-in the figure in front of him - shifty eyes, height about right for Zubke, but too much weight: perhaps it's the coat. "Remove the scarf and the hat please, Gazda or whatever your name is."

Under the hat was unruly, greying, curly hair. As the scarf unwound a pointy beard appeared - not Zubke.

"Sergeant Friedmann I presume."

"So, you are, Gazda."

"Only my friends call me that." He reached towards the inside of his coat. Bea clamped his hand. There was no resistance.

"Frisk him."

"Clean, Sarge."

"If I may, Sergeant, I was going to get my identity card, so you know who I am."

Gazda took out the card and handed it to Bea. "Madam."

Bea read the name and handed the card to Jochim.

"Rudfolf Affolter I'm arresting you on suspicion of instigating the murder of Felix Braun. You do not have to say anything, but ..."

"Hello, Lisa?"

"Yes."

"Beatrice Menna, I have some news for you."

Not surprisingly, the arrest of Rudi Affolter caused quite a stir in ZFFM. The Swiss newspapers were, as usual, cautious in their reporting. They only said Affolter was being questioned about a death in The Lipstick Club. Most readers showed little further interest in the case: The Lipstick Club was part of the seedy side of Zurich life, a side that many Zürchers didn't like to admit existed.

Everyone at ZFFM except Erna had forgotten about the theft of Christopher's briefcase in August 2008. When she heard about the arrest, she immediately telephoned Lisa.

"Affolter's a criminal, we were right. Why don't we telephone the police and tell them about him stealing Christopher's briefcase."

"I hardly think there'd be any interest in that. Anyway, Christopher saw the news and asked me, told me, not to go around reminding people about his stolen bag and my, our, suspicions about Rudi."

The Trial

29 January 9 May 2009

Jochim Friedmann predicted Rudolf Affolter would go on trial quickly, but as he and the Public Prosecutor put the case together, evidence emerged that it involved more than the murder of Felix Braun.

Lisa and Christopher assumed that their abductions would be part of the charges Affolter would face. Jochim avoided the topic, even with Bea. His superiors still knew nothing about the abductions. Although the two 'cases' had many people in common, and that had helped him to identify and arrest Gazda, he thought it would be easier to put him in prison on the murder changes. He thought, adding the charge of abduction might dilute the case against Affolter.

Two months into the investigation Jochim knew he had to talk to Lisa and Christopher.

"Sorry it was spaghetti Bolognese again."

Christopher shook his head. "You don't need to apologise for something so delicious Jochim."

Jochim took a deep breath. "As you know, I can't discuss the investigation with you. What I can say is that we've made some significant discoveries. I think we're going to be able to put Rudolf Affolter away for a long time."

Lisa clapped. "Good, very good."

"I think the case is so strong that I'm going to suggest that we don't confuse it by including the abductions."

Three pairs of eyes stared at him. Lisa's and Bea's mouths started to fall open.

Bea recovered first. "Are you suggesting–"

Lisa finished the sentence. "that Affolter gets away with what he did to me, to us?"

"No ... no not for one moment, but we would need to do a lot of investigating to be able to prove a case against him."

"'Prove a case against him'? I've ... we've told you what happened."

"Lisa, I believe you, of course, but proving it in court is different to believing. Bea and I both know that."

Bea nodded. "Do you think it would be that difficult?"

"Not easy. We'd almost need a confession from someone who did the abductions. And we don't know who did them."

"Affolter. It was Affolter."

"He ordered them, Lisa. What Jochim is saying is how does he prove it in court."

"So, you agree we should just forget about what happened to us, Christopher?"

"No, that's no–"

"No, Lisa, we won't forget what happened. It's just that I won't charge him at the moment."

"So he gets away with it."

"No, he w–"

"You just said you're not going to investigate and therefore you can't charge him."

"I said I was suggesti–"

"Suggesting? Suggesting?"

"Lisa, let Jochim finish."

"You agree with his 'suggestion', Christopher?"

"I want to hear the reasons behind it first, Lisa."

Lisa folded her arms heavily across her chest and glared between Jochim and Christopher.

"Lisa, I know how you feel. I would feel the same way. But, if the prosecution is successful Affolter will be going away for a long time, much longer than on a charge of abduction. I'm just a bit afraid that presenting what is really a completely separate situation in parallel might confuse or dilute the case."

"So, what are you going to charge him with?"

"I can't tell you that, Lisa."

"But it's more important than two abductions."

"Not more important, just worth more, much more, in terms of prison time. That will be his punishment, losing his freedom."

Lisa continued to glare.

"Presumably, Jochim, the abduction charges could come later, when he's in prison?"

"Bea's right. And ... and it's possible that some things may come out in the trial that will help to prove his involvement in your abductions."

"And that would mean more years added on to his sentence."

"You're sure, Bea."

Bea looked at Jochim. He nodded.

"So, you agree with Jochim, Bea?"

"I don't know any more about the charges than you, Lisa, but I trust Jochim's judgement. And not just because we're ... because of our relationship."

Christopher could see Lisa's anger was beginning to subside. "And you and I won't have to go to court and describe waking up in a certain condition in a certain hotel."

Jochim smiled. "I'd have to know about that to charge Affolter."

Lisa also smiled. "This wine's very good Jochim, but I'd need something much stronger before telling you about Hotel zum Kirsch." The smile was also for relief: thank goodness she'd managed to persuade Erna not to go to the police about Christopher's stolen bag.

The trial finally got under way. It was expected to last no more than two weeks. Lisa and Christopher took holidays, which raised a few eyebrows and some pointed comments from Erna. Lisa tried to convince her that it was just coincidence, but she knew Erna would continue to believe and talk about 'Lisa and Christopher being together, at last'. Lisa, surprisingly, found herself not feeling uncomfortable about it.

As the trial entered its third week, Lisa and Christopher went back to work and attended only a few days each until the end.

The Public Prosecutor conducted the trial from the present backwards. She described what happened in 2008 followed by the background. Jochim explained this was to impress the judges with the seriousness of the crimes. For Lisa and Christopher this meant they missed much of the history of Rudi Affolter, which for them was more interesting.

Fortunately the revelations from the trial were such big news for Switzerland that SRF 1 took the unusual step of preparing a documentary. Scheduled for broadcast the day after the verdict, it would tell the story in chronological order.

The judges delivered their verdict on 30 April 2009: guilty.

"Do you want to watch before or after eating Christopher?

"How long is the recording?"

"One hour."

"Might be better to watch afterwards. We'll probably want to keep stopping to discuss."

"OK."

"What are we eating?"

"I've prepared a special dish with frutti di mare and full of exotic Mediterranean flavours."

"Ah, your famous spaghetti vongole."

"Oh, I wanted it to be a surprise."

"A surprise would have been if we were not having your piatto d'autore."

"My only dish."

SRF 1
presents
Zurich in shame

The twenty-three day trial of Rudolf Affolter ended yesterday. The judges returned unanimous verdicts of guilty on all three charges - instigating the murder of Francesca Kardomah, instigating the murder of Felix Braun, and criminal organisation of prostitution. Sentencing will take place next week.

"To a long time in jail, I hope."

Rudi Affolter was born in 1952 in Birmensdorf, Zurich. His mother, Lejla Dedeić had fled war-torn Yugoslavia at the age of nine with her six-month-old brother Anto. She married Franz Affolter, a Swiss shoemaker, in 1951. Franz Affolter was a strict disciplinarian and Rudi grew up hard edged. Even at school his contemporaries, he had few friends, knew not to cross him.

He left school at sixteen and, despite pressure from his father, showed no interest in shoemaking. He drifted through several jobs, ending at Zurich Flaschen Fullungs Machinen (ZFFM), where he eventually became the Marketing Manager. The people we talked to at ZFFM said he was friendly, but short-tempered. They never felt they got close to him. There was something mysterious about him.

He doesn't seem to have formed any permanent relationships with women, preferring the services of Zurich's ladies of the night. In 1980 he met Krystal Wissler in a nightclub.

"Rudi Affolter knew André's mother?
"Listen Lisa."

Krystal was someone he'd seen many times, but never been with. He'd had more than usual to drink, celebrating having just landed the job at ZFFM, and for the first time, he didn't wear a condom. For Krystal too it was the first time she'd had unprotected sex with anyone, client or friend. So when she missed two periods, she knew who the father must be.

"What? What? Affolter is André's father? I thought that was Grindel?"

Affolter refused to have anything to do with her.

"Typical."

and told her to have an abortion.

"By some backstreet quack no doubt."

Krystal named the boy André, yes André Wissler, the local football hero.

Lisa dived for the remote control and pressed pause. "Can you believe this? Do think André knows? And, I've been working with the father of my ex-husband. I can't believe it."
"OK Lisa, calm down, let's—"
"Calm down, Christopher, calm down?"
"Let's listen to some more." He pressed 'play'.

As soon as she got out of the hospital Krystal turned up on Affolter's doorstep. At first he shut the door in her face, but for some reason the

350

Gazda

bundle in her arms fascinated him. Perhaps it was
the recognition of the Affolter nose.

"I knew there was something familiar about him."
"Shush, Lisa."

They ordered blood tests. Krystal, André and
Rudi were all 'O' group, which eliminated 60% of
the male population as the father. Rudi have a
contact at a private clinic in Zurich and got him
to carry out the newly developed HLA (Human
Leukocyte Antigen) test. This showed 80 to 90%
chance that Rudi was the father of André.
There was no way a family was going to tie down
Rudi. But he made sure Krystal had the finances to
support her and the child. He kept in regular
contact with Krystal through a lawyer, but
insisted that André never knew about him.

"There's the answer to one of your questions."
Lisa smiled. "Shush, Christopher."

Affolter guided Krystal in important decisions,
such as schools. When André showed a real talent
for football, Rudi used his contacts to start
André's career. But he never changed his mind
about André not knowing who his father was.
His many years as a customer meant he knew many
of the girls and their pimps. When important
business contacts and visitors were looking to be
'entertained', he could be the intermediary - good
for business and good for Rudi Affolter, with the
generous 'commissions' he received. From there it
was a small step to running his own girls, and
then setting up the Discrete Escort Agency, where
the 'ladies' can cost over 1,000 Francs a night.

"That's the agency Sabina came from. Didn't she charge you
1,500? You should have negotiated with her."
Christopher started to blush. "I just gave what she asked for. I
wanted to get it over as quickly as possible."

By the late nineteen nineties he was
controlling most of the prostitution in Zurich,
both on the street and at the high end. All, of

course, hidden from his friends, family, colleagues at ZFFM, and the tax authorities. In his secret world Rudi Affolter took on the name 'Gazda'. In Serbo-Croatian this means master or boss, a small nod to his mother's native tongue.

In 2001 André Wissler transferred from Grasshopper Club Zurich to Aston Villa in England. The move did not please Rudi. He could not exercise so much control over André's life at such a distance. When André returned to FC Zurich in 2003 with an English wife Rudi was even less pleased. He'd harboured thoughts of André marrying into one of the respected Zurich families, and then perhaps revealing himself as his father.

Lisa pressed pause. "I'm surprised the press haven't been chasing me as the ex-wife of Affolter's son."

"If this had have been in England they would have been."

"So, when I came back to Switzerland with André, Affolter must have been more than disappointed. He probably pressured Krystal to intervene in our relationship and push André towards divorce."

"That might be extrapolating too far, Lisa."

"You think so? I'm not so sure, Christopher. But he must been happy when it happened."

"Happy for a short while at least."

"Why?"

"Because it backfired didn't it. From what you told me and what André told Jochim, he blamed you for spoiling his world cup chances."

"Yes, of course. And what does the father think of the woman who spoilt his son's chances of glory? This is starting to explain a lot."

"It's a big step from blaming you for spoiling André's chances to having us and then you abducted."

"Is it? Revenge must have become an obsession."

"And when you started working at ZFFM he knew it was only a matter of time before he found a way to satisfy his obsession."

"You know, thinking about it now, I always felt he was a bit ... I don't know ... strange with me. Not unfriendly, just strange. The way he looked at me sometimes. As though he was seeing inside me."

"I wonder how much he knew about your 'investigation' of him after the theft of my briefcase. That must have made him really angry."

"You see, Christopher, it is starting to explain a lot."

Christopher took the remote from Lisa and pressed play.

Gazda

André Wissler divorced in 2005 and this gave Affolter back some control over André's life. Wissler missed going with the Swiss team to the World Cup in 2006. The divorce process probably accounted for his loss of form.

In 2007 Wissler decided he wanted to buy a jazz club. He liked jazz and some football colleagues had told him it was a good investment. Word got back to Affolter through the lawyer, Herman Zubke. Affolter had been using Zubke to stay in contact and transfer money to Krystal Wissler. Affolter was against the idea because it put Wissler a little too close to his prostitutes working in the Niederdorf area. But he knew he couldn't stop him, and he probably liked the idea that his son had inherited his love of trad jazz. Through Zubke, Affolter 'owned' several clubs and decided to sell Wissler The Celler. He probably thought he'd be able to keep an eye on him through the bar manager, who had worked for Affolter for many years. Zubke, who Wissler knows as Uncle Herman, recommended The Celler and arranged the purchase.

Affolter made sure his girls stayed well away from the streets immediately surrounding The Celler. But, in early September 2008 it came to the attention of the police that prostitutes were working The Celler. They raided the bar on 16 September.

The three prostitutes arrested, including the one who had tried to solicit an undercover policeman, received police cautions. KRIPO Sergeant Jochim Friedmann told the judges the raid sent a warning to other bars that prostitutes working inside bars would not be tolerated.

The police investigation following the raid focused on who had given permission for the women to be in The Celler. As the owner, André Wissler was the main suspect. In several interviews he denied all knowledge.

The police knew from the beginning that a 'Felix' was a pimp working in the Niederdorfstrasse. They also knew that Felix worked for Gazda, but had no idea who these people were or where to find them. On 1 November, one month after the raid, police traced Felix Braun and

353

interviewed him. And that's what started the chain of events that put Rudi Affolter in court.

This time Christopher pressed pause. "Was the prosecution case convincing about what happened next?"

"What do you mean?"

"How much was fact, how much invented, and were the witnesses credible?"

"That was the basis of Affolter's lawyer's argument. The prosecution convinced the judges."

"And you?"

"I was at the time, but I know I had a 'slightly' biased mindset. Let's see how it comes over now."

Felix Braun had told the 'ladies' to go into The Celler. Affolter's, Gazda's, anger with Felix Braun opening The Celler and André Wissler to investigation significantly increased when the police questioned Braun. Gazda feared the police might be getting closer to him. He assumed someone must be talking to the police. His suspicion fell on one of the prostitutes arrested after the raid on The Celler.

Intuition or lucky guess on Affolter's part? It was certainly not lucky for Francesca Kardomah. It was her who had given the names of Felix and Gazda to the police. She was brutally beaten and died. According to the testimony of KRIPO Sergeant Jochim Friedmann, Ms Kardomah gave a positive response to him when he asked her if Felix Braun had attacked her.

Christopher pressed pause again. "I wasn't sure about that, 'a positive response'."

"The nurse confirmed there was a peak on the pulse monitor."

"I suppose it was only a small part of the evidence that Felix Braun killed her."

The police investigation showed that Felix Braun killed Francesca Kardomah on the orders of Rudi Affolter. In summary the evidence presented to the judges was:

- an eyewitness account of a heated argument between Felix Braun and Francesca Kardomah just after two am on the 4 November in the Hotel Stein. Near the end of the argument Clive Pritt, an employee of the hotel, said he heard Braun say 'Gazda's fucking angry about you talking to Friedmann. He wants you silenced.'

- two prostitutes, who gave their evidence from a screened witness box. They witnessed the attack in the labyrinth around the Hotel Stein, behind the area known as 'prostitution allee'. They were close enough to hear Braun say 'You won't be fucking talking to anyone else Francesca. Gazda's going to be fucking pleased with me for silencing you'.

- the autopsy on Francesca Kardomah showed the savage attack was with bare fists. There were two small indentations in her stomach, which the pathologist proved matched a ring worn by Felix Braun.

Both Lisa and Christopher reached for the remote control. Christopher got there first.   "OK, convincing evidence that Felix killed Francesca, but I still think the link to Rudi was weak."

"Can we call him Gazda? I don't want to think of him as Rudi anymore."

"OK."

"Three people heard Braun say Gazda's name."

"But the defence questioned the credibility of those witnesses. I can only think the evidence presented later to show how Ru– Gazda used Braun to muscle the prostitution business persuaded the judges about his involvement in the murders."

Lisa pressed play. "Let's see if this programme picks that up."

The prosecution star witness, Mr A, gave his evidence surrounded by a screen. Mr A is a serving police officer, and for some years received money from Affolter for supplying information about police activity in the Neiderdorfstasse and Langstasse. On 5 November Mr A told Affolter about the search to find and arrest Felix Braun for the murder of Francesca Kardomah. Affolter told Mr A he would find Felix Braun before the police and 'silence him permanently'. Mr A described several telephone calls in which Affolter asked if the

police were making progress in finding Braun and
repeated the threat to silence him permanently.

Lisa was almost jumping up and down in her seat. She pressed
pause. "What I whispered to you in court, I can now shout: that's not
what happened. Grindel sent Cousteau to kill Felix Braun, on Gazda's
instructions. So he's just as guilty of, what did they call it, instigating
the murder, as Gazda."

"So, why was it presented this way in court? We'll hav–"

"So the police can protect one of their own."

"I don't believe that of Jochim, and I don't think you do."

"He must have come under pressure from above."

"We'll have to ask Jochim."

When paramedics examined Braun's body in the
toilet of The Lipstick Club on 6 November, they
found so many stab wounds they could not determine
where one ended and another began. He died on 11
November without regaining consciousness. Police
quickly identified the killer as Henri Cousteau,
known as the Mad Frog. Cousteau fell down a
stairway and died while in custody.

When Mr A heard about what had happened to
Felix Braun he decided to cooperate with the
police to identify and arrest Gazda.

Christopher could see Lisa shaking her head. "Shall I stop the
recording?"

"Yes."

"What's wrong?"

"Hearing this again confirms what I said to you in court, Grindel
looks like a hero. Not only is he getting away with his part in the
murder of Braun and what he did to us, but now he's the mysterious
avenger. What happens next? He gets promotion?"

"I don't think so. His identity's a secret so there're no reactions
from Gazda's friends. As Jochim said the main idea was to put Ru–
Gazda away for a long time. Grindel's evidence and involvement were
vital."

"Gazda's not put away for a long time, yet."

"The verdict is guilty."

Lisa folded her arms across her chest and sighed.

Gazda

A long line of witnesses give evidence about the way Rudi Affolter controlled the prostitution business in Zurich and Bern. Prostitution is, of course, legal in Switzerland. Individuals can apply for a licence to work in various designated areas. Organised groups of prostitutes can also apply. Trouble starts when one group tries to dominate.

Affolter used the threat and demonstration of violence to control who worked the streets. Several prostitutes described how Affolter had personally told them they must work for him or get off the street. Three who ignored him came forward with details of injuries, confirmed by hospital records, inflicted by Affolter himself. Felix Braun was one of several pimps in Zurich. His violent nature made him an important figure in Affolter's organisation. Until Braun invited some of his ladies into The Celler.

The defence did not plan to call ...

"I don't understand why the defence didn't call any witnesses, Christopher?"

"I think that's what they're about to explain."

"Go back a bit."

The defence did not plan to call any witnesses. SRF has learned that several people at ZFFM refused to appear as character witnesses. The case for the defence, put forward in the opening and closing presentations, was there was no physical evidence to connect Rudolf Affolter with either of the murders or the criminal organisation of prostitution. The prosecution obviously thought they had enough to connect Affolter to the murders. A key witness to establishing Affolter's involvement in prostitution was his lawyer Herman Zubke.

The news about when André Wissler was to appear in the witness box leaked out and a small crowd gathered outside the Zurich Cantonal Court. He refused to comment and, unusually for him, would not sign autographs. On the witness stand he simply confirmed that Herman Zubke had arranged the sale of The Celler to him.

357

Lisa was hugging the remote control. She pressed pause. "André looked very reluctant to answer the questions."

"I should think that he was still getting over the shock of Ru—Gazda being his father, Lisa. Did you see how Gazda stared at him all the time he was in the witness box?"

"And André refused to meet his eye."

"I didn't see André's mother in court. Was she there?"

"Only on the day André gave evidence. She sat at the back of the public gallery and stared at Gazda the whole time."

Herman Zubke was called by the prosecution. Other than confirming his name and occupation, he refused to answer any questions about his relationship to Rudi Affolter, claiming client and lawyer confidentiality. Persuaded his evidence was important to showing Affolter's connection with the Zurich prostitution and criminal world, the judges allowed the prosecution to treat Zubke as a hostile witness.

The prosecutor led Zubke through a list of clubs and backstreet hotels that Affolter owned through Zubke. To each one Zubke simply answered, yes. His only No answer was to the statement that he knew what the properties were used for. This prompted a rare moment of amusement in the court. One of the judges commented that Zubke must be the only person in Zurich who did not know what they are used for.

In his closing remarks, the prosecutor brought together individual pieces of evidence to paint a picture of Rudi Affolter. A picture of a man who ruthlessly controlled most of the prostitution in Zurich and Bern, and as someone who stopped at nothing to take revenge on those who crossed him.

The judges clearly agreed with the picture, and took the short time of three hours to reach their verdict - guilty.

SRF sources expect life sentences for the murders, considering the premeditation and cruelty.

"How do you manage to get the spaghetti to taste the same every time, Bea?"

"Secret ingredients, Lisa."

"She means me, Lisa."

"You're only part in the secret, Jochim, is you keep supplying me with the same wine when I'm cooking."

"But seriously, what is the secret?

Bea put on her best Italian accent. "I could tell, but then I would have to kill you."

There had been no mention of the trial during dinner. Not surprisingly it was Lisa who broke the 'curfew'. "Pleased with the verdicts, Jochim?"

"We'll have to see what the sentences are, but yes. It's never easy to prove instigation of murder, because of lack of physical evidence to connect the accused and the victim, as the defence argued. The judges agreed we provided enough evidence that Rudolf Affolter–"

Lisa winced.

"Are you OK, Lisa?

Lisa shook her head. Christopher answered "We've decided not to use his name. We refer to him as Gazda."

"OK. The judges agreed–"

"Sorry, Jochim, can I just explain?"

"Of course, Lisa."

"When I heard what had happened to those two people, I couldn't help thinking what he could have done to me."

"We understand, Lisa." Bea reached out to touch Lisa's arm.

"As I said, the judges greed we provided enough evidence that Gazda had the motive and the means to have two people removed."

Silence. Four people in deep thought.

"So, you think your decision not to include our abductions was correct?"

Jochim had wondered how long it would be before Lisa asked this question. "Yes, I do, especially with the result we have. The prosecutor expects the maximum sentences. And we've got–"

"I still don't like that he's getting away with it."

"He's not, Lisa."

"You said that before, but–"

"Let Jochim finish, Lisa. You were saying 'and we've got'."

"Lisa, we can still charge Gazda with the abductions. You remember when we discussed at the end of January I said we needed someone involved to start talking. Well we have that and more.

Gazda

"Two things happened during the investigation that will be key if Gazda goes on trial for the abductions. As you can imagine, I spent many hours interviewing him. With his lawyer present I had to be careful to stick with questions about the charges. One of Gazda's outbursts revealed more than most of my questions.

```
Transcript of video interview
20 March 2009
DS  Friedmann,  DC  Weber,  Rudolf  Affolter,  Mr
Baumgartner (lawyer)
Friedmann: Let's talk about your son, André
           Wissler.
Affolter:  I've told you, leave him out of this.
           It's got nothing to do with him.
Friedmann: But you sold him The Celler and the
           raid on The Celler was the start of
           this investigation.
Silence.
Friedmann: You haven't been a good father, have
           you, Rudi?
Lawyer:    I really don't see what this has to do
           with the charges against my client.
Friedmann: Oh you provided money. Money from your
           prostitutes. But where was the fatherly
           love, Rudi?
Lawyer:    Sergeant, I must ask you to direct your
           questions to the charges.
Friedmann: But it must have been a big
           disappointment when your boy missed the
           World Cup.
Affolter  pushes  back  chair,  stands  and  leans  on
table.
Affolter:  Because of that English bitch.
Friedmann: Mr Baumgartner, you should advise your
           client to sit down or I will have him
           handcuffed.
Lawyer:    You can't do that.
Friedmann: Try me.
Affolter  sits  and  leans  across  the  table  towards
Friedmann.
Affolter:  I will not have André brought into
           this. It's-
Friedmann: I'll decide who's brought into this, as
           you put it.
Affolter:  He has nothing to do with this.
```

Friedmann: To do with what exactly?

Silence.

Friedmann: You want to tell me about, what did you
            call her, 'that English bitch'?

Silence.

Friedmann: Was it one of your prostitutes?

Affolter: André goes nowhere near my
            prostitutes.

Friedmann: So, the first admission that you
            have prostitutes.

Affolter: Fuck you, Friedmann.

Friedmann: I think your lawyer will advise
            you to curb your language.

Silence.

Friedmann: Sounds logical to me. Like father,
            like son. Can't keep away from
            prostitutes.

Affolter jumps to his feet. His lawyer tries to
restrain him.

Affolter: That fucking bitch Lisa Stern isn't a
            prostitute, but she needs a good hard
            fucking. Her fucking divorce process
            stopped André going to Germany. If the
            fucking bitch goes anywhere near André
            again she'll pay.

Affolter sits.

Friedmann: The same fate as Francesca Kardomah
            and Felix Braun?

Affolter: Worse.

"Wow."

"Yes, Lisa, wow. We did consider using this is in court to show Gazda's temper, but then we would have needed to explain who Lisa Stern is. Plus, his lawyer was right, I should have been sticking to the charges. I just saw an opportunity. We can use it."

"You said two things happened that will be key when Gazda goes on trial."

"Yes. You saw from the newspaper reports that three people were arrested with Gazda. Well, it's not quite true. We took Gazda and his bodyguards into custody, but only Gazda and two of his henchmen were charged. The third person had not shown any resistance, so we couldn't immediately charge him with anything, except being with Gazda. Mikos Varga, a distant cousin of Gazda's was inter–"

Gazda

"Lisa, what was the name of that six feet of muscle at Ru—Gazda's dinner party?"

"Herman Munster you mean, Christopher. ... Mikos, Aha!"

"Herman Munster's a good description, Lisa, because despite his size and tough outward appearance, Mikos Varga's good-natured, clumsy and quite naive, just like Herman Munster. I left the initial interview to my DC, Peter Weber . Peter's the good cop."

"And Jochim's naturally the bad cop. Aren't you darling?" The first time Bea had said the word 'darling' except when they were alone.

Jochim blinked twice. "Sometimes. We had nothing on Varga, but Peter told him he could be going away for a long time. Obviously the idea of prison horrified Varga, and he started talking immediately. Peter had difficulty to slow him down."

```
Transcript of video interview
24 November 2008
DC Weber, Mikos Varga
Weber:  You realise, Mikos, that this is an
        informal  interview.  Your  two  friends  are
        charged  with  threatening  police  officers,
        but you're not charged with anything, yet.
        You can have a lawyer present if you
        choose.
Varga:  I've done nothing.
Weber:  As I said, you're not charged with
        anything, at the moment.
Varga:  OK.
Weber:  How long have you worked for Gazda?
Varga:  Mr Affolter you mean?
Weber:  OK, Mr Affolter.
Varga:  Five or six years.
Weber:  He's going to have some serious charges
        brought against him, you know.
Varga:  I haven't done anything.
Weber:  The judges are going to find that difficult
        to believe. You work for him. He has people
        beaten up and killed.
Varga:  But I didn't do any of those things.
Weber:  What exactly do you do Mikos?
Varga:  I frighten people.
Weber:  By beating them up?
Varga:  No. Look at me. I look as though I could
        beat people up. That's always been enough.
Weber:  And if it hadn't been?
```

Varga: I told Mr Affolter. I told him I couldn't harm anyone. He said it didn't matter. He said he could always get someone to ... someone to ...

Weber: Do the strong-arm stuff?

Varga: Yes.

Weber: The judges won't believe it.

Varga: Mr Affolter will tell them.

Weber: There's even less chance they'll believe him.

Varga: So, so what?

Weber: You'll go to prison.

Varga: Prison! I can't go to prison. I can't go to prison.

Weber: I'm afraid you'll have no choice.

Varga: But you don't understand.

Weber: What don't I understand, Mikos?

Varga: I suffer from cleithrophobia.

Weber: You mean claustrophobia? You'll still go to prison.

Varga: No cleithrophobia.

Weber: And what's that?

Varga: I'm frightened of being trapped or locked in an enclosed space. Unlike people with claustrophobia I can go into small rooms as long as I know I can leave when I want to.

Weber: Just a moment.

DC Weber speaks to someone on the telephone.

Weber: OK, the police doctor confirms what you said. Doesn't sound ideal for someone in prison: headaches, nausea, rapid heartbeats, even death sometimes.

Varga: I can't go to prison.

Weber: Hmm, difficult. With the violent charges against Mr Affolter, prison's going to be difficult to avoid.

Varga: I told you, I never did any harm to anybody.

Weber: Never?

Varga: There was only one time ... two times, when I did more than frightening people. I can tell you about them if it'll mean I don't have to go to prison.

Weber: I can't make any promises.

Varga: Mr Affolter had some guests at his house. He-

Weber: When was this?

Varga: I don't remember exactly ... we sat
outside, so it must have been warm, maybe
the end of August, the beginning of
September last year.

Weber: Who were the guests?

Varga: Mr Affolter introduced them as his work
colleagues Lisa and Christopher, I think. I
don't know their full names.

Weber: Who else was at this party?

Varga: Not a party, a dinner. There was Mr Zubke,
Mr Affolter's lawyer, his wife, two—

Weber: What was the name of the wife?

Varga: Ekaterina, she's Mr Affolter's niece. There
were also two, young, American ladies.

Weber: Names?

Varga: I can't remember.

Weber: So what happened?

Varga: Mr Affolter wanted to question the two
colleagues. He said they were asking too
many questions about his business and he
had a score to settle with the woman. He
put something in their drinks.

Weber: And what did you do?

Varga: Nothing. The idea was for me to threaten
them, so they'd tell Mr Affolter what they
knew about his business. But the
combination of alcohol and the drug meant
we couldn't revive them enough.

Weber: Go on.

Varga: Mr Affolter decided to embarrass them. We
took them in a taxi to a hotel in Zurich,
dressed them for sex, and left them in a
room with a few empty bottles. I went to
The Celler, which Mr Affolter used to own,
and told the barman to say they'd been
there drinking if anyone asked.

Weber: And that's it?

Varga: I felt sorry for them, they seemed nice.

Weber: You said there were two times you did more
than frighten.

Varga: The second time also involved this lady
Lisa. Mr Affolter told me to go and pick
her up in Zurich. He said I should drug
her. I held her in a chair while he
questioned her in the cellar of his house.

> Then I drugged her and put her back in her
> own apartment.

"So, André's innocent of everything?"

"Yes, Lisa, André Wissler had nothing to do with prostitutes in The Celler or your abductions."

"Pity."

Christopher shook his head. "Careful, Lisa, sounds as though you want revenge on Wissler. He didn't do anything."

"Hmm."

"The events of the last few months have put Wissler off ownership of a place like The Celler. It's up for sale."

Lisa smiled and nodded. "Good. But you also didn't want to use this Varga evidence to show Gazda's vicious nature."

"No. If I did I'd have to put you and Christopher on the witness stand. I told Weber I didn't think it would add anything to the case we already had against Gazda. We put Varga on police bail and took away his passport. We have the recording and transcript for future use."

"What about Grindel? What's going to happen to him? It didn't come out at the trial about Grindel, Mr A, arranging the accident for Cousteau. And, in fact, arranging for Cousteau to kill Felix Braun."

"No, there was no need, Christopher. Grindel's evid–"

"Another one who's getting away with what he did to me, us."

"I know that's what you might think, Lisa, but Grindel's evidence was vital to the case against Gazda, so we wanted to keep him 'clean' as it were. That he'd been working for Gazda and was now giving evidence against him strengthened his credibility. Bringing out his direct involvement would have weakened it."

"Gazda knows who Mr A is. His lawyer didn't even cross-examine him. Didn't try to discredit him by telling the court that he arranged the killing of Felix Braun, and then killed Cousteau?"

"I think I can answer that Christopher. That would be almost like admitting Gazda's involvement in the murders."

"Lisa's right."

"But it means he gets away with murder."

"Right again, Lisa. But, and I wouldn't want anyone outside this room to know I said this: the world is a better place without Henri Cousteau, and to some extent Felix Braun."

"But isn't this corruption of evidence?"

"Strictly speaking yes, Christopher. But again, it puts Gazda away."

"So, the end justifies the means."

365

Jochim took a deep breath and nodded.

"Jochim, I'm worried, this could get you into trouble."

"Bea, you know this is not the first time it's been done. And that's something else better left in this room. Neither Kullmer nor Müller know about this. If they did they'd probably unofficially agree.

"Kullmer and Müller?"

"Jochim's bosses, Lisa. But doesn't Peter Weber know about the tape of Grindel pushing Cousteau?"

"Yes, but not about Grindel's involvement in Felix Braun's murder. There's no record of what Grindel told me. I've talked to Peter about the tape. We agreed the push and the words spoken by Grindel were not conclusive."

"Sounds a bit like what you once called 'the English all knowing wink', Jochim."

"The Swiss equivalent, Christopher." Jochim could see that Lisa wanted to say something else. "Lisa?"

"So, what does happen to Grindel now?"

"He leaves the police force. Early ret–"

"With a nice big pension no doubt."

"No, Lisa, not with a big pension. There'll be no charges against him, in return for his help in putting Gazda away, but he'll leave only with the money he paid into the pension fund, not the canton's contribution. He'll sign a piece of paper to say he has voluntarily agreed to this for 'personal' reasons. It's happened in the past, but usually with senior officers."

"Who knows he's Mr A?"

"You and Lisa, Christopher, and us of course. Plus Kullmer, Müller, Weber, the prosecutor's office, and probably other people in Grindel's department."

"And, of course, Gazda."

"As you say Lisa 'and Gazda'. That puts him in danger of reprisals from Gazda's 'friends'."

"Good."

"He's leaving Switzerland. Now he knows he's not Wissler's father there's nothing to keep him from doing what he's probably been wanting to do for some time: go to Thailand."

"Thailand?"

Bea smiled. "Sergeant Grindel has a certain liking for prostitutes Lisa."

"What about lawyer Zubke, Jochim? He was just carrying out Gazda's orders?"

"To a certain extent, yes, Christopher. He must have known what was going on in the properties he bought for Gazda."

"What will happen to him?"

"The question is, how much did he know about the operation side of Gazda's business? At the moment, I can't see anything to charge him with Lisa, but–"

"Another one getting away with it."

"I understood Jochim to mean he hasn't done anything against the law, Lisa."

"Christopher's, right. But Zubke knows we're watching him. Other than putting the properties in his name, his main work for Gazda was to channel money and advice to André Wissler through his mother."

"What's going to happen to the Lipstick Club and the other places?"

"They're on the market, Bea."

"There's another person who was once one of our, or at least my, suspects of being Gazda–"

"Anto Dedić, Christopher?"

"Yes, Jochim. What's happened to him?"

"It came out at the trial that he's Gazda's uncle. Once upon a time he was quite a big player in the Zurich drugs market. He got Felix Braun the job as a pimp after Braun did him a favour in prison. As far as we can see he retired from crime and lost all his money gambling. I pretty sure he knew Affolter was Gazda, but there's nothing to tie him to the 'business'. We'll keep an eye on him. He probably gets handouts from Gazda and told him about my questioning."

"So, we'll just have to wait for the sentencing now. Sometime next week?"

"Wednesday we expect, Christopher. Then Gazda won't be able to hurt anyone else."

"Or steal any more briefcases."

"I think we can forget about that now, Lisa."

"Maybe you can Christopher, but–"

"Lisa, please."

Silence. Lisa fumed, Christopher shook his head, Bea and Jochim exchanged puzzled looks.

Lisa glanced at Christopher and slowly nodded. "Jochim, in your interviews did Gazda ev–"

"Lisa, please."

"Did Gazda ever mention a briefcase?"

"A briefcase?"

"We, I, think that Gazda stole Christopher's briefcase from his office."

"When was this?"

"Lis–"

"August last year. It just a few weeks before–"

Christopher sighed heavily.

"before that night at Gazda's house when he drugged us."

"Why would Gazda steal a briefcase? Seems a strange thing for someone like him to do."

"To get at–"

"You're right, Bea. It seemed strange to me at the time. With what we now know about Gazda it sounds ridiculous. Lisa thought–"

"And Erna."

"Lisa thought he did it to get back at me because he and I had a disagreement at a business meeting." Christopher smiled. "The Gazda we now know would have probably had me beaten up if he wanted to get back at me."

Jochim could almost hear Lisa's teeth grinding. "Do you have any evidence that he stole the briefcase?"

"He used Christopher's credit cards to buy new clothes."

"Lisa, I don't think Gazda needed to use my credit cards."

"Why do you still defend him, after all he's done?"

"I'm not def–"

"Yes you are."

"I'm not."

"Hey you two. If you continue like this you won't have properly digested my spaghetti bolognese and be ready for Jochim's speciality, tiramisu."

Lisa and Christopher laughed and chorused "Sorry."

"Jochim makes tiramisu?"

"No Lisa, but he knows the best little Italian shop in Zurich where to buy it."

Following the SRF documentary the interest in the Rudi Affolter case was high. Jochim told Lisa and Christopher the public gallery would be full for the sentencing. They arrived an hour and a half before the schedule start and only just managed to get a seat.

Die Täglichen Nachrichten
Daily Diary
8 May
Bernd Zolliker

Yesterday saw the sentencing of Rudolf Affolter, known as Gazda. The boss of one of the biggest groups of prostitutes in Zurich will never see the outside of the prison walls again.

In his summary of the evidence used to find Affolter guilty, the presiding judge stressed the cruel and vicious nature of the murders committed under Affolter's orders. Francesca Kardomah and Felix Braun both met their end after sadistic attacks. So, it was no surprise Affolter received life imprisonment for each one. What was surprising was the sentences are to run consecutively. The eight year sentence for criminal organisation of prostitution will run concurrently.

The questions I asked in the Diary in September last year, if there was a new clampdown on prostitution in Zurich and whether this was in the best interests of Switzerland, remain open.

Christopher went to the other side of the taxi, slid in beside Lisa, and said to the driver, "The Kronenhalle please."

"Have you been to the Kronenhalle before?"

"No, you?"

"Supposedly one of the best restaurants in Zurich. A bit beyond the budget of a poor secretary."

"Rud– Gazda suggested we take a group of visiting Russians once, but–"

"He would."

"But they never arrived for some reason."

Jochim held out his hand to Lisa, but also leant forward for the Swiss three, cheek kiss. Christopher followed his lead with Bea. Lisa and Bea exchanged kisses, and Jochim and Christopher two-handed handshakes.

"Thank you for the invitation."

"You're welcome Christopher. We wanted to thank you for all your help. Have you been here before?"

Lisa and Christopher answered together "No."

"We come here all the time."

"Not all the time Bea, only once a week." Jochim winked.

Christopher caught on. "Ah, when we said no we hadn't been here before, we meant not on a Saturday." He nodded towards Lisa.

"Yes, in fact we always sit at this table."

A waiter appeared and filled Lisa's and Christopher's glasses with champagne.

Jochim raised his glass. "Lisa and Christopher, and Bea, thank you for all your help in putting away a dangerous criminal."

"Cheers."

"Cheers."

"Cheers."

"So, the maximum sentence, as expected."

"Yes Christopher. What we hoped for, but didn't expect was the sentences to run consecutively."

Lisa took another sip of champagne. "'Life' means what exactly in Switzerland?"

"I thought you might ask that, so Bea did some research."

"There's no rule, but it seems people serve 15 to 20 years. Parole is possible from year 15. With consecutive life sentences parole seems unlikely. Even if it is after say 15 years, it still means a minimum of 30 years. How old is he now? Fifty-seven?"

"Good."

The waiter appeared again, refilled the glasses, and asked Jochim if they were ready to order.

As they finished their coffee a small nod passed from Christopher to Lisa, and from Bea to Jochim.

Lisa and Jochim started speaking at the same time.

"Lisa, there's something—"

"Jochim, we've been—"

"Go ahead Lisa."

"We, Christopher and I, have been talking." Lisa looked at Christopher, who smiled encouragement. "You know I've been the one determined to get revenge on Affolter. Well, now that he's put away for a long time we, I, have been wondering if it's worth pursuing the abductions. It's not that I'm not still bloody angry about what he did. Excuse the language: must be the champagne. But having seen what goes on in court, it'll be a lot of hassle for us, for me. In a way it'll be like Affolter hurting me again. Am I making sense?"

Bea and Jochim exchanged faint smiles, and, Christopher thought, small sighs of relief.

Bea touched Lisa's arm. "Perfect sense and Jochim—"

"Do you realise you just called him 'Affolter' twice, not Gazda."

"Don't think that means I've forgiven him Christopher."

"Oh I know, otherwise you'd have said Rudi."

"Never."

"Jochim has something to say."

"Lisa, we've also been talking. I've always had doubts we would get far with charges of abduction. Don't get me wrong. I wasn't just leading you along with all the talk about not bringing what happened to you into the trial, and waiting for a 'confession' from someone involved. I wanted to take a hard look at what we had to see what the chances were of making the charges of abduction stick. Am I making sense now?"

Lisa smiled and nodded.

"The outburst of Gaz— Affolter and what Mikos Varga said are significant, but I can imagine lawyers arguing the outburst was obtained during unreasonable questioning of a prisoner. They could argue the first 'abduction' was a practical joke among friends after a heavy night's drinking. I know it wasn't, but do you see what I mean?"

Again Lisa smiled and nodded.

"The second time, which was an abduction, would not be easy to prove. We only have what Varga told us, and what you experienced of course."

Now Lisa reached for Jochim's arm. "Jochim, don't look so worried. I understand what you're saying. We came to something like the same conclusions."

"So, Lisa, are you saying we don't go ahead with the abduction charges?"

"Yes Bea, that's what I'm, we're saying.

Jochim's gave a pronounced sigh of relief "OK, would anyone like another cognac?"

Glances all round, followed by yeses.

"There is a big reason I decided not to go ahead. I haven't told Christopher this."

Christopher's eyes widened.

"You said Jochim, that to charge Affolter you'd need to know more details about Hotel zum Kirsch. I can't imagine standing up in court and describing the picture of Christopher that greeted me when I woke up. He was–"

"Yes, thank you Lisa."

Bea and Jochim leant forward and whispered together. "Some other time Lisa. We'd like to hear." Everyone except Christopher laughed.

Christopher changed the subject quickly. "I hope we will have other times, not for Lisa's revelations, but for us to meet now that Affolter's in prison."

Again Bea and Jochim spoke together. "We hope so too."

"Cheers."

"Cheers."

"Cheers."

"Cheers."

"Oh, by the way, I almost forgot, we think we can settle your argument."

Lisa and Christopher looked at each other and shrugged.

"Tell them Bea."

"Clever Sergeant Jochim Friedmann, soon to be Inspector Jochim Friedmann, found–"

"Congratulations."

"Congratulations." Lisa blew a kiss.

"found a report–"

"By accident."

"from the Bern police—"

"The Bern city police."

"Can I finish the story Jochim, otherwise we'll be here all night."

"Not a bad place to be all night."

"Christopher, let Bea finish."

"The Bern police charged eight people from an office cleaning company based in Bern with stealing things from SwissPost headquarters. All the items were low value: general office equipment and personal belongings of the staff. But it had been going on for a few years. The total could run into many thousands of Swiss Francs. When they appeared in court they asked for 524 other offences to be taken into account."

"Five hundred and twenty-four? They kept a record?"

"The leader did Christopher. Tell them what you found Jochim."

"Normally I wouldn't have time or interest to read all the report, but on scanning the opening paragraph I noticed the company worked in Bern and Zurich. So I—"

"I think I know what's coming."

"Yes, Lisa you can probably guess. '11 August 2008, ZFFM, Zurich, briefcase, passport, wallet - cash and credit cards'."

"Belonging to Mr Christopher McLendi."

"I don't know that Lisa, but everything fits."

Lisa looked at Christopher, who tried, but failed to hide a broad grin. "OK. I could have been wrong about Affolter."

"'Could have been'?"

"Without hard evidence we can't be sure. Isn't that right Bea? Jochim?"

"Yes Inspector Stern."

THE END

More from Trevor Johnson

Sorry's not enough

How many times can you say 'I'm sorry' and then do the same thing again? The alcohol-fuelled torrent of words that pour out of Graham

hurt Jennifer every time, but this type of domestic abuse leaves no scars, no bruise on bruise. Graham can't or won't see the abject misery building in Jennifer. He does say 'sorry', every time, but without really knowing what he is saying sorry for. Jennifer sacrifices her job in Geneva for a return to England, and for a time the verbal abuse stops. Then the emotional roller coaster of good time-abuse-sorry-silence-good time-abuse starts again, but the peaks are less frequent and the troughs become lower and lower. Why do abused women allow it to continue? Jennifer goes inside her head to try to find an answer to why it is happening and what she can do about it. In spite of all the hurt she feels the same love for Graham as she had at the beginning, but can she learn to live with his demons, and stop their marriage breaking up?

Trevor's Shorts Vol 1, 2, and 3

The three volumes of 'Trevor's Shorts' are a collection of the stories I've written over the years. Some were created for competitions, some because an idea occurred to me, and some just for fun. There's no real common theme: flirting, ambition, St Swithin's Day, Brexit, falling in love, Sat Nav, dreaming of fame, a voice from the grave, birth of a brother, a woman scorned, a night to remember, a night to forget, and saying sorry are all in the eclectic mixture.

All books are available at Amazon as ebooks and paperbacks

Printed in Great Britain
by Amazon